"HOLD!"
COMMANDED THE SHEE.

"You are a brave man," she said. "I like you." She slowly unfastened a gold pin holding her dress together at the shoulder.

Sandy was very much impressed, and scared down to his toes. The shee was tall, slim, and regal; looking every inch a goddess. Her teeth were ivory with the slightest hint of emerald, her hair greenish black, and her skin a creamy green satin beaded with tiny scales. Her eyes were midnight black and strangely sorrowful, and her lithe body full yet graceful.

"I am death and I am _____," she said as she drew closer and e_____

PRAISE FOR D____
PREVIO____

"Fast paced and fun"
Locus

"Starts off as a fantasy quest
run by the Wild Bunch,
but quickly turns into a spectacle
Spielberg would love.
And after that, it gets **really** interesting!"
Craig Shaw Gardner,
author of *A Malady of Magicks*

"Soars into new dimensions of imagination"
Marvin Kaye,
author of *A Cold Blue Light*

Other Avon Books by
Donald Aamodt

A NAME TO CONJURE WITH

Avon Books are available at special quantity discounts for bulk purchases for sales promotions, premiums, fund raising or educational use. Special books, or book excerpts, can also be created to fit specific needs.

For details write or telephone the office of the Director of Special Markets, Avon Books, Dept. FP, 1350 Avenue of the Americas, New York, New York 10019, 1-800-238-0658.

A TROUBLING ALONG THE BORDER

DONALD AAMODT

AVON BOOKS • NEW YORK

If you purchased this book without a cover, you should be aware that this book is stolen property. It was reported as "unsold and destroyed" to the publisher, and neither the author nor the publisher has received any payment for this "stripped book."

A TROUBLING ALONG THE BORDER is an original publication of Avon Books. This work has never before appeared in book form. This work is a novel. Any similarity to actual persons or events is purely coincidental.

AVON BOOKS
A division of
The Hearst Corporation
1350 Avenue of the Americas
New York, New York 10019

Copyright © 1991 by Donald Aamodt
Cover illustration by Daniel Horne
Published by arrangement with the author
Library of Congress Catalog Card Number: 91-92076
ISBN: 0-380-75827-X

All rights reserved, which includes the right to reproduce this book or portions thereof in any form whatsoever except as provided by the U.S. Copyright Law. For information address Donald Maass Literary Agency, 64 West 84th Street, New York, New York 10024.

First AvoNova Printing: December 1991

AVONOVA TRADEMARK REG. U.S. PAT. OFF. AND IN OTHER COUN-TRIES, MARCA REGISTRADA, HECHO EN U.S.A.

Printed in the U.S.A.

RA 10 9 8 7 6 5 4 3 2 1

This book is for:

Sue Paterson, who likes my writing and has the first book I ever autographed.

The staff of the Brooklyn Center Social Security Office for putting up with me for so long.

The Award Processing bunch for having done it even longer.

Don Maass because he is a friend, a much put-upon agent, and lets me bamboozle him in cards.

And especially Britt and Jennifer Aamodt, who gave me the experience needed to create Anala.

A TROUBLING ALONG THE BORDER

1

THE Goddess threw a pebble into the water. The ripples spread quickly to the far corners of the pool, bounced back from the surrounding wall, and slowly disappeared into nothingness. In quick moments the surface of the pool became unnaturally smooth and still.

The Goddess looked deeply into the water. At first she saw only its startling clarity, like that of an unflawed blue-white diamond. She spoke a word and the water instantly became clouded and opaque. Gradually it cleared, forming an image as it did so.

A scrawny figure was running bare-ass naked through the night. Behind him in the distance was the flare of torches, the gabble of angry voices, and the bell-like howling of Askeni hunting dogs on the track of fresh prey. The man stopped for a moment and listened, then turned and ran faster as he heard the dogs getting closer.

Zhadnoboth the sorcerer rounded a corner and then ran faster as he saw his objective in sight. The next instant he howled and began hopping around on one foot, holding the big toe of his other foot in his hands and moaning in pain. In his agony he hopped off the trail and onto a long-needled plant commonly called traveler's friend.

The sorcerer let out a heartrending screech and abruptly sat down. Cursing obscenely between moans, he started yanking out as many of the long spiky barbs as he could find. Suddenly, the trailing dogs began roaring and bellowing in earnest as they smelled his blood on the wind.

The sorcerer cursed, sprang to his feet, and fell back down

1

to his knees, crying in agony. Cursing and moaning, he got to his feet gingerly and began hobbling away.

Finally he reached his destination, a signpost where two trails crossed. He sank to his knees and crawled the last few feet to clutch the post. He rested a brief moment and then yanked a bloody thorn from his foot. Quickly he scratched some runes upon the wood.

"Curse those damned bitches," he muttered. "And doubly curse that fat-bellied husband of theirs. They'll pay for this. They'll wish they had never been born." He heard the dogs yowling for blood just around the turn of the trail. "You don't have me yet, you misbegotten bastards," he yelled. "My staff might be broken, but I still have magic in me."

Furiously he scratched a few more signs on the old wood. He picked up some dust and threw it in as many directions as he had time for. The final two pinches he threw up into the air and down to the ground.

A pack of dogs burst around the corner, saw their prey kneeling in the moonlight, and loosed bloodcurdling howls as they charged for the kill. Zhadnoboth hurriedly began chanting as many spells and spell parts as he could remember, throwing them together into an ungodly hodge-podge of mismatched magic. The masters of the sorcerer's guild would have been horrified at the way Zhadnoboth in his fear mangled and perverted the rules of their discipline. But they were *not* there, and it was not their lives on the line. Besides, his spellmaking worked . . . in its own way.

The first dog bared its fangs and went for the sorcerer's throat—

—And the next instant the slavering brute found itself running down a rutted road between high banks of snow, head-on into the chest of a giant and very surprised ice bear. The other dogs suffered much the same fate as they charged in for the kill, suddenly finding themselves on other roads and trails, some of them very strange indeed.

The last dog, a chronic laggard from birth, saw the fate of its fellows and tried to stop, digging its paws into the dirt and trying to skid to a halt. Instead, maybe hitting a stone or a hole, it went tumbling head over heels to go crashing into the sorcerer—or where he should have been. The dazed animal picked itself up, looked where it had been, stuck its tail between its legs, and ran howling in terror up the strangely lighted road it was on.

Down below Zhadnoboth looked in bewilderment at the dog running up a moonbeam. He glanced at Zarathandra's bright and ghostly moon and wondered what its inhabitants would think when an Askeni hound came running down out of the sky. He looked around, puzzled, back up into the sky, and then shrugged. This was not quite the spell he had been trying for, but it worked—and thank the Goddess for that. He sat down and started to pick up the remaining thorns out of his feet, forgetting his thankfulness and cursing the fate that had brought him here.

Sitting on the edge of her pool, the Goddess watched him and smiled. The sorcerer was a conniving scoundrel and an indifferent worshipper at best, but she could not help but like him. Maybe because he was so ineptly great at being both a sorcerer and a knave. And he was one of her best, if unwitting, henchmen. He had served her well in the past, and she needed him again—both him and the outlander he had accidentally brought to this world. She grimaced—the outlander was clearly a whim of destiny; one of its dark-humored jokes.

Zhadnoboth looked up, suddenly realizing the hubbub caused by those following him had gotten a lot closer. Several dark-skinned men carrying torches came trotting around the corner of the trail, followed by several spearmen. One of the spearmen gave a yell and charged forward.

Zhadnoboth recognized him as a poor relation of the king he had offended, a proud man out to make a name for himself as his only way out of poverty and obscurity. The spear flashed forward to impale the sorcerer. He flinched, his head knowing his spell still protected him, but his heart yammering in terror. Zhadnoboth was brave, but only when backed up into a corner.

The spearman fell forward as his spear failed to meet flesh. Swiftly he was back on his feet and ready to attack again. After a moment he dropped his spear to his side and stared in terror and astonishment at his surroundings. He was in a dimly lit tunnel that seemed to come from nowhere and lead nowhere. He cocked his ear as he heard the raucous noise of feasting coming from one direction. Ashen-faced, the spearman faced the noise and began to march toward it. Thus began the long and illustrious career of Bornhu the Troll-slayer.

The rest of the tribesmen stopped dead when they saw their companion disappear, several of them later saying that the had seen him run down a road heading for hell. They gabbled nervously to themselves and spread out in a semicircle around the sorcerer, none of them coming too close. Two of the braver ones threw spears. But after the spears disappeared into nothingness, they joined the rest in backing a little further away.

Zhadnoboth glowered at his pursuers and wondered what to do. He had planned on getting this far and working one of the spells he could do without his staff, a crossroad spell that let him choose a road to more hospitable places. However, in his panic, he had created a different spell, a real doozy of a spell. He could dimly see roads galore radiating from this spot, but damned few looked inviting, especially the one at his feet with flames shooting up from it.

Suddenly, the grim-faced tribesmen facing the sorcerer ceased their excited gabbling and fell back to each side. A tall and skinny oldster strode out from their midst. His body was covered with rubbed-in ashes, his eyes circled by white paint, and a string of monkey skulls encircled his neck. His only garment was a codpiece of spiked leather protecting his privates. In his left hand was a gourd rattle filled with human knucklebones; in his right, a silver-hafted dagger, its edges black with poison.

He glared at Zhadnoboth and snarled contemptuously, then began to dance in place; howling magic curses in his native tongue, shaking the rattle continuously, and making menacing slashes with the dagger.

The tribesmen began gabbling excitedly as the many roads leading from the crossroads became visible to them and they could see where some led. One tough old warrior glanced down the fiery road at Zhadnoboth's feet, turned white, and keeled over backward. Several of the tribesmen turned tail and ran, while the others backed even further away. This only made the witch doctor angrier and he danced harder.

At first Zhadnoboth stood up to the magical attack confidently, certain that any sorcery of his was superior to anything this savage could throw at him. Slowly his confidence dwindled as he became entranced by the show put on by his opponent, and he began to feel uncomfortable. He felt something at his feet, glanced down, and started. Red-eyed snakes were rising from the ground, their bodies misty and indistinct, but for brief moments becoming flesh—and those brief moments were coming more and more often.

Zhadnoboth panicked. He reached down, grabbed some dust, and threw it at the witch doctor. Then he ran for it, hurriedly choosing a road that looked promising.

He found himself on a desert path climbing up to a low ridge. "That showed that savage," he muttered, feeling much braver now that he was out of the frying pan. Zhadnoboth limped to the top of the ridge, saw a milestone beside the road, and smiled. The symbol at the top represented the Rithian Empire—a long safe distance from where he had started.

He looked off into the distance and saw the moonlight shining off the whitewashed adobe of a small desert town. He would go there tomorrow, get supplies, and then head out of town to look up a certain demon. That demon owed him. If it hadn't been for that demon, he would be rich and not be forced to go selling his services to ungrateful savage kings.

Zhadnoboth shivered, suddenly realizing the desert night was cold and he didn't have a stitch on. He began twirling the bronze ring on his left little finger and softly chanting a spell through chattering teeth. At least he would get his robe back and the magics concealed within it. Wouldn't those ungrateful bastards be surprised when that part of their loot disappeared.

The Goddess nodded in satisfaction and clapped her hands. The image in the pool shivered and disappeared. An old evil was stirring again and once again she must act to right a balance long ago set awry. She had cast her first die. Zhadnoboth was within the southern borders of the Rithian Empire; soon he would help unleash her own personal demon against her enemies.

A pang of memory tore at the Goddess, opening ancient wounds. Even immortals could err; and for their sins, worlds suffered. Grimly, she set her teeth and steeled her heart. Now and for all time the matter must be set right, despite the cost to herself.

She looked again at her pool, a tear trickling from her eye.

2

Two men, heavily cloaked against the predawn chill, knelt atop a stony ridge and looked toward a dark splotch ahead in the night air—a sleeping village. Behind them their killers crouched by their rudhars and waited for orders. Out of the darkness in front of them a burly figure appeared. He was dressed in a sand leopard pelt and not much else. There was blood at the corner of his mouth and matted into his beard.

"They only had one sentry and he was barely a stripling," the burly man growled. "He'll get no older."

Yargath rose to his feet and turned to his killers. "Take the girl and slay the rest, especially the old man." He paused, then added in a deadly voice, "If anyone even scratches her, I'll hang him by the balls." Then he mounted his rudhar and started toward the village. The killers split into three groups, one following him and the other two circling to each side.

The burly man and Yargath's companion watched them go. Then with catlike grace they stalked into the darkness after them, their forms fluidly shifting from man-beast to kill-beast.

Slouching wearily in their saddles, Sandy and his nine border troopers rode north. Nearly a month of hard travel through a blistering desert, reminding its turbulent inhabitants that they were still part of the Rithian Empire, had taken its toll. Now all that kept them going was the knowledge that Kimbo-Dashla and some well-earned leave lay less than a day ahead.

Though the Kri Yitheni of the middle desert were famous for their loose women and lavish hospitality, there was bad to go with the good—the palavering with shifty and stubborn

7

headmen, the thankless hours spent listening to proud tribesmen offended by the way the empire or its citizens treated
them, and always the keeping of an eye open for trouble brewing.

Patrol work along the border was a boring and dirty job.
There was fighting to be done and raiders to be hunted down,
but just being there was what it was all about—it gave the
desert folk tangible proof they were getting something for the
taxes they so reluctantly paid.

The thought of fighting made Sandy grimace. He could
already see the disapproving look and hear the hard words
from his colonel when he reported his patrol's skirmish with
Yartazi raiders. His bad reputation was going to get worse. A
little trouble was expected now and then, but he was the only
borderer who found it on every patrol. He was going to be a
junior officer forever and he didn't blame them, not with his
record and disregard of authority—not to mention that general's daughter he'd dallied with. Still, it wasn't a bad life, and
they weren't about to get rid of him. He was too good at this
borderer crap.

Sandy took a drink of water from his canteen and made a
face. It was lukewarm and tasted like old bathwater. For the
millionth time he cursed the sorcerer who had five years ago
accidentally yanked him into this world at the back end of
nowhere. What he wouldn't give to be back on Earth and
drinking a cold beer! Thank god they only had to show the
flag in one more village. Then they could make for Kimbo-
Dashla with its cool wine and open-thighed tavern wenches.

Sandy glanced back at his bastards and smiled in satisfaction. The men of the Desert Legions were a hard-bitten lot,
and the borderers were even tougher. It was a rough life on
the southern fringes of the Rithian Empire; if thirst, sand-
storms, snakebite, or solitude didn't get you, there were always plenty of rebellious tribesmen or raiders from beyond
the border to do you in.

Every one of his troopers had bellyached about the lonely
and thankless patrols, but he knew every mother's son of them
would keep on reenlisting until death or old age chopped
them down. They were proud, thinking themselves ten times
better soldiers than anyone else—friend or foe—and maybe
they were. They would die to the man to keep this pride,
knowing without it the desert and its inhabitants would de-

vour them alive. It was this and the evenhanded justice they handed out that kept the southern border stable—mostly.

Sandy shifted in his saddle, trying to ease the soreness in his muscles, and silently damned the beast he was riding on. Rudhars were unmatched for desert cavalry work, but like their less streamlined relative the camel they had their short-comings: foul tempers, a pacing gait which shook every bone in the rider's body, and mule-headed stubbornness.

He cast a searching eye over the hill surrounding them, looking for any sign of trouble; but there was also a kind of love in his gaze. It was a bleak land, though far kinder than the deep desert they had left the day before. These were the foothills, lying between the true desert to the south and the mountains which shielded the lush heart of the empire from the wilder lands. The rocky bones of the country jutted through the skin of dirt everywhere, coloring the landscape with swathes of burnt yellow and rusty brown. Here and there stunted brushes grew, surrounded by tufts of coarse grass and scattered clumps of dragon's-tongue thistle. The only sounds were the faint wailing of the wind and the occasional cry of a sand dove.

Sandy suddenly stiffened in his saddle and then barked out a command to his troopers. They spread out into a skirmish line. He looked to his sergeant and pointed to the sky ahead—circling were the black and ominous forms of vultures, above what should be the village they were headed for.

Fifteen minutes later they were spread out on a ridge to the east of the village. Its buildings, of fieldstone plastered with adobe, were charred ruins. Faint wisps of smoke still rose from some of them. In the village square were the crumpled bodies of its seventy or eighty inhabitants: men, women, and children. Even from their distance they could see the remains were little more than blackened cinders. Nailed to a fig tree overlooking the square was the naked body of an old man.

Sandy looked down at the ghastly scene and scowled. There was magic here. His sixth sense, part of the baggage forced on him when he got shanghaied to this world, could feel it—Chanzi magic. It had been years since those shapechanger wizards had openly dared to venture into the empire from their lairs in the High Artages. Something bad had to be brewing for them to get so bold. Much as they hated the empire and the Goddess, they usually were not this bold about showing it.

He studied the terrain carefully, looking for any sign of an ambush, and saw nothing. Turning to Hojeen, his ancient and desert-wise scout, he asked, "What do you think?"

The wizened little man chewed on the tip of his mustache and thought a moment. "Nothing there, but not feel right."

Sandy nodded and motioned for Hojeen and two troopers to scout out the village. He and the rest of his troopers watched, weapons ready, as the three quickly searched through the few buildings. When nothing turned up, they cautiously rode down to join them.

Sandy looked at the white-bearded old man nailed to the tree and cursed obscenely to hide his grief. The old man had died hard. His limbs had been twisted out of their sockets and the wrinkled flesh was almost hidden by the charred furrows scored into it by a white-hot iron. When they had tired of that sport they had nailed him, still alive, to the tree and ripped out his entrails. The Hagba Khamliss had been a kindly and loving man—and more, a good friend. Sandy made a silent vow that those who had done this would pay in blood.

He stared around uneasily, but saw nothing except his mounted troopers spread out in a ragged skirmish line and Hojeen nosing over some tracks like a bloodhound. But he could sense strong magic somewhere near—and something else, something he could not quite place his finger on, bothered him. Then he glanced up into the sky—

The vultures! They should have been feeding when the patrol got here, but something had kept them away.

Casually he raised his left hand and wiped sweat from his brow, letting the ring on his little finger touch his eyelids. It was a plain silver ring inset with a tiny chip of emerald, a piece of loot from a fiasco he'd been roped into after being yanked from Earth to this world. It was the Ring of Uncertainty, most of whose powers he still didn't know—though he had accidentally found it could give him the ability to see through *what seemed to be* to *what was*. While not appearing to, he scanned the land surrounding the village with his magically enhanced sight, stiffening imperceptibly when he found what he was looking for.

Casually he called his sergeant over, a burly outlander from far away in the western islands. With his voice he said, "Aku, take three men and search the other end of the village again."

But while he spoke, his hands said something different in the sign language that was the lingua franca of the desert.

The sergeant nodded his understanding and gave a salute. He rode his rudhar from one of the skirmish line to the other as if trying to decide who he wanted on detail with him, unobtrusively signaling with his hands *be ready to attack* to each trooper he passed.

When Sandy saw his men were ready and roughly headed toward a fruit orchard facing the open end of the square, he made his move. He roared a bloodcurdling battle cry, loosed an arrow toward a decrepit-looking fireplum tree, and charged toward the orchard. In almost the same instant, his troopers joined in the war cry, loosed a volley of arrows toward the orchard, and charged hell-for-leather after him.

The arrows struck the trees at the front of the orchard, breaking the spell that hid their true shapes. The foremost trees were now a dozen Jadghuli tribesman, half of them now dead or wounded and the other half demoralized by suddenly finding themselves on the wrong end of an ambush.

Sandy whipped out his saber and, moving with supernatural speed, fell upon the nearest Jadghuli. He slashed left and then right, his razor-sharp blade and demon strength decapitating one foe and severing the wrist of another. The Jadghuli were tough and blooded warriors, but no match for someone damned—or blessed—with being more than merely human.

Before he could finish off his second foe, his rudhar tripped and sent him flying head over heels from the saddle. Only the steel cap hidden under the hood of his burnoose kept him from cracking his skull—that, and a more-than-normal toughness. As it was, he staggered drunkenly to his feet and looked around through dazed eyes for a foe.

But the skirmish was almost over. It had been a slaughter. The only Jadghuli not down was the one Sandy had maimed, and he was fleeing full tilt westward, Aku at his heels.

The outlander rose in his saddle, yanked a javelin from the quiver by his right leg, and flung it at the Jadghuli. The javelin hit the raider between the shoulder blades, its head coming to a halt only after it came out his chest a foot or more.

The Jadghuli screamed hoarsely and tumbled from his saddle.

As Aku leaned over from his saddle to retrieve his javelin, the tribesman moaned. The sergeant offhandedly cut the Jadghuli's throat and then with a show of strength jerked his javelin from the body with one yank.

Sandy quickly checked on his other troopers. Most were still mounted and alert for trouble. One was on the ground nursing a wounded arm while Hojeen was moving from body to body, cutting the throat of any foe who still showed signs of life.

Aku rode over and said, "Thank the Goddess these Jadghuli bastards are too proud to wear armor, otherwise they might have bloodied us more than they did." He paused and added, a faint question in his voice, "It's even luckier that you spotted their ambush."

Sandy nodded and lied a bit. "I spent time working for a sorcerer and developed a nose for magic. Those trees just didn't feel right. Besides, the Chanzi raise an awful stink when they work magic."

Aku sniffed the air and wrinkled his nose. "Aye, I can smell ranguli ointment. There's no mistaking that rancid stench." He paused, then went on thoughtfully "I though you could never smell ranguli ointment until a Chanzi spell was broken."

Sandy laughed and replied, "You can if you know what to smell for. I got well acquainted with stinks when I worked for that sorcerer."

"He taught you well. You're a lucky man to serve under, even if they don't think so in Kimbo-Dashla. Colonel Zurtkel says the only safe place to put you is in the front line of a battle—at least there you can't make things worse."

Sandy laughed once more. "I imagine this little set-to will screw up my promotion again. Especially with the Hagba Khamliss dead and the lulzi—" Then he remembered, and swore an obscene oath. To Aku he snapped, "Get the men ready to ride and tell Hojeen to get his butt over here double-quick."

Hojeen was by his side in moments. Sandy barked, "Tell me what sign you found—especially what sign you found of the lulzi."

"Maybe twenty more Jadghuli than we slew were here. When they ride away, they have two prisoners: lulzi girl and somebody else—old man by way he walks. Two Chanzi wizards with them.''

Sandy nodded. The scout was a spry old man with only a fringe of dark hair around the top of his head, and scrawny as a plucked chicken but as tough as old shoe leather. He was more than old, though his hair was unsullied by any gray; so old not one knew when he had joined the Desert Legion— he'd always been there. Some said he'd lived forever—a trooper Sandy knew swore that his grandfather had served with Hojeen and that the old scout had been ancient then. Whatever the rumors, there was no doubt about his ability as a tracker and scout; drop a grain of sand in the desert and he could find it if he wanted to.

''It not good a sign that Jadghuli and Chanzi run together,'' Hojeen said. ''They much rather shed each other's blood. Big trouble has to be brewing.''

The old bastard was sharp and, if rumor was true, heard whispers from the Goddess on occasion. Certainly some very powerful people paid heed when he warned of trouble. Not that Sandy needed any warning about trouble *this* time. Just having the lulzi missing was a disaster.

Damn, he should have been prepared for something like this when Hojeen had decided to go with this patrol, though the two other occasions he'd done so nothing really horrendous had happened—except maybe for that witch who had hexed Janiphar's band. Still, associating with one the Goddess favored was chancy, especially for Sandy. He wished this was Earth where the gods and goddesses, if they existed, kept their fingers out of human affairs.

Aku rode up and gave an offhanded salute. ''The men are ready, all except Chirarri. His sword arm is slashed to the bone. Azil slapped some healing salve on and sewed up the wound, but he'll not be much use in a fight for a while.'' He paused and added, ''We rounded up the Jadghuli's rudhars. Most are the bobtailed trash they usually ride, but they should make useful remounts if we have a long chase.''

Sandy nodded. ''Hojeen says there are about twenty more raiders and that they have the girl Anala with them. Thank the gods for small favors—there would have been hell to pay if they had slain her.''

Because desert tribes took their religion seriously, they revered those the Goddess had chosen as her lulzi. The empire would be in trouble enough for letting her be kidnapped.

Sandy made a face. "Damn that lame-brained vixen! The Hagba Khamliss told me that he was about to send her to Kimbo-Dashla to study with the city's high priestess. I don't doubt it's her fault and she was still here. She's as boneheaded and stubborn a brat as I've seen."

"She is an orphan, and only fourteen years old," protested Aku.

"That's no excuse for being one of the worst pains in the rear I've ever come across," Sandy snapped. "Anyway, we have to bust our guts trying to save her—or the governor will hang us high for letting her be kidnapped."

Sandy turned to Hojeen and asked, "How much of a lead do they have on us? Where do you think they are headed?"

The old man scratched his chin. "They'll head southwest toward barren ground. That's what I'd do in their place. Fastest way to their home tents, but little water on the way." He paused and added, "Tracks say the same thing. They have maybe three hours on us. If we push hard we might catch them."

"We'll do it," muttered Sandy, "We have little choice."

Hojeen pointed north. "Company coming. Maybe hour away. Pilgrims to see the Hagba. I can see sunlight glinting silver on prayer banners."

Sandy nodded and turned to Aku. "Send Chirarri to me. You and the men go with Hojeen after the raiders. I'll catch up to you."

Aku looked at the stony and seemingly trackless ground and then at Hojeen questioningly.

The old man cackled and said, "Don't worry, younker. If I can't find their spoor, I'll *smell* the bastards out."

As his other troopers rode off, Sandy quickly gave instructions to a pale-looking Chirarri. "Don't push yourself, but make sure you get to Kimbo-Dashla and report to the colonel. When you pass the pilgrims, tell them what happened and then push on."

Sandy quickly caught up with the rest of his troopers, who were riding at a steady mile-eating pace. As he passed from the rear to the front of the column, he glanced at the remounts they had acquired. That old scoundrel Hojeen had managed to latch onto the only Jadghuli rudhar that was much more than dogmeat. It was a dun-colored beast with faint black stripes on its legs; a chiragutta courser, by the look of it. He wondered how the Jadghuli had got hold of it; the Kri Shandri clans didn't sell these beasts and had been known to spend years tracking down thieves who had dared raid their herds.

As Sandy took a position beside Aku, the sergeant asked, "Why is this girl so important? The desert folk revere her, but I don't see why. Of course, I am an outlander, and know little of this land."

"Neither do I," Sandy said sourly. "Supposedly she is a lulzi, a sort of wisewoman and witch combined. Though as far as I can tell, she is neither. The desert folk say that long ago the Goddess promised that to each generation of desert folk a lulzi would be born."

He made a face and added, "Anala is barely into her teens and has an opinion on everything, especially if she doesn't know anything about it."

Aku laughed. "You seem to know her well."

"Do I ever. At the end of every sweep my patrol makes through the desert, I have to stop in and check on her. She can talk the hind leg off a rudhar and never pause for a breath." He gave a wry smile and then joked blackly, "After having her for a day or two, maybe the Jadghuli will pay us to take her off their hands."

Aku got serious. "Won't they slit her throat if we get too close?"

Sandy shook his head. "They might try, but I doubt that bad penny would be so easy to get rid of, especially since she has the favor of the Goddess."

Sandy eyed Aku thoughtfully, a grin spreading slowly over his face. "She has her eye on you," he said. "My last trip through here, while I was having dinner with her and the Hagba Khamliss, all she could talk about was my new sergeant and how brave he had to be—mot to mention how handsome. Now that she is fourteen I wouldn't be surprised to see her put her shoes at your door, especially since she knows that someday you are going to be an important somebody in this army—you brought quite a reputation from the islands, and the powers-that-be are keeping an eye on you."

Aku flushed a bit and said, "I am only an outlander."

"Try your bull on somebody else," Sandy jabbed back in

a knowing tone. "You know the court prefers its competent generals be outlanders—they're easier to control. And you certainly are more than competent, even if the stories of your military exploits in the islands are only half true."

Aku changed the subject. "What is this about shoes at my door?"

Sandy gave a wry shrug. "It's an odd custom these desert folk have. If a woman is rich or important enough, she can force a man to marry her by placing her shoes at his door. The pretext is that he has slept with her and is obligated to make an honest woman of her. Since she asks marriage, legally her allegation cannot be questioned, even if she is still a virgin."

Aku shook is head and muttered, "Crazy barbarians."

"It usually doesn't work out too badly," Sandy said. "Since she asked for the marriage, the woman must support the man while they live together. If she asks for a divorce, she is obligated to give a tenth of her wealth to him. It's not that common, these desert wenches are tight when it comes to money and think twice before they try shoe marriage. Besides, a man can usually wiggle out of it if he knows the right palms to grease, except if the woman doing the asking is a lulzi or a priestess of the Goddess."

"I wouldn't say *no* if she asked," Aku said, laughing. "I'm willing to take the easy way to the top if it is offered. Though I do have two wives and five children back in the islands—not to mention that widow I've been tupping back in Kimbo-Dashal."

"Doesn't matter. These desert wenches prefer an experienced man for their first husband. If she does ask, all I can say is, better you than me."

Sandy looked around at his patrol and then called a halt. "Change mounts," he ordered. "I want our rudhars to be fresh when we catch up with the Jadghuli."

Hojeen spoke to him before taking over the point position again. "Three more Chanzi shapechangers with them now. Come from south."

Sandy nodded and barked out marching orders. "Column of twos. Zim-Adada bring up the rear and Aku ride beside me."

As he rode beside Aku, Sandy gave him some advice. "If we do recover the lulzi, it might be well for you to get on the good side of her. They usually assign sergeants to me if they are thinking about promoting them, but any little extra pull you can get wouldn't hurt. Just remember me when you are a marshall of the empire and I'm the oldest subaltern in the army—and with something cushy, not with the dirty assignments.''

Aku laughed and said, "I promise. Not that I'll ever make it that high.''

"You will,'' Sandy told him seriously. "Not only the generals have their eye on you, the Goddess does to—that's probably one reason Hojeen joined my patrol this time, not that I wasn't glad to have him along. Besides, you have that something which makes men want to follow you to hell if need be—that, and brains to go with it.''

"You're a cynical bastard,'' Aku said.

"No, just a realistic one. The Rithian army needs you, the Goddess wants you, and I'll do what I can to help you.''

Aku laughed. "I suppose the generals hop to it when you ask them. And what do you expect for this help?''

"Nothing,'' Sandy said, "except maybe a drink for old time's sake once in a while.''

Aku smiled and shook his head. "I really have it made,'' he said in a disbelieving tone, "hobnobbing as I do with two of the Goddess's most powerful bullyboys. I only wish that the next time we sit down to a feast of hard bread and jerky you two will change your perfumes. You've both been using stale sweat and old dirt too long.''

Half an hour later Sandy had fallen back to ride rear guard. When he had an opportunity, he cocked an eye toward the heavens and said in an undertone, "How about throwing some help our way? We're good, but we'll need more than that to catch those Jadghuli. Besides, it will show what an all-powerful goddess you are.''

There was no reply from the heavens, not that he expected one.

By changing mounts on the hour they were able to set a killing pace. The western horizon was streaked with red when Sandy rose in his saddle and yelled, "Halt!'' In a quieter voice he added, "Take ten.'' He motioned for Hojeen to come over and join him.

Chewing on dry sausage and sipping lukewarm water, the two men knelt on the ground to talk.

"How far behind are we now?" Sandy asked.

Hojeen screwed up his face and looked toward the west, where the air now had that indefinable quality of dusk which is halfway between darkness and light. "They're only two hours ahead. Their rudhars are tired and they have no remounts. Their spare rudhars stampeded into desert about an hour after they left village. Very odd, but happens. Good for us; we might catch them."

Sandy took another drink from his canteen, made a face, and replied, "I saw where it happened. There was the smell of sorcery in the air. Not Chanzi magic, but real sorcery." He added uneasily, "I'd sure like to know who their other prisoner is."

Hojeen nodded. "Don't know. Not a desert tribesman—walks like city man. Wears those rope-soled sandals they make in the savannas south of here."

Sandy grimaced as a memory flashed through his mind: the memory of a scruffy-bearded old reprobate he'd once known. "It would just be my luck if it is him," he muttered to himself. To Hojeen he said, "Can you follow their trail at night?"

The old scout's face broke into a grin. "Darkness better for us. The moon is almost full and the power of the Goddess waxes stronger when it shines. Jadghuli will be blind this night, but I will see."

Sandy just hoped the Goddess was taking enough interest in mortal affairs to put a spoke in the wheels of Anala's kidnappers. If she didn't, not even Hojeen's supernaturally keen night sight would help much. In his mind a soft voice whispered, *Luck comes to those who work for it.* Sandy made an obscene comment.

He hurriedly finished the hard biscuit he was chewing on, washed it down with water, and got to his feet. "Mount up," he yelled at his troopers, perversely enjoying their bitching at having to move stiff muscles; if he wasn't in charge he'd be bellyaching too.

They kept up a hard steady pace for nearly three hours. Hojeen, in the point position, never once lost the trail. Around midnight, the scout halted and motioned Sandy to come forward, then pointed to the rocky ground at their feet. As he did so, the moon seemed to shine more brightly, its rays illuminating scuff marks in the earth with silvery sparkles.

Most of the marks headed off to their right, but some went straight ahead.

"They split forces," Hojeen said. "Jadghuli who go north have four Chanzi with them. Other group has prisoners, one Chanzi and few Jadghuli—they head for the hills ahead."

"Why did they split?" Sandy asked.

Hojeen thought for a moment before replying. "Tullicantra caves just to the north, maybe a two-hour ride. At full moon there are always Kilbri tribesmen there. They worship Goddess as *Cloimiry-Fina the Old*. This is the time they initiate new warriors into manhood. Jadghuli might go to steal rudhar. Or, maybe, they meet someone."

The scout pointed ahead into the darkness and gave a bloodthirsty chuckle. "Goddess smiles on us, gives us enough Jadghuli to make killing easy."

"Yeah," Sandy agreed sourly. "I've heard *that* story before." He strained his eyes against the darkness, trying to see the hills Hojeen said were ahead. "I don't see anything."

"Hills there for those with young eyes," Hojeen said in a deadpan voice.

Sandy gave the old scoundrel a withering look. Hojeen smiled innocently and didn't wilt a bit. Sandy absentmindedly played with the ring on his little finger and looked again. This time he saw a vague mass looming ahead in the darkness.

"I see the hills," he said. "What do you know about them?"

"Salt flats and treacherous ground to north of hills. Jadghuli will follow trail to south of hills. Maybe they will stop at Taz Makil. There are caves and a rock tank there. Many times, but not always, there is water in tank. I think their rudhars are too tired to go much further." He paused before adding, "From the north there is a way through hills to Taz Makil. Hard, but on foot we could make it."

Sandy thought for a moment, weighing his options. Then he called Aku to his side and explained the situation. "Hojeen and I will sneak in from the north," he concluded, "and try to rescue the girl. You take the rest of the troopers and circle south. Hide there and be ready to charge in if I give a signal.

"And don't be seen," he added quickly. "That hoyden

may have the luck of the damned, but luck doesn't stop a sharp knife.''

Sandy and Hojeen, on foot and each leading two rudhars, picked their way along the north edge of the hills. The ground was almost impassable, a combination of rubble torn from the hills by flash floods and salt-encrusted playas filled with corrosive mud. Sandy was wishing he had gone south with his troopers—at least they had solid ground to ride on.

An hour later the two of them were easing down a dry ravine on the south slope of the hills. They had hobbled their rudhars and left them behind on the north side of the hills, since the trail was hardly fit for mountain goats. The ravine they were in was not much more than a crack and slanted down at almost forty-five degrees, but at least it led down instead of up.

Sandy looked at his companion and swore softly. That dried-up old scoundrel hadn't even worked up a sweat, while Sandy was puffing and getting rubber-legged. Hojeen had to be made out of steel and leather instead of flesh.

The ravine turned a corner and opened out onto a rocky ledge which faced south. Hojeen motioned Sandy to get on his belly, then they both crawled cautiously to the edge of the ledge and looked down on the place called Taz Makil.

Below was a large embayment in the side of the hills, surrounded on all sides except the south by steep cliffs. In the bright moonlight they could see clearly what was below, except for an area just under their ledge.

On the left side of the embayment, at the foot of a cliff, was a shallow cave. Four men were seated in a circle in front of it, taking turns smoking a slender foot-long pipe. A stray breeze brought the sharp biting smell of pickled dhargyul weed to the ledge.

Sandy smiled: Here was something in their favor. When aroused the four would fight like madmen, but without reason or caution. A lot of desert tribes used the drug to put themselves into a frenzy before battle, thinking it gave them extra strength and endurance. Maybe it did, but it also put them at a disadvantage if they had to think.

Standing off to one side and looking disgruntled was a squat, bearded figure who wore a loincloth and the pelt of a sand leopard instead of a hooded burnoose like the Jadghuli.

Sandy could smell him, too, on the same errant breeze which had before brought the pungent scent of dhargyul weed. The man stank—a rank bestial smell mixed with the stench of long-unwashed human.

Hojeen touched Sandy's arm and pointed to the top of the cliff overlooking the cave. Sitting there was a huddled figure keeping watch on the desert, but with its back to them: a Chanzi.

Hojeen whispered into Sandy's ear, "There's another cave— at the foot of this cliff and left."

Sandy nodded and cautiously pulled himself forward until his head stuck over the side of the ledge. Looking straight down and to the left, he saw a narrow opening in a dark angle of the cliff. Hunkered down in front of the cave was another Jadghuli. Sandy's lips parted in a grim smile. The odds were seven to two against them and it was going to be tough to rescue the lulzi—but it could be done. The Jadghuli weren't expecting trouble, and that would make it easier.

"I kill guard below," whispered Hojeen. "You take his place." He didn't wait for an answer, but started crawling along the ledge to the left. It quickly narrowed to nearly a thread and ended at a spot almost directly over the guard's head. Hojeen came to a halt there and crawled into a sitting position.

Carefully and silently he pulled a bundle of thin sticks from his robe and began fitting them together. When he was done he had a three-foot blowpipe in his hand. He pulled a small dart and copper tube from a leather pouch at his waist, dipped the point of the dart into the tube, and inserted the dart into the blowpipe. Then he put the blowpipe to his lips and patiently waited his chance—and did it all as easily as if he had been standing on level ground.

Sandy started to crawl closer to Hojeen, but the guard heard the faint scuff of his boot against stone and looked up. Hojeen puffed on the blowpipe; the dart hit the guard in the throat. He jerked, tried to scream, and then collapsed backward.

With catlike agility, Hojeen was off his perch and climbing down the cliff face, dropping the last ten feet in a light-footed leap. Sandy hurried down the cliff after him. Holds were plentiful except for the last few feet, and Sandy had to let go and leap to the ground also. He landed almost silently, but looked up quickly to see if any of the raiders had been alert enough to hear. Fortunately their attention was focused on other things.

Sandy shoved the guard's body into the shadows at the foot of the cliff, then hunkered down to replace him. In the dark and from a distance Sandy's huddled figure should be indistinguishable from the dead Jadghuli. A moment later one of the Jadghuli from the circle looked up to check on him and quickly looked away, satisfied that all was well.

Hojeen rose from the dark shadow where he had been hiding, pointed to the sentinel on the cliff, and made a cutting motion with his hand across his throat. Sandy nodded yes. The scout found a handhold on the cliff and then another and soon was scuttling up the rock face like a human spider, silently working his way to the left. Sandy watched in amazement as Hojeen's wiry fingers found holds upon the sheer rock.

One of the Jadghuli took a puff of dhargyul weed and casually looked upward. Hojeen froze to the stone. Sandy's heart jumped up his throat and he loosened his saber in its sheath. To his eyes, the shadowy lump which was Hojeen was as visible as a candle in a dark room. But the Jadghuli saw nothing, and turned back to make a joke to his companions. They guffawed loudly and the Chanzi turned from staring out into the desert to glare at them.

The Chanzi suddenly went stiff, listened, and then swung around to stare out into the desert again. Sandy made an obscene comment under his breath and pulled his poniard out; the Chanzi's wizardly senses probably had detected Aku and his troopers.

The shapechanger hurried over to circle of the Jadghuli and spat out some indistinct words. The Jadghuli staggered drunkenly to their feet, drawing their sabers. When they turned and faced the desert, Sandy began to breathe again. In moments the fat was going to be in the fire, but at least the raiders had no idea they'd been infiltrated from the rear.

The Chanzi made a disgusted comment, showed a bow into the hands of one of the Jadghuli, and then came loping toward the cave Sandy was guarding. Sandy rose to meet him, just as another Jadghuli stuck his head out of the cave.

"It's your turn to suffer with the brat," he growled.

Sandy turned casually. With his actions hidden from the Chanzi, he shoved his left hand over the surprised Jadghuli's mouth while using his right to slip his poniard between the man's ribs and into his heart. While the dead Jadghuli collapsed back into the cave, Sandy turned to face the Chanzi as though nothing had happened. The wizard, preoccupied with his plans for the lulzi, hadn't noticed the murder.

"Get that bedamned hoyden out here," he growled, and started to push Sandy aside. Then he reared back as he caught the smell of blood. Sandy's poniard lashed out, but only raked the Chanzi across the ribs. Instantly the wizard thrust out with his staff, catching Sandy in the gut and sending him staggering backward, gasping for air.

The wizard pointed his staff at Sandy and said a word of power. A flickering pale green light sprang from the staff and surrounded the wizard with a body-length halo. The wizard began saying a second word of power. Sandy tried to ram his poniard into the Chanzi's gut, but the thrust was stopped an inch from its target by the bending yet unbreakable greenish halo. The wizard tried to point his staff at Sandy again. Sandy shoved it aside and tried to skewer his opponent again—with the same result. The Chanzi muttered another word of power, making it seem like an obscene curse. There was a flash of light and a cloud of thick black smoke hid him from Sandy's view.

There was a muttering from inside the cloud and Sandy's poniard started to turn red with heat. Sandy swore and threw it with full force into the heart of the black cloud. There was a loud *thunk,* followed by an angry curse, and the sudden and complete disappearance of the cloud.

The two of them glared at each other. Sandy's throw had hit the wizard, and he was bleeding freely from a cut on his brow. Apparently the spell which had heated up the poniard had nullified the Chanzi's protection spell—though not completely, for the melted weapon lay smoldering on the ground.

Sandy attacked, jumping forward to wrap his fingers around the wizard's throat. It wasn't easy because the Chanzi was covered from head to foot with the ointment he and his brothers used for their magic. But eventually Sandy gained a choke hold and began squeezing the life out of him.

Desperately, the wizard croaked out the first word of power he had used and touched his neck with his staff. Immediately the green force field reformed about his body.

Sandy's hands were pushed away from the Chanzi's throat by the force field. He spat out a curse and squeezed harder.

His demonic strength was starting to overpower the wizard's protective aura when the magic ring on his little finger unexpectedly became active. There was a shower of blue sparks as it touched the green force field, a stench of burning flesh, and the protective spell disappeared. Quickly Sandy reached forward to throttle the wizard, now a fire-blackened and screaming thing. He gave a practiced twist of his wrists, there was the snap of breaking bone, and the Chanzi dropped to the ground, dead.

Sandy tossed the dead wizard one away, his charred staff the other, and then yanked out his saber to face what Jadghuli remained.

There were none left. While the Chanzi had been coming toward Sandy, Hojeen had scuttled the rest of the way up the cliff and surprised the sentinel. When Sandy engaged the shapechanger wizard, he'd given a war cry and tossed the sentinel's dead body down among the other Jadghuli, who had turned to go to the Chanzi's aid.

Confused by foes behind and above them, the drug-fuddled Jadghuli had been easy meat for Sandy's troopers charging in from the desert.

There was a scrabbling sound from the cave, and Sandy whirled, ready to strike.

A bedraggled teenage girl, a smudge of dirt on her left cheek and her dark curly hair in snarls, stuck her head out and glared at him.

"Put that thing down," she snapped. "You're here to rescue me, not chop my head off. And it's about time you got here—I might have died of old age if you'd been any slower."

Sandy didn't pay too much attention to her cutting words; he expected her to be a pain in the butt. Besides, the scrawny figure climbing out of the cave after her had most of his attention. It was a scheming, conniving sorcerer by the name of Zhadnoboth: the inept master of magic who had yanked Sandy out of Baltimore and into Zarathandra by mistake and then helped strand him on this world forever.

"You miserable no-good bastard!" Sandy roared.

The sorcerer gave a startled gasp and shrank back into the cave.

The girl turned and yelled indignantly, "Don't you swear

at me, you incompetent pot walloper. I am a lulzi and should be treated like one, not insulted by a mannerless oaf.''

Sandy gave Zhadnoboth one last glare, silently promising there would be a later accounting, and turned to soothe the lulzi, steely forbearance on his face and an urge to strangle in his heart.

3

THE Goddess stared intently into the aquamarine depths of her scrying crystal, smiling as she watched the meeting between Sandy and her lulzi. It was time the two became better acquainted—much better acquainted. Possibly they'd rub the rough corners off each other, but at the least they'd begin learning how to work together. They were an ill-matched pair, but she needed both of them—one to speak for her and the other to be her man of trouble.

A fond smile played about the Goddess's lips as she looked on Anala. She loved all her lulzis, doting on them as though they were her own children. This one should become the greatest of all, if she could harness her talent—and if she could learn that others had their worth. Sandy would be good for her; she'd find it hard to either bully him or beguile him.

As she stared at the half-grown Anala, unbidden memories rose, and a shadow touched her heart. Children were special. They had inside themselves the makings of wonder, the ability to become many things. Each had something to give to the world, even if it was just a smile at the right time or one line to a song. They could be so much and that was the saddest thing; for how few became even a little of what they could be—and some became much worse. She'd loved her own children deeply, but not wisely. She remembered her two youngest, as children and as what they grew into, and she wept softly for a time.

At last, with fierce determination, the Goddess pushed her sorrow away. There was a shee, one of the demigods who'd so disturbed ancient Zarathandra, to be dealt with. This would be the last of their many encounters. It was long past time to put an end to this malevolent creature—and that leftover god who was her sometime ally.

The southern frontier of the Rithian Empire was erupting into rebellion, and the Four had come together: The time of the prophecy was at hand. Ancient of days, man of magic, wise maiden, and reluctant warrior; in their hands was the shee's fate or hers. She, who was so nearly all-seeing and all-powerful, depended on these four—because the Goddess had a peculiar weakness when it came to this shee. Only through her Four could she overcome it.

Now also was the time of tempering for the Rithian Empire and the man she had groomed to lead it to renewed greatness. It could become a glorious memory or head into an even more glorious future. Her fate and its destiny were intertwined, as were the fates of the rebels and Jara Greenteeth.

Everything depended on an ill-assorted group of maybe-heros and a scapegrace general.

The Goddess stared intently into the crystal, her eyes watching while her mind was a million miles away—scheming for the future and mulling over ways to twist destiny to her advantage.

4

SANDY patiently listened to Anala's nonstop complaints for several minutes. Then he turned to Hojeen and said, "Take the lulzi over to the rock tank and if there is water in it, get her cleaned up."

"You . . . you can't do that," sputtered Anala. "I'm no serving wench, to be brushed off at your whim."

"I can and I will," Sandy said, deadpan, as he successfully suppressed a smile. "Now get, while I figure how to get you to Kimbo-Dashla in one piece."

She stuck her hands on her hips. "Be a *big man* then, but we all know you're doing it because you're not half the man your sergeant is. Your own troopers say he cut down two Jadghuli by himself. What did you do?" Then she turned her back insultingly and stomped off.

Sandy looked after her, rolled his eyes, and shook his head as if asking *why me*. Hojeen gave a quiet chortle and trotted after the lulzi. Sandy sent a look filled with evil wishes after him.

The sorcerer was hovering nearby, polishing the surface char off the Chanzi wizard's staff and trying to look inconspicuous. Sandy stalked over and cornered him against the cliff. "What are you doing here? Did you run out of other innocent souls to hornswoggle?"

"Innocent soul!" the sorcerer howled. "I'd be the richest man in the whole world of Zarathandra if you hadn't botched things up. It's because of *you* I have to work magic for coppers—and for ungrateful fools. I fled north from the cities of the savanna to save my neck, not look for you," he added, twisting the truth a bit. "But now that I am here, there is the matter of what you owe me."

"I owe you a kick in the rear!"

"You should be grateful. Instead of being a minor demon suffering torment in some hell, you now breathe the sweet air of Zarathandra."

"I am not a demon. I'm just a poor slob you magicked from his world to this back end of nowhere."

Zhadnoboth gave a disbelieving snort. "And it's a fine mess you landed me in. If you and your troopers had done your job right, none of this would have happened. When a harmless traveler can't go on his way in peace, then something is wrong."

"Keep quiet," Sandy growled. "I have enough trouble without being chewed out by harebrained brats and motheaten sorcerers. Just stay out of my way and don't try to be useful. It's easier to survive your conniving than your help."

The scrawny sorcerer bounced up and down on his heels, reminding Sandy of a bantam rooster getting ready to attack. "You ungrateful cur," he howled. "I *made* you what you are."

"Yeah," Sandy agreed. "A no-account officer on a forgotten frontier."

"You are more than that, and you know it. You have the favor of the Goddess and a magic ring—and all because of me. I should have some reward for bringing you good fortune instead of being nearly killed by blackguards."

"If you want," Sandy said sarcastically, "I'll finish the job they botched, by hanging you as a menace to the empire."

Just then Anala came barging over, still dripping from a hasty washing at the rock tank. "Leave the poor man alone," she ordered. "He's worth a dozen ruffians like you. It was due to him the Jadghuli lost their remounts. What's more, he also managed to free me before you showed up. And if you hadn't blundered in, no doubt the two of us would have made a better job of those raiders than you did."

Sandy made a wry grimace. "If that incompetent's sorcery scared off the rudhars, it was by accident. When he works magic, it's a miracle if his spells do what he wants them to. Usually it rains frogs—or something worse."

Anala gave a ladylike sniff and said, "You're jealous. He

is a sorcerer and a man of honor, while you are"—she paused, trying to find the right words—"a lowdown ruffian."

"Man of honor!" Sandy shook his head. "Zhadnoboth would sell his own grandmother as a ten-year-old virgin if he could."

Their argument was interrupted as two Jadghuli came riding hell-for-leather out of the desert and into their midst. They almost rode down Aku before they realized they were among enemies instead of friends.

The sergeant grabbed the boot of one rider and flipped him out of the saddle. Then he whirled, yanked out his dagger, and ran the other Jadghuli through the gut. The Jadghuli doubled over and rolled from the saddle.

Meanwhile, Aku barely had time to unsheathe his saber before the first Jadghuli attacked him. There was the clang of metal against metal and the flash of steel in the moonlight. For a few brief moments the Jadghuli held his own. Then the sergeant saw an opening, stepped inside the guard of his foe, and with practiced ease skewered him through the heart. It was a masterful bit of fighting for the outlander; apparently he had learned his soldiering well in the islands.

By the time Sandy got there, it was over. Aku was already cleaning his blade on the cloak of his last foe. Sandy bent over to make sure both Jadghuli were dead and then yanked an ivory cylinder from the waist of the Jadghuli Aku had gutted.

But the sentry Sandy had posted at the top of the cliff was scrambling down pell-mell. "Riders," he gasped. "Plenty of them. Coming from both east and west."

Sandy spat an angry curse and turned to Aku. "Take the troopers and ride straight south into the desert. Just buy Hojeen and me some time, so we can sneak the lulzi out the back way." He smiled and added dryly, "Just make sure those bastards see you."

Aku grinned, threw a what-the-hell salute, and began barking orders at his men. "Get off your dead rears, boys, and into your saddles. We have to run like hell if we don't want those Jadghuli to feed us to the vultures."

Sandy raced over to where Hojeen was standing with Anala. "Grab the lulzi and take her back over your so-called trail. I'll follow and protect your ass."

Anala charged up to him and screamed in his face, "You

coward! How dare you send brave men to their deaths while you skulk off to safety?''

"Shut up!" he roared. "My job is to get *you* to safety!"

She started to shriek a protest. With a disgusted snort, Sandy grabbed her, slung her over his shoulder, and stalked off to the back of the embayment, while Anala screamed angrily and beat her fists on his back.

At the back of the embayment was a man-wide crack leading up to the trail Hojeen and Sandy had followed to get to Taz Makil. The scout spryly scrambled up the crack to the ledge he and Sandy had used to spy out the embayment. Sandy followed and shoved the lulzi up to him, adroitly dodging a kick she aimed at his head.

He yelled to Hojeen, "Get this bonehead moving. We don't have much time."

"They'll hear about this in Dar-Esh-Rith," Anala promised furiously.

"No doubt," Sandy said dryly. "But I don't give a damn as long as you get your pretty butt moving up the trail."

She would have said more, but Hojeen grabbed her and pushed her ahead of him up the ravine, whispering to her. Whatever he said did the trick and she began climbing up the trail on her own.

Sandy heaved a sigh of relief and stood guard at the foot of the trail, waiting to make sure no foe was close on their heels. He tightened his grip on his saber hilt when a figure came running toward him.

"What about me?" squalled the sorcerer in a terrified voice. "If those barbarians find her gone and me here, they'll skin me alive!"

Sandy thought, *good riddance,* but grabbed Zhadnoboth and shoved him up the crack by main force. The sorcerer scrabbled frantically to get a good grip on the rock. For a moment he almost tumbled back into Sandy's arms, but an angry growl did wonders for his climbing ability.

Sandy waited a couple of minutes more and then followed. After climbing for a while, he paused to listen. He heard nothing. Grunting in satisfaction, he continued with his climb. Maybe Aku's charge into the desert had done some good.

Sandy climbed for twenty minutes more, until he was near the crest of the hills, then paused to wipe the sweat from his brow and check the back trail again. He shivered as he saw the ominous look of the land in the predawn moonlight. The hills seemed to crouch like silvery gray beasts waiting for unwary prey.

He turned to go on; then stiffened and cocked his head. A faint sound came to his ear. He swore, unsheathed his saber, and waited for who or what was coming—glad of the narrowness and steepness of the trail at this point.

Moments passed—moments during which a deep inner dread grew in him, and the hair on his arms began to stand on end. He'd had this feeling before and had learned to trust it: Whatever followed wasn't human or even natural. His mind told him it had to be shapechangers, his instincts said *run*.

Finally he caught a glimpse of a fast-moving shape silhouetted against the trail below. Nervously Sandy wiped the sweat off the palm of his sword hand and gripped his saber tighter. He leaned closer to the boulder he was crouching by, then jerked away as it shifted under his weight.

Sandy looked at the boulder, gave a savage grin, and pushed on it again. The rock seemed ready to break free, if he shoved it hard enough. Just below him the trail sloped down at a steep angle and then turned a corner—a perfect place to ambush his foes with the boulder.

He patiently waited for the Chanzi to arrive. Suddenly a huge beast, its rough fur stained silver by the moonlight, bounded around the corner and charged up the trail toward him. It was a sand leopard, twice the size of any he'd seen.

Sandy rose and gave a mighty heave on the boulder. For an instant it resisted, then with a grinding roar it came loose, bouncing down the trail like a charging elephant before smashing into the werebeast. There was a scream of agony, bestial and yet undeniably human. Then the boulder and the leopard plunged over the cliff that bounded the left side of the trail.

For a second, Sandy could hear the Chanzi's agonized screams—then an immense crash as the boulder hit something—then silence.

An involuntary shudder ran up Sandy's spine. He had expected a werebeast and seen one, but the actuality was soul-chilling.

Just as he picked up his saber again, two more werebeasts charged around the corner and up the trial. One followed the beaten track, while the other found purchase on the steep wall bordering the trail on the right and tried to flank him. Sandy surprised the werebeast coming up the wall by attacking—he hurled himself into the air and downward. The sand leopard reared to meet him, but not quickly enough: Sandy's boots crashed into its chest, knocking it backward toward the abyss.

The werebeast clawed wildly at the rock as it tried to save itself from going over the edge. For a brief moment it teetered there as its talons caught hold on the rough shaly rock. Then the top layer of the rock split off and the wereleopard toppled over into the abyss. Sandy could hear its bestial screams of terror echoing upward as it fell. Then there was a heart-stopping screech, a sickening thud, a rattle of falling stones, and then silence.

Meanwhile, Sandy flung away his saber and grabbed desperately for a hold, as his momentum carried him downward and toward the edge. He barely managed to save himself, falling to his knees and pulling himself to the center of the trail as some of the rotten rock at the edge collapsed under his weight.

He heard a snarl and saw the last werebeast pouncing down on him from higher up the trail. It was young and made a misjudgment because of the slope, almost sailing over him instead of hitting him. At the last moment, it twisted in the air and managed to knock him over with a blow from its forepaw.

They both rolled down the center of the trail in a wildly thrashing tangle of limbs as they fought for advantage, forgetting about the abyss that rimmed the trail. Somehow Sandy managed to get inside the reach of the thing's talons and wrap his legs around its middle and his hands around its thick-corded neck. Their downward momentum was stopped when they smashed into a sort of pocket in the rock, just about where the trail turned the corner.

For an instant they lay there stunned, then renewed their desperate struggle. The werebeast roared in frustration as it fought, because it could not get at Sandy. Its claws tore the back of his burnoose to shreds but couldn't penetrate the mail shirt beneath, while the viselike grip of Sandy's hands about its throat kept it from tearing him apart with its teeth. It tried to get its hind legs up and under to rip out his belly and privates, but couldn't quite do it—Sandy's rear end was flush against its hind legs, preventing this movement.

But Sandy was not doing much more than holding his own. His arms and hands were immensely strong, but the neck muscles of the wereleopard were like twisted steel cables and he couldn't make a dent in them. He tried to crush its ribs with his locked legs and got nowhere. As long as he held on he was all right, but his muscles were becoming one giant ache.

The werebeast shifted its attack, giving up its futile clawings, and began forcing its slavering jowls toward Sandy's face. He resisted with all his might, but grudging inch by grudging inch the beast forced its teeth closer. Soon the yellowed fangs were only the width of a hand from his face and its foul breath was making him gag.

The wereleopard, feeling Sandy's grip loosen, opened its mouth wide and snapped its head forward in attack. An instant before, Sandy had pushed himself suddenly back. As the beast's head shot toward him, he rammed his right fist into its mouth and then down into its throat. The wereleopard gagged and tried to jerk its head away, but Sandy relentlessly kept shoving his fist deeper into its throat. Frantically, the werebeast tried to close its jaws and bit his arm off, but Sandy had leverage and it couldn't close its mouth. The werebeast panicked and it frantically tried to do several things at once— spit Sandy's arm out, ravage him with its talons, break away from his death grip, and get air. This went on for several moments, then the beast realized it was dying and a savage vindictiveness calmed it down. Doggedly it started to drag its body and the man wrapped about it toward the cliff edge. Inch by agonizing inch it forced itself forward.

It got to the very brink of the cliff. One more surge from its muscles would topple them over. Sandy released his scissors hold and dug in his heels. For a moment which seemed to last an eternity it was muscle power against muscle power— Sandy did not win the contest, but neither did he lose. He just held the werebeast to a standstill, and that was enough.

Hope faded in the eyes of the wereleopard and they clouded over. The next moment a violent shudder shook its body and it collapsed. For minutes Sandy kept his hand shoved down the beast's throat, refusing to give the unholy thing even the slightest chance of reviving. Then, finally sure the thing was dead, he yanked his arm from its throat, wincing—the skin on his hand was hanging in shreds.

The beast was lying halfway across Sandy's body so that he could hardly breathe. He tried unsuccessfully to budge it, but all strength seemed drained from his muscles. He rested a moment, then became irrationally furious at his predicament, and with a sudden surge threw the carcass off himself—anger finding strength his conscious mind couldn't tap.

Gingerly Sandy got to his feet and almost immediately fell into a fighting crouch when he saw the beast's body quiver. The wereleopard's alien flesh was flowing and remolding itself from beast shape to man shape—becoming the corpse of a youth barely out of his teens.

Sandy tried to climb up the trail and sank to his knees, finding himself weaker than he had thought. As he rested he consciously became aware of his wounds for the first time. His left thigh was bleeding profusely from a deep ripping cut, his right hand had hardly any skin on it, and his back under the mail shirt was an aching agony. The only blessing was that the wounds weren't mortal—he certainly didn't relish the thought of dying yet again.

He heard a scraping sound from below and then a rock falling. Instantly he was alert and on his feet. A glimmer of metal caught his eye and he hobbled toward it—to find his saber jammed into a crack in the rock. He cautiously edged over to the cliff and looked down.

At first he saw nothing. A dark something moved and he saw it, looked closer, and swore. About forty feet down were two glaring green eyes filled with hate. There was a snarl, and he knew for sure it was the werebeast he'd knocked over the cliff. Somehow it had survived its fall and now, powered by an unearthly vitality, was crawling back up the cliff to get him.

Sandy picked up a hand-sized piece of rock and heaved it down at the werebeast. There was a thud, an agonized snarl, and a frantic scratching of claws—but the man-leopard held on and stubbornly started coming again. He looked around, saw a larger piece of rock, hobbled over to pick it up, and then staggered back to heave it over the edge. This time there was a crunch, a wailing screech, and then a diminishing series of thuds as the creature bounced off projecting pieces of the cliff on its way to the bottom.

"Die, you bastard." Sandy stared hard into the abyss, now graying with the approach of morning, and nodded with satisfaction when he heard one final thud. The thing just possibly might survive, but it would be in no shape to come after him.

So he sat down and began tending to his wounds as best he could. Sandy healed far faster than the average person, but it didn't hurt to help the healing along. After fumbling with a pouch on his belt, he pulled out a round tin, pried the lid off, and began rubbing the malodorous brown salve into his wounds, cursing all the while. Abraggi's salve was a godsend to the Rithian army—if given time, it could cure a soldier of almost everything except death. But it was a brutal medicine, biting like liquid fire when it was applied, but quickly scabbing over an open wound. A hundred-year-old joke in the Rithian army was that any wound was less painful than the cure.

Eventually Sandy looked up the trail toward the top of the pass, said a few well-chosen curse words, and started up the steep winding way. His whole body ached and his legs were like jelly by the time he got to the crest and could look at a path that led downward.

The sun was just inching up over the eastern horizon, coloring the swirling morning mist crimson. One patch of mist clumped together so it resembled a tall lean woman cloaked in a blood-red hooded robe. Sandy turned to it and snarled, "Why don't you get somebody else to do your dirty work?" He paused and then added, "It's about time you showed up."

There was a soft laugh, and a voice as melodious as silver chimes said, "Because there's no one better at it."

"Bullshit!"

"My lulzi must be saved—without her, Zarathandra will be a lesser place. I can't intervene directly—even goddesses are bound by certain laws and necessities. *You* must do this." As though it were an afterthought, she added, "And maybe teach her some of what she needs to know."

Sandy looked sourly at the shadow figure. "Cut the soft soap. I'll do my best to get her to Kimbo-Dashla, but nobody is going to teach that loudmouth anything—she thinks she knows it all."

"We all get older and wiser. Give her time and she'll blossom."

"Yeah," Sandy said sardonically, "from an obnoxious brat to an obnoxious battle-axe."

The Goddess laughed. "You're a good match for her. She needs an ornery bastard to bring her into line."

"I'm not ornery. I just don't like being continually dragged into your schemes, especially when I get saddled with wet-nursing a hoyden who sinks her fangs into me every time I see her."

The Goddess laughed again, which only made Sandy's temper hotter. He tried to step up the argument, but she deftly cut the ground from underneath him.

"No wonder you're in such bad humor," she said as she touched his bad hand with a gentle caress, her shadowy form now become warm flesh. "You're hurt."

"As if you didn't know."

She ignored his comment and with elegant grace made a pass with her hand. His clothes and gear fell in a heap to the ground beside him. Crooning a soft chant, she began running her hands gently over his wounded flesh. He started to protest through chattering teeth, but she said, "Keep still. How am I supposed to heal you if you spoil my concentration?"

Sandy kept still, though ungraciously. Her healing touch did feel good, but he was in no mood to admit that to her—and the morning air was cold.

Under her touch his lacerated flesh reknit itself, forming unblemished hide where before had been bleeding wounds. As her fingers gently kneaded his deeply bruised back, sore and knotted muscles relaxed and healed themselves. In five minutes his body was as good as or better than new—and his temper had changed from sour to sunny.

The Goddess stepped back and admired her work. "Now you look good." She paused before adding, "*Very* good."

"Maybe I do, but I'm bare-assed and freezing my butt off." He reached down to pick up his clothes.

She put a hand on his arm. "Why hurry? You have a little time to squander."

He gave her a sidelong glance and said ironically, "Whatever happened to the randy Goddess who just grabbed and jumped on? You must be mellowing with age."

The Goddess gave a bawdy laugh, rubbed her suddenly naked body up against him, and whispered into his ear, "Aren't we lemans? I should have my privileges—shouldn't I? Besides, a goddess of love *must* have it." She nibbled on his ear and gently pulled him to the ground.

Sandy gave in to her gently aggressive seduction, not altogether unwillingly. There was a lot to be said for having a goddess as a lover—she was as ingenious and lusty a lay as he'd ever bedded. But she wouldn't take no for an answer and there was no way to dump her if he wanted to. Still, despite her being a high and mighty bitch at times, he did kind of like her—or, god forbid, even love her.

Sandy let loose a lurid curse when he pulled on his left boot and found a stone had rolled in. The Goddess laughed and said, "You need a wife—somebody to look after you. You'd certainly be less cross-grained."

"No thanks," Sandy muttered as he yanked off his boot. "I'm stuck with you and that's more than enough."

The Goddess looked at him musingly. "Marriage would give you a certain place in society. It's time you lost your reputation as a lusty rogue who has diddled with every wife and wanton on the border."

"Whose fault is that?" Sandy demanded as he yanked his boot back on. "You've worked hard to make me notorious—lord knows why."

She ignored his comments. "You should be known as a solid citizen who does his womanizing discreetly." Her voice started to fade out. "I know just the woman to be your chief wife, a crafty conniver who'll get you the best marriages." After her almost-inaudible last word came an empty silence.

The meaning of what she had been saying finally penetrated Sandy's mind. His body froze for an instant, his face turned red as his temper started to sizzle, and then he jumped to his feet and whirled around to give her a piece of his mind.

He was too late. Her tall hooded figure was just the faintest shadow . . . and then was gone.

"Come back here," he yelled to empty air. "Damn that scheming rig," he muttered. "What harebrained plan has she got up her sleeve now?"

Sourly he picked up his burnoose and put it on, noticing that she had taken the time to mend it with her magic—in fact, it was in better shape than at any time since he had bought it. That was her to the T: do him all kinds of little favors and throw him to the wolves when she wanted something done.

The rest of the journey was easy, mostly downhill—not that

he noticed; he was too busy stewing. He knew damn well she was up to something, not even counting this idiotic marriage junk. He could feel it in his bones that *interesting times* were ahead, and he cursed—couldn't he be blessed with a dull time for once? Why hadn't she had the sense to draft a hero into her service instead of a former bureaucrat from Baltimore?

The sun was barely all the way over the horizon when Sandy came stumbling down a ravine and into the midst of his companions. They were mounted and impatiently awaiting him.

"What have you been doing?" Anala said peevishly, though there was a touch of worry in her voice. "While you dallied, the whole Jadghuli nation could have come down on us."

Sandy was in no mood to be chewed out, especially by a know-nothing young girl. "Lord, I should have let those raiders keep you. They'd have found out there are things worse than death."

His words cut Anala to the quick. A lulzi and thus very holy, she was used to getting the proper respect.

She drew herself up in the saddle and in a voice she meant to be grand and chilling said, "Your superiors, the emperor, and the Goddess shall hear about this discourtesy. After they are though with you, maybe then you'll have some manners."

"I run this show. If a certain snot-nosed brat doesn't like it, that's too bad. Once I dump you off in Kimbo-Dashla, you can be as high and mighty as you please. Until then, pretend I know enough to come in out of the rain." He saw her po-faced look and added, "Of course you can bitch as much as you want to, behind my back."

His words shocked the lulzi into silence. If her stormy looks had had any force, they would have killed Sandy excruciatingly a hundred times over. Yet under the anger lurked a kind of fear and even a smidgen of respect.

Sandy turned to Hojeen, who had watched the argument with wry amusement, and said, "Let's get going. I had trouble along your back trail. The Chanzi and those Jadghuli raiders, the whole kit and caboodle, must be on their way to intercept us by now. Something big is brewing; there are too many of the bastards around for it to be a simple raid." He added more quietly, "*She* said as much, though getting any solid fact from her is a miracle."

Hojeen nodded, knowing who *she* was without being told.

Sandy and he had never talked over each other's relationship with the Goddess, or even acknowledged it, but had come to an unspoken understanding that they served the same mistress.

Zhadnoboth interrupted them. "How long do I have to ride this abominable beast?" He pointed beneath him to Sandy's remount, a moth-eaten and cantankerous-looking rudhar who seemed to like the sorcerer as little as he liked it. "I'm an old man and not up to riding an animated butter churn for any longer than I have to."

He looked pointedly at Anala's rudhar, the smooth-striding Chiragutta courser loaned her by Hojeen. Maybe resenting his words, the rudhar he was riding twisted its neck around and tried to take a nip from the sorcerer's leg. Zhadnoboth swatted it on the nose. The man and beast exchanged fish-eyed stares, each silently promising there would be a day of reckoning.

"You're free to stay here," Sandy said curtly.

The sorcerer seemed to be thinking over the stories he'd heard about the Jadghuli. With ill grace he said, "I'll go with you."

Hojeen pointed to the east and west. "No good going either way. Enemy be coming from both directions soon. Have to go north into Tolk Gilzad. A bad place—I know of only one man who came out of it alive."

They looked north and saw a wasteland of salt flats, sand, and foul ground. It looked evil—the ground generally colored a sickly looking yellow-brown, what plants there were had wicked-looking thorns and clung close to the ground as though waiting in ambush.

"When we enter, follow close and do what I tell you," said Hojeen. "It is evil; many men have died here. Water is filled with salt and alkali. If you walk the wrong place, the ground can swallow you. Many bad things live here—not friendly to humans or to each other."

"Don't worry," Anala said. "You have a lulzi with you—the Goddess will look after you."

"We appreciate the protection," Sandy said sardonically. "But we'll also watch our step and do what Hojeen says."

Anala gave him a withering glance. "Be an unbeliever, barbarian, but don't crawl to me for protection if she appears."

Sandy shrugged. "For now, let's follow Hojeen. He knows this land and we don't."

Anala gave him a look which could have boiled lead, but held her tongue. She was hardheaded and full of herself, but could see sense when you hit her between the eyes with it.

A faint smile tugged at the corners of Hojeen's mouth as that tough old man led them carefully northward, though he continued to treat Anala with the reverence the desert folk had for their lulzi.

The Tolk Gilzad was badlands and not true desert, but that might have made it worse. The ground was rough and treacherous, sparsely covered with haggard vegetation. Here and there were pools of black foul-smelling water, many stretches of ground white with alkali and salt, and strewn everywhere were razor-sharp fragments of rock. The most common plant, a rust-red and rounded clump of sticks armed with two-inch-long hooked thorns, polluted the air with a stench of iodine and rotten eggs.

Hojeen pointed to one of the bushes and said, "Don't touch. The thongs of assassin bush can slice boots to ribbons, flesh to shreds. The poison in the thorns makes wounds fester and burn." He pointed to things that looked like thumb-sized ash-black puffballs. "Don't step on firefoot. Sap will eat a hole right through a boot—and then foot." As they went along he pointed out several more plants, all of which were obnoxious if not dangerous in one way or another. As he had said, the life in the Tolk Gilzad was not friendly.

They made slow progress as the old scout more often than not went sideways and roundabout instead of straight ahead. Some of the things he avoided were obvious, but more often only he could see the dangers that surrounded them.

It irked Sandy to make such slow progress, especially knowing pursuit must be close at hand; but at least they weren't getting themselves killed. He wished they were out in the true desert. It was harsh, hot, and merciless; but at least the danger was out in the open, not lurking in ambush.

About an hour after they had entered the Tolk Gilzad, they heard Jadghuli war whoops ringing out behind them. Sandy turned in his saddle and looked back. A way behind them, and on the other side of a salt-encrusted flat of dry mud Hojeen had avoided, were a dozen or so hard-riding Jadghuli. He cursed and reached for the bow case attached to the rear

of his saddle—but stopped in mid-grab when he glanced at
Hojeen. The old scout was calmly riding along and ignoring
the foes closing in on them.

Well, if that wily old bastard wasn't worried, then neither
was Sandy. He barked out orders to the sorcerer and Anala,
who both showed signs of getting ready to bolt: "Keep riding, slowly."

The Jadghuli raced ahead until they were almost parallel to
them across the mud flat. Then their leader gave a signal with
his arm and they charged in a body across the mud flat toward
Sandy and his companions.

They were a fearsome sight with their bloodcurdling war
crys and flashing weapons—

—And without warning, the ground collapsed under their
feet. Rudhars and riders went tumbling head over heels, disappearing into a mushrooming dust cloud thrown up by the
collapse.

Through the dust came screams of agony and horror—the
crunch of breaking bones, the sound of living flesh being torn
apart. Soon the boiling dust cloud was streaked blood-crimson
and venomous black. An incredibly messy eater was having
his lunch; bloody pieces of men and rudhars sprayed in all
directions as it fed. A breeze blew from the roiling cloud
toward Sandy and his companions, and they gagged, then
gulped clean air gratefully when the wind changed again.

With horrified fascination, Sandy caught occasional
glimpses of what was doing the feeding. Sometimes he saw
a writhing black tentacle tipped with a three-pronged claw
and lined with a double row of sucking mouths—hundreds of
them. At other instants there was a gigantic talon covered
with innumerable razor-sharp barbs, many of which had
bloody shreds of meat and splinters of white bone clinging
to them.

Sandy turned away, feeling sick. After five years in Zarathandra he'd seen his share of death, but this seemed worse
than any slaughter he'd experienced. Anala and the sorcerer
were as white-faced as he felt.

Hojeen said impassively, "They now good Jadghuli." He
turned and started leading Sandy's party deeper into the bad-
land.

About an hour later they rode over a small rise and saw
spread before them batches of cheery green. Scattered across

the plain at irregular intervals were many small hillocks, each holding a bush which sent exposed snakelike roots in every direction. These crawling roots kept to their own territory, never intruding into that of a neighbor—almost as though the bushes observed a sort of truce. Their woody bark was a rich reddish brown and sprouting out everywhere, from branches and roots alike, were slender leaves colored the waxy green of holly.

"Touch-not bushes," Hojeen explained. "They're friendly . . . almost. We'll be safe in their territory for a while." He started forward, carefully maneuvering his rudhar through the spaces between the outstretched roots.

As he got close to the bushes, Sandy noticed a pleasant vinegary odor in the air, a welcome change from the stenches most of the plants in the Tolk Gilzad seemed to exude. He looked and saw tiny lavender flowers concealed in a multitude of crevasses which veined the surface of the bushes' gnarly wood. And there were translucent many-barbed thorns tipped with drops of ruby-colored resin and hidden at the base of the leaves.

Sandy liked the no-nonsense savagery of the touch-not bushes. You knew immediately where you stood with them.

Hojeen pointed to the resin tipping the thorns. "Poison. It will burn your skin, but not kill you."

They carefully threaded their way through the touch-not bushes for nearly an hour, coming finally to an open space surrounded on all sides by battalions of the pugnacious plant. The clearing was rocky, the ground mostly crumbled pieces of yellow-brown shale, and not inviting looking—but it was a place to rest.

Scattered here and there through the clearing were boulders of blue-speckled granite, ancient and greatly weathered, yet resembling late-coming intruders to this place. Hojeen stopped by the largest boulder, a piece the size of a small hut, and said, "We rest here for a bit. This place is old, very old. Magic lingers—hides this place from prying eyes. It would be best we don't travel until sun lowers. For next two hours it will be time of small-death-that-flies, but they don't go near touch-not bushes. They'll leave us alone. When sun is there—he pointed to a place high in the western sky—"they'll return to nests."

"When do we eat?" Anala said after doing a fancy dismount, a flashy roll and jump such as the emperor's crack palace troops did. "I haven't had a decent meal since yesterday." She looked around demandingly, expecting someone to jump to serve her.

Sandy dismounted from his rudhar in a leisurely manner, nodded at her words, and said, "You're right. It's time we ate. Hojeen can make even sawdust seem tasty, so he'll cook. I'll see to the animals, Zhadnoboth will help me, and you'll gather firewood." He looked around and added, "There's enough deadwood around so it shouldn't take you too long."

Anala listened in stunned silence—then her inner fires erupted. "I'm not your slave girl!" she yelled. "Do your own dirty work! I'm a *lulzi*, not some trull you can kick around."

Sandy stared down his nose at her, then turned to Hojeen. "Cook for three. The lulzi will look after herself." He began to uncinch his rudhar's saddle.

Anala choked on her anger. Eventually she managed to croak out, "You can't do this, you bastard son of a whore. No bugging—"

"No work, no food," Sand interrupted. He yanked the saddle off his mount and threw it to the ground. "We're four. We have no time to wait on each other. Everyone does his fair share." He paused and added bitingly, "A lulzi should act like a lady, not like a drunken hussy who's crawled out of the gutter."

Dead silence for a moment, then Anala said in a strangled voice, "You're one to talk." She gave him a contemptuous look, turned on her heel, and stalked away. As she gathered brushwood, she muttered a constant stream of profanities and dire curses. Once she even turned, pointed a finger at Sandy, and shouted, "You don't have proper respect!"

Sandy only shrugged, hid a smile, and went on with his work.

Hojeen ambled over and pointed to the touch-not bushes. "What's above ground is poisonous, but underground parts are not. They have a rose-colored rootlet which makes a good drink if chopped up and brewed in hot water."

Sandy turned to Zhadnoboth, who was loitering nearby and trying to appear busy. "Dig up some of those root things Hojeen has been talking about. If you have any questions, ask him." Sandy turned his back and began unsaddling another of the rudhars.

The sorcerer gave him an exasperated stare, then went to do what he was told. He had too much experience to mistake Sandy's quiet tones for softness. After he had been scratched a couple times by touch-not thorns, he too was cursing Sandy—but much more quietly and less profanely than the lulzi.

After he had finished unsaddling the rudhars, Sandy turned his ear back to Anala for a moment. A constant stream of verbal abuse still came from her, as she threw everything except elephants and toads his way. She bitched about his temper, the world, men, women, bad food, the wrong weather, the way he combed his hair, the time she stuck a needle in her thumb, that he was ugly, why was it day and not night, how pretty some people thought her, he didn't know how to treat his betters, he wasn't always right, and a thousand other things—some of which made sense. He listened for a while, shook his head, and began rubbing down the rudhar he had just unsaddled.

Later on, after he had finished with the rudhars, Sandy dumped some gear near the fire Hojeen was building and paused to rest for a moment.

The old scout glanced at his hands and said, "That's new skin, like from healed-over wounds. Maybe you heal very, very fast?"

Sandy gave the dried-up rascal a smile. "You should know how it is, old man. You sometimes have to bleed if you soldier for a living."

"Some don't bleed enough." Hojeen grunted.

"And some old men take too long to die—way too long."

The shadow of a smile touched the scout's lips. "The Goddess looks after her own."

"Yeah, that she does."

Just then Anala stomped up and dropped a load of dry sticks on the ground. "Look at my hands," she said plaintively, waving them under the men's noses. "Half my nails are broken and it will be weeks before the scratches heal."

Sandy nodded and said to Hojeen in a deadpan voice, "Slow healer."

A chortle burst from the old scout's lips.

Anala flushed, stomped her foot, and snapped, "What are you two simpletons laughing at?"

Sandy suppressed a chuckle. "Nothing that concerns you."

"Doubtless it would concern no one but a halfwit."

Sandy shrugged, sat down, pulled off his boots, and began to leisurely rub night-toad fat into the shoe leather.

Anala gave him an incensed look, pointedly turned her back, and began chattering away at Hojeen—mixing complaints with gossip about anything that popped into her head. Hojeen listened patiently, giving a grunt now and then to make her think she had an interested audience.

Sandy continued to work on his boots, glad the lulzi had blessed him with the silent treatment.

5

FROWNING, the Goddess rested on her silken couch and thought about Sandy. His coming to Zarathandra had been a bolt from the blue, a long-expected savior in an unexpected form. Through him she had finally been able to destroy Kels Zalkri, a demon god from elsewhere, who for a thousand years had been trying to wrest Zarathandra from her. The accident of Sandy's true name, which meant nothing on Earth but was a great name of power on Zarathandra, had furnished the fatal weapon. It had also bound their fates together inextricably. Her true name and his were two parts of a greater whole. He was still human, but also something more. And she too had changed, gaining a humanity that made her an even greater goddess than she had been before. She held the upper hand, but he had more power than he knew—and that galled her.

She needed that damned scapegrace, and someday she would teach him proper respect. Still, she thought, he was a most useful weapon to have in her quiver. But he should show the proper pious deference. She silently damned destiny for choosing him, and paying no heed to her wishes.

As the Goddess mulled over her plans for Sandy, a wicked smile came to her lips. He needed to be taken down a notch or two, and Ree-Mahim was the one to do it. She would plot and finagle Sandy into the corner where he belonged. A feeling of almost maternal love spread through the Goddess as she thought of Ree-Mahim. She was a special person—always looking for the main chance and loving conniving for its own sake, yet she did it with such zest and goodwill that even those she cozened had to like her. She'd be good for Sandy, and one way or another she'd obtain for him the rank and prestige he needed to be the sword of the Goddess.

—Not that Sandy would appreciate it. The Goddess quietly chortled as she thought of how he'd howl when her trap was sprung.

She permitted herself a few more moments of pleasant day-dreaming, then turned her mind to serious matters. Jara Greenteeth had to be dealt with once and for all, and the uprising along the Rithian Empire's southwestern border needed seeing to. Now was the time for Aku to be brought forward, but more importantly the lives of the Four needed to be entangled with that of the shee. She could count on her priestess Belissa to knowingly do her part, but the sorcerer would be chancy. She had cast the runes a thousand times and most of her readings said that by mischance and mistake he'd do his part. Still, she was uneasy. The wild unpredictability of Zhadnoboth's sorcery made him one of her most effective agents. It also made her want to pray every time it was unloosed.

But thoughts of Mem-Jara-Shil turned the Goddess's mood black. Memories of the shee's sneering voice and murderous deeds were swiftly followed by a red cloud of anger. Their feud was an old and bitter one. This time there would be no pity, no mercy.

The Goddess's mood became blacker still as she brooded. Though her hatred for the shee was an unhealing wound, still her heart was heavy. Destroying Jara Greenteeth would rid Zarathandra of a bloodthirsty monster.

Yet the Goddess could remember a time when Jara had been innocent.

6

SANDY ate with gusto the meal Hojeen had prepared. Anything would have tasted good, but the old scout had whipped up an almost-feast. From the small rosy tubers of the touchnot bushes he had brewed a tea—true, it had an odd musty flavor and looked like scummy pond water, but it tasted better with every sip you took. It was odd that something so good could come from a poisonous plant, but then not *that* odd once Sandy thought about it. After all, the leaves of a potato plant could kill you, but that did not make potatoes any less tasty.

From the coarsely ground five-grain meal which every Rithian soldier carried as part of his field rations, Hojeen had baked some surprisingly good biscuits—eaten with slices of gumlike Zahada cheese, the biscuits were both delicious and filling. Of course the rest of the meal, strips of jerky and the sun-dried prunes of the sand plum, was rather humdrum fare. Still, they made the rest of the cookout seem that much better.

While they ate, Hojeen and Zhadnoboth played battles, a board game popular for centuries in the inns and taverns of the Rithian Empire. The two old codgers gossiped happily as they diced and placed pegs in intricate patterns in the hundreds of interlacing holes drilled in the board. Until this moment they'd been more than a bit standoffish toward each other, but now they found a common ground and were fast becoming cronies.

Anala watched and tried to give advice on strategy, but they quietly ignored her and played their own games. Finally, she gave a disgusted sniff and walked over to sit by Sandy.

49

"You're an unmannerly crank, but at least you hear what I say."

Sandy bit off a piece of jerky and slowly chewed on it, giving no indication he had caught her words.

Unfortunately his pretended lack of interest did not discourage Anala, who was sure she had an audience. She prattled on about a couple of inconsequential things and then started to gush about Aku.

"You are lucky to have such a man serving under you. I've heard travelers say he was a great hero and warrior in his homeland. And he's so handsome . . . why, any hot-blooded woman would come running if he looked her way. Did you see the way he finished off those two Jadghuli? There's not many a warrior who could have done it as well."

Sandy grunted and said, "He is a very able soldier."

Anala leaned closer and whispered in a conspiratorial tone, "I know the emperor himself is keeping an eye on him. If Aku makes a name for himself as a common soldier, he'll rise high and fast in the army. The emperors have always favored outlanders as generals; they are less of a threat to the throne than an able and popular Rithian." She paused and added smugly, "When they hear from me about how great a warrior he is, he will be on his way to the top."

Sandy nodded in agreement. Maybe she was a bit stuck on herself, but she rightly knew how much weight a lulzi's word carried in the empire, especially along its southern border.

Anala was starting to prattle inanely about what a piece of manflesh Aku was when her tone changed abruptly. A rapt expression came over her face as she said with quiet certainty, "Fortune's favored child—greatness in war shall be his, but greater in peace shall he be. Aku! Aku! Your name shall ring fair and sweet down through the ages."

The hair along the back of Sandy's neck prickled as he heard Anala speaking not as a half-grown girl but as a lulzi— as one in touch with the mysteries.

As suddenly as it had come, the trance left her, and she prattled on as if nothing had happened. "When I first saw him I knew here was man fit to bed a lulzi. He stood out from among your troopers like an eagle amid crows." A gentle smile flickered across her lips and she said dreamily, "It would only be right that a great lulzi be made a woman by such as he."

Sandy shook his head and rolled his eyes skyward, wondering once again if the world of Zarathandra would ever be the same once this piece of baggage really got rolling. He interrupted her babbling, trying to bring her back to earth. "What about the wives and children he left behind in the islands, and the woman he keeps in Kimbo-Dashla? What if he doesn't want you?"

Anala jerked her head up, looked at him as if he was a simpleton, and said indignantly, "A man does not refuse a lulzi. It is not done. As for the women, they should be glad that a lulzi should choose to honor their man."

"No doubt you are right," Sandy said dryly.

Anala was too sure of the fitness of things to catch the irony in his voice and rattled on. "I'll be the greatest lulzi there ever was, renowned for my wondrous deeds and many loves. Aku will be remembered for being the first and one of the most sublime of these loves. I'll have a dozen children, sired by the best Zarathandra has to offer, and they'll be as famed as their mother."

A picture of Anala, a baby on her hip, aggressively pitching woo as she backed a reluctant suitor into a corner, flashed through Sandy's mind—and an involuntary smile played across his lips. "Only the best?" he asked sardonically. "Sometimes the dregs have more to give a woman than the great—and are less likely to be in love with themselves."

Anala stuck out her lower lip and glared disdainfully. "Big man!" she said. "You're nothing, and will always be nothing, and that sticks in your craw. You have to sneer at others because that's the only way you can be their better."

Sandy looked at her, wondering what burr had got under her saddle, then shrugged and said, "I only meant to say it's better to lie with someone because you like him than because he's famous."

"You fear Aku because there is greatness in him."

Sandy shrugged again and replied in a voice edged with irritation. "Aku is all right. He can be a bastard, but most men can. But he has talent and drive and I've told the big brass that. I don't envy him. Let him be great and famous, just so I can go my own way."

"To be a little man with little problems." Then abruptly she changed tack. "You don't approve of me, do you?"

Sandy tried to get his thoughts in order, confused by the

swift way she had changed the ground they were fighting over. He didn't think he exactly disapproved of her, though she was a pain in the rear. "You're passable," he said, deadpan. "You'll be better when you've gone down the road a little further."

His words did not please her. "I am a lulzi—I don't need gray hair and wrinkles to be wise. I am far more than any common lout can ever hope to understand." Abruptly, she shot off on another tangent. "And who are you to talk? Half the floozies in Kimbo-Dashla are panting after you, if I hear right. And no reason for it. You're not rich, handsome, or much of a lover. Why the widow Ree-Mahim, the wealthiest woman in the city, takes to you I can't see."

Sandy wondered what mortal sin made him deserve the lulzi. "Who I hobnob with is no concern of yours," he said shortly. "I only want to save your neck and then palm you off on somebody else as soon as possible."

Anala reddened and stared poutily at him. Tears welled up in the corners of her eyes and she began to sob softly. "I miss the Hagba Khamliss. I could talk to him and he would understand. He knew what my heart meant even if my lips said the wrong thing."

Sandy sighed in exasperation. He could sense her inner pain and felt sympathy, while at the same time he wondered how she could be such a scatterbrained brat. He supposed there had to be some sense to the way her thoughts skipped around, but he couldn't see it. He prayed for an early deliverance from his guardianship and placed his arm around her shoulders to comfort her.

Sobs racked her body convulsively, as for the first time she openly mourned a friend. Sandy sensed that deep feelings, suppressed until now, had broken through the barriers she had erected, and she was at last admitting to her inner self that the Hagba Khamliss was dead and she'd never see his gentle smile again or hear his soft voice teaching her bits of wisdom as they ate breakfast.

With the sixth sense which was a byproduct of that strange and indefinable relationship he had with the Goddess, Sandy could feel the terrible aching emptiness within her.

He held her tight, giving what comfort he could. Gradually her sobs died down as her inner storm subsided to a quiet agony. She would remember her grief, but now she would be able to live with it.

"I'll miss the Hagba also," Sandy said in a brooding voice. "He was special, a true friend. His kind are few. You could talk to him about your doubts, fears, and least noble parts of your inner self and know he understood."

Anala nodded, then suddenly aware that his arm was around her, pushed it away and glowered at him. "Keep your hands off me," she said arrogantly.

"They're off," Sandy snapped, as angry at himself as at her—it served him right for being a sentimental fool. He finished his meal in silence and pointedly ignored the lulzi when she stalked off to be by herself.

When he had finished a last cup of tea, Sandy pulled from his belt the ivory tube he had taken off one of the dead Jadghuli. His erratic sixth sense was still working rather well and he could feel a glow of importance emanating from it. Almost reluctantly he gave the tube a quick twist. It came apart as he had intuitively known it would. Two objects fell out: a ring and a roll of parchment.

He picked up the ring, stared at it for a moment, and then felt an uneasy shiver travel up his spine. It was of age-mellowed gold inset with a dark ruby carved to resemble an eyeless face. He had spent a lot of time studying ringlore trying to learn about the Ring of Uncertainty he wore, and he recognized this new ring. It was called the Daughter's Ring, though none of his sources had said why it was so named. If even a part of the tales about the ring and its owner were true, the odds against them might be even bleaker than he had thought. Though legend said that long ago she had been destroyed, the evidence in his hand said legend lied.

He left the ring lie in the palm of his left hand and tried to touch it with his mind. A flash of insight—mostly of an immense power and unimaginable antiquity. He also felt subtler impressions, emotions imprinted by the mind of the ring's owner—rage and lust and cruelty were among them—and oddly a tinge of sadness. Sandy shivered once again and quickly stuffed the ring into his belt.

Almost gladly he picked up the roll of parchment. It was two documents, one rolled up within the other. The outer document was in code, but he read it easily—his reluctant, though special, relationship to the Veiled Goddess had given

him many strange and useful abilities. Then Sandy swore
vehemently and threw the parchment to the ground.

He stewed for a moment before unrolling the second parchment. It was cracked with age and written in an archaic language. He read it through twice, wondering where that bastard
Zadar Kray had found it. What he read was interesting—and
just possibly helpful.

He glanced over and saw that the crafty old scout and the
even less honest sorcerer were still playing their game, engrossed in trying to out-finagle each other. He picked up the
parchment he had tossed to the ground and called, "Hojeen,
come here."

The scout heard the urgency in his voice and hurried over,
followed by the sorcerer—who never passed up a chance to
stick his nose into other people's business.

"The whole damn southwest border is going up in flames,"
Sandy said in a voice hoarse with anger. "The loyalty of the
Kilbri tribes is what held this section of the frontier together.
Now Zadar Kray has slain his uncle and his cousins and become the headman of the Kilbri. He's leading a rebellion
against the empire. Besides the Kilbri, the Red Branch Zenori
and the Black Branch Zenori have joined the revolt. He's allied himself with the Chanzi and the Jadghuli from across the
border. And a couple of renegade Kri Shandri clans have
joined with them."

"That's bad," muttered Hojeen. "It's not right that Kilbri,
Zenori, and Jadghuli fight side by side. They enjoy killing
each other too much."

"It's that damned prophet Krizzan Tham-Shanek; he's bewitched them with his wild ravings and puny miracles. No
doubt they'll end up eventually sinking their knives into each
other. The question is, can we and the empire survive until
they do? What were those fat-assed bureaucrats from the
Walled House doing to let this happen? If Ublachak the Lame
were still in charge, both Zadar Kray and the mad prophet
would long ago have been found with their throats slit." Sandy
paused and added, "The only good news is that the White
Branch Zenori and the Kri Rithi clans are still loyal to the
empire. That and *this*," he said, pulling the ruby ring from
his belt and showing it to them.

Zhadnoboth gasped and turned ashy white. Hojeen stared
stonily at the ring for several moments, then an unreadable

look came into his eyes and he bowed his head and said what might have been a prayer.

The sorcerer recovered quickly and turned on Sandy. "See what you've done, demon. I was peacefully minding my own business and the next thing I know I'm dragged into war. That was bad enough; but now I find out a demigoddess, who supposedly died centuries ago, may be looking for blood." He stomped up to Sandy and shook a bony figure at him. "It's your duty to get me out of this mess. It's a fine how-do-you-do when an officer of the empire puts a citizen's life in danger for no reason." Sandy's gaze caught his and he backed down a bit. "Well, maybe once there possibly could have been a reason."

Sandy gave him a hard stare and said, "You should think some more." He added caustically, "And you are not a citizen of the Rithian Empire."

"I am as much a citizen of the empire as of any place else on Zarathandra."

"That's not saying much," replied Sandy. "Only that the empire has not got around to booting you out yet." He favored the sorcerer with another hard stare. After a moment Zhadnoboth wilted under the pressure and backed away. "It's time you started paying your way," Sandy said, his voice just barely threatening. "I can't keep protecting you unless it is worth my while."

"You want me to pay!" screeched the sorcerer. "You! Whose blundering incompetence once lost me a king's ransom in treasure—and you want me to pay you?" Then he added sanctimoniously, "And after all I did for you."

"Oh, come off it," Sandy said. "You've never done anything in your life unless you thought there might be a profit in it. Besides, I'm just asking for a little of your sorcery. If I say you did it for a good purpose, that should square it with the judges."

"What judges?" sputtered Zhadnoboth.

"The ones who might be trying you for unlicensed use of sorcery, treason, and for some of your various other crimes."

"What crimes? And what do you mean treason? I'm not a citizen!" Then he caught on to Sandy's game, reddened, and shouted. "This is blackmail! I won't do it. When did I do any sorcery? What do I get out of it?"

"Your life, some goodwill, and I won't make mention of your falsely claiming citizenship."

"That's highway robbery," the sorcerer said. He added in a slightly wheedling tone, "I should at least get expenses and a fee suitable to a sorcerer of my ability."

"I'll mention it to the brass," Sandy said dryly.

"If I live that long," Zhadnoboth grumbled. "The way you make things sound, we'll be lucky if we're only chopped to pieces."

"That's where you come in. Your sorcery is going to get us out of this pickle. Think of what you'll gain! You'll save your neck and earn the gratitude of the empire in the bargain."

"Gratitude rides lightly in the pocket and buys no bread," Zhadnoboth replied.

Sandy shrugged. *"So."*

The sorcerer stewed for a moment. "I'll do it. But you better make mention of my services to somebody who counts."

Sandy nodded.

"There is just one small problem," Zhadnoboth said in a suddenly too-smooth voice. "My sorcery of late has been a bit uncertain." He saw the black clouds forming on Sandy's brow and quickly added, "I no longer have my staff, and without it I have trouble controlling my spells. I did some work for a petty king far to the south of here, and that fat ingrate broke my staff when he wasn't satisfied with the result. It wasn't my fault the fertility spell took hold of his wives when he wasn't around."

"I'll chance it," Sandy said sardonically. "It can't be any worse than your usual run of sorcery."

"I am a great and very powerful sorcerer."

"Yeah, but if you call for rain one never knows if you're going to get wine or wine jugs falling from the sky. You get results, but I doubt even the gods know what they will be."

The sorcerer glowered, but could think of no suitable reply.

"I saw you latch onto the staff of that Chanzi wizard I slew," Sandy said.

Zhadnoboth snorted. "It's a poor substitute for mine. Those Chanzi incompetents use green pipewood to make their staffs instead of pipewood which has cured for seven years in a mixture of vinegar and gall. Still, it is better than nothing."

"Let's get on with it," Sandy said as he covertly looked around for suitable places to take cover.

"What about me?" butted in Anala, once again showing a talent for turning up at inopportune moments.

Sandy cursed silently, wondering why she wasn't still off somewhere pouting like any normal brat would be.

Like a snub-nosed martinet, Anala began pacing back and forth in front of them, lecturing them on what they should do. "With my help the sorcerer will make a sending to the Goddess's high priestess in Kimbo-Dashla. I will tell her what we know. Then the sorcerer and I will use magic to clear our way through our foes and get us to Kimbo-Dashla."

"I'll believe it when I see it," said Sandy. "Especially with every Chanzi wizard in the area on our tail and maybe Jara Greenteeth too."

Anala stamped her foot. "The power of the Goddess is within me. Nothing can stand against her. Certainly not any scruffy shapechanging wizard or a bogey who has been dead for a thousand years. Trust in the Goddess and she shall prevail."

"Especially if your sword is sharp and your wits even sharper," Sandy said. "She can't be everywhere, nor is she all-powerful. There are worlds and there are worlds and only in one does she rule—and not always unchallenged."

"You outland heathen," Anala cried. "Beware that your blasphemy doesn't damn you for eternity." Without any warning she was in a state of grace, speaking as a lulzi touched by the Goddess. "I see her, standing between heaven and earth. Her hand reaches out and rests on you."

Hojeen and Zhadnoboth stared in awe as they caught a glimpse of one of the great mysteries of Zarathandra.

"So she touches me. So what? We still have to save our own asses." He deliberately spoke harshly, hoping to jolt Anala out of her trance.

It worked. Anala blinked dazedly, staring about in confusion.

Sandy kept talking, trying to drive home his points while the lulzi was too befuddled to interfere. "You're right, we should contact the high priestess and tell her what we know, then sneak out of this corner we're backed into. You and the sorcerer are powerful, but so are our enemies, especially if they have Jara Greenteeth behind them. It would be best to challenge them *only* if we know we have an advantage.''

"When is that—when they are safely in their graves?" Anala scoffed. "We can't win by being cowards. And I for one don't fear a long-dead shee.''

"Mem-Jara-Shil lives," Hojeen interrupted. "That I know.''

"I fight when I have to," Sandy said, replying to Anala's backhanded slap at him. "I also know when to back away. Of all the shee Jara Greenteeth is the most dangerous. Several times she has challenged the Goddess. Each time the shee was defeated, but never slain. The last time the Goddess only brought her down with the help of a desert shaman seeking vengeance. If the Goddess can barely defeat such a being, can a lulzi not yet full grown do better?''

Sandy's words made Anala think instead of react and her arrogance quickly evaporated. She was just a fourteen-year-old girl again, nervous and unsure of herself. "The Goddess threw the shee from the mortal realms and into the nether-worlds long ago, barring the gates against her return," the young lulzi said in an unsteady and hopeful voice.

"Banishment to the netherworlds doesn't have to be for-ever," Sandy replied. An unpleasant memory flashed across his mind: Things had gotten very sticky before he and the Goddess reached an understanding. Once again, he silently cursed Zhadnoboth for shanghaiing him into this damned world of too-real magic. Aloud he said, "When there is a strong enough will, a way can found—and nobody has ever said that bitch was weak-willed.''

He held up the ruby ring. Anala's eyes grew big as she saw it for the first time. "I don't know how Zadar Kray got this, but he was offering to return it to Jara Greenteeth in return for her aid in the revolt. If we just hold onto it, we might strike a greater blow at the revolt than any army. Without it the shee cannot fully return to mortal realms.''

"I don't like it," Zhadnoboth said. "It's impossible that it should fall into your hands at this moment just by chance.''

"Either the Goddess or the shee is playing games," Sandy agreed wryly. "Maybe both. However that may be, we are still sitting in the frying pan.''

For a moment there was a glum silence as they thought this over. Then Anala babbled out, "But it's our chance to do something great. We'll become part of legend like the Witch of the Singing Sea or the Seven Warriors of Sunset."

Sandy shook his head in exasperation. She was going to be a greater problem then he had ever dreamed—you could squelch her for a moment and then she bounced back and was off on another goddamned tangent. Now she seemed bound and determined to make them heroes, even if she had to kill them to do it.

One of the parchment rolls fell from Sandy's belt, where he had carelessly stuffed it. Zhadnoboth's eyes lit up with avarice and with the agility of a pickpocket he reached out and grabbed the document in midair. The moment his fingers touched the parchment it burst into greenish flames. The sorcerer howled in pain and began blowing on his seared fingers. What was left of the parchment drifted to the ground as blackened ashes.

Sandy had no sympathy for Zhadnoboth. "Serves you right," he snapped. "You never could keep your hands off what belongs to others."

Hojeen grabbed Sandy's arm and pointed south where a black cloud loomed large in the sky, slowly moving toward them. Bolts of jagged red lightning poured from it to lambaste the ground underneath. A continual booming thunder, sounding like barrage after barrage of heavy artillery, began to reach their ears. However, the cloud's advance was not smooth. It moved in fits and starts as though something was resisting its forward march.

"That's not Chanzi magic," Zhadnoboth said. "It's sorcery, but of a kind I am not familiar with."

"Whoever that sorcerer fellow is he'll be in bad trouble if comes straight at us," Hojeen said laconically. "Tolk Gilzad is dangerous to attack with magic. Old war left many bad things behind." He gauged the distance. "Maybe in an hour he will get to Red Heart. We better be far away if he tries to hammer his way through there."

Sandy nodded. "You get the animals ready." He turned to the sorcerer and Anala. "We'll hold back on Zhadnoboth's sorcery for a moment." He gave the lulzi a wry grin and said, "Now we'll see if you're all wind or not. Do a sending and see if you can contact the high priestess. The sorcerer and I will give what aid we can."

Anala gave a disdainful sniff and sat down on the ground

in tailor fashion. Zhadnoboth sat down at her left side and assumed the same position, grumbling all the while. Sandy sat down facing her and touching almost knee to knee.

"My way is not magic," she said reverently. "It is something much greater—the way of the Goddess."

She placed her hands in her lap, closed her eyes, slowed her breathing, and softly began to chant a prayer. Gradually her voice trailed away to nothing as she drifted into a light trance.

To Sandy's eyes she still didn't appear to be anything out of the ordinary—just a snub-nosed, curly-headed, and passably pretty girl just sitting around. Then the hairs on the back of his neck began to prickle. His sixth sense detected a faint and intangible aura of power beginning to glow within her. It had a strange heat which his inner self felt, but which left his skin cool. Slowly it spread outward, waxing stronger by the moment, until she was radiating psychic energy like a human sun.

She raised her closed eyes to the sky and called out, "O Veiled One, send forth my spirit and protect me on the way."

There was a moment of unbearable tension—and then they were elsewhere. Sandy found himself in a endless, featureless void. In front of him was a glowing aquamarine essence, flanked by a paprika-red cloud—Anala and Zhadnoboth.

We were to aid you, not be dragged along, huffed the sorcerer's thought; Sandy was thinking the same thing. Anala ignored them and turned her thoughts toward Kimbo-Dashla and the high priestess. As she made contact, her consciousness shot off in that direction as a gossamer thread spinning out from her spirit body. She pulled Sandy and Zhadnoboth along as if they were bound to her with steel cables.

Sandy cast a startled look back and for an instant caught a glimpse back into reality. He saw his body, Anala's, and the sorcerer's frozen in an instant of time.

Out in the featureless darkness surrounding them, something sensed their presence and attacked. It came out of the void like an emerald-hued comet, sizzling with energy and spitting green sparks. It slashed with talons of light, shot off to a safe distance, and began to circle them.

At the touch of the icy-cold talons, the blue essence that was Anala instinctively huddled close to Sandy. She bawled in confused pain, more surprised than terrified.

Sandy reacted by thinking *mean* and slashing out, he didn't know with just what—but something. It worked; the green thing didn't like the touch of the claws he'd thought up, and it backed further away.

Then it was a cat-and-mouse game as the green menace and Sandy feinted and slashed with immaterial but razor-sharp fangs and talons. There were no bodies to hurt, but their minds felt excruciating pain each time a blow or bite scored. The thing kept trying to get at Anala, and the sorcerer and Sandy kept frustrating its attack.

The green thing would circle menacingly and then charge in like a wolf going for the throat of its prey. Sandy would block the attack and riposte with a slash at the other's ghostly throat. Then the whole rigmarole would start over again. Despite ferocious assaults and sly ambushes by both, neither could gain an advantage. The green predator couldn't do much damage, but neither were they able to make any progress toward their goal.

After a while Sandy became aware of biting pain traveling up the wispy thread connecting his consciousness to the far-away thing that was his body. He turned a portion of his mind that way and realized the magical silver ring, the Ring of Uncertainty, was throbbing with energy. Almost unconsciously he called to it with his mind—and it, or maybe its ghost, came to him. He felt suddenly stronger, faster, and meaner.

With new confidence he renewed his attack on the green slayer. Now his mind-made talons were edged with a crackling blue fire that left the other's psychic flesh smoking each time they struck.

The thing gave a scream and fled out into the void. There it stopped and circled them, far, far out, almost beyond the range of their senses. It wanted desperately to attack again, but shrank back as it remembered the pain. Eventually it came to a halt and they felt its mind turn their way.

There will be another time, warrior. I see this. There will be no one to aid you and no talisman to wield; only you and I. What then will save you from my hunger? The icy thoughts were those of a woman—malicious, savage, and utterly sure of herself. It was She Who Hungers—Jara Greenteeth.

There will be a next time—for me, Anala said, talking big. *It will be your last.*

A mocking laugh echoed through their minds. *When I fear a child just past mud pies and diapers, I'll not be fit to live. Crawl back and snivel on the shoulder of* Mama Goddess, *baby thing.* Then she was gone.

That bitch! screamed Anala.

Get us to the high priestess now, Sandy ordered with a steel-sharp thought. He turned his attention to the sorcerer. *And what the hell are you along for? You haven't done anything to pay the freight.*

I'm here in case of need. There was no need.

Yeah, and a man walks better on one leg than two.

I can't find the high priestess, interrupted Anala's panicky thought. *I lost contact when that thing attacked me.*

Sandy suppressed his exasperation and sent a calming order. *Mesh your mind to mine. Think of us as separate strands coming together to form one rope.* He sent a sharp thought to the sorcerer. *And you too.*

Uncertainly their minds groped around, trying for the strength of oneness, yet instinctively shying from such intimate contact. The soul only cares to stand naked in its own sight.

Think of Belissa, the high priestess, Sandy ordered, trying to give them at least a common focus. *I know her, and well. With memory and the power of three minds we can find her.* He hoped he knew what he was talking about.

His thought provided a catalyst and for a brief instant their minds became one. It was enough. In that moment they were no longer marooned in limbo, but transported to the temple of the Goddess in Kimbo-Dashla—at least spiritually.

Sandy glanced around and saw they were in the Dak Tibka, the holy of holies, the fane deep in the center of the temple. Only priestesses dedicated to the Goddess and those the Goddess considered her own could come to such a place and leave unscathed.

It was a small room, with arches starting from the floor at each corner and meeting at a point twenty feet over their heads. The stone of the arches was milk-white marble, contrasting with ceiling and walls which were tiled; the small tiles were subdued in tone, but glowed with every color of the rainbow. In the south wall was a brass-studded door which led to the public parts of the temple. Near the north wall was a altar of the same milk-white marble as the arches. Overhead, near where the arches met, were four stained glass windows which illuminated the room with many-hued light.

In front of the altar a tall lean woman knelt. She wore a light-blue hooded robe whose edges were embroidered with silver thread. It was the distinctive garb of a priestess of the Goddess, and the silver thread meant that she was the high priestess of a temple. Around her brow was a band made from three silver wires twisted together, a sign that she was a high priestess recognized by the Rithian Empire. Her long narrow face was strong boned and unlined—a face you would remember, but handsome instead of beautiful. Though she was only in her mid-thirties, her rich brown hair had many fine streaks of gray in it. She had the same feel as the room— hard, yet with an inner warmth.

She arose and turned to face them with the languid grace and hidden power of a contented tiger. Her deep-seeing eyes recognized the true semblances behind the three ghostly presences visiting her. "Welcome, Anala." There was a slight pause and she added, "And your two bravos also. You were expected."

"And I love you too, Belissa," Sandy muttered.

"Bravo?" Zhadnoboth asked.

The high priestess ignored them both and spoke to Anala. "It is time you came to visit, little sister. Soon you will be coming into your full powers as a lulzi. There are many things we should talk about."

"I have no time, my lady. War and death are loose along the border." Anala spoke proudly and confidently, wallowing in the respect given her by Belissa—and also at the chance to show Sandy and the sorcerer she was their better.

"We worried when the sacred lamp kept lit for the Hagba Khamliss went out and our sendings couldn't find you," Belissa said in a respectful tone underlain by a hint of amusement. "I rejoiced when our Goddess spoke to me and said that a certain scapegrace soldier had taken you under his wing—though I could wish you were in more reputable company."

Sandy's immaterial face quirked in a smile. The priestess and he went back a way and they both enjoyed taking sly digs at each other on occasion. "Let's cut the gossip," he said. "We don't have forever. Tell that fat-bottomed governor of ours that the commandant of the Shepherd's Gate has sold out and plans to let the rebels in tonight.''

"Tell the emperor that Mem-Jara-Shil has returned," Anala interrupted in a pettish tone, miffed because Sandy had dared steal her thunder.

The high priestess inhaled sharply. "Are you sure?"

"That insolent *bitch* tried to ambush us as our spirits journeyed through the space beyond the worlds."

Belissa frowned, apparently liking neither the news nor Anala's childish rancor.

Sandy spoke up. "Fate delivered two parchments and the shee's ring into our hands. One parchment was an ancient document making prophesies about her and her eventual fate, the other was a letter from Zadar Kray offering alliance and the ring. That conniving bastard probably didn't care if Jara Greenteeth accepted his offer or not; with the ring in her hands she was certain to become a thorn in our sides."

"Your read that?" the priestess said. "I didn't think Zadar Kray was foolish enough to put so much in writing."

"The letter was in code and there was a protective spell, but such things can be gotten around. Besides, Zadar Kray has only one life to lose. And he has already put that on the line."

Belissa looked at his shade with increased respect. "The Goddess and I have talked much about you. She said you were more than an interesting rogue. Then I believed her; now I know for myself."

Sandy glanced sharply at the priestess. There was an odd undertone in her voice he couldn't identify—a certain happy satisfaction that appeared to have nothing to do with what they were talking about. She and the Goddess had something cooking and he wished he knew what it was.

Then Belissa put aside humor and became deadly serious. "I'll get word to the Jeweled Court about the shee and to the governor about the traitor. But you three must do something also. Those of the desert people still loyal to the empire are gathering at the Seven Wells, but they need someone to lead them—someone who has no feuds going with any of the Kri Rithi clans, the White Branch Zenori, or the Kri Yitheni."

"That's asking a lot," Sandy commented wryly. "I can't think of a general on the border who hasn't stepped on somebody's toes."

"Your sergeant Aku could do it," Belissa said. "He's war-wise, angered no one yet, and has the favor of the Goddess. This sorcerer can get him to where he is needed."

"For a price," Zhadnoboth said quickly. "I do have a bezoar from a dragon's gizzard, but it cost me dear."

"You shall have just reward for your services."

The utter certainty in her voice must have convinced Zhadnoboth, for he seemed to start mulling over spells in his mind.

"So we get him there," Sandy said matter-of-factly. "Why will the desert men accept him as their leader? He is only a sergeant here, despite the experience he had as a general in the western islands."

Balissa replied, "The tribesmen have been gathering at the Seven Wells for a week. The Goddess came to them in their dreams and said a warrior destined to lead them to victory would appear in their midst and the prophecy will come true."

"Very conveniently," Sandy said sourly. "Especially when an army is gathered to crush a revolt before it begins."

"The ways of the Goddess are wondrous," Belissa said piously, though the hint of a smile twitched at the corners of her mouth.

"That they are," Sandy growled.

"They are wondrous," piped up Anala. "And miracles are miracles even if you help them happen. Our Goddess cannot know everything, but she can know trouble is brewing."

For once the lulzi's various thoughts almost hung together, not that Sandy was willing to believe the girl. He trusted the Goddess less than he did Zhadnoboth, though she was honorable in her own way. All he said was, "Let's get back. We have things to do."

"Wait," protested Anala. "What of Jara Greenteeth?" she asked the priestess. "You are said to have the sight. Can you tell us anything?"

Belissa drew in on herself for a moment. "I see nothing clearly. But this I can say: You shall decide her fate and she yours."

"I will decide it," Anala said determinedly. "This is a time of legends, a time for lesser mortals to step aside, a time for a lulzi to take hold of destiny."

"And a time to go," Sandy added.

Belissa made a motion of blessing and they were yanked back into the void. They shot like arrows across the nothingness, back to their mortal bodies. Anala, stung by the way Sandy had made her fine words seem foolish, forged out ahead of the others.

From the furthermost reaches of nowhere, an emerald streak of fire shot in to attack her while she was out beyond Sandy's protection. However, this was a different Anala from the one who had been so shaken by the original attack—minutes older and as grouchy as a starving bear. Her anger became talons of ice-blue fire and she shredded the onrushing Jara Greenteeth to ragged ribbons.

The shee screamed and fought back, scalding Anala's soul with venomous bile and tearing it with steely malice. The lulzi ignored the onslaught and redoubled the fury of her own attack. The void became lit with an unearthly radiance, as a maelstrom of whirling green fire, blue fire, and the ruby-red glow of rage came together and then exploded outward like a small sun going nova.

The furious skirmish lasted only an instant, breaking up the moment Sandy jumped into the fray. Jara Greenteeth shot off like a comet bent for hell. Anala started to go after her, but Sandy grabbed her by some spiritual scruff of the neck and stopped her in her tracks.

No!

Her anger turned on him, engulfed him like a river of lava. He shoved it right back at her. Before the confrontation could go any further, they were yanked back to mortal Zarathandra.

Their souls didn't just slip back into their bodies, but crashed back in. The sorcerer yowled and gently cradled his head between his hands. Sandy groaned and would have carried on, but Anala didn't let him.

"You yellow-bellied fool," she yelled. "I had that craven piece of scum on the run. If you hadn't stopped me I would have finished her off."

"She'd be picking what was left of you from between her teeth by now if I hadn't stopped you. You should thank me."

Anala looked at him with contempt, muttered "coward," and then turned and marched off furiously.

"Good riddance," Sandy growled, watching her go. Gingerly he got to his feet, stumbled over to his rudhar, and started rummaging through his saddlebags for something to kill a splitting headache.

Moments later he sipped on a leather bottle of jackberry

brandy and cast a worried eye toward the sorcerous storm approaching from the south. He unrolled the remaining parchment and read it again, wondering what the old document was trying to say.

The Four will come and her time will be upon her.

One she will hate.
One she will love.
One she will fear.
And one she will know.

One shall betray.
And one shall slay.

7

The Goddess knelt on a tiled mosaic of jade and rock crystal and looked into her pool of seeing. She watched Sandy down another slug of brandy and then touched the black water with her fingertip. Ripples erased the images pictured there, and for a moment the water's surface was jumbled confusion of tiny warring tides. Abruptly it went mirror smooth and another scene appeared.

It showed the shee sitting slumped over at a marble-topped table. Her face was haggard, and sweat stained her white silken gown and pooled on the table beneath her arms. Cupped in the center of the table was a large sphere of moss-green crystal, its color matching exactly the many mossy streaks coloring the cool white of the marble. The sphere began to emit short rapid pulses of emerald light.

Jara Greentooth's body stiffened; she sprang to her feet and whirled around to face the unseen Goddess. "If it isn't the great mother goddess," she sneered. "No doubt watching to see how her puppy bitch did. She did well, nipped at me a bit—when she had a dog with more teeth to back her up." Jara added sneeringly, "Someday we two will meet again, and I'll have bitchhide for my shoes and dogmeat for my belly." She gave a shark's smile, her pointed teeth gleaming wickedly. "And someday I'll hang the mother bitch's carcass from my wall—beside the rotting bones of all her whelps she's sent to slay me."

Righteous anger exploded within the Goddess and she replied in a voice of fury, "When I send someone to slay you, shee, they'll not be such easy meat. You won't have a well-meaning bumbler to slaughter or an innocent messenger to betray. See then who whines.''

The Goddess hit the water hard with her hand and the shee's offending image disappeared as armies of miniature tidal waves fought a no-quarter war upon the surface of the pond. The Goddess rose to her feet, spoke a word of power, and clapped her hands. There was a crash like thunder and the pool and its surroundings shattered into a million fragments, replaced a moment later by piece of rocky desert no different from the rest of the land that surrounded her.

The Goddess bowed her head and meditated a moment to cool her temper. Of all her enemies the shee always had been the best at knowing how and where to rub the salt in. She glanced around the desert, taking in the red, raw earth, the pitted and weathered rock, a few tough and thorny plants. . . . How she loved it. This was her land, this and all Zarathandra—she'd let no thing, no being befoul it or suck its inhabitants' life's blood unchallenged.

The Goddess turned her thoughts to her lulzi and smiled proudly. Anala hadn't done well, but that was expected. She had started to find herself and that was all to the good, especially since she'd managed to rile Jara Greenteeth. The shee had brushed off Anala's efforts as nips, but those nips must have stung to cause such a strong reaction. Whatever her words, Jara Greenteeth would be wary of the lulzi in the future.

Anala was just emerging from childhood, both as a person and as a lulzi. More and more she would come into her own power as she grew older and was tested by adversity. And if her mind and soul grew with her power she would be very special indeed.

Still the Goddess grieved, for Anala's progress reminded her of past might have beens. She could unobtrusively guide the beings entrusted to her, but she couldn't take them in hand and mold them; then they would only be a second-rate shadow of what they could have been. They had to face the sledgehammer of fate by themselves and be pounded into steel or slag, depending on what was within. And even the steel could be broken.

For a while the Goddess brooded about destiny. It was often neither kind nor just nor fair. In her blacker moments she wondered if fate was only the whim of an uncaring universe.

The Goddess threw off her black mood and began considering the future. A time of challenge and opportunity was beginning. Anala and her companions had to measure up, or they would plunge both themselves and Zarathandra into disaster. Aku must be delivered to his army and the Four to their own special battleground—each to fight their different but interconnected wars. Her chosen would decide: doom to the shee, or a greater doom to Zarathandra?

8

Hojeen's arrow flew high, and with a scream of agony the creature came cartwheeling down from the skies. It hit the desert floor with a bone-cracking crash, sending high a cloud of red dust.

Sandy rode his rudhar close and looked at what had fallen. The thing had a saw-toothed beak, red and purple wattles, and feathers the color of old ashes. It was some kind of vulture, though in size it came nearer to an airplane than a bird. Dark black blood dribbled out from where the arrow had buried itself just under the wishbone.

Hojeen rode up, bow in hand and a grim smile on his lined face. The thing, despite its terrible injuries, glared at them with hate-red eyes. It tried to stagger to its feet and attack them, but was too injured to move. The scout vaulted down from his rudhar, strode over to the wounded bird, grabbed hold of its neck with one hand, and slashed its throat wide open.

Hojeen knelt down and pushed his dagger of blackened steel into the sandy soil, cleaning off most of the gore. Then, he wiped the blade against his pant leg to remove what blood was left. He pulled out a whetstone, spit on it, and began honing the dagger's edge.

"Chanzi are hard to kill," he said laconically. "But this dagger is special. Long, long ago a holy man blessed it. It does a good job of killing unnatural things."

Sandy looked at the blackened steel blade with its inlaid silver runes and recognized the work. He glanced knowingly

71

at Hojeen. "Its killing prowess wouldn't have anything to do with who smithed it?" he asked.

"That too," Hojeen agreed.

Sandy heard a gasp from Anala and turned. There was a sick look on her face and one hand was over her mouth, a shaking finger on the other was pointing toward the ground. He looked that way and saw that the werething now was a writhing abomination. Its flesh was halfway between that of a dead bird and that of a man—and still changing. Hastily he looked away.

"Our enemies no longer have eye in sky," Hojeen said with satisfaction. He pointed west. "We must go that way. Other ways have bad feel to them."

Sandy nodded, cast an eye toward the sorcerous storm threatening from the south, and then turned to Anala and the sorcerer. "Are you sure you don't want to do the transportation spell now?"

"I can do it any time you like," Zhadnoboth replied.

"Now is not the time," Anala said, biting her words off quickly. She still hadn't forgiven Sandy for stopping her chase of the shee—and for maybe being right. "As darkness touches the sky, that will be the time. As a lulzi I know this." She paused and added cuttingly, "It's fortunate that you have fell warriors such as Hojeen and Aku to serve you."

Sandy nodded impassively, not quite suppressing the smile that tugged at the corners of his mouth as he turned and followed Hojeen toward the west.

As they rode along, Sandy stared sourly the bleak landscape and mused. This direction seemed no better than any other, but he trusted the scout's instincts. Besides, he'd be glad to get out of the Tolk Gilzad. It was shelter of a sort, but he'd prefer a place where you could sit down and not have to worry about putting your butt on a monster or a sinkhole.

Anala and the sorcerer rode behind him, the lulzi bending Zhadnoboth's ear with a continuous chatter, the sorcerer nodding his head at appropriate moments or making a noncommittal grunt. "I showed that shee," she said, raising her voice to make sure Sandy heard her. "She'll think next time about attacking a lulzi. Of course she has bad blood, but that's no excuse for her to be the way she is."

"Never disparage an enemy," Sandy said, as if to himself.

"Fear your foes until they are dead. That way you don't get your throat cut by underestimating them."

"You're a fine one to talk," Anala replied hotly. "A warrior who doesn't fight unless the odds favor him. You should have been a clerk instead of a sick-stomached soldier."

"A soldier like that lives to fight another day," Hojeen said.

"If one calls that living."

Sandy stood up in his stirrups, motioned the others to silence, looked back along their back trail, and listened with his inner senses.

"What do you hear?" jeered Anala. "Your conscience?"

"You talk too much," Sandy said offhandedly. He hollered up to Hojeen, "Take care of these two. I'm going to stay behind for a while."

The lulzi gave a disdainful sniff and rode past him, managing to jostle him with her rudhar as she did so. Zhadnoboth gave a fearful look backward and hurried to catch up to Hojeen, worrying about what had spooked Sandy.

Sandy watched them disappear from sight, then pulled a javelin from the quiver strapped to the side of his rudhar. Lolling lazily in the saddle, he started to check the fastenings binding the head of the javelin to the shaft. To his left the air thickened, and soon a vague shadowy figure could be seen.

He whirled in the saddle and threw his javelin full force at the menacing figure. With incredible grace and speed, the figure's hand flashed out and snatched the javelin in midair. "Well thrown, warrior," the Goddess said, laughter in her voice.

"If it was well thrown, you'd have been spitted."

The Goddess laughed again and sidled closer, managing to seem provocative despite her long hooded robe.

"*Now* why are you here? What's the bad news this time?"

"That's my Sandy—always fearing the worst when I show up."

"I've had experience with you, that's why," Sandy told her sourly. "Trouble is never far behind."

"I've only come to say that demons must be as sure of their footing in this world as any mortal," she said innocently. Then she playfully tossed the javelin back at him, letting her robe fall open. He had a teasingly brief glimpse of her wanton nakedness and then she was gone as if she'd never been.

"Bitch!" Sandy yelled after her as he caught the javelin. "And I am *not* a demon!" He stewed for a moment and then grumbled to himself, "What in hell was that all about?" Still frowning, he dug his heels into the sides of his rudhar. The beast sulkily started off in the direction Sandy wanted to go.

"I wish this accursed adventure was over," Sandy muttered as he rode along. "It's one damn thing after another—and that half-grown piece of baggage in the bargain." He looked up at southern sky and swore. The sorcerous storm was now almost upon them.

He dug his heels into the flanks of his rudhar, and it finally broke into a fast canter. Then he shook his fist at the sky and bitched to the Goddess, "How about some help for once?" He paused to give added vehemence to his next words: "And take that damned lulzi off my hands!"

A sudden, violent wind engulfed Sandy and his mount in a miniature sandstorm. Man and beast staggered stubbornly through the maelstrom for a minute or so. Then Sandy spat out an obscenity and said, "All right, I apologize. And damn you to hell." The gale hesitated, gave one last fierce gust, and was gone.

Sandy caught up with the others just where the touch-not bushes finally petered out. Riding up to Hojeen, he pointed at the threatening black clouds which were now so close.

The old scout looked at the approaching storm. "It'll be big trouble very soon. Hit the ground and take cover." He suited his action to his words, getting his rudhar to flop down on its side and then lying beside it with his head holding its neck down.

The others followed his example. Anala's beast went out of its way to be nice to her, lying down with dainty grace and raising no fuss. The sorcerer's beast went down kicking, snorting, and saying bad things in beast talk. Zhadnoboth replied in kind, with some very telling comments about the rudhar's probable ancestry. Sandy's rudhar wasn't any happier about the situation, but did more than complain. It grabbed hold of Sandy's arm and bit down, refusing to let go until he pinched a nerve at the back of its neck.

"You just wait, you pile of crap," Sandy said. "If we ever get out of this I'm selling you to the first butcher I come across.'' Then rudhar and man lay on the ground, glaring at each other eyeball to eyeball.

The sorcerous storm crept closer and closer, the crash of thunder so loud and so constant that they couldn't make themselves heard over it. Then the storm stalled just to the southeast of them as the sorcerer directing it ran into a snag. The black clouds piled up higher and higher as the storm strove to advance. Then there was a pause in the thunder and lightning, followed by an immense barrage of crimson lightning shooting down from the clouds. Million-bolt burst after million-bolt burst came with machine gun rapidity as the sorcerer directing the storm tried to overwhelm some obstacle.

The fierce barrage continued for almost five minutes. Without warning, the frenzied attack came to an abrupt halt and was replaced by an intense stillness. The silence was so profound that Sandy could hear his beard scraping across the back of his hand. The stillness held until an unbearable tension had built up; then the storm let loose a titanic blast of lightning that turned the air blood-red for an instant.

There was another silence. Sandy's hair stood on end, crackling with electricity. An instant later an immense shock wave rolled over them, engulfing them in a choking cloud of dust. Then it was past, leaving behind a sulfuric stench and many odd bits of debris—some of it bloody bits of flesh and bone.

Zhadnoboth stumbled to his feet and shook a fist toward the southeast. ''You numbskull! You're a disgrace to whoever taught you storm magic. I could do better before I was out of diapers.''

The storm clouds still hung over the southeast horizon; but they were now limp, graying, and rapidly beginning to disperse. Then, without warning, an immense pillar of fire and black smoke erupted from the ground beneath the clouds. Higher and higher it rose until it hit the clouds and exploded in a ball of red fire. Sandy and his companions were temporarily blinded and hurled to the ground.

As their sight came back they saw a fine white ash falling all around them. The humans were forced to cover their mouths and noses in order to breathe. Their rudhars coughed and spit a bit, but that was mostly for show—their bodies handled ash just as well as the blown sand they were used to.

Hojeen looked toward the southeast and gave an evil

chuckle. "That's one sorcerer fellow who was no match for Tolk Gilzad."

"I wouldn't call him a sorcerer," Zhadnoboth said sourly. "I'd call him incompetent."

Sandy gave a cynical smile, thinking Zhadnoboth was a fine one to talk. He seemed to operate on the principle of throw anything in the pot and see what happens. What was irritating was that his sorcery worked wonders in an ass-backward sort of way.

Anala brushed the dust off her robes and came bustling over, bent on trouble, just as Sandy turned. They collided and she was knocked over, sitting with a thump on the desert floor. She gave a scream, bounced right back up, and started dancing around and yowling—all the time plucking wildly at her rear end.

Sandy was stupefied for an instant. Then he saw a flattened long thorn plant on the ground and began to laugh. Anala stopped her pained dancing, gave him a look filled with concentrated venom, and hauled off and punched him in the stomach. He stumbled backward, clutching his tomach and trying to regain his breath.

"Why did you do that?" he gasped, backing away. "It wasn't my fault."

"You laughed!" Anala glowered at him with blood in her eyes.

Moments later, after Anala had calmed down some, Hojeen began pulling the long and slightly hooked thorns from her rear end with a tweezers. His face was deadpan, but he was having trouble breathing as he forced his chortles back down.

Anala looked up from her bent-over position and spat out, "Keep that smirk off your face. I'd like to see you laugh if your backside was the pincushion." Hojeen pulled another thorn out and she yowled in pain. She heard a smothered snicker and yelled at Sandy, "Just you wait."

"It's time to go," Sandy said, remounting his rudhar and waiting for them to do the same.

Soon they were riding west again, the lulzi in a crouched position. A constant stream of complaints drifted Sandy's way. He turned a deaf ear her way and his smile toward the desert.

About an hour later, Hojeen called a halt. In front of them stretched a broad and level sandy area. The scout dismounted and picked up a stone. "No matter what, don't ride on this sand," he said, tossing the stone onto its surface. The stone hit the sand, bounced to a stop, and then disappeared with a small pop as the sand sucked it under.

Hojeen began moving them right, going as much west as possible while still avoiding the sand. The ground they traveled over was rocky: the rudhars kept trying to drift over to the softer sand, while their riders kept yanking on the reins and forcing them back. For an hour it was guerrilla warfare between the blockheaded beasts and the sorely tried humans. By the time they came to the end of the sand and saw they could head straight west again, they were as bitchy and uncooperative as their animals.

Something flashed by them and was gone, moving too swiftly to leave more than an impression of strawberry-hued light. For a moment there was nothing more and then it flashed by again.

"I knew it," Sandy crabbed. "I just knew it. Things can't go right for us for more than a minute." He looked at the sorcerer and asked, "What the hell is it now?"

Meanwhile, the red menace was bouncing rapidly about in a herky-jerky fashion—coming and going to all points of the compass, but always getting nearer and staying longer. Then it suddenly settled in one spot, pinning them between it and the treacherous sand. Now that it was still they could see it was a reddish colored spot, about sixty feet in diameter—a sort of hole in the air.

Zhadnoboth got one good look at the spot and twisted around in his saddle, desperately searching for the best way to skedaddle. He jerked the head of his rudhar around and rammed his heels into its sides.

Before his mount could move a step, Sandy grabbed the reins and said, "No!"

"You don't know what that thing is," Zhadnoboth said frantically.

"Tell us and I won't shove you headfirst into it."

The sorcerer wiped some sweat from his brow. "It's a gate to elsewhere—one of the lower hells, if I guess the color right. It's Shenyagi magic, though what one of those sorcerers is doing so far from the Pearly Sea I don't know."

Sandy gave him a grim smile. "You're a sorcerer—do something."

"I can't whip up a spell like a cook making puffed pudding. Sorcery is no catch-as-catch-can art; it needs to be thought out."

"Botch something up," Sandy said impatiently. "It isn't going to be any worse being blown up by one of your spells than it is by one of theirs."

Anala pushed her rudhar between them. "Stand aside. I'll do it." Her tone was the strong and confident one of a poker player holding a royal flush. "I can feel the power of the Goddess bubbling strong within me."

She turned to where the gate was trying to open, and hesitated for a moment, as if unsure of how to apply the strength she felt within her. Then she smiled and spoke a word: "Stop."

A magical force in her voice reached across the distances to the sorcerer controlling the gate. It hit with a jolt that must have rattled the Shenyagi's teeth, because the magical backlash certainly did that to Sandy.

The gate trembled violently and rapidly began to fade. But the Shenyagi sorcerer was not so easily cowed. Sandy could feel his anger, and the gate stilled its motion and became a blackish crimson. Sandy instinctively sensed that the gate was just an instant away from opening.

Anala was just as stubborn as the Shenyagi sorcerer and was galled by his refusal to knuckle under. She raised a finger and waved it angrily at the gate. "Don't you do that," she said, chiding her opponent as though he were a bratty child. "Begone, you quack magicker, before I burn your cullions off." The gate faded to an almost invisible pink. Anala smiled gleefully, reveling in the voice magic she had found within herself.

The Shenyagi sorcerer had staying power, if nothing else, and he rallied his forces and struck back. A sudden wave of force buffeted the lulzi. For a moment she lost her concentration and the gate waxed strong again. Through its redness they could almost see what lay beyond.

"Hold!" Anala yelled, the force of her voice rocking the gate. "Go! Go away to nothingness," she commanded. The gate started to fade once again.

Once again the Shenyagi counterattacked and almost forced the gate open, but Anala's voice stopped it and shifted the balance the other way. For long minutes the battle went on that way, the gate waxing and waning as one or the other momentarily got the upper hand. Several times each almost won, but could not quite pull it off. The battle was a stalemate, though one in a constant state of flux.

Anala kept up a constant chatter; threatening, berating, ordering, insulting, ridiculing, and bullying her opponent—just the use of her voice, not what she said, seemed to be what made her newfound magic effective. There was a joyous exuberance in the way she used her voice, a joy like that of a child learning to talk or a bird making its first flight. She tried all kinds of variations of tone, volume, mood, timbre, and whatever else she could think of—stretching her abilities to the utmost and finding the full range of her power.

The Shenyagi sorcerer was a worthy opponent. He didn't have the one overwhelming power that she had, but he knew a thousand ways of magic and a thousand variations of each. He would pummel her one moment, confuse her the next, and beguile her after that—all the while stubbornly and unceasingly trying to force the gate into full reality. He had the skill, but the lulzi had a one-track mind which wouldn't swerve from its purpose.

After one episode where the world split into millions of fragments and scattered to the four winds, Anala rose in her saddle and commanded ''Begone and be nothing! Become ash in the fire of the Goddess.'' From somewhere her girlish voice had obtained a thunderous volume which shook earth, sky, and her companions to the core—and shattered the immaterial substance of the gate, turning it to burning fragments which began collapsing in on themselves.

From some deep well within himself the Shenyagi sorcerer found the strength to resist—just barely. Almost dissolved into nothingness, the gate drew itself together, deepened its color to a blackish crimson, and charged like a runaway express train at the lulzi and her companions.

Zhadnoboth took one look and dove for the ground. Sandy paled and clutched at the hilt of his saber. Even the imperturbable Hojeen backed away a step. Only Anala did not flinch.

The onrushing gate was almost upon the lulzi before she shook an angry fist at it and said, ''Back! I command you!''

The gate came to an abrupt halt, but trembled as it strove to advance. Beyond its red haze, they could halfway see something monstrous struggling to get out, but Anala refused to let it overwhelm them. She blistered it with a constant flow of fierce words and began forcing it back, slow inch by slow inch.

The Shenyagi sorcerer controlling the gate grudgingly let it be backed up, trying to lull her into the belief that he had shot his last bolt, then swiftly moved the gate to one side and shot it toward them.

Anala blocked the flanking attack with a renewed outburst of words and forced it a little further away. Now the battle settled into a new phase with the Shenyagi sorcerer constantly shifting the gate from one side to the other as he tried to catch the lulzi unaware. Anala met every challenge and determinedly forced the gate further and further away—but at a snail's pace.

Sandy suddenly remembered the Goddess's words. "Use your brains!" he yelled out. "Maneuver the damned gate over the sand and let go. Let whatever is behind it tangle with the sand. Then jump back into the battle."

Anala gave him a resentful glare but heeded his advice. She kneed her rudhar, urging it back down the way they had come. The gate followed, moving toward the treacherous sand. By constantly berating and yelling insults at both the gate and the Shenyagi sorcerer, Anala finagled the gate into a position well over a hundred yards away from solid ground. Then she abruptly ceased her magical browbeating.

The Shenyagi sorcerer was caught completely unaware by her change of tactics. The gate exploded into full reality and opened a way between the worlds the instant after Anala let go, giving the Shenyagi sorcerer no time to choose the exact moment he wanted it open. The vague redness of the unformed gate had now been replaced by a gaping hole that looked into a place of blackness only faintly illuminated by flashes of crimson light. A hot wind roared from the gate, bringing with it the stench of brimstone and rotting flesh.

The noisome stench engulfed Anala; she turned green and began heaving. Her rudhar gave a strangled scream of outrage and ran headlong for some place beyond the reach of the foul wind. When the beast came to where Sandy waited it stopped. There a violently sick Anala hung over the side of her rudhar—in no shape for further voice magic.

In the meantime a huge amorphous blob, looking like clear

jelly tinged with inky black, had oozed through the gate. Thousands of eyeless heads kept forming, disappearing, and then reappearing on its slimy surface. Each head was mostly mouth, filled with needlelike teeth. The mouths opened and shut with spastic rapidity, their teeth clicking and sending iridescent green spittle flying. It slithered rapidly over the sand toward them, bringing with it a ravenous hunger so enormous they could feel it as a nearly physical force.

The avalanche of rapidly moving alien flesh seemed unstoppable, but as it got closer it also seemed to lose momentum. Nearly thirty yards away from them, it stopped dead in its tracks. They got an impression of puzzlement, then fury, An angry chittering came from its thousands of mouths, and its flesh rippled as it tried to moved closer to them. It got nowhere and now its enormous bulk seemed somewhat less.

Sandy looked toward the sand and saw that where the creature touched it, a stormy battle was going on: The atoms of alien flesh and grains of sand were fighting a no-quarter battle. Sand by the barrelful was turning white hot and then melting to nothingness, but the creature also lost a tiny bit of substance for each sand grain destroyed—a price it couldn't pay, because enormous as the hell thing was, its bulk compared to that of the sand was like a raindrop to an ocean.

Zhadnoboth, confident of his power now that the creature was on its last legs, entered the fray. He pointed the staff he had appropriated from the Chanzi wizard, muttered a word of power, and a bolt of purplish lightning came from the sky and smote the creature. The hell thing screamed in agony and a greasy cloud of black smoke rose from a burning wound. Zhadnoboth looked at the staff, puzzled, gave a what-the-hell shrug, and let loose a barrage of the odd-colored lightning.

The beleaguered monster, under attack from both above and below, didn't last long. There was an immense sucking sound and the wounded hell creature was gulped down by the sand, leaving behind only the stench of burned flesh. For several moments the surface of the sand bubbled and boiled, spewing forth wisps of fetid smoke and fiery pieces of protoplasm, as the monster fought to escape from the belly of the sand beast. There was a shrill series of screams rising to an earsplitting crescendo and then silence for several moments. Suddenly the surface of the sand split apart as an immense bubble of reeking and incandescent gases exploded outward. Rapidly the sand settled back down and there was the quiet of death.

Zhadnoboth glared disgruntled at the sand, quite obviously angry because it had robbed him of what he considered his rightful victory. When he saw that the gate was still open, he petulantly, and without thinking, hurled an enormous bolt of the purple lightning at it. The bolt hit the gate and smashed it as though it had been made of fiery glass. The strangely silent explosion that followed flattened Zhadnoboth, his cohorts, the rudhars, and anything else that was standing around.

Sandy picked himself up, spit sand out of his mouth, and hobbled over to his rudhar. The frightened and spiteful beast bit at him. Sandy cuffed it hard across the nose and climbed back into his saddle before it could retaliate. He turned to the sorcerer, glowering. "You did it again, you witless bastard—almost killed us."

Zhadnoboth straightened. "I destroyed the gate, didn't I?"

Sandy stared down at him for a long moment with no expression on his face. "Yeah," he rasped, his caustic tone saying more than a thousand words.

"Nor will that Shenyagi blunderer bother us for a while. When the gate shattered I could hear his screams. It will be months before he'll be fit to cast a spell."

"Let's hope so," Sandy replied. "We have trouble enough as it is—and I wish I knew why. We're being hounded much more than seems reasonable, even if the lulzi is with us."

Anala was white and none too well, but she wasn't about to let Sandy scoff at her without a fight. "A lulzi is not some catchpenny witch they can ignore. They fear me—and with good reason." She paused and added, "Not like some people who sit on their rear ends and let others do the dirty work."

Sandy snapped, "They're panicking and letting fly with everything they have. There has to be a reason for their desperation. You are part of it—they *did* kidnap you—but there has to be something more."

"Maybe you and that trinket of Jara Greenteeth's you hold," Anala said sarcastically.

Hojeen spoke enigmatically. "Krizzan Tham-Shanek is a prophet. Sometimes he believes his own prophecies."

They all looked at him.

"His mother was priestess to old, old god, Hothum of the

Dark Places. He has few worshippers. To a handful he gives gift of true prophecy—sometimes.''

Sandy waited for more. When it didn't come, he asked, "So, what do you mean?"

"I think, maybe, that Krizzan Tham-Shanek has made a prophecy. Maybe about lulzi, and maybe that lulzi is key to war."

The scout's words made Anala's day, instantly replacing the self-confidence she had lost. She perked up and forgot about her nausea, remounting her rudhar as if she were a queen.

Zhadnoboth vigorously nodded agreement to Hojeen's words and hurried over to Anala. "Are you all right, my dear?" he asked unctuously. "I have a potion which will settle your stomach and put the rose back in your cheeks. Would you like to try a drop?"

Sandy grimaced, annoyed both at the way the sorcerer was buttering up the lulzi and the way she couldn't seem to get enough of it. Now she'd be even more of a handful to control.

Anala did not deign to notice his grouchiness. Instead she replied to the sorcerer in a grand and yet properly demure voice, "No, I am quite well now." She paused to give subtle emphasis to her next words. "Today has truly proven that Hojeen and you belong on this undertaking." There was a magical power in her voice which made it seem to sing, to hint at profound mysteries, to whisper of the deep and sublime beauty of life—the magic all the more potent because she was unaware of it. "A time of testing and of greatness is coming. We are chosen; we must be found worthy—this I see." Then she added in a soft, yet caustic tone, "Even those of us who have so far made themselves far less than they could be."

Sandy gave a wry smile and wondered if he ought to look around and see who, besides himself, constituted *us*.

As they rode once more to the west, Zhadnoboth edged his rudhar up beside Sandy's. He pulled a notebook from his robe and scribbled awkwardly in it as he also tried to hold on to his mount's reins. "That was some spell I used to destroy that hell thing. I've marked the details of the incantation down—and how much I should be paid for creating such a masterful bit of sorcery. When I get to Dar-Esh-Rith lesser sorcerers will pay through the nose to learn the details of the spell."

"That should be reward enough, especially since you didn't know what the hell you were doing—and you didn't do much of that."

"There you go agian," Zhadnoboth crabbed, "carping about my magic and trying to cheat me out of what I am due. What other sorcerer could you name who gets such great results?"

Sandy didn't reply. There was not much he could say, either good or bad, and not be wrong. That conniving bastard always screwed something up and yet got amazing results, though what they would be not even the Goddess knew. It was as though Zhadnoboth had attained a certain mystic level of ineptitude that transmuted his blunders into something special, something wonderful.

The sorcerer's voice lowered to a conspiratorial growl. "They say that the Walled House pays well for certain secrets. If you said the right word, we could gouge them for a fortune in gold—and half would be yours."

"I'm not a spy."

Zhadnoboth arched any eyebrow and wheedled, "No, but Hojeen says you have their ear. Just think of all that lovely gold going to waste in their cellars."

"Hojeen's an unwashed dotard who doesn't know what he is talking about. And I'm only a minor officer in a forgotten corner of the empire."

"Or so you both seem."

Sandy didn't reply.

"All right, be that way; but don't come crying to me when I have all the gold and you have none." In a huff, the sorcerer dug his heels into his rudhar and rode off to join Hojeen.

Sandy called after him, "With you counting, my half share of a treasure chest would be one gold coin—or less."

A contemptuous snort was Zhadnoboth's only reply.

Sandy lolled easily in his saddle, glad for a chance to rest and enjoy some peace. Then he heard Anala's rudhar, hurrying to close the gap between them.

Anala's exhilarated voice piped up from beside him, "I showed I was a real lulzi, didn't I?"

"I thought you weren't talking to me."

"I thought so too, but decided you just can't help being jealous of me. You're only a man and I'm a lulzi."

"And I'm the only one you can talk to," Sandy said, needling her gently.

Anala pouted for a too-brief second and said, "You're hopeless. But I did show that I was a lulzi."

Sandy gave a slow nod and replied, "Yes, you did prove you're a lulzi. But that's easy. What's hard is finding out what you're going to be when you're not working miracles—a stuck-up pain in the butt or a person worth talking to."

"But I'm a lulzi, and should be respected."

"Everyone is important to themselves. Remember that, and others will see the worth in you."

Anala reined up her rudhar and fell behind, complaining, "You're no fun to talk to. And what right has a down-at-the-heels soldier got to lecture me?" Then she yelled, "Just you see—I'll be the best lulzi there ever was!"

Sandy smiled ruefully. He *had* been a little hard on her; she could be almost human at times. One day she was going to be one hell of a lulzi—she had certainly showed him the talent was there. He decided to be nicer to her, then quickly changed his mind; she had begun talking again, seemingly to herself, but more than loud enough for him to hear every word.

"We lulzi don't have magic. We have a greater power: the grace of the Goddess and the wisdom to use it."

"It is said the wise speak little and do much," Sandy opined.

Anala ignored him and blithely went babbling on about wisdom, lulzi magic, and whatever else occurred to her— preferring an unwilling audience to no audience at all.

Hojeen led them on a crooked path westward as he avoided the myriad hazards of the Tolk Gilzad. At one point they zigged by a stony flat crawling with tiny scarlet scorpions.

Hojeen pointed to the scorpions as they passed, and in his sloppy Rithian said, "Desert folk call them sting fellows. The lesser Hagbarak slew the great he-dragon, Anzark-Ot, with an arrow poisoned with their venom. The old tales say the worm lay paralyzed in the desert for a month and slowly wasted away."

Zhadnoboth hastily moved his rudhar further away from the scorpions.

"That's terrible," Anala said sadly. "How that poor beast must have suffered."

"He brought it on himself," Hojeen said laconically. "Ate too many children; couldn't get off the ground."

A half hour later they circled around a large hollow. As they passed they could see the bottom was littered with the mummified remains of innumerable birds and beasts—and one thing that might once have been a man. A stray gust of air came his way and Sandy felt a fierce stinging in his nose and eyes, followed by a sick queasiness. He kneed his rudhar and hurried on by, but it was several minutes before he felt right again.

As dusk approached they came over a hill and saw a wide area of low dunes stretching to the horizon both to the north and to the south. Scattered on the surface of the dunes were many pieces of broken bone, some white and new looking, but most yellow with age. In the distance, on the far side of the dunes, they could glimpse the barren and rocky ground that lay beyond the Tolk Gilzad.

"Bad place," Hojeen said, pointing to the dirty gray sand. "People—beasts sink in. Later bones are spit up."

Sandy looked at some of the bones lying nearby. They seemed to have been eaten at by acid. "What if we get across the sand," he asked Hojeen. "What lies beyond?"

"Just desert. Maybe enemies, maybe not. I doubt they expect us to leave the Tolk Gizard alive, let alone cross sand." He pointed at Zhadnoboth and said, "Now's the time for him to do his stuff."

"I don't like it," crabbed the sorcerer. "There is an ancient magic here I don't understand—a baneful thing which hates anything that lives."

"Quit complaining," growled Sandy. "I've seen you get around worse things." With grim humor he added, "I will see that you get paid for any magic you do here, even if I have to dig open your grave to put the gold in your hand."

The sorcerer gave him a baleful glance and started rummaging through his robe, finally coming up with a book bound in a moth-eaten green leather. Muttering to himself, he began paging through it.

"Now is the time to send Aku where he belongs," Anala ordered.

Zhadnoboth looked thunderstruck. "That's it. I move Aku and at the same time get us out of here. I know just the spell." Eagerly he went back to paging through the spellbook. "Here it is. Now you'll see what a real sorcerer can do."

Moments later they had dismounted atop a small hill overlooking the dunes. Zhadnoboth drew two circles on the ground with the tip of his staff and then drew a larger one to surround them. Nervously chewing on his beard, he consulted his spellbook, then muttered a word of power and touched one of the circles. It lit up with a faint orange glow. He did the same with the other small circle. But there was a glitch in procedure when he touched the circle that surrounded them, and it lit up with a sickly yellowish glow. Zhadnoboth cursed and jabbed at the circle with his staff. The glow reluctantly turned orange, but Sandy noticed the color was not quite the same as that of the two smaller circles—though the sorcerer appeared satisfied with the result.

He now pulled from his robe a yellowish black stone, the size of a child's fist and with a pebbled surface. "This is a bezoar from the gut of a rogue dragon. With my aid he was slain and I received this stone as a reward."

"No doubt they knew they were giving it to you," Sandy said cynically. He was wise to the sorcerer's ways and knew the best way to squelch a long-winded spiel before it began.

Zhadnoboth started guiltily and said, "It was a just reward." Then, mumbling muffled curses, he began rummaging around inside his robe, pulling forth what else he needed for the spell—a small copper kettle, some charcoal, a tightly corked vial of blue glass, and an earthenware pot of sulfur paste.

Hojeen and Anala goggled as Zhadnoboth assembled the spell's ingredients, wondering how such bulky junk had caused no bulges in his robe. Sandy wasn't surprised: He had seen the robe trick before. Someday he was going to give in to the temptation to hold the sorcerer upside down by the ankles and shake him to see what would fall out.

Zhadnoboth made a cone-shaped pile of the charcoal and put the copper kettle on top of it. He touched the charcoal with the tip of his staff, said a minor word of power, and it began to burn with an odd bluish flame. Next he carefully placed the bezoar in the bottom of the kettle, opened the blue glass vial, and poured twelve drops of a dark oily fluid on the stone.

Soon a stomach-turning stench filled the air. Sandy wrinkled his nose in disgust, both at the smell and the memories it brought back. The sorcerer had once dosed him with a few drops of the foul stuff—tincture of bloatfish—and he would never forget it: As bad as it smelled, it tasted far worse.

Zhadnoboth dug into the pot of sulfur paste with his forefinger, scooped out a glob, and then flung it into the kettle. This he did twelve times. As each glob went in, he chanted a number in a voice as melodious as a rusty hinge—counting down from twelve to one. Soon the air within the circle was almost unbreathable as the sulfur fumes mixed with the stench of overheated tincture of bloatfish.

Zhadnoboth began dancing in place and reciting with staccato rapidity the names of all one hundred and thirteen demons from whose bones Omdad the Creator had made the earth and sky. As he recited each name a nimbus of watery blue light built up around him until he resembled a rather scruffy angel in full glory. When he had said the last name, he stepped back, extended his staff until its tip was over the kettle, and said Kythornak's third word of power.

There was a moment of electrifying quiet. Then the aura surrounding him contracted and sank into him. An instant later it flowed like water from the end of his staff and down into the kettle. For the next moment nothing happened, except the air was suddenly sweet and breathable again—then a thick column of bluish gray vapor erupted from the kettle and rose to form a large cloud just over their heads.

After about five minutes, the copper kettle made a sort of hiccup and ceased smoking. The sorcerer threw a smug smile Sandy's way, raised his staff and rammed it into the cloud above their heads, and then slowy spoke Kythornak's thirteenth word of power. The churning blue-gray vapor rushed to the staff and was absorbed into it. When about a third of the overhead cloud was gone, Zhadnoboth lowered his staff and pointed it at one of the other circles. This time he recited Kythornak's thirteenth word of power in reverse, unsaying what had been said before. With a whoosh the vapor was expelled from the staff, shooting across to the smaller circle and filling it with a fifty-foot-high column of restless and turbulent smoke. Then he repeated his spellwork and filled the second small circle.

Finally, he stuck his staff into what was left of the original cloud, spoke the thirteenth word once again, and rapidly whirled his staff about in a circle, making three rotations. The cloud abruptly settled to the ground, blanketing so thickly they couldn't see more than an inch from their noses.

Zhadnoboth chanted doggerel in a high-pitched voice, "Aku, Aku be the first; oh Seven Wells, oh Seven Wells be the second; and let the third be us."

The air around them cleared; and the turbulent vapor which had filled the other two circles was also gone. Inside these two circles there no longer was just bare dirt, but scenes from other places. In one, Aku and three of Sandy's troopers were huddled about a small fire, looking tired. Each of them bore freshly bandaged wounds. In the other, a grim bunch of desert chieftains was sitting in a circle, wrangling hotly.

Then, in sudden surprise, the people in both circles looked toward them.

Anala seized the initiative. She stepped forward and in her grandest and most ladylike voice said to the assembled chieftains, "Men of the desert, look at me. I am the lulzi whose time has now come."

The desert men stared at her in stunned awe for a moment; then one, two, and finally all of then bent their heads and touched hand to heart in reverent respect.

"I bring you a general who will lead you to victory," Anala continued in a commanding voice, giving the chieftains no time to think.

She pointed to Aku.

The desert men raised their heads and stared in surprise at Aku, apparently seeing him for the first time. But they were no more surprised than Aku, who sat by his fire in thunderstruck silence.

"Aku of the Isles is a mighty man of valor," the lulzi went on. "A man of battles, a man of wisdom, a man favored in the sight of the Goddess. Listen to him, and follow him. *This* the Goddess commands."

For a moment there was a tense silence. Then a chieftain, wearing the red headband and white headcloth of the White Branch Zenori, rose to his feet. "I will follow him," he said. The next moment a Kri Yitheni chieftain joined him in swearing allegiance. Then chieftain after chieftain was rising to his feet to offer his loyalty and that of his fellow tribesmen.

"You have done well, my children," Anala said in a grand

yet affectionate voice, touching the men's souls as they sensed the worth she saw in them.

Sandy envied her for a moment. He could get men to follow him, but he could never win their hearts as she had, so swiftly and so effortlessly. They hardly knew her and yet they seemed ready to follow her to hell if she said the word. Then he smiled wryly. He was himself—and that was what he most wanted to be, flaws and all.

"Make ready your swords," Anala said, her voice full of a quiet magic. "I shall bring you your lord. Aku of the Barren Earth I name him."

Sandy was certain she had made up the title on the spur of the moment, but by destiny or maybe by chance she had struck a deep chord within the chieftains. They looked toward the other circle and Aku with a mixture of mystic awe and impassioned eagerness. The lightly given title had a deep meaning for them. Sandy wondered what kind of beast Anala had released.

The lulzi made an imperious gesture at Zhadnoboth, implying he now had to make her words true by transporting Aku to the Seven Wells and his destiny.

The sour-faced sorcerer, disgruntled because she had stolen his thunder, hesitated for a second and then extended his staff. He touched the ground at her feet with its tip, then pointed the staff at Aku and said a word. A bridge, seeming made from the swirling blue-gray vapor which had so suddenly vanished, now formed first at her feet and then arched through the air to complete itself at Aku's feet.

Aku stared at the insubstantial-looking bridge and didn't move.

"Cross it, you fool," Zhadnoboth hissed. "It won't last forever."

Aku hastily scrambled to his feet, tested the span with a wary foot, and then ran across. The bridge started to fade and Sandy's three other troopers darted across—dead scared of crossing the insubstantial span, but not wanting to be left behind. The bridge dissolved under their hurrying feet and they fell, but landed within the larger circle.

"Now what?" Aku whispered to Anala, back to being a practical man once he'd got over his astonishment.

"Lead your desert bastards to victory," Anala whispered back. "With your experience and ability it should be easy."

"I'll do it, but war is never easy."

"You have the Goddess behind you, and her lulzi." She paused, eyed him boldy, and said in a suggestive voice, "A successful general who knows a lulzi—knows her well—could go far."

Aku gave her a slight nod, showing he had caught her meaning.

She looked at Zhadnoboth and pointed imperiously at the circle in which they could see the assembled chieftains. The sorcerer raised his staff and created another bridge—but there was a peevish look on his face and Sandy knew the old coot was going to demand an arm and a leg for this day's services.

Anala strode boldly across the bridge of vapor, Aku at her side, tall and grim. Sandy's three other troopers brought up the rear.

When they stood within the circle of desert men, Anala spoke up, "Here is your lord. Swear now your oath to him."

One by one each chieftain came forward, the unwritten but rigid rules of desert etiquette determining in what order they came. Each knelt and kissed her hand with reverence. Then each, in an ancient ritual, placed his sword at Aku's feet—silently swearing obedience to him.

When the last sword had been laid down, Anala raised her hands and said, "In the name of the Goddess I bless you, my children. Now follow your leader to victory." She turned on her heel and impressively marched back over the bridge Zhadnoboth had created for her.

Sandy marveled at how reverently and unquestioningly the desert men accepted being called children by a mere child. Still, she had impressed him, brat or not. The lulzi part of her was quite something. Now if she could only get the human side of herself to be a someone you wanted to know.

The moment Anala stepped back into their circle, Zhadnoboth raised his staff and pointed it at circle she had left. He spoke Kythornak's fourth word, the word of dissolution, and a bolt of red lightning sprang from the tip of his staff and blasted the other circle. It disappeared in a glorious burst of red and rose fire, leaving behind only an ordinary bit of desert floor—and a vapor bridge that went nowhere. Zhadnoboth gave the orphan bridge a malevolent glare and then cursed it out, as though it were at fault for being there. Still fuming, he swatted at the end of the bridge anchored near his feet.

Instantly the bridge dissolved into billions of tiny motes and then was nothing.

"Now you see I am really something, soldier," Anala said to Sandy in a bullying voice.

"You are that," he agreed as he kept a worried eye on the sorcerer. He had a bad feeling, but he couldn't quite put his finger on the *why*.

The sorcerer, still in a foul mood, abruptly spat out the word of dissolution again and struck the ground at their feet with his staff. The instant it happened Sandy knew what had been bothering him. The spell felt out of balance—even more so with only one of the lesser circles destroyed. He threw a curse Zhadnoboth's way and threw himself to the ground.

There was a soundless explosion and Sandy felt himself being sent a million different directions at once. He blacked out and when he recovered consciousness, found himself tumbling head over heels through the air, going hellbent to somewhere. Occasionally he caught glimpses of his fellow travelers as he whirled dizzily about.

Their speed kept increasing until everything seemed a blur. Then, suddenly, they hit some kind of barrier and burst through. Their wild tumbling stopped and now they raced like four rockets over a barren landscape full of rocky crags and sheer-sided ravines—a land whose outlines seemed to subtly change from one second to the next. The sky was a purplish haze filled with light that seemed to come from a sun of many scattered parts.

"Bad," Hojeen croaked. "This is Land Beyond the Edge. Not Zarathandra or any mortal realm. This is lost place which lies between. Place where Greenteeth is."

The sorcerer gave a terrified screech.

Sandy jerked his head around, and his innards turned to ice. Dead ahead, atop a might crag, with a grim fortress, weirdly there and yet not there. One instant it seemed very real and the next the merest ghost of that reality.

And they were being flung full force at the jagged cliff face beneath that citadel. Sandy snapped his eyes shut, preferring not to witness his own annihilation.

The next instant there was an icy shock and he felt himself slowing down. It was like he was being forced through a sieve made of cold Jell-O as his atoms flowed through the spaces between the molecules of the rock. There was a *pop* and he felt himself falling.

Sandy opened his eyes and stared wildly about. He saw a shifting blackness, a blackness lit by flaming torches. A howl of pain burst from his lips as his feet slammed hard onto a slanting surface. He went tumblong down, caught a glimpse of a worked stone wall, and then ploughed into it. For a moment he lay there unmoving, but conscious—then a knobby something slammed into him. As he passed out, he heard Zhadnoboth gibbering in terror.

9

SANDY came stumbling through the mist, looking dazed. The Goddess gave a wicked smile. For once her wayward liege-man might be easy to handle.

When he saw her shadowy figure he came to a stop. As he took in the midnight blue of her hooded robe and her throne of aquamarine crystal, the light of reason slowly appeared in his eyes. Then he knew her, knew himself. The simple-minded mildness disappeared from his face and was replaced by wary vigilance. "Now what?" he asked.

"You're now within Jara Greenteeth's fortress. The Four have come to the time foretold. On you and your companions depend the shee's fate and the future of Zarathandra."

Sandy looked around with untrusting eyes. "This doesn't look like a damned fortress to me. All I see is pearly gray clouds, you, and your fancy chair floating on nothing."

"This is but a dream. Your body lies in the dungeon depths of the shee's fortress. Here you are outside time and beyond her ken."

"Why am I here?"

"Four is the number and each has a part to play."

"That tells me a hell of a lot," Sandy replied.

Hidden by the hood of her robe, the Goddess smiled, enjoying his disgruntlement. "You are my demon, my man of battles, chosen by destiny to be my sword in times of need."

"I keep telling you and that pipsqueak sorcerer that I'm not a demon."

"Oh, but you are a demon. You are more than merely

human, with powers and abilities no human has. You can die, but always live again. What else can you be but a demon?''

Sandy scowled. "Call me what you will, but in my heart I know what I am. As for destiny—I'd call it something else. That miserable excuse for a sorcerer only hooked me by mistake when he cast his spell. It could have been any poor schnook who was in the wrong place at the wrong time. Hell, if he'd roped in a half-blind hunchback, you'd have latched onto him.''

"You are what I got; you will have to do.''

Sandy's scowl grew blacker.

The Goddess glanced lecherously at his naked body and again wondered what she liked about him. He was only passably handsome, not much over average height, moderately well muscled and as compliant as a rusty hinge. Still, he did have curly hair and a wry good nature—not that these made up for his many faults.

"You through giving me the eye or are you going to drool all day?''

"You're nothing to look at.''

"I agree, but you still look.''

"That's my nature and my privilege," the Goddess said with an awesome majesty.

Sandy was having none of it. "Save your act for someone else. As for privilege, if you weren't a goddess, I'd call you a floozy.''

She made an exasperated motion with her hand and he was clothed in a rough brown robe. "Watch your tongue, man," she said vehemently. "Or you'll learn the price of my anger.''

Sandy cooled his temper, but didn't back down an inch. "I've already learned, and where did it get you? Nowhere. You need me and I'm stuck with you, so tell me what you want and I'll do the best I can.''

The Goddess mulled over her options, weighing in her mind how her words might affect the future. She did not want to say too much, yet saying too little could work against her.

Suddenly it all came together, and the Goddess knew what to say—the words that would best mislead and maneuver him into doing her will, but also would leave the crucial decisions up to him and his companions.

"Long ago, in the days of the shee's youth, a prophecy was spoken.''

Sandy gave a snort of disgust. "I don't want to hear words you put in somebody's mouth."

"Prophecy comes from beyond; neither I nor any other being can bring it about or control it." Her voice was as clear and sharp as a rap on the knuckles. "It was said there would be four, and together they would determine the fate of the shee and which way destiny would fork."

"What is her fate?"

"I don't know. This I do know: The four of you must contend with the shee and attain some sort of victory."

Sandy shook his head. "In other words you don't know what's coming down the pike, but you want us to wing it as best we can."

"That might sum it up." The Goddess was pleased with herself. She had said only one thing that was less than the truth and yet had managed to get his thoughts turned the right way. Now for another matter, while he was here and the time was right.

One moment the Goddess was a queen on her throne and the next a wanton sidling up to him, gently letting him feel her nipples pressing on him. She ran her hand through the curls of his hair.

Involuntarily, he started to back off. She didn't let him go, but crowded him with her flesh. He stopped and looked squarely at her. "Damn it! Stop that. You're going to give me some answers, not weasel out by taking me for a tumble." His face had started to redden and his body to press against hers.

She laughed and stroked him. *"No* is not for you. You're easy."

"Yeah, but not all the time," he protested.

"This is a dream and in dreams anything is possible."

"Oh hell!" Sandy said. He grabbed her, ran his hand down her flank, and with savage gentleness pressed his body to hers.

10

SANDY groaned and opened his eyes. For a moment his heart stopped. A vague shadowy mass surrounded him; all he could clearly discern was the glimmer of hungry teeth. Frantically he clutched for his sword hilt.

"It's about time you woke up," said Anala. "You're too much dead weight to lug around." Belying her words was the anxiety in her voice.

Sandy's vision cleared and he saw that the pack ready to tear him apart was only his companions plus three pale-faced strangers. Beyond them he could dimly see a low ceiling of rough-cut rock and walls made from close-fitting stone blocks.

"Which corner of hell is this?" he asked as he sat up.

"Dungeons of Cimber-Tal-Gogna," Hojeen grunted. "I've been here before. Great, great fortress that no one has completely mastered, not even the shee. She rules the heart, but there is more to this stone house than she knows." His eyes clouded for a moment. "Once she was not here."

"What!" Sandy shot to his feet, fumbling for his weapons.

"She does not know we are here," the scout said impassively. "Dungeons old and have many dark corners she can't see into."

Sandy growled, "So you say. More likely, we've jumped from the frying pan and are now ass-deep in the fire." He swung around and snapped at Zhadnoboth, "What kind of mess have you got us into this time?"

The sorcerer flinched, then retorted, "It was as grand a piece of magic as I've ever done—even a mere soldier should see that. We're where we want to be, in the heart of our enemy's stronghold. Here we can most damage her. Any other sorcerer would have spent weeks getting you here.'' Zhadnoboth put on his best face, trying to appear haughty and unjustly maligned at the same time. He almost pulled it off, mostly because he was gulling himself as well as the others.

Sandy snorted, ''Get off it, old man. Admit it was one of your usual botches.''

Zhadnoboth drew himself as tall as his scrawny frame let him. ''I am as great sorcerer as you'll ever see. The hand of fate touches me and makes my magic even greater.''

''The sorcerer is right,'' piped up Anala. ''We're where we must be. Destiny has chosen us to bring doom to the shee. We should bless Zhadnoboth. His great sorcery has brought us to where we are needed.''

Sandy choked, then said vehemently, ''Destiny be damned! You don't climb a mountain by jumping into a pit. Thanks to this jackass of a sorcerer we'll have to do things the hard way.''

''No doubt you'd prefer fighting the shee from some whore's bed in Kimbo-Dashla,'' Anala said insultingly.

Sandy glowered at her. ''There's better places to be—and better things to do. You tell me how we break out of this stinking dungeon.''

''There's only one way from these dungeons and she controls it,'' said a sullen voice.

Sandy turned and saw a thin-faced man, his skin pale from the lack of sun, staring at him. Backing him up were two companions of much the same ilk. Sandy started to speak and then cocked his head and looked puzzled at the man. There was something about the voice and the face that seemed familiar.

The man scowled and said, ''Remember me? I'm Talim Shenyanda.''

Sandy gave a curt nod and replied, ''I do now.'' How could he forget such a stuck-up bastard? Talim was the casual by-blow of a minor Rithian noble, some sort of shirttail relative to the emperor. Talim had never let anyone forget he had royal blood flowing in his veins. He was also a holier-than-thou prig, a whoremonger, a dandy, and a damned good soldier.

Sandy and Talim had never been friends, although they'd both been in the same training outfit and survived together the most sadistic bunch of sergeants this side of hell. A year out of boot camp, Talim had made officer, pegged as a real comer by those in the know. Then he and his troop had left on a routine patrol through the desert and neither he nor any of his men had ever came back.

"I've rotted in this damned dungeon since a sandstorm swallowed up my patrol and dumped us in this borderland of hell," he said savagely. "There's only one way out and it leads to Jara Greenteeth and the walking dead who serve her. There's no way through or around the dead—you cannot slay cold meat or escape eyes that never close. And if you could— then there is the shee. After that bitch feasts on body and soul—a man is less than even her dead." His voice was bitter and trembling with anger.

Sandy could feel his despair and the rage underlying it. If Talim ever got a chance at revenge, he'd make the shee pay in spades for what she had done to him.

"Wrong. There are three ways from the dungeons," Hojeen said matter-of-factly. All eyes turned toward him. He held up one finger and said, "Steel gate." He held up another finger and said, "Secret gate." He held up a third finger and said, "Hidden gate."

"You're a fool, old man," sneered Talim. "I've been over these dungeons a thousand times. There is only one entrance."

"Three gates," Hojeen replied in a quietly stubborn voice.

"Where are the other two?" Sandy asked.

Talim grabbed Sandy's arm, shook him, and yelled, "Are you going to believe this stinking peasant or a gentleman and officer?"

Sandy yanked Talim's hand from his arm. "I listen to anyone who has something worth saying. Not to someone who thinks only his words are worth hearing."

Talim went deadly pale. "If we ever escape from these dungeons, you'll answer to me and my sword, you baseborn bastard." He paused and added, "Unless you run for cover with your tail between your legs."

Sandy shrugged. "If you want to die I'll not stop you. Till then it will be hard going to get out of here. Let's try burying the hatchet in the shee before we bury it in each other."

Talim sneered, but nodded yes. Sandy brusquely turned his back on him and asked Hojeen, "How sure are you about these three gates?"

"This place not always belong to shee. This old man once run dungeon for him who was before. Maybe Hojeen still knows its secrets."

"Cut the bull," Sandy snapped. "Just spit out what you know."

"That old fool knows nothing," Talim scoffed.

His ill-timed words pushed Sandy over the edge. He swung about and stomped down hard on Talim's foot. Talim screamed in surprise and pain, involuntarily reaching down to clutch his injured foot. Sandy's fast-rising knee caught him on the chin. There was a crunch, Talim's head snapped back, and he collapsed in a heap.

Sandy turned to Talim's fellow prisoners and snapped, "Take care of this fool."

They nodded dumbly and jumped to obey.

Hojeen squinted down at the unconscious Talim, gave Sandy a crooked smile, and walked over to the nearest wall. He looked carefully at the stone blocks and then thumped one three times on its left edge. It swung open like a door, revealing a small dark hole. The old man gave a satisfied cackle and reached inside and pulled out a dusty bottle of mottled green glass. He rubbed the dust off on his robe, pulled the cork with his age-yellowed teeth, took a deep draught, and then smacked his lips and gave a sigh of satisfaction.

Sandy took the bottle from him, carelessly wiped its mouth off, and took a long swig. His breath caught for an instant as the liquor hit the back of his throat, then he smiled and took another and longer shot. He handed the bottle back to Hojeen and commented, "That's proof you're too long unhanged, but your hooch does hit the spot."

"How about some for me?" Zhadnoboth whined. "Nobody thinks about a poor sorcerer dragged into adventures he wants no part of."

Hojeen took another swallow and passed the bottle to Zhadnoboth. The sorcerer grimaced and fastidiously cleaned off the bottle before he poured a generous slug into an earthenware mug he had dug out of the deeper recesses of his robe.

"And what about me?" Anala said.

Zhadnoboth started to hand her the bottle.

"Don't!" ordered Sandy. He reached forward and snatched the bottle from the sorcerer's hand. "She's trouble enough without having her flat on her rear end."

Anala's temper flared. "What are you afraid of, that I'll show you up? I'm a lulzi and can drink any ten men under the table—especially an underhanded knave who doesn't know how to fight like a gentleman."

Sandy was puzzled for a moment. Then he shrugged and said, "Talim needed a lesson. Besides, I fight to win—not to get my teeth knocked out." He gave her a disbelieving look and asked pointedly, "When have you drunk anybody under the table?"

"Not yet. But—"

"Well, you're not starting now."

Anala was not taking no. Her eyes squinted in determination and she aimed her forefinger at the bottle, saying in a voice that rang with equal measures of authority and pettishness, "Come here!"

The bottle was almost jerked out of Sandy's hand by the magical force in her voice, but he held on and then jerked it back. For the next few moments their impromptu duel went on, she chattering nonstop commands and Sandy stubbornly resisting—the sweet tones of enchantment against brute muscle. The battle seesawed, first he'd be dragged bodily toward her and the next instant he'd regain control and obstinately back away. Finally, things came to a standstill as magical pull and brute force canceled each other out.

The bottle writhed like a live thing in Sandy's hand and then began to emit a screeching howl as the tortured molecules pulled apart. The sound rose to an ear-splitting level—and then higher—to a piercing silence. Tiny chips of stone began flaking off from the rock walls and falling from the ceiling. Suddenly the bottle disappeared into nowhere, leaving behind a cloud of overheated liquor that exploded outward in a fine mist.

Zhadnoboth stared in horrified disbelief. "You imbeciles," he screeched. "That was the finest bragberry brandy—drops of the thirdwater from the northern reaches of Yimberhay. Usually only royalty gets to drink such a nectar."

"Come off it," Sandy crabbed. "I wouldn't call the stuff you stash away for yourself rotgut. I've drunk from your private stock—I should know."

The sorcerer looked hatefully at Sandy and retorted, "May you roast in the deepest hell. Such perfection is to be rolled on the tongue and slowly enjoyed, not wantonly squandered as if it was bilge water.'' He added spitefully, ''And don't think I'm not keeping track of what's owed me—be it liquor or gold.''

Hojeen gave them an enigmatic appraising look. Then he shrugged, stuck his hand back into the hole in the wall, pulled out another bottle, elbowed the stone door shut, stalked over to Zhadnoboth, and shoved the bottle into his hand. The sorcerer hastily slipped it inside his robe. As usual the robe was much bigger on the inside than the outside—not a bulge to show where the bottle was stashed.

''What about me?'' Anala demanded.

Sandy said patiently, ''Where I was raised children did not drink—ever.''

''Children!''

''I'll show you the hidden gate,'' Hojeen interrupted. He turned and walked out the rough-cut doorway of the chamber.

Caught between anger and befuddlement, Sandy turned and barked to the larger of Talim's fellow prisoners, ''Follow me! And haul his butt along too,'' he added, jerking his thumb at Talim. Then he strode from the room, giving no time for protest.

The big prisoner yanked the groggy Talim to his feet and half carried, half dragged him after Sandy. Zhadnoboth and the other prisoner followed right at their heels. Anala glowered after them for a moment. Finally she gave a peckish sniff and reluctantly followed.

Sandy stopped outside the doorway of the room and knelt down beside Hojeen, scanning the dungeon. The main chamber was almost a block long and about a third as wide. The ceiling was a good ninety feet above their heads. He could see it had been a giant cave which had been reworked into a hall. The wall opposite them was made from huge blocks of red granite, so close-joined he doubted a knife blade would fit between the stones. The other walls, the floor, and the ceiling were of fine-grained cave limestone—smoothed just enough to look worked.

Leftward, scattered at floor level, many dark openings pierced the walls of the hall. In front of them lounged a scattering of prisoners, pale-skinned and scrawny. There was only a handful of them, but the immense size of the main hall made them seem even fewer. They paid little heed to Sandy and his companions; they'd long ago lost their spirit and curiosity.

Near the ceiling and circling the entire cave was a row of man-tall brackets, bronze and stained green with age. Each bracket held a burning torch—their flames giving a flickering reddish tinge to the light in the cave. Now, for the first time, Sandy noticed the powerful redolent odor of pine tar. It was a refreshing stench, one more dungeons could have used. He frowned and sniffed the air questioningly, wondering why his nose had just now smelled an odor thick enough to be cut and stacked.

"Torches only stink up big room," Hojeen said. "When place first made a mighty magic was put on them—never do they go out. They burn and make air good." He added in an offhand and subtly different voice, "When last torch dies, Cimber-Tal-Gogna dies."

Sandy gave a half-heeding nod and carefully scanned the far wall. A narrow stair, made from huge blocks of cave limestone, hugged the red granite of the wall and led up to a large stone platform overlooking the dungeon. Ten feet higher was the ceiling. At each end of the platform, one of the torches burned. Embedded in a dark recess in the cave wall, midway between the torches, was a huge steel door. The left and right halves were each five feet wide and nine feet high. There was no way of knowing how thick the door was, but it had a ponderous look and Sandy estimated that it might be half a foot or more thick.

He eyed it closely, noticing deep gouges in the metal. The door had held, but something monstrous had once attacked it.

Hojeen pointed at it. "Steel gate. It now belongs to shee." He nodded toward the left. "Secret gate that way. It also belong to shee." He nodded right. "Hidden gate this way. Belong only to itself." On silent feet he stole off toward it.

Sandy gave an uneasy upward glance toward the steel door and followed the scout. Hojeen's unconcern about being observed by Jara Greenteeth made no sense, but felt right. Sandy was going to have to corner that old sinner and get a few questions answered—or try prying them out of the Goddess. The thought of the Goddess lit a fire in his belly and he threw a venomous comment skyward: "And don't think, hussy, I don't know whose finagling has got me into this mess." He hoped she heard him—it would do her good to listen to something besides the verbal pap her worshippers gave her.

As Sandy followed Hojeen, he noticed that the chamber gradually began to change character. The ceiling got lower and the walls rougher, until at the far end the room was all cave. There the ceiling abruptly plunged earthward and the walls came together, leaving a small opening barely four feet high and maybe wide enough for a fat man to squeeze through. Hojeen never hesitated, but popped through the opening and was gone.

Sandy stopped, not liking the look of the rough doorway, then gave a rueful smile as he caught the thick musty odor common in old cellars. It brought back pleasant childhood memories of his grandmother's house—of shelves loaded with dusty jars of pickles, of bins loaded with new-picked potatoes, of crocks full of fermenting sauerkraut, and of small barrels of homemade wine waiting to be bottled.

He stooped and hurried through the opening, paying more attention to his fond memories than his footing. The next moment he was cursing Hojeen as he slid down a steep water-slickened slope of loose shale. He arrived at the bottom amid a shower of mud and loose rock, but in one piece. Still grumbling, he headed for the flickering red glow he saw at the end of the tunnel.

The tunnel twisted and turned downward out of the shale and into limestone. A tiny stream flowed along the floor of the tunnel, switching from one side to the other as the whim took it. After he had crossed it for about the twentieth time, Sandy growled, "Make up your damned mind about where you want to flow." He got no response from the stream, though for the rest of the way it dutifully hugged the lefthand wall.

The tunnel took an abrupt right turn and Sandy found himself in a dingy and rather down-at-the-heels grotto. Instead of the multicolored and jewel-like limestone found in many caves, nature had carved this one from a fragile yellow-brown limestone which fell apart at the touch. The floor was ankle-deep in rock chips, the walls were pitted with jagged scars, and the cave itself was fairly small—maybe the size of a neighborhood theater.

The grotto's only exceptional feature was at the far end. There, the streamlet had formed a small pool of clear water.

Just beyond the pool the back wall of the grotto was fronted by a foot-wide crevasse. Every one or two seconds a red sheet of flame erupted from the depths of the crevasse, flowed up the blackened wall, and out a narrow shaft which split the cave roof.

Hojeen was squatting beside the pool and gazing intently at the flames as they went up the natural chimney. Sandy knelt beside him. "You figuring the quickest way to turn us into burnt toast?" Absentmindedly he cupped his hand, dipped it in the pool, and brought the water up to his lips. He spat out the lukewarm stuff almost as fast as he had drunk it. "God, this water tastes like somebody's soaked their old socks in it."

A hint of a smile twitched at Hojeen's mouth. "Better than no water." Sandy nodded and dipped some more water out of the pool and drank it, made a face, and drank some more.

There was a scuffling sound behind them. Sandy turned and saw the rest of his companions stumble into the cave. Zhadnoboth, Talim, and the other two prisoners all shared the same bad temper—and mud-soaked clothing. Anala was as bespattered as the rest, but an impish grin played about her lips and an inner glow seemed to radiate from her.

"Now what!" Sandy snapped.

"It's what we get for following you," Zhadnoboth replied peevishly.

"More likely because this half-pint got you to make mud pies." Sandy gave Anala a raking glance, though an unvoiced laughter tempered its fierceness.

"It's more than you ever did," she retorted. "Besides, it's old sore-tooth's fault anyway."

Sandy was all ears waiting for the rest of the story, but Hojeen interrupted. "Be ready. The Maki-Maki-Noor will be near soon."

"Who the hell is Maki-Maki-Noor?" Sandy snapped, wanting to hear what cock and bull Anala would come up with.

"The Maki-Maki-Noor are the people of light," Anala said.

Hojeen nodded agreement.

"Rightly they are called the Machimacanar. In the cold spaces between the worlds and the moons is their country. Of gossamer and moonshine are they made. Starlight and sunshine is their food and drink."

"Quit quoting your schoolbooks and tell us something useful," Sandy broke in. "Like what are these Maki things doing here?"

A quirky smile flashed across her face for a moment, then Anala remembered who she was. Frowning, she said in a sulky voice, "Hojeen must be wrong. The Maki-Maki-Noor never leave the void which is their home."

"I think this place is holy for Maki-Maki-Noor," Hojeen said. "It's not all rock and mud here. If you turn the right corner, you can find a big emptiness. Legend is that in the old, old, old times all this place was between stars. Now in scattered places some of the nothing which was before still exists. Maki-Maki-Noor visit those places. Maybe as pilgrims, maybe not. They must shrive souls, must purify selves, must haggle and trade. Then they can return to big emptiness beyond moon."

"That's hogwash," Zhadnoboth said disgruntledly. "Nursery tales. And what would you trade to a cloud of vapor some star burped up? Glass beads? Furniture polish?"

Hojeen shrugged. "Long time ago, I see them. They came and they traded."

"So they trade," Sandy said. "What good does it do us?"

Hojeen chuckled softly. "You can trade for trip. Maki-Maki-Noor can take you from here to other places."

"What other places?"

Hojeen shrugged again. "Other places. Maybe one pace away or two paces away. Maybe much more. It's all same to them. They don't know the difference between a hairbreadth and a Rithian mile."

Sandy looked disgustedly at the old scout. "You dragged us here for that!"

Hojeen replied laconically, "It's a way out."

A rapt expression appeared on Anala's face. "I can feel the power of the Goddess," she whispered. "This is the place of destiny, the time of greatness, the way to glory."

The hairs on the back of Sandy's neck stood on edge at the eldritch tone in her voice.

He wasn't the only one who heard it. Zhadnoboth gasped and stared fearfully at the young girl. Talim and his fellow prisoners looked at her in awe. Only Hojeen seemed unaffected, gazing her way with expressionless, almost sleepy eyes.

"We are with you, little one," Talim vowed. "This is our chance for atonement, our chance to destroy a great evil." There was desperation and madness in his voice.

"How do we do it?" Sandy asked bluntly, trying to still the magical craziness of the moment.

He succeeded. Anala blinked and looked confusedly at him, now merely a girl again. The others relaxed and looked grumpily at each other.

Anala stared angrily, and a little sadly, at him. "You have the soul of a worm and less heart. You feel nothing and make fun of those who do."

Sandy shrugged off her words. "Mystical madness has its place, but so does common sense. I'm responsible for you idiots. Maybe we're supposed to be great heroes, maybe not. But as long as I'm in charge we'll go forward with our eyes open and our heads out of the clouds."

"You should dream a little."

"I do, but not all the time."

Sandy turned to Hojeen and asked, "How do we talk to these Maki-Maki-Noor?"

Sandy, Anala, Hojeen, and Zhadnoboth stood by the edge of the pool, looking across it toward the intermittent sheet of flame on the other side. Talim and the other two prisoners hung back, guarding the entrance to the grotto.

"Maki-Maki-Noor will be here soon," Hojeen said as he pointed toward the latest gust of flame. "See, the fire is starting to turn green. When they're all the way here, we'll make ourselves known. Then we'll haggle. And they'll try to diddle us." He gave a crooked smile. "Don't laugh when they try to cheat us out of nothing."

"What do we trade?" Anala asked, looking speculatively at Zhadnoboth.

The sorcerer looked back at her and clutched his robe to himself.

"The Maki folk are strange. Value a thought, a whim, a way of looking. Want to trade for odd nothings. Maybe very valuable to them." Hojeen shrugged expressively.

The bursts of flame gradually came faster and faster, until there was an almost continuous wall of pulsing fire along the back wall of the cave. At the same time the flames changed from a bright red-orange barely tinged with green to an aquamarine blue streaked with brilliant threads of emerald. A hot coppery smell began to fill the cave. Then there was a vague shimmering which was both in the fire and beyond it.

Hojeen sat down cross-legged, with the pool in front of him, and ritually rubbed his face and neck with its water. This done, he closed his eyes and began moaning out a chant that sounded like the croak of a bullfrog with sore tonsils. Still, it seemed to work. The shimmering in the fire began to take on a pattern.

After a couple minutes of this serenade, he stopped, drank a handful of water, and began the whole ritual over again. He did this once more, but there was no apparent strengthening of the pattern hidden in the flames.

"This is the most idiotic magic I've ever seen," Zhadnoboth said.

Hojeen opened his eyes and shook his head. "Not magic, talk."

The sorcerer gave a snort and muttered something under his breath.

"It is time for me to speak," Anala said brashly. "Is it not written that a lulzi speaks for the Goddess and all shall hear her?"

The sheet of flame suddenly exploded outward, engulfing them in a cloud of fiery sparks. Billions of multicolored pinpoints of light overwhelmed them, shot through them, surrounded them, moved them. Shimmering atoms of bronze, vermillion, topaz, Tyrian purple, cobalt, ocher, Turkey-red, bottle-green, and a million other colors lived, died, and were reborn again in an immense universe. A universe enormously empty, a universe enormously full, a universe of black velvety nothingness, a universe of light. It was the sky, the sea, the land, all creation, nothing, their souls, their breath, their bodies. If death, if was a painless and glorious death.

Slowly, in the chaos surrounding them, they discerned a faint pearly glow. It had a rhythmically shifting shape they couldn't quite bring into focus. It was a part of the whole and yet distinct. One moment it was unaware of them and the next its attention was fixed on them.

Its mind brushed against Zhadnoboth's, and in a swirl of

mustard thought moved on. It touched Talim and jagged sable images filled their minds. It moved on to Anala.

Her mind spewed forth a stream of instructions and commands, all in a very confident and chatty manner. "I am Anala, a lulzi of the Goddess. I am here to talk to you and tell you what we need. You have to take us out of here and help us on our quest. It is a time of destiny and now is your time to play your part."

The Maki-Maki-Noor recoiled from her, leaving behind a cloud of sulphurous purple thoughts. It moved on to Hojeen and there was a gentle mingling of lemon, lavender, and sweet ginger friendliness. Wry burps of multihued thought bounced between the two of them.

Sandy could sense they were a couple of good old boys meeting again after a long separation. No matter how bizarre this Maki-Maki-Noor turned out to be, Sandy knew one thing: It had to be a bit of a scoundrel. No bosom buddy of Hojeen's could be anything else.

There was a burst of butter-rum thought and Hojeen and the Maki-Maki-Noor parted. It turned its mind Sandy's way and was with him. Thin wisps of aquamarine thought meandered through his consciousness, rousing an awareness which was not words, thoughts, or images but a constantly changing combination of all three.

"Yilm. Me not you, maybe you. Tuch-Seven-Circle-Ti-Blue much me. Yowlly harsh. Yilm give. Yilm get. Much, much now."

"He be *Tuch*," Hojeen said. "He wants to swap. Some of his yilm for new yilm."

The scout's gravelly voice in his ear made Sandy realize he was still standing on the cave floor—he could feel it through the soles of his boots—though his mind insisted he was floating in some chaotic universe of light.

"Yilm is part of Maki folk. Sometimes not part—he wants to add yilm. Dicker with Tuch, get what you want. Make a tough swap."

Sandy gritted his teeth, irritated by the amusement in Hojeen's voice. "Just let me haggle with him."

A honey-silver thought touched Sandy's mind. "Tuch-Seven-Circle-Ti-Blue be I." The name was a soft sapphire cloud, yet sharp as salt herring and tart as rhubarb.

"Trade yilm." There was a hesitation, as if the being was

dissatisfied with what it had expressed and fumbled for something better. "Me five strands star gleam give. Some happy aroma. You what?"

Sandy was caught off guard by the outlandish offer and didn't know what to say.

The creature took his dumbfounded silence as tough bargaining and sweetened its offer. "Five squares love, two circles other love." There was a pause and it added a bit more. "Sip of darkness."

Sandy mentally shrugged, said what the hell, and plunged into the screwy dickering. "Pinch of chagrin, a blush from Anala, and ten meals remembered."

The creature mulled this over. Its thoughts were an olive mist with faint flashes of excited red, as if it was secretly chortling over the deal shaping up.

"Not enough. Want three blush. Something more." These latest thoughts were sharp obsidian-black slivers hidden in a goose down mist.

Sandy countered with an offer of half a drop of dew, three baskets of goodwill, and some off-color limericks. His thoughts went out as ripples of good-natured nut brown with tiny raisins of bawdy cinnamon embedded in them.

Chartreuse billows of foam huffed from the creature. "Tuch no fool he. No cheat he with bad-rotten offer. Want basket of dew, some goodwill, many limericks, and two blushes."

Sandy was now really into it. He had only the foggiest notion what he was trading, what he might be getting, or where in the bargaining he was. He was drunk with the mellow fizz of thought and enjoying the dickering for itself. Still, he kept being otherwhere as one of his objectives.

Offers, counteroffers, swaps, generous concessions, sly deceptions, and tooth-and-nail haggling lit up this strange universe which surrounded them. Mists, tight spirals, sludges, billows, and occasional blocks in many shapes, tastes, and colors surged back and forth as the trading got hot and heavy.

"I'll tell you what," Sandy said. "You give me one more morning glimmer and move the whole kit and caboodle of us somewhere else and it's a deal."

The creature pondered for a while. "Glimmer too much." His thought-words were a bland saffron, but an eager orange lurked behind them.

"No glimmer, no deal," Sandy replied, his thought a hard-nosed cobalt.

For a long moment the creature considered the deal or at least tried to give that impression. *"Done."* The salty crimson thought rolled like thunder through their minds.

Sandy was pretty well contented with the deal. He had got what he wanted and had a bit of fun doing it. The creature had palmed off a couple real dogs on him, but he in turn had snookered the Maki-Maki-Noor on one or two items. That wine of yesterday's memory had been a real steal, worth a lot more than a trip out of here.

"Yilm for yilm. My yilm. Your yilm."

The creature reached into Sandy's being and was gone the next moment. Sandy felt infinitesimally lighter, as if the odd-ball things he had traded had weight and now were no longer there.

A swirl of tiny motes of light, many-colored and sparkling, left the creature and engulfed Sandy. For a moment he looked like some spectacular firework set off for the Fourth of July. The sending sunk into his being and was gone.

Now Sandy felt curiously fuller, even though he knew he had traded for nothings. He shrugged it off and turned his mind to more important things, like deciding where he wanted the creature to send them.

"Final tidbit," came the mellow brown thought, full of the kind of contentment you get after having finished a great meal. "Almost forget to move you other place."

The universe swirled and surged, seized hold of them, and swept them elsewhere. They tumbled through space and time for what seemed both forever and only an instant. A black hole appeared before them and they plunged into it.

Sandy felt himself drop violently. He hardly had time to get scared before he belly flopped to a landing. He rolled to a sitting position and tried to catch his breath. He looked around confusedly and saw he was in an immense room.

Then a whole mess of kicking humanity—his late-arriving companions—landed on him.

All was confusion as for the next few moments they tried to sort themselves out.

Sandy remained pinned until Zhadnoboth suddenly gave a screech and rolled off his chest. Sandy sat up again and saw the sorcerer dancing around and shaking his hand. A finger poked him in the ribs. He looked around and saw Anala sitting across his legs and giving him a mock glare.

"Now where have you landed us?"

"Look what she did to me," Zhadnoboth waved a bloody finger in Sandy's face, showing the deep indentations made by Anala's teeth.

"He deserved it," Anala said as she picked herself up gingerly and brushed the dust from her clothes. "He should learn to keep his hands to himself."

"Me!" Zhadnoboth shouted. "She's one to talk. Where were her hands?"

Anala's face reddened. "I was only trying to dig my way out of that pileup." Her voice was muted and lacked its normal cocksure tone.

The sorcerer muttered, "A likely story."

Before Zhadnoboth could add more, Anala turned her back on him and launched an attack on Sandy, leaving the angry sorcerer high and dry. "Where have you dumped us now?" she demanded.

"I don't know," Sandy said grudgingly. The room was large with a high-vaulted ceiling of closely fitted stonework. The walls were hung with tapestries, once rich, but now ragged and moth-eaten. A massive T-shaped table made from a dark wood and inlaid with gold dominated the center of the room. Scattered were the matching chairs, many overturned and some broken. Over everything was a centuries-thick layer of dust, undisturbed except for the marks they had made.

"That was some bargain you made," Anala said sarcastically.

The hard looks the rest of them were giving Sandy, left no doubt they felt much the same way. Hojeen got him off the hook.

"This was the grand dining room. Jara has no use for it."

"We're still in her hold," Anala said eagerly. She turned to the others and shouted, "We are the chosen. It's our destiny. The shee is doomed!"

The magic in her voice was powerful. For a brief moment they shared a oneness, a oneness unique to them and at the same time a part of something older and greater. Destiny had grabbed hold of them and they knew they could not escape its grip.

"Yeah, we're stuck," Sandy said. He pulled his sword from its scabbard, sat on the edge of the table, and began honing the blade with his whetstone.

His laconic words and matter-of-fact attitude curbed the wild ardor of the others, but made it no less powerful. Talim glared scornfully at him and then knelt before Anala.

"Swear us into brotherhood, my lady, like the first lulzi did with the Seven. Do this and bless us. We will be a band whose like has not been seen since the days of old." He paused and added quietly, "May our deeds be as great." There was a strange mixture of humility and arrogance in his words, but above all a profound sincerity.

Anala stood silent, somehow taller. Her true being loomed larger than the flesh that contained it: human and more than human, a gentle maid yet regal as a queen, a mortal with a spark of divinity smoldering within her. She held out her right hand.

Talim stood up and placed his right hand on hers. "I pledge my heart, my blood, and my soul to this brotherhood. May the bond be forever. May I never be untrue to it. This I, Talim Shenyanda, pledge." His words rang with single-minded intensity.

Silence fell over the room and for a moment no one moved. Then Jatro, the larger of Talim's fellow prisoners, came forward and placed his hand atop that of Talim. He swore the same oath with a quiet vehemence.

Shamdad, the other prisoner, joined the circle next. He spoke his oath with a joy and religious enthusiasm, as though with this moment he had found himself.

Hojeen shook his head sadly, gave a sort of sigh, and marched up to be next. There was no hesitation as he took his place in the circle and put his right hand atop the others. There was a deep somberness in his voice as he spoke the oath. There was also a hardness, a give-no-quarter savagery, which boded ill for the shee.

Zhadnoboth hung back for a moment, then darted forward and swore his oath with a fevered speed.

Magical energy filled the room, restlessly surging about it, seeking completion. Tiny tornadoes of dust swirled across the floor, over the furniture, and up the walls, collapsing and reforming. Streamers of light blue static flowed from every corner of the room to dance over the skins of Anala and the oath swearers. A faint odor began to permeate the air, lavenderlike, but with the bite of ozone added.

Sandy kept whetting his sword, seemingly unaware of what was going on around him. The others watched him with a quiet intensity. He inspected the edges of his blade. Satisfied with the edge he had achieved, he wiped it off, stood up, and shoved his sword back into its scabbard.

"Are you going to join us?" Anala hissed impatiently, momentarily dropping out of her role as an aloof and mystically inspired lulzi.

"I'm coming." Sandy walked at a deliberate pace toward his companions, put his right hand atop theirs—and an electric shock surged through the group. Their muscles gave a tremendous jerk and they froze into position. Slowly mistlike streamers of aquamarine light rose from their bodies to enclose them in a common halo.

"One we will become and one we shall stay until our time is come. This I say for us. This I say for the ones who have walked this path before. This I say in the name of the Goddess." There was a rapt and dreamlike tone to her voice. Her words were magic, not heard by the ear, but spreading through their sinews like warm fire.

The moment Anala finished her invocation, the glowing radiance was gone and they could move again. They parted and looked at each other in a sort of wonder, seeing their companions as they had never seen them before.

Again Talim took the lead. He knelt before Anala and said, "Bless us now, my lady."

Anala flushed, no longer a lulzi possessed by her power, but an excited and slightly bewildered girl. Then she screwed herself up and stepped forward like a queen. She drew an invisible sign with her finger on Talim's forehead and said, "In the name of the Goddess I bless you and give you strength." Then with each of the others she repeated this ceremony until only Sandy was left.

A faraway look came into her eyes as once again Anala spoke with the power of a lulzi. "You I do not bless. It is not needed, as the oath was not needed. You are who you are, and the Goddess had chosen."

Sandy smiled bleakly. "I know."

As suddenly as it had came, the power left Anala. She stared confusedly at Sandy, knowing she had spoken to him, but not remembering the words—only that they were important.

11

THE Goddess stood before a table, closed her eyes, and cast the dice a third time. She held her eyes shut for a moment longer and then opened them slowly. A quick scowl crossed her face as she looked at the roll. Neither the dice's position on the table nor the numbers shown were to her liking.

The tabletop was round and divided into thirteen pie-shaped segments. Seven segments were of a lemon-colored wood. A wood very similar to mahogany had been used for the other six. In the center where the wedges came together was a thirteen-pointed star of silver. Thirteen symbols were inset in the wedges, each symbol made of a different gemstone.

Two dice rested on a dragon of black onyx—Narkild the Devourer, sign of the thirteenth month. The third lay between the two heads of Yanoyan Who Looks Two Ways, the sign for the seventh or middle month of the year. Narkild's numbers were two threes. The serpent's number was one.

The Goddess stared intently at the dice. Three times now they had totaled seven, and that was the wrong number. Something was awry; it should have been four. Still, things could have been worse.

Each time the roll of six had varied. Each of the three combinations was different, though they totaled the same. And each time the six gravitated to a different symbol. Themrys the Blind had captured the first roll, Ilyannan the Child the second, the dragon the third. None was to her liking, but Narkild's roll boded the most ill.

Yanoyan was the one constant. Whatever path to the future she took, his sign would influence it. An ill-omened sign, speaking of treachery or uncertainty, but one she had expected. Here, at least, the ancient prophecy still held true.

The Goddess frowned and rolled the dice around in her hand, wanting to try again. Instead she placed them atop the silver star in the middle of the table. Any further casts would only make one of the three futures certain. She could feel it in the dice, in the air, in her bones. Better to leave things as they were, with some freedom to choose and maybe manipulate.

The Goddess turned from the table and began walking the halls of her palace, mulling over the possibilities, unaware of anything but her thoughts. When she roused from her revery, she was in her garden staring into the emerald-watered pond in its center.

The Goddess knelt down on the tiled edge of the pond and plucked one of the flowers floating in it. Carefully, she tore the flower apart and selected seven petals. These she placed in the palm of her hand, then held it to her mouth and spoke a name to each petal. She inhaled gently, and smiled with pleasure at the sweet and yet tart aroma of the flower. She held her breath for seven beats of the heart and then let it out with an explosive puff.

The petals went tumbling through the air. Some settled to the earth almost immediately; others drifted for long moments; eventually all but two came to rest. These two found a hidden wind and floated over the garden wall and into the unknown.

The Goddess pursed her lips and frowned. Sandy she could understand—he was a contrary bastard and she expected a contrary result. The other, however, was a surprise. Still, five could be counted on to be themselves.

Now, having an inkling of what to expect from the future and from the seven who would serve her, the Goddess began planning her strategy. She would start with some subtle meddling, adding a seemingly insignificant something to the stew already boiling. A something too tiny for the shee to bother with. A something that could bend destiny just enough in her favor.

The shee was strong, clever, and ruthless; but with her strengths she also had weaknesses. The greatest of these weaknesses was to equate power with deadliness. She would come to know of the seven and she would count them for nothing.

"Jara, Jara," the Goddess murmured. "You were always the most cunning, the sharpest witted, but you were never wise. You fear the bite of my sword. You have yet to learn that pinpricks can be as deadly." She laughed softly.

The Goddess turned her thoughts toward Aku. He was doing well. Already his troops had won several skirmishes and caused dissension in the councils of the enemy. Kimbo-Dashla was still under siege and the border still being harried, but the pressure was less. Warriors who should have been at the siege had been sent to crush Aku and his army of tribesmen.

The force sent was strong; six clans of Red Branch Zenori, the Dry Water clan of the Kilbri, some two hundred Yartazi raiders, and a dozen Chanzi shapechangers. But Zadar Kray had overreached himself when he had named Krizzan Tham-Shanek to command this force instead of Kas Marzak of the Zenori. The mad prophet was a formidable foe, but no soldier.

Still, so much depended upon what would happen in the shee's citadel. Whatever happened there would be reflected in the struggle going on along the border of the Rithian Empire.

12

Sandy sat with his back against the wall, munching on some flinty bread and string cheese. Beside him on the floor was a jug of cold bragberry cider. He was content; the food was filling and reasonably tasty, while the spicy tang of the cider hit the spot nicely.

Then a shrill and demanding, *Squeak! squeak! squeak!* sounded to his right. It seemed to come from a white ball of fur crouched next to the wall, staring at him with beady red eyes. Sandy blinked—he'd been looking that way only a moment before and there hadn't been a sign of the creature then.

Squeak! squeak! squeak! the thing said insistently.

Sandy glowered at the creature. It didn't move. It started to squeak again and he broke off a piece of his bread and threw it toward the animal. "All right, have some."

The creature backed off skittishly, then darted forward and snatched the bread. Hurriedly it backed off a safe distance and began chewing methodically on its loot, all the while keeping a watchful eye on him.

Sandy reached for the jug and the creature scuttled out of reach. He laughed and drank a slug of the cider. "Don't worry, piglet. You're not on today's menu." He arched an eyebrow and added, "Of course, if I was hungry enough . . ."

The dumb beast caught the drift of his words and edged closer to him. It sat up and began squeaking in a demanding manner.

Sandy gave a disgusted grunt and twisted a piece off a string of cheese. "By god, you are a piglet. Here, have some cheese." He went on sternly. "But that's the last crumb you bum off me." He threw the cheese toward the creature.

His piglet caught the string of cheese in midair and then dropped it. It gave Sandy an accusing stare and began to sniff at this odd-smelling loot. Hesitantly, it nibbled at the cheese. After a few bites, the piglet was chewing with gusto. When it was finished, the piglet sat up, brushed off its whiskers with its front paws, gave a contented burp, and looked hopefully at Sandy.

"Go find another pigeon," he told it.

The piglet shook its head and squeaked again. Sandy scowled at the creature and pointedly chewed on a string of cheese. The piglet gave an outraged squeal and began bouncing up and down on its four feet.

Sandy watched the piglet's conniption fit for a moment and then threw it a piece of bread. "You know the world is going to pot," he muttered to himself, "when you get bullied by a ball of fur."

Hojeen came over and hunkered down beside him. "Time we talk some."

"If my piglet lets me," Sandy said. He looked where the creature had been and did a double take. It was gone, leaving behind a solid wall and solider floor, and nowhere it could have gone to. Even the dust was undisturbed. "Did you see it?" he asked Hojeen.

The old scout gave him a peculiar look and shook his head.

At that moment Anala burst through a door at the far end of the room, and came running over. "Let's go," she said eagerly. "We've found an open way into the rest of the castle. There's a hidden stairway leading up at the back of the pantries. We can attack when she's not expecting us."

Sandy began firing some down-to-earth questions at her. "Where do we attack her? What forces does she have? Are just we seven going take on Jara Greenteeth and her minions? What plans do you have?" Sandy paused to take a swig from his jug. "As it is, we have about as much chance as a snowman in hell when we do go against her. So let's not cut our throats before we even start."

Anala gave him a cross look, miffed as much by his common sense as by his lack of enthusiasm. "If we attack at once we will surprise her."

Sandy gave a disgusted snort. "Surprise must be planned

for, otherwise you're the one most likely to be surprised.'' He took another swallow from his jug of cider, wiped off his mouth with the back of his hand, and waited for a reply.

Anala stewed for a moment. Then, gritting her teeth, she acknowledged he had made his point. ''All right, we need to plan. And you're better at it than me. And we could use some help.'' She stopped speaking for a moment and then added, ''But that doesn't mean we shouldn't attack.''

''We have to attack. There's nowhere to run to.'' Sandy reluctantly got to his feet. ''Round up the others and bring them back here. It's time we held a war council.''

His words and tone did not sit well with Anala, but she nodded and went off to fetch the others.

Sandy called after her offhandedly, ''Bring back some food and drink when you return.''

Anala stopped dead in her tracks and swung around to face him. ''I am not your slave girl. I don't come at your beck and call. ''I—''

Sandy interrupted. ''Thank god for small favors.''

His words struck Anala speechless. She was infuriated by his calling on a god instead of the Goddess, by his disrespectful attitude, but especially by his opinion she wasn't worth having. She groped for words and finally came up with something to say. ''Heathen!'' she shouted, and stomped off, her shoulders bent forward and her fists clenched.

Watching her go, Hojeen commented laconically, ''She's a bad enemy.''

Sandy nodded. ''Still, I don't know if I could take her as a friend. Just having her around is enough of a cross to bear.''

Hojeen took a gulp of the bragberry cider and rolled it around his tongue before swallowing. ''She has her own cross. *You*.'' He grinned and added, ''Good for her to have disrespect. Best way to learn value of respect.'' He nodded to himself and had another slug of the cider. ''She's good for you too. You learn much.''

Sandy took the jug from his hands, wiped the lip off, and chugged down a long swallow. ''Quit being a philosopher, old man. Let's put our heads together and do some figuring before she returns.''

They clustered around the head of the table watching Hojeen draw a rough map in the dust. ''We're here, off to one side, near the top of fortress. Dungeons are on the bottom. Greenteeth is in the middle, between the throne room and main halls are where she rules most strongly.''

Talim shook his head and said scornfully, "No castle has a banquet room tucked off in a corner like this. We have to be closer to the shee than he says.''

His words didn't bother Hojeen. "This fortress is very odd. Things are not always where they should be. Rooms move if they are not wanted.''

Talim gave a disgusted snort. "This is a building, not a bunch of walking stones.''

Hojeen gave a slight shrug, his gesture saying plainly that Talim could believe what he wanted, but that didn't make it the truth.

Talim clutched at the kitchen knife stuck in his belt, stung by the old scout's attitude. Hojeen watched his gesture with an unworried coolness.

Before the situation could get worse, Anala stepped in to soothe their feelings. "The building doesn't matter. What matters is getting the shee however we can, or getting around her if it comes to that.''

Her words calmed the storm between them. What she said was not important; it was the way she spoke: a subtle magic woven from tone and syllable. It was a gentle, healing magic, a magic made irresistible because it came from the heart and she was unaware she used it. Old pains were soothed and minds cajoled into reason.

Like a silken mist it seeped through Sandy's soul and brought tranquility. He was aware of it, yet for a moment let the magic ease his mind. And he gained a certain respect for her. She might still be a pain in the rear, but she did have possibilities.

Shamdad, the smaller of Talim's fellow prisoners, spoke up. "Hojeen is right, Gogna's House is a strange place. Old beyond time, already ancient when the shee first was.''

Everyone stared at him in surprise.

A wry, sad smile flickered across Shamdad's face. "Once I was a scholar. I spent my days searching old books and manuscripts for knowledge. Then I found a book, *The True and Exact History of Cimber-Tal-Gogna* by Jeshovan the Caitiff, in my lord's library.'' He gave a shrug and added, "That book was my downfall. I was lucky to escape with a whole skin. Or, maybe, not so lucky, since what I had learned led me here and eventually to Jara Greenteeth's dungeon.''

''All very interesting,'' crabbed Zhadnoboth, ''but it doesn't tell us much.''

Shamdad got on with his tale. ''It was Jeshovan's contention that with every change of master the geography of this citadel shifted—rooms vanished and others appeared.''

''They didn't vanish,'' Zhadnoboth muttered grumpily, revealing more knowledge than he'd let on previously. ''They just got shoved out of the way. Jeshovan said that every part of this citadel that once was still exists somewhere. If your feet can find the ways, you can still go to them. There are many odd places tucked away in here, places the shee has never been or even heard of. And, if Jeshovan is right, there are still some very strange inhabitants left behind in the forgotten parts of the citadel.'' The sorcerer paused and wet his lips. He resumed speaking in a conspiratorial voice, ''Rumor says there are fabulous treasures hidden away in the lost corners of the place.''

''You've got treasure on the brain,'' Sandy said digustedly. ''The shee's been here a couple thousand years. Do you think any stray treasure is still lying around? And if you find treasure, where are you going spend it? First we have to deal with Jara Greenteeth, first we have to survive, then we can find time to be greedy.''

''Easy enough for you to say,'' Zhadnoboth said heatedly. ''You might prefer to hoist tankards with death, but the rest of us like to keep body and soul together.''

''Some of us more than others,'' Sandy said sarcastically.

''What's the harm in taking what's due you?'' retorted the sorcerer. Then he changed tack abruptly, managing to sound reasonable and somewhat put upon. ''I'm all for this crusade, but if some gold finds its way into our pockets along the way, so much the better.''

Anala had had her fill of their bickering. ''Some war council,'' she said acidly. ''You should listen to Shamdad, like I did, instead of going on about treasure. He wandered these halls for many days before he was captured.'' She pushed Shamdad forward. ''Tell them what you told me.''

''There is a way to the dungeons that bypasses the shee and the dead warriors who serve her.''

"And in the dungeons are what's left of my patrol," Talim said. "And maybe ten or twenty others who could help us."

"We just left the dungeons," Sandy said disgustedly. He turned to Shamdad and asked, "Where does this way lead?"

"Parts of the citadel exist in other whens, other wheres. Some know the shee, most do not. In certain places you can move from where you are to another where. One such place is in the guardroom, just outside the steel door that seals off the dungeons."

Sandy nodded and asked. "Who stands guard?"

Jatro broke into the conversation. "I know better than anyone." He straightened up like a noncom giving his report. "There are eight of the dead and their commander. He's a half-breed troll of some sort, about twice as big as me." Jatro was an inch or two over six foot and built like a rhinoceros. "He'll be hard to kill, but at least he can be killed. As for the dead, they'll keep fighting until doomsday."

"Tell me more about this half-troll," Sandy prompted.

For the first time Jatro showed some emotion, hate deepening and giving a rough edge to his voice. "He's a drunken bastard who hates everyone and everything, himself most of all. He's kicked to death two prisoners that I know of. And he's usually so soused he can hardly stagger, but even dead drunk he's a match for any ten ordinary men."

"You know him well."

"I should," Jatro said bitterly. "I've had to swab out the guardroom enough times and take his bullying. I had a set-to with him a month ago and got my butt stomped. It was a week before I could crawl out of bed."

"My sergeant does not say enough for himself," Talim said. "No one else has lasted even a minute against Rom-Skola. He lasted five and even floored that damned cullion once." Talim's voice had an odd mixture of praise and condescension in it, as though he thought it unworthy to be proud of a subordinate—and yet the pride was there.

Sandy thought for a moment and then asked, "How well does he do his job?"

Jatro smiled and answered, "About as well as you suppose. He's careless and does as little as he has to, but he's never had to worry about an attack."

"He does now," Anala said.

"What about the dead?" Sandy asked.

Jatro frowned and thought a moment. "They're fell fighters, but don't think for themselves. Still, they are more aware than some give them credit for."

"When we get through with them, they'll be chopped to pieces," Anala said with enthusiasm.

Sandy said, "With what? Hojeen and I are the only ones here with weapons. Those knives you picked up in the kitchens won't do much against foes armed with sword and spear."

"Even less against warriors already dead," Zhadnoboth added. "What you need is magic, and I can give it to you."

Sandy turned a suspicious eye toward the sorcerer. He had yet to see the sorcerer be generous, except if it was to his advantage.

"Under cover of my magic we can sneak up against our foes and catch them unaware. And these walking dead are not invulnerable. Magic has quickened them into a semblance of life, but my magic can give them back to the Keeper of Souls."

"What kind of magic is that?" Sandy asked. "What spells and cantrips will you use?"

The sorcerer gave him an annoyed look. Then, beginning to see doubt on the faces of the others, he hurriedly went on. "Well. Er. There are several spells I could use. Spells of deceit and misdirection might do, but a spell of invisibility would be best." Now he was waxing enthusiastic, as excited by his spiel as those he was trying to con.

He snapped his fingers, as if he had just thought of it, and said excitedly, "I have just the thing—a conjuration taught me by my old master." A tear showed in his eye and he sighed, "Ah, those were the days to be young."

"And these are the days to come up with something besides hot air," Sandy said sarcastically.

The old sorcerer turned red. He shook a finger in Sandy's face and shouted, "Just you wait, you scum of an unbeliever. I'll show you. There's not a sorcerer on Zarathandra that's my match!"

Sandy nodded, making Zhadnoboth even angrier. "It's true you have no equal," Sandy mocked. "Sometimes the costs of your services are also without equal."

Zhadnoboth glowered at him and then by an effort of will put on his best smiling and virtuous face. "A master is worthy of his hire," he said reasonably. "But," he went on, grandiloquently waving off any potential protest, "ours is a great and holy cause. Such causes demand sacrifices, and I will give freely of my magic. It is only just and fair I do this."

Anala jumped up and gave a loud hooray.

They all gave a start and looked at her.

"With such dedication and courage we can do what must be done," she gushed. "We can do what is right. The shee has been a scourge for too long. Now is the time for justice, a time to rid Zarathandra of a great bane."

Her heartfelt passion mixed with the magic of her voice to stir them deeply. They felt a nobleness of purpose, a mutual sense of destiny, a great rightness in their souls. Exhilaration filled their hearts and they felt nothing could stand in their way.

Sandy brought them back down to earth. "So we're pure in heart. That still doesn't put weapons in our hands or gain us allies." He had been as moved as any of the others by her words, but he was stubbornly practical. "If we must do great deeds, then let's do them with as much firepower as we can gather."

Anala gave him a caustic look. The others were none too happy with him either. For a brief moment they'd been something more than what they knew themselves to be and he had reminded them they were only human.

"In the old days," Hojeen said, "weapons were hidden under this place." He walked over to the wall and pulled aside the tattered tapestry which hung there. Behind was a wall made from small blocks of green-flecked marble. He looked the wall over carefully and then turned to Talim. "Knife."

Talim hesitated, then with ill grace pulled out the butcher knife he had stuck in his belt. He tossed it, hilt first, to Hojeen.

The old scout deftly caught it and rammed it into a crack between the stones. For a moment nothing happened; then with a groaning noise a door-sized section of wall began sliding backward. After it had moved inward about six feet, the wall stopped with a thud which rattled the table.

On the left side of the doorway there was just more wall, but on the right was a dark opening. The floor beyond the opening was of red granite except for a circular piece of milk-white quartz the size of a half dollar in its middle. Hojeen stepped forward and stomped twice on the quartz insert. Instantly a soft white light filled the opening, revealing a stair leading downward.

Hojeen looked toward his companions expectantly. Sandy loosened his sword in its sheath and stepped forward. He and the old scout went down the stairs side by side. For a moment the others didn't move, then Zhadnoboth muttered something about gold and rushed to the stairs and down. The rest of the party followed after.

At the bottom of the stairs, they found a large room with walls and vaulted ceiling of red brick. Through the massive arched doorway in the opposite wall there seemed to be another room of much the same sort. Racks of weapons covered the walls. There were swords of every description, spears, war axes, daggers, halberds, and bows of all sizes. This was no small cache of weapons, but an armory.

Hojeen and Sandy were nowhere in sight, but the sorcerer was routing through the brassbound chests stacked at the foot of each wall and in the middle part of the room. First he'd open one, rummage about, make a sound of disgust, and then rush to open another one. Finally, after about his sixth or seventh failure, Zhadnoboth sat down on a chest and stewed.

"What's in the chests?" Talim asked.

"Armor and more armor," Zhadnoboth snapped. "Nothing worth looking at a second time, just plain workaday gear."

Talim knelt by a chest the sorcerer had rummaged through and pulled out a byrnie of silvered steel. He held it up and looked it over. "These chests might not hold what you want, sorcerer, but what's in them is worth more than their weight in gold."

Zhadnoboth gave a snort of disgust. "I'll take gold any day."

Soon Talim, Shamdad, Jatro, and even Anala were going through the room like children in a toy store, stringing bows and testing the pull, getting the heft and feel of this sword and that sword, trying on cuirasses and mail shirts.

The sorcerer watched their antics with a sour face, refusing to get involved. Instead he pulled a flat blue glass bottle from his robes and swigged on it. Suddenly he sat up straighter and his nose began to twitch. He bounded to his feet and trotted over to the arched doorway where he saw a room much like the room behind him, except each wall was pierced by an arched doorway identical to the one he stood in.

Zhadnoboth looked around peevishly, momentarily unsure of which way to go. Then his nose twitched again. He smiled to himself and headed off to the left, following his nose like a youngster on the trail of fresh-baked cookies.

He went through three rooms before he found Hojeen and Sandy digging through a large chest carved from orange jasper. Its massive marble lid and various objects from the chest were lying on the floor around them: alabaster statuettes, brass pots, a dagger with an ivory hilt and a ruby pommel, about thirty gold rings strung on a loop of wire, an open wooden box filled with candles, and what looked like a set of toy building blocks.

Zhadnoboth maneuvered his way through the odds and ends, stashing the dagger and the gold rings in his robe as he went. Curious, he peered over Hojeen and Sandy's shoulders. The old scout absentmindedly handed the sorcerer a coral necklace and went back to rummaging in the chest. Zhadnoboth looked puzzled for a moment, shrugged, and shoved the necklace into a pocket.

Hojeen's face lit up, and he pulled a bunch of keys from the chest. They were strung on a ring of silver and there were twenty-one of them, twenty of gold and one of iron. "Master keys. Open all doors in citadel."

"What's the iron one for?" Sandy asked, an edge to his voice. He had seen a key like it once before—a key he still held.

Hojeen shrugged. "Don't know."

Sandy took the key ring and looked closely at the iron key. It began glowing with a faint blue light and tiny silver runes could be seen. He held it close to his eyes to read the almost microscopic writing, silently moving his lips as he deciphered each word of the inscription.

"Well, what does it say?" Zhadnoboth demanded.

Sandy looked around at the sorcerer. "I should have known you'd show up." His eyes swept the floor, noticing what was missing, and then the sorcerer, though he said nothing.

Zhadnoboth was not to be sidetracked by either derogatory comments or accusing looks. "What does it say?"

"It's a language and a script I've never seen before."

The old sorcerer gave a snort and said, "So what? You can read it anyway, demon."

"It doesn't make much sense. It says the key will be used three times. Once at the beginning and once at the end."

"What's the third time?" Zhadnoboth was exasperated.

"That's the confusing part," Sandy replied. "It says something about being used once when it is time for neither."

Zhadnoboth nodded and began to search around inside his robe, finally coming up with a small book. Its cover was yellowed and age worn, but its thin pages seemed as crisp and clear as though printed yesterday. He hurriedly leafed through it, found the passage he wanted, and swiftly read it. "I have to find our companions," he said in what he thought was a calm voice. Then he turned and scooted off.

"Now what's he up to?" Sandy said. "I'd like to know what he knows about this iron key." He paused and added, "And why he left it behind."

Hojeen didn't answer directly. "Key never shone for anyone. Until now." He gave Sandy a shrewd look. "It is said there will be a man of the Goddess who knows all tongues."

"I've never heard that," Sandy said.

"Old, old prophecy."

Just then Zhadnoboth came shuffling back into the room. "Could I borrow that key ring?" He shifted about nervously on his feet. "I'd like to show it to the others."

"We'll *all* go and show it to the others," Sandy replied. "I think it best that it stay in my possession."

His words galled Zhadnoboth, who turned on his heel and marched off.

Sandy watched the sorcerer stomp away and a smile crossed his face. Ruefully shaking his head, he muttered, "The Goddess only knows why I like that old conniver. He's got to have some redeeming qualities, but damned if I can think of any of them."

"She doesn't know either," Hojeen said enigmatically.

Sandy turned toward the old man, surprised. Once again he wondered who or what Hojeen was.

"How would you know?" he asked.

"Same way as you."

Warily they looked at each other. In the borderlands, the less said about oneself the better. Enemies were common enough without adding yourself to the list.

Tacitly acknowledging the standoff, Sandy said, "Let's go join the others."

Hojeen nodded and they set off for the entrance room, a strange companionship between them.

"It's about time you two got here," Anala said as they came into the room. "We're ready to go."

She looked the part. There were two daggers in her belt, another strapped to her left arm, a quiver on her back, a bow in her hand, and a steel cap on her head.

"Do you know how to use that bow and those daggers?" Sandy asked.

"I was the best bowman in the village," she said in an insulted voice.

"Bowgirl," Sandy corrected her.

This only increased her anger. "Best bowman. I hit the bull's-eye twenty out of twenty times at a hundred paces."

"Have you ever shot at a target that shoots back? Or one that is charging at you?"

"No. But I can learn."

"Probably over our dead bodies," Sandy replied. He turned from her and shouted, "Over here."

The rest of their companions snapped to immediately and assembled around him. There was no mistaking the authority in his voice. They knew without being told that he was taking charge and there was to be no nonsense.

Only Anala protested. "This isn't fair. You have no right."

"No, it isn't, but that's the way it's going to be. There is fighting ahead and I am a warrior who has been up the creek and seen the bear. If you want to win, if you want to live, I'm the only choice you have."

Sandy stared at each one of them, silently challenging them to step forward and disagree. None did. They had already decided, even Anala, that he was the one to lead them into battle. His words only made official what they had unconsciously agreed on.

Sandy turned to Talim and said, "You'll be second in command."

Talim gave a curt nod. He was dressed now in a brigandine of burnished steel and a Norman-style helm chased with gold designs. His armor was like him, slightly flashy, but very serviceable. He looked twice the man he had been before—and thought himself much more than that.

But Sandy was happy to have him along on this adventure. There was no better warrior to have alongside you when the crunch came. It was the lulls you had to worry about.

Quickly he gave Talim his orders. "If we win our fight at the dungeon door, you and Jatro are to round up what prisoners you can and get them out as fast as possible. The rest of us will hold the door. We'll have some time before the shee can react, but it won't be long."

Sandy noticed the recurved bow reinforced with silver wire which Shamdad had chosen for himself. "Can you use that bow?"

Shamdad replied, "I do well enough. In my youth, I spent two years as a bowman in the armies. I've sent a goodly number of foes to meet their maker."

"You and Anala hang back when we attack and use your bows as best you can."

"They burn," Shamdad said.

Sandy gave him a questioning look.

"The dead men, I mean. I saw one brush against a torch. His flesh burned like candle wax."

"Then we'll have to make fire arrows of some sort," Sandy said. "Two rooms down and one room to the left I saw enough arrows to supply a thousand armies." He cast a sideways glance at Anala, who seemed ready to spout off again. "Take Anala with you," he said to Shamdad, "and see if the necessary makings for fire arrows are there."

Shamdad nodded and started trotting off. Anala glanced crossly at Sandy; then, surprisingly, she took herself in hand and said nothing as she went after Shamdad.

Sandy watched her go, a hint of approval in his eyes. There just might be hope for her. He turned to Hojeen and Jatro. "Talim, you two, and I will be the main assault troops. Shamdad and Anala will provide covering fire if needed." He nodded toward Zhadnoboth. "The sorcerer will use what magic he can on our behalf. We should catch them by surprise, since they won't expect an attack from within the citadel."

"Surprise won't do us much good," Jatro said suddenly, a shrill edge in his voice. "Nor will swords be much use. Cut the dead and they don't care. You've never seen them fight. They keep coming despite wounds that would stop anything mortal. What's to stop them? Nothing!"

"Oh, but swords are very effective against them," Sandy retorted, swiftly taking control of the conversation. "You can't kill them, but they have their weaknesses. Cut their hamstrings and they can't walk, blind them and they can't see, cut off their hands and they can't fight."

"You've never fought them," Jatro's voice was trembling with dread. "You haven't felt their cold eyes on you. You haven't seen them just keep coming, and coming, and coming. Have you felt your guts turn to water, your legs refuse to move, and your hands shake so bad you can't hold a sword?" Sweat stood out on his brow and the color had left his face.

"I've fought them," Sandy said savagely. "And they fall just as live men do. You don't fight toe to toe with them. You fight smart and dirty. They don't react well, so you move about and come at them from all directions." He paused before adding, "They can't kill you any deader than anyone else."

His words seemed to hearten Jatro. The big man's face lost its ashen hue and he nodded; then with black humor he joked, "Let's go to it, then. If we're going to be scared spitless, we might as well do it with sword in hand."

"All this babbling about the terrible dead is hogwash." Zhadnoboth snapped, suddenly as brave as a bully after breakfast, though moments before he'd been as terrified as Jatro. "Use the right spell and they're only dead meat. And I know the right spell," he added smiling slyly. He paused, awaiting comments and maybe a little praise.

Sandy obliged with the comments. "What is the right spell? And why haven't you mentioned it before?"

"Dardannan's seventh cantrip," he said huffily. "And no great sorcerer goes around telling one and all what magic he plans. He keeps his thought secret, husbands his strength, and strikes when the time is ripe."

"Yeah," Sandy said unenthusiastically. "Who's Dardannan and what does his spell do?"

"Who's Dardannan! Don't you know anything? He was the greatest necromancer this world ever knew. Every spell for raising and animating the dead, he knew or created."

Sandy sighed in exasperation. "Okay, he was great. But we want a spell for laying the dead."

"That's what the seventh cantrip *is*," the sorcerer told him.

"Even necromancers don't want the dead cluttering the land-scape all the time."

"Can you do this seventh cantrip?"

The sorcerer drew himself up and said blithely. "There are only the words and the right gestures. Any competent sorcerer can perform the seventh cantrip."

Sandy nodded grudging approval and said, "We'll use your magic, but we'll keep our weapons ready just in case we need them." Sandy knew better than to wholly trust the sorcerer's magic. His spells worked, but sometimes too well, and rarely the way they were supposed to.

The sorcerer gave a derisive snort. "When I loose the seventh cantrip, the walking dead will be done for. You'll have nothing left to fear except a drunken troll."

Instead of replying, Sandy sat down and began honing the edge of his sword. This got the sorcerer's goat as no words could have. Mumbling maledictions, Zhadnoboth wandered off to a corner and began reading scraps of parchment he pulled from the hidden recesses of his robe. The others worked on their gear or rummaged around the armory to see if anything better was available.

After a while, Anala and Shamdad came wandering back, both carrying two quivers on their backs. She walked up to Sandy and said, "We found what you wanted. Is there any other chore you want done?" Her words were soft and good-humored, but there was an edge to them.

Sandy inspected the edge of his sword, put it back in its scabbard, and said, "No." He got up from the box he had been sitting on and yelled for attention. "Get what gear you're taking and lug it upstairs." He looked over to Hojeen. "Take them to the old kitchens and get them provisioned."

"I wouldn't feed that slop to my worst enemy," Talim grumbled.

"Neither would I," Sandy agreed. "But it's all we have."

When the others had left the armory, Sandy pulled out the silver key ring and stared thoughtfully at it. Then he placed it on the lid of a chest, the gold keys bunched on one side and the iron key by itself.

Around his neck, on a chain of small silver links, hung a small bag of soft leather. He pulled the bag up out through the top of his burnoose, opened it, and carefully shook out the iron key inside it. With a clink it dropped onto the chest lid near the key ring.

He pulled out a dagger and with its point moved the iron key close to its counterpart on the key ring. As he had thought, they were nearly identical. With dagger point he moved the keys closer together, and both began to glow with a faint blue light. He nodded and put his key back into its bag, being careful to touch it only with the dagger and not his hands.

From the moment he had seen it, he had suspected that the iron citadel key was important. Now he was completely sure. The key he held in trust had immense powers—he had seen it hold a god at bay—and this key must have like powers. He shivered as memories of his desperate struggle with Kels Zalkri returned.

The citadel key had a feel to it both similar to and yet different from the key he held. The power was there waiting to be used—but who would use it? If it was like the key he held, it needed a master. And Sandy had a sinking feeling that the master it chose would not be to his liking.

He put the key ring away and sat down on a chest to think for a moment. Absentmindedly he pulled a small package from his pocket and tore the wrapping off. Inside was a rolled up strip of dried fruit. He looked suspiciously at it—it was like no fruit he'd seen before and its sickly green color was not appetizing—shrugged and began chewing on it. To his surprise it had a sour tangy taste which really hit the spot.

Chewing on the fruit strip, Sandy stared unhappily at the floor. Both keys had the same maker, of that he was certain. But who had that maker been? And were there only two keys? What worried him even more was that he had found the citadel key *right now*. It was just too convenient. Either the Goddess, the shee, or both were setting things up for the kill. Well, he was going to be damned sure he wasn't the kill.

Suddenly he blinked and jerked his head back in surprise. On the floor, right where he had been staring, was the white-furred pest who'd bothered him before. It hadn't been there a second ago, he was sure. It almost seemed to have appeared out of thin air.

The pest stood up on its hind legs and looked at him with its beady red eyes, trying to melt his heart with a woebegone and suffering look. He ignored it and kept chewing on his fruit roll. The creature then tried some soft squeaks, full of tearful pleading. When this routine got it nowhere, it had a snit fit. It chirped, it bawled, it threw itself on the floor, it squalled, it rolled over and kicked its legs in the air, it drooled like a feebleminded lunatic; all the while keeping a weather eye on Sandy.

"All right, damn you," he said finally, throwing his arms in the air. "I'll feed you." He tore off a piece of the fruit roll and tossed it the piglet's way.

While it ate, the creature sat on its haunches and stared with fearful greed at Sandy. Gone was its demented behavior; apparently eating was serious business.

Sandy watched his piglet for a moment, shook his head, and headed for the stairs. The creature sent a demanding squeal after him, glared accusingly, and then rushed to gulp down the rest of its booty.

Sandy climbed unhurriedly to the top of the stairs, looked back down, and yanked the knife out of the wall. The stone door slid shut with a crash which sent puffs of dust swirling through the room. Sandy stared intently at the now-hidden door, an enigmatic look on his face. "Let's see if you get through that," he said to himself.

There was a shrill squeak at his feet. He looked down and saw an angry ball of white fur wiggling its nose in hunger and glaring demandingly up at him. He made an obscene comment and stomped off towards the kitchens. The piglet waddled after him, keeping up a continuous chittering protest as it did so.

13

THE Goddess smiled in satisfaction as she turned from the pool. The mad prophet had declared Kas Marzak a traitor and had him beheaded in front of his fellow tribesmen. By force of will and his great personal magnetism, the prophet had carried the day, making even the Red Branch Zenori believe this was a just and holy act. He had won full control of his army and by so doing doomed it to defeat: The wily and battle-scarred Kas Marzak had been the only one in this small army who was a match for Aku as a general.

She had great plans for the Rithian Empire, and Aku was the linchpin on which they hinged. By winning the coming battle his career in the Rithian army would be well on the way. His star was rising and that of Zadar Kray was already on the wane.

With a frown the Goddess turned back to her pool of seeing. From the cream-colored crock of salt-glazed stoneware beside her, she pulled a handful of multicolored dust—a mixture of pollen carefully harvested in early spring from twenty-three different flowers she grew in her garden. She said a word of power and scattered the dust over the water.

Gentle swirls and ripples formed on the surface of the pool. At first there was confusing mix of colors as the different pollens were moved about by the water, but gradually a picture formed. It showed Sandy and his six companions traveling down a dusty corridor. Then a riptide suddenly surged through the pool and destroyed it, leaving only jumbled patches of sodden pollen which quickly sank out of sight.

A wicked smile played about the Goddess's lips. She had seen what she had wanted to see and at the same time had caught the attention of the shee. Once again she had reminded Jara that not even in her citadel was she beyond the reach of her deadliest enemy. More importantly, she had turned the shee's attention outward, away from the doom stalking her from within.

Now, if Sandy would do what the Goddess expected of him, her triumph would not be long delayed. He had the key and the shee's ring; add the third talisman and the magic of threes would come to be.

But with Sandy anything could happen. She could only influence him, not control him. The Goddess silently damned his contrary streak, though it was one of the things that made him so valuable.

The Goddess's mind turned back to the seven keys: Did they control her destiny, or she theirs? In some indefinable way they were tied to her, yet she could not control them. If she could only remember beyond that ancient day when she had awoken with the seven keys in her hand. Perhaps she would soon, for the time of gathering had come. She thought about the ancient doggerel.

> *Seven keys at my lady's belt.*
> *One for the desert lord.*
> *One for the mountain hold.*
> *One for the shadow—*

But enough of that. Now was the time to deal with the shee.

> *Seven keys at my lady's belt.*
> *One for the desert lord.*
> *One for the mountain hold.*
> *One for the shadow dark.*
> *One for the northern cold.*
> *One for the forest deep.*
> *One for the warrior bold.*

One for the maiden wise.
Seven locks, seven keys, and seven days.
Then shall be regained what was lost,
and lost what is not held dear.

14

Anala and Shamdad stood in the middle of the corridor, looking toward its far end. The little man had a scowl on his face and kept muttering under his breath. Anala hopped from one foot to the other, impatiently awaiting his decision. Sandy and the rest of the group, all experienced campaigners, were sitting and getting some rest.

"Well!" Anala demanded, unable to wait any longer. "Is this the place or isn't it?"

Shamdad shook his head. "It's not quite right. It's not the same as before." He did a quick count on his fingers. "This is the seventh corridor past the court with the dry fountain, but it is different."

Hojeen ambled over. "Many *if* places in citadel. Shee rules the great *if*, the heart. There are other and lesser *ifs—ifs* that were, might be, or never were. They change, move, grow, fade away, and are born. If you think right, you can move from great *if* to other *ifs* and back again. Sometimes get short-cuts to parts of great *if*."

"But we must choose the right way," Anala said heatedly.

Hojeen merely shrugged and said, "If you walk long enough, you come to great *if* all the time. All ways lead there."

"But we don't have the time," Anala said. "You don't go out the front door, around the house, and in the back door, just to cross a room. We could be old and gray before we find the shee."

"Not much chance of that," Sandy said as he took a drink

139

from his canteen. "If you're born to be hanged, you don't lose your way to the gallows."

Anala marched over to him. "I suppose you can lead us out of here."

Sandy took another drink from his canteen. "Yeah, I can."

"Big man," Anala said bitingly. "One day here and you know more than Shamdad, who's been here for years. If you're so good, lead us."

Sandy slowly got to his feet, stretched, gave her a wink, and started walking down the corridor. Dogging his heels was a perplexed Anala. He stopped by Shamdad.

"What's one of these turnoffs like?"

Shamdad frowned and thought a moment. "I can't tell you. It's a way of thinking. There are places that are both here and some other place. If you come upon one and your mindset is right, you can move from one reality to another and not even know it. Such a place is ahead of us. I know this and yet I don't think it's right, and I don't know why."

"You make about as much sense as a toad on Tuesday," Sandy groused, and started down the corridor. His on-again off-again sixth sense was working after a fashion and he didn't like the signals he was getting from it. He knew they'd find their way to their destination and that there was trouble brewing. Damn the Goddess, anyway. If she was going to stick him with a gift, the least she could do was make it reliable. His damned sixth sense never worked the same twice in a row and never seemed to be working when he really needed it. He muttered another curse and made sure his sword was loose in its scabbard.

Anala hurried up to trot beside him. She was so excited she could hardly keep still. Her nose wiggled, her hands wove patterns in the air, her elbows and knees were all over the place, and her feet danced about. "You've done it," she said excitedly, her anger already forgotten. "We're in a new place."

"Looks like the same endless corridor to me," Sandy replied.

Anala made a disgusted sound. "You men—you can't tell a tub from a thimble. Just look around. Use your eyes."

For a moment Sandy saw nothing. Then he noticed the walls: They were still stone, but now they were polished marble instead of dust-covered sandstone. He looked again, and then toward both ends of the corridor. "Where the hell is Zhadnoboth?" he yelled.

Anala and the others looked around and saw what he had seen: There was only six of them and nowhere the sorcerer could have gone.

Sandy walked back down the corridor. It remained unchanged, almost endless, and with no sign of Zhadnoboth. Cursing the sorcerer, Sandy walked back to the group.

"Magic man had wrong thoughts," Hojeen said offhandedly. "Go some other way."

"We've got to find him," Anala said, a faint edge of panic in her voice. "He could be dying or in desperate need. We must save him or our fellowship will be broken."

Her words had whipped the others into a fine fettle and they were ready to dash off in all directions. Sandy stepped in and stopped that.

"That numbskull could walk into a snake pit and come out unscathed," he commented acidly. "Wherever he is, I know he considers *us* lost, not him. Damn him! He's more trouble than a pie-eyed dragon and half as useful." Despite his exasperation, there was a slight undertone of worry in his words.

"You're a fine one!" Anala stormed. "He's *your* friend, and now you want to abandon him!"

"I didn't say that," Sandy replied. He turned to Talim. "Lead them down this corridor until you find a good stopping place. I'm going back to find that booby and wring his scrawny neck."

"That's right, go off gallivanting just when we need you." Anala stepped forward and started to wave a finger at him.

Sandy put his hands on her shoulders, spun her around until she was facing the other way. He handed her to Jatro. "Make sure the lulzi goes with you. Now, get going."

He watched them tramp off. Anala glowered back at him and dragged her feet, but went along, helped by the strong hand of Jatro on her shoulder. Talim didn't seem too happy either: Doubtless he'd been raised to honor and respect lulzis, not frog-march them hither and yon.

As they disappeared around a curve in the corridor, Hojeen looked over his shoulder and gave Sandy a roguish wink.

Sandy walked back down the corridor for quite a way. When nothing happened, he stopped and cursed the sorcerer again . . . and gradually became aware of a tingling in his left little finger. He glanced down and saw that the tiny emerald on his silver ring was glowing. He moved his hand about and noticed that the light became brighter when he pointed in the direction he had come from.

"Well, that's something else you can do," he said to the ring. "But what the hell is it."

He thought a moment and then again pointed the ring in the direction from which he had come. Closing his eyes, he began walking. The tingling sensation in his finger got stronger and stronger as he moved forward; then suddenly stopped.

Sandy's eyes snapped open and he looked around. He was in an arched doorway looking into a huge hall. The bare stone walls were black with age and the floor was thick with dust. He heard a faint chittering and looked up. A hundred feet or more above was a vaulted ceiling, but so shrouded in gloom he could barely see it. Something flitted through the air and then disappeared. Then another did the same thing. "Bats," he muttered.

There was no sign of Zhadnoboth except for some footprints leading to a bronze door at the far end of the hall. He followed the tracks until he stood before the door. It was green with age, almost a foot thick, and stood open a crack.

Sandy's sixth sense was going strong, and he felt a great unease. He strung the ivory bow he'd picked up in the armory and nocked an arrow. Carefully he eased through the door and into a long narrow room lined with stone shelves. Each shelf was loaded with large red earthenware pots; one had been knocked off its shelf and among the shards was a pile of copper coins. Sandy picked one up; six-sided and with a square hole in the middle, it was like no other coin he'd ever seen. Absentmindedly he put it in a pocket and went on.

The doorway at the far end of the room had been closed off by a bronze grille—a bronze grille that now stood wide open with a jagged hole blasted in the lock. Sandy gave a satisfied grunt. He knew the sorcerer's work when he saw it.

A long hallway lay like a *T* across the doorway. At regular intervals down each side of the hall were more grilled doorways. At each end of the hallway was a massive door—one of silvery metal and the other gold tinted. A couple more grilles had been blasted open, but there was no other sign of the sorcerer, and Sandy decided to go down the corridor to his right. The door at that end was the gold-colored one: Zhadnoboth would have been attracted to it like a moth to a candle flame.

He glanced in one of the grilles which had been blasted open as he went by. The walls were lined with swords and daggers, many adorned with jeweled hilts and scabbards. A bare spot on one wall showed the faint outline of a sword and scabbard and Sandy wondered what made that particular sword so valuable to the sorcerer.

Sandy paused at the foot of the low stair leading up to the golden door. The surface of the door was smooth and unmarred by keyhole, latch, or handle—but a lever was sticking out of the left hand wall.

This was too easy. Gingerly he pushed down on the lever; it wouldn't budge. He studied the wall and found three keyholes, one above the other, just to the right of the lever. He pulled out the key ring and wondered which key or keys to use. Then he knew which gold key it was and how to use it: His vagrant sixth sense was working again. He put the key into the middle keyhole and twisted it to the left, then he did the same with the top and the bottom keyhole. He ended the sequence by replacing the key in the middle keyhole and twisting right. There was a whoosh of displaced air and the door swung ponderously inward.

"It's about time you got here," Zhadnoboth said as he came stomping out. "If you had waited much longer I'd have joined them." He pointed backward to several piles of dry bones. A faint clinking accompanied his gestures, and he wore several heavy gold necklaces, and his every finger bore at least one jeweled gold ring. In his hand was a staff carved of a dark red wood.

Over his shoulder he carried a straight sword in a gold scabbard sprinkled with thousands of tiny rubies. The hilt was of tightly wound gold thread; at each end of the gold-chased crosspiece was a ruby the size of a robin's egg. The pommel was another ruby, this one as large or larger than a hen's egg, and worth a king's ransom. The sword was worth kingdoms.

Zhadnoboth walked down the stairs and the door slammed shut behind him. Before it closed, Sandy caught a glimpse of what was inside: chests spilling over with gold coins, walls festooned with gold chains, jewelry, bowls, shields—and most impressive, a golden statue of a broad-shouldered giant.

"When I need you you are never around," the sorcerer complained. "If I had to rely on you I'd be dead meat now." He walked by an open-mouthed Sandy and then abruptly stopped. Turning, he took the sword off his shoulder and handed it to Sandy. "You carry this. I'm too old to be lugging around such hardware."

Without thinking, Sandy grabbed the sword. A cold shock ran through his arm and for a moment he forgot Zhadnoboth. He stared hard at the sword, knew it for what it was, and then slung it over his right shoulder. "You *would* pick a magical sword."

"Why else would I carry around a hunk of steel? I'm no lunkhead of a warrior." The sorcerer was clearly in a fouler temper than usual, and wanted no questions asked.

Sandy shook his head disgustedly. "If this keeps up I'll be hip-deep in magical whatnots before this adventure is over—and so far I don't see what use they are." He glanced back at the sword hilt and shook his head again. "If you had to get a magical sword, couldn't you have picked a less gaudy one?"

Zhadnoboth said, as if speaking to an idiot child, "Don't you have any sense? What do you think I'd get for a plain magical sword? Not much! But for something fancy like this, I can name my price and have them begging to pay more."

They walked in silence back toward the entrance to the treasure house. Outside the bronze door, Sandy stopped and unstrung his bow, thinking unkindly about his sixth sense. The only menace which had turned up was Zhadnoboth.

With a crash the bronze door of the great hall swung open behind him. Sandy yanked out his sword and spun around, ready to fight. Coming toward him was the gold statue: eight feet tall and half as wide, a sword in one hand and a mace in the other.

The gold man moved forward ponderously until Sandy could see that gold was his color and gold his substance. The statue's hair was fine strands of spun gold, his skin a ruddy beaded gold. His teeth were sharp spikes of white gold and his massive muscle, layers of corded gold. And gold was his soul. Only his eyes were more than metal: One was an emerald the bright green of early spring, the other a sapphire the clear blue of winter skies. In both burned star fire.

"Hold, man," he thundered in a melodious gold-toned voice. "No one may leave my master's treasure house without settling accounts with me. Each is welcome to take what they please, but each must pay in their own coin for what they take." When he ceased the silence seemed to last for eternity. "What do you pay?"

"I don't pay a damned thing," Sandy retorted, and threw the magic sword to the floor. "This is the sorcerer's loot, not mine. I answer only for my own debts."

"Then pay," the gold man said.

Zhadnoboth watched the confrontation for a moment and quietly scuttled off to safety, only stopping when he reached the doorway at the far side of the hall.

Sandy saw this out of the corner of his eye. "What about him?" He pointed toward Zhadnoboth. "Is your law only for the hindmost or is it for all?"

"We have settled accounts, he and I," replied the gold man.

Sandy threw a scathing glance Zhadnoboth's way. The sorcerer flinched guiltily. "Then I'm going," he said. "I took nothing and I pay nothing."

"What of the coin in your pocket?"

Sandy reached in his pocket, muttered an obscenity, and threw the copper coin to the floor. It bounced and then rolled into the gloom. "Take your damned coin. I only robbed you of it by accident. If I had wanted to snatch some treasure, I'd have taken something worth having, not a piddling copper coin."

"Large or small, each thing taken must be paid for, and for each the same price." The gold man's voice was implacable and unforgiving, and he moved forward menacingly.

"You mean you're out to get me because of one miserable copper piece?" Sandy was outraged. "That's as fair as sending me to hell for breathing."

The gold man said nothing. Swinging sword and mace, he kept advancing. Sandy threw down his bow and quiver and began circling to his right. The gold man just kept coming.

For long moments they danced this silent dance, Sandy circling and keeping out of range, not anxious to test the strength and skill of his opponent. The gold man kept stalking him, gradually backing him into a corner.

Sandy gave his foe a savage grin and jumped forward, attacking. There was a swift fake one way and then a backhand stroke which lopped the head off the mace, and then he and the gold man were going at it hammer and tongs.

Eventually Sandy, weary and battered, backed off and began circling again. He had barely held his own with the gold man, but he had accomplished his purpose: He was no longer boxed in.

Untiring and remorseless, the statue kept coming after him. Patiently he stalked, never letting up and never giving an opening. Time was on his side and he knew it; eventually he'd wear Sandy down or trap him in a corner.

Sandy knew the gold man's strategy and that only made him more stubbornly determined to win. That thing from hell was going to pay a price. And if Sandy lost, then the statue would find the war far from over—there was more than one demon here.

Sandy fought with all the knowledge and skill at his command, knowledge gained from years of no-quarter desert warfare—circling for a while and then making fast and furious attacks, the hall resounding with the clash of metal against metal. More than once against his ponderous foe, Sandy landed a telling blow, only to have his blade bounce of the statue's hide. No ordinary army steel, no matter how powerfully wielded, was going to bite into the gold man's magical flesh.

Sandy wiped the sweat off his brow with the back of his left hand and wondered how long he could last. His sword arm felt like it was ready to fall off, the sword itself was notched, and it was becoming an agony to breathe. He smiled through gritted teeth at his opponent. He hadn't hurt that bastard yet, but he would, somehow.

Sandy attacked once again. He rained blows at the gold man, but his foe parried them and attacked in turn with sledgehammer blows which jolted Sandy to the core. During a savage exchange of blows, Sandy's blade, a piece of the finest steel forged in the empire—snapped in half.

Sandy looked at the stump of his sword and then at his foe. For the first time the gold man smiled, and he moved in for the kill. Sandy stepped inside the gold man's blow and grabbed the his arm. He fell backward and used his leverage and demonic strength to flip the gold man over his shoulder. The statue went flying and landed on his back with a thunderous crash.

Sandy got to his feet and then bent over, trying to get his breath. It had taken every ounce of strength he had to throw the gold man and he still didn't know how he had done it— trying to move his foe had been like trying to pick up a mountain. He looked over toward the gold man and saw that he was groggy, but getting to his feet. Sandy grinned: At last he had hurt that tough bastard.

He straightened up and looked around for a weapon. The magical sword Zhadnoboth had stolen was lying nearby. That gaudy piece of junk would have to do. He hobbled over, tore the sword from its scabbard, and nodded with satisfaction. The shimmering blue steel blade was the work of a master smith; even if it had not been magic it would have done the job.

Power seeped up through the hilt and flowed into his body. Sandy's breathing eased and the burning in his lungs ceased. Strength returned to his muscles as weariness fled. Around the edges there was still some fraying, but nothing to worry about for now.

Sandy flexed his arm and the sword moved with ease—and hummed as though eager for action. "All right, you're a magic son of a bitch," Sandy muttered to the sword. "But let's see how you do against the magic of this gold bastard."

He heard the statue's heavy tread and turned to face him. The gold man kept advancing until he was about ten feet away. There he stopped and gave Sandy and his new weapon the once-over.

"Your sword will make no difference, man. Such a weapon is only as good as the wielder. Neither matches me." His golden tones were confident and unfearing; too confident, too unfearing. "You will die, man, and you will be nothing."

Sandy shrugged. "All men die—we are born dying. It's how we die that counts."

"Death is death; there is no return. Coward or hero, it makes no difference. Each is as dead."

"It makes a difference to me." Sandy smiled grimly and added, "Besides, you give me no choice." Without warning, he charged his foe.

"No!" wailed Zhadnoboth. "You'll damage my sword!"

The great hall rang with the sound of their blades crashing together, and with another sound: the banshee wail from the sword in Sandy's hand. It sang a wild steely song as it split the air; as it went through thrust, parry, and riposte: sometimes as soft as a whisper and other times shaking the very stones with its roar—and at all times a screech. It wasn't pleasant to the ear, but there was a kind of music to it nonetheless.

For long moments Sandy and the gold man fought, neither able to gain an advantage. Sandy was fast and a master swordsman, but his opponent matched him in skill and far overmatched him in strength. Then Sandy's blade got inside his foe's guard and raked him across the chest. The magic edge of this sword sliced through the charmed flesh of the gold man and left a long gash. Tiny gold droplets oozed from the wound and fell to the floor, hissing and crackling when they touched the cold stone.

There was another flurry of action and then they backed away for a moment, resting and staring at each other. Even with his demonic vitality and the magical power flowing from the sword into him, Sandy felt fatigue slowly creeping through his muscles. And the gold man was moving slower. Apparently even magical and inhuman flesh had its limits.

"You fight well, man. I will be sorry when I slay you."

"Not as much as I will," Sandy replied. "Not that it will do you much good."

The gold man rushed forward and they went at it again. Sandy fought hard, but the gold man kept hammering away and forcing him backward. The lightness was gone from his feet, and he could only keep fighting doggedly and wait for a chance to land a telling blow. And that was getting harder and harder to do. His arm felt like a piece of numb lead and he could barely move it.

The gold man's sword nicked him on the arm and drew blood. Sandy saw the handwriting on the wall. He backed off, flipped the sword to his other hand, and went back to battle left-handed. For a while this tactic worked to his advantage—at least this arm didn't feel like it was going to drop off, and his foe had problems fending off a southpaw attack. He managed to wound the gold man again, slashing him across the face. Soon, however, his weariness caught up with him, and the gold man began forcing him backward.

Sandy stumbled over something on the floor. For a moment he was off balance and was unprepared when a sledgehammer blow from his foe smashed into his sword. The weapon went flying, and Sandy, deprived suddenly of his magical energy, collapsed to the floor in utter exhaustion. The gold man's sword whistled through the air where he had been but a moment before.

Something was under Sandy's right hand, and instinctively he grabbed it, only realizing a moment later that it was an arrow. The gold man was towering over him, sword high, as he staggered to his feet. Sandy came up inside his foe's reach and drove the arrow into his sapphire eye. The gem splintered under the blow and the arrow buried itself deep inside the eye socket of the gold man.

The statue screamed and dropped his sword. Sizzling gold blood spurted from the wound, burning Sandy's hand. He jerked away, but was trapped as the gold man's arms wrapped about him. He heard his right arm crack and then his ribs, but he felt nothing; he was beyond pain. He reached behind his neck with his left hand and pulled out the throwing knife he kept concealed there. Rearing back, he plunged it into the gold man's emerald eye.

His foe screamed again and his arm tightened spasmodically. Sandy felt his back break and lost all sensation from the hips down. Gold blood spurted into his eyes and blinded them. Then the gold man dropped him and staggered backward to fall with a crash to the floor. Sandy collapsed in a broken heap, thought, *I got the bastard,* and then passed out.

Sometime later he was aware of someone holding him. He could see nothing, his right arm was useless, and his lower body was unfeeling dead weight. Hard experienced hands probed at his body and then he was dropped to the ground.

"Some warrior," Zhadnoboth said. "You're no use this way. It will take days for you to heal and be any use. You're better dead." He yanked Sandy's poniard from its sheath and with a single stroke sliced his throat open from ear to ear.

Sandy found himself walking through a netherworld of fire and fury: a world of interconnected volcanic caverns, walls glowing with heat and streams of liquid sulfur pouring down them to collect in bubbling pools. Small lizards, nostrils spurting fire and steam, scampered from pool to pool, gobbling up the millions of darting gnat-sized sparks hovering over the boiling sulfur. Here and there runty demons with cinder-black skins stood guard over herds of salamanders grazing on fiery coals. They gazed at Sandy curiously, but stood aside to let him pass.

He wandered aimlessly through the fiery caverns for an eternity, yet knowing that he was going somewhere. Where, he didn't know. Just that he'd reach it someday, some century.

Eventually he came to a large cavern which had in its center a lake of molten lava, white-hot, with a surface constantly erupting in fountains of fire. In the shallows of the lake the gold man, his eyes now blue-white diamonds, sat bathing, luxuriating in the pleasant fires.

Sandy marched to the shore of the fiery lake and started wading out to where the gold man was. He was almost on top of the gold man before the metal being saw Sandy. He looked in disbelief at his mortal foe, now larger than he. Sandy walked up to him and punched him in the belly. The force of the blow bent the gold man double. Sandy picked him up, raised him high above his head, and threw him belly first into the bubbling magma. The gold man hit the surface of the molten lake with a tremendous splash. Gobbets of burning lava splattered everywhere, hissing angrily—and evaporating into nothingness if they touched Sandy.

He grabbed the dazed gold man by his wiry hair and dragged him out of the lake. On shore Sandy picked him up and rammed him headfirst into the nearest wall, smashing the stone and punching a hole through to the cavern on the other side.

"The next time you pick a fight, remember that some men are demons," Sandy told the gold man. "All for a damned penny," he grumbled as he walked away.

Suddenly there was a darkness in front of him. Formless at first, it quickly shaped itself into the figure of a woman wrapped in a hooded robe. Her face was hidden in the depths of the hood, but he could feel malevolent eyes glaring at him.

"What are you doing here? You're needed in Zarathandra, not in some second-rate hell."

"Taking care of unfinished business."

"My business is your business, not piddling feuds with minor devils. Zarathandra needs you. Now go!" And with that she disappeared.

"Dammit!," Sandy roared. He paused and then muttered to himself, "If I had to get stuck with a goddess, why did it have to be a double-dealing battle-axe?"

Sandy turned his thoughts to Zarathandra reluctantly; in these netherworlds he could be anything he wanted to be, but in mortal realms he was only a man. He visualized the dim-lit hall where he had fought the gold man. There was a flash of blinding agony and the next moment his naked body tumbled to the floor where he had died.

As he got to his feet, he saw Zhadnoboth bending over what seemed to be the crumbed remnants of the gold man's earthly body. The sorcerer ran his fingers through the stony fragments and grumbled loudly, "Fool's gold." He picked up a piece and threw it angrily toward the end of the hall.

Sandy came up behind him and gave him a boot in the rear. The sorcerer went sprawling. Sandy followed after, picked him up, turned him upside down, and began shaking. Gold pieces, rings, jeweled necklaces, several gold-hilted daggers, and even a gold pot large enough to cook a chicken in dropped out. When he had a pile of treasure a foot and a half high, he dropped the sorcerer.

"Now your jingling won't wake the dead when you walk," Sandy said.

Zhadnoboth jumped to his feet spitting tacks. "That's my treasure, fairly won. You can't take it from me."

"I'm not. I'm just leaving it here."

"That's not fair," screamed the sorcerer, almost crying. "You don't need gold, but what do I have? Nothing! When I am old and decrepit who will take care of me? Do you want me to end my days scrabbling for a piece of moldy bread some housewife threw out? I want to spend my old age peacefully sitting by the fire, with enough coppers in my pocket to buy a bit of cheese or a bottle of bragberry brandy when I need them."

Sandy eyed the disheveled sorcerer, still wearing a gold collar and the jeweled rings he'd found, and just shook his head. For Zhadnoboth, too much would never be enough. "Serves you right. I owe you one for cutting my throat. Someday I'll return the favor."

"I only put you out of your misery," Zhadnoboth protested. "You'd have lingered for days, dying breath by breath, if it hadn't been for me. Besides, you're only a demon."

The sorcerer's last words struck a sore point with Sandy, partly because there was some truth in them. "What I am is an unlucky bastard you shanghaied into this godforsaken hole by mistake."

The sorcerer gave a disbelieving sniff. "If you're not a demon I can't tell the difference. I've seen you do things no mortal should be able to." He paused and then added, *"And you don't stay dead."*

Sandy slowly steamed for a moment. "That's because of your damned Goddess. She needed a henchman to do her dirty work and I just happened to be handy. That's another thing I owe you."

"Huh!" The sorcerer snorted. "A gift men would give their souls for and you're unhappy. Even a newborn babe wouldn't believe that." Then he asked acidly, "Why don't you tell the Goddess you want to be a mere mortal?"

"I can't count the times I've tried," Sandy said disgruntledly. "But once that she-wolf makes up her mind, she won't change it. A mule is reasonable compared to her."

Zhadnoboth's silence said more about his disbelief than words ever could.

"All right," growled Sandy, "so there are advantages to being what I am. But I never asked for the job and I don't like ending up ass-deep in alligators. I'm all for adventure, as long as it is someone else's adventure." He glowered at the sorcerer. "And we still aren't lugging that treasure of yours with us!"

They bickered a bit more, with Zhadnoboth coming around to Sandy's point of view; he wasn't given much choice.

"I'm not leaving my property lying about for some villainous treasure hunter to pick up," the sorcerer grumbled. He pulled out a handbook of spells and paged through it until he found what he wanted.

Holding the spellbook in one hand and his new staff in the other, he read through a spell and wove intricate patterns in the air with his staff. As he spoke the words to the cantrip an amber glow gradually surrounded his gold. He spoke the final mystic word and poked the end of his staff into this glow. Instantly, it and the treasure it contained shrank to an amber crystal the size of a golf ball. Zhadnoboth picked it up and threw it toward the far end of the hall. As it went, it rapidly diminished in size and with a faint pop disappeared into nothingness.

"You have to be careful with treasure," he explained to Sandy. "There's always unscrupulous characters who will try to make off with it."

"Yeah," Sandy said dryly. He looked around and saw that the door to the treasure chamber had disappeared as if it had never existed. His clothes and gear were lying in a pile not far away, where they had dropped when his previous body disappeared.

He quickly dressed and slung his bow and quiver across his back. In the meantime Zhadnoboth had retrieved the magic sword and was checking every inch of it with a critical eye. Sandy headed his way.

"Look here," he said peevishly, pointing to a faint scratch on the cross hilt. "What are you going to do about that? How am I going to explain that to buyers?"

"Tell them it was put to good use," Sandy said, plucking the sword from the sorcerer's hands. He shoved it into its scabbard and belted it on.

"What are you doing?" howled Zhadnoboth.

"I need a sword and this is the only one available."

The sorcerer started to howl some more, then swiftly changed his mind. A crafty look crossed his face. "You can use the sword." He paused. "But I need some assurance you will return it."

"I'll use this magic hunk of junk only as long as I have to," Sandy replied testily. "When I find a sword more to my liking you can have it back."

"That might be forever."

Sandy cast a scathing look at the gaudy sword belted at his waist. "Not likely."

"Still, these magic swords grow on one—even a lesser one such as this," Zhadnoboth said in a silky voice. "If I had some token you valued, I would rest easier."

A crooked smile played about Sandy's lips for a moment. He slipped the silver ring off his little finger and pressed it into Zhadnoboth's palm. "Here, take the Ring of Uncertainty. It will be my bond that I will return what is yours."

A brief grimace crossed the sorcerer's face. He had lusted

after the ring ever since Sandy had acquired it, but just now he'd been angling for something of more immediate important. "Thank you," he said disgruntledly, stuffing the unexpected prize away inside his robe. The ring was worth a thousand swords, yet he knew that somehow he'd been had.

"Follow me," Sandy said. "And keep your mind on me, not on your daydreams."

Zhadnoboth made a vulgar comment about behinds and trotted after him. Somewhere along the way they made a transition and found themselves traveling down the marble corridor where Sandy had parted from the rest of their companions.

He held up a hand, signaling for Zhadnoboth to stop, and dropped to a knee, scanning the corridor floor. A frown appeared on his face and he chewed on his lip.

"Well? What is it?" Zhadnoboth asked.

"They went this way, but there are other tracks here. Very faint, very light, and going the same way." He looked more closely at the floor. "There are more of the tracks and they are old. Or at least the tracks of our companions overlay them."

"I never knew you were a tracker," Zhadnoboth said sarcastically.

"I wasn't," Sandy replied, "until I got dragooned into the Rithian army. You learn such skills when you're stationed on the southern border. Or you don't last long."

He looked both ways down the long corridor, said, "Come," and began trotting silently in the direction their companions had gone.

Zhadnoboth muttered a few curses and hobbled as fast as he could after him. He caught up with Sandy where the corridor ended, a small balcony with a broad stair leading down from one side. "I'm an old man," he wheezed. "I can't take this silly dashing about."

Sandy motioned him to silence and looked at the scene below. The stair led down to a broad hall, dusty and abandoned looking. Several small bodies were scattered about the floor, and off to one side was a dead something. In the center of the hall were their companions, with Anala kneeling down and holding a small still form in her arms. Otherwise the hall looked empty—until Sandy looked twice. Then he could see many small figures crouching silently in the nooks, crannies, and shadows in that part of the hall nearest their companions.

"Ningerlings," whispered Zhadnoboth, who had moved up to stand near Sandy's elbow. "Their spears look none too friendly."

From below Anala was crooning a wordless melody: a gentle sound, a healing sound that eased the soul and coaxed life to burn brighter. Her tune changed and she chanted words of healing. "Oh mother who loves the great and the small, lend me your power to heal this little one. Make life flow unsullied through his veins. Restore his heart. Heal the wounds of his body and of his soul. Strengthen his flesh and make pure his blood. Help him to be whole again." There was a catch in her voice and she was silent for a moment. "Oh healing mother do this, work through me to do thy will." There was another silence and then she began her velvet-toned crooning once more.

The crooning went on for a moment more. Then the figure in her arms stirred and sat up. A wondering sigh came from the watchers, quickly replaced by quiet and excited chattering.

Sandy strung his bow and began stealing down the stair. As he got closer he could see that the ningerlings were about four feet high with a stringy scrawny build, no hair on their heads except a kind of Mohawk crest, and pointed ears which were vaguely elflike.

An old man came out of the shadows and walked toward Anala. His gray-tinged skin was folded and creased like old parchment; his wispy white hair was pale and almost colorless. If there ever had been fat on his body, it was long gone: He was thin as a whisper and yet seemed tough as old leather.

He knelt down by the figure Anala had been holding and ran his hands over the boy's body, lingering over the long red slash across the boy's belly and a large round wound on the side of his neck. Both injuries were already starting to heal. He muttered a word and the boy scuttled off as though his tail had been singed.

After seeing a small family of ningerlings welcome and hug the stripling, the old man turned to Anala. He bowed his head and spoke in awed and reverent tones. Anala looked blankly at him, for once not knowing what to say.

"He says only a great warrior could slay the urgach, but

only a greater healer could heal its wounds," Sandy said, coming down the last treads of the staircase. He spoke a few words to the old ningerling and listened to his long reply. "He says that she who is unseen has blessed you and is strong in you, that you are strong of soul and heart. He says that the Sandcreeper sept of the Yimsi are blessed by your coming. Your song is theirs and their hearts to command."

"Tell him I only did what I could," Anala said wearily. Her young face was drawn, and her hair was plastered to her head by sweat.

Sandy turned to the old ningerling and said a few words. The ningerling listened and then rattled off a quick reply. Sandy nodded, but before he could translate these last words, the ningerling cocked an eye Anala's way and added a few comments. There was a bawdy tone to his words and he gave Sandy a knowing wink as he finished.

Sandy guffawed and crackled off a retort. The old ningerling gave a whoop and a holler, then chortled out the joke to his clansmen. Their laughter rocked the deserted hall.

Anala turned beet red. "What was that all about?" she demanded angrily.

Sandy carefully choose his words. "He said a holy woman such as you should have many daughters." For a moment he almost burst out laughing, but after a short struggle he forced it back down. "He says he'd be happy to oblige." Sandy tried to keep his voice deadpan and almost succeeded.

"You know damned well that was not what I meant. What did you say?"

"I just agreed with him."

Anala stomped over until she was belly to belly with him, the top of her head even with the middle of his chest. She looked up at him and shook a finger in his face. "You said more than that." She backed off and pointed to the old ningerling. "You tell that old lecher to keep his business to himself." She gave a disdainful sniff and added, "Even you are preferable to that old goat."

Sandy turned to the ningerling and spoke a few words. His tone was grave and respectful.

Now Anala's temper really sizzled. "You tell him what I said, not that sanctimonious garbage you're spouting."

"I was just saying your words in a more tactful way."

"You have as much tact as a mud toad." She pushed Sandy

aside and started telling the ningerling what she thought. She went on for a couple minutes, spewing out a lot of choice words about dirty old men in general and him in particular, also what she thought of underhanded connivers who laughed at her.

She paused for breath and the old ningerling touched his hand to her lips and blessed her. Then he spoke what sounded like words of condolence to Sandy.

"Now what did he say?" she choked out.

"How sad that so many of the truly holy are mad."

"Mad!"

"He also invites us to share a feast with him and his clanspeople. And asks if there is anything they can do for you."

Anala stewed silently for a moment and then a smile almost broke through. She caught herself and said, "You deal with him, you're his type of riffraff." Then she did her best to stalk off, mumbling about bastards never getting their just desserts.

Sandy caught Talim's eye and motioned with his head toward Anala. Talim gave a sullen nod and went to stand near the lulzi. The rest of their company drifted over to be near him and Anala. Meanwhile Sandy and the old ningerling, Tak Tak ab Craxidour, had a chance to talk.

"She is a great lady, very young, but very holy," the Craxidour said, a smile on his lips but reverence in his voice. "The Yimsi are much honored that one the Goddess has touched has come to us."

Sandy lied a bit and said, "We are honored to travel with her. She is on a mission for the Goddess."

"Yimsi will help."

"She travels to meet the great shee, Jara Greenteeth, and destroy her."

There was dead silence for an instant. Then the Craxidour said grimly, "The green lady is very bad. She kills many ningerlings. The Sandcreeper sept will help you. I will talk to other Yimsi septs and to septs of other ningerling tribes."

"We'll settle for a guide," Sandy said.

"You will get more." There was a very determined look on the Craxidour's face.

They had wandered over to where the dead creature lay. It was an ugly manlike brute covered by irregular patches of long yellow hair. Instead of nails its hands had long talons and it had a round mouth filled with many sharp teeth, much like the mouth of a lamprey. On the fur, the talons, and around the mouth were scattered gouts of drying blood. Between its great saucer-sized eyes the haft of an arrow jutted.

"Only a great warrior can kill the urgach. They poison the soul and cloud the mind. A true heart, hard mind, and strength which comes from deep inside are needed to fight it—and, maybe, win. Long ago Ingoldoron, the last king of Ty-Brummigar, stared the urgach in the eyes and died—and he had slain dragons and walked the Paths of Doom. Your holy child looked the urgach full in the eye, yet slew it with first shot. But greater still is one who can heal someone wounded by the urgach. Ingoldoron lingered for days and not even the greatest healers could ease his pain or cure his wounds. She is greatly blessed by the Goddess. There is death in her hands, but also life. She is great and will be greater."

Sandy smiled wryly. "It's the getting there that's the problem."

The Craxidour chuckled. "To be young and to be a fool are almost the same thing, but only if you have been a fool can you become truly wise." He shook his head sadly. "And only the fool can do the impossible. He does not know it cannot be done or the price that must be paid."

"That's what I'm for," Sandy told him. "To knock some sense into her head and save her bacon."

The Craxidour smiled and replied, "That's what all we old fools are for, isn't it?"

They had a laugh together, a laugh that was all the merrier for the sadness that was beneath it. Then they gabbed for a while and parted friends for then and forever.

Sandy walked over to his companions. "The ningerlings will lead us to the dungeon door," he said. "But first we must go with them and feast."

"We don't have the time." Anala jumped to her feet. "We have a quest to achieve. We don't have the time to fritter away on such foolishness."

"We don't have the time not to," Sandy replied. "We can use whatever help we can get, be it a guide or a few cut-throats. And if it means spending a little bit of time guzzling and gorging on good food, I'm willing to suffer."

"Suffer!"

"All right, I'll enjoy myself."

Talim butted into the conversation. "Kas Sandro is a good enough soldier, my lady. If you can tear him loose from either the brothels or the dinner table. To him fighting is an unpleasant job a soldier has to do now and then."

"A good soldier only fights when he has to," Sandy replied. "He doesn't go looking for trouble, because he knows it will find him. Just because we've been tapped on the shoulder by destiny, doesn't mean we have to ignore the good things in life."

"That's not my type of good soldier," Talim snapped.

"It's my type."

The two men faced each other for a moment. Talim was wound tight as a drum and ready to chew steel spikes.

"How long are you going to go on with this silly nonsense?" Sandy asked in exasperation. "I've had a hard day and I've got better things to do than stare at your ugly puss."

Talim backed off, puzzled and unnerved by Sandy's attitude. Anger or fear he could deal with, but not being treated as if he was a pain in the behind.

Anala stepped in, a moment late, but with all the right intentions. "Stop this squabbling. We are chosen by destiny. Are we going to deny it by fighting among ourselves?"

Talim saluted her. "I'll gather the others." He glowered at Sandy and then said to Anala, "But only because you are along will I hold true. Today you proved yourself a warrior, much more than others who were not here." He turned and started getting the others ready to move.

"I guess he told me," Sandy remarked. He looked Anala up and down. "And where did you get those grand words?"

Anala flushed, started to speak, and then hesitated for a moment. "I sort of cribbed them from a book I once read," she said, shamefaced.

Sandy laughed. "Even if they weren't all yours, they sort of fit."

Anala brightened. "Did you see that creature I shot? His stench was so bad I probably could have hit him dead center with my eyes closed. Was that a shot! I got him right where I aimed. That'll teach him to mess with my mind."

Sandy smiled to himself and waited to hear more. She deserved her moment of glory. Let her savor it while she could.

Five minutes later Anala was still babbling and Sandy was

wondering if his ears would hold out. He gave a sigh of relief when he saw the Craxidour coming over.

"We must go to our place now," the ningerling said. "We would be honored if you and your companions would go with us."

"It is my companions and I who would be honored," Sandy said, putting on his best manners.

Picking up Talim and the rest of their companions, Anala and Sandy followed the Craxidour out of the hall. Anala walked along babbling away happily, for the moment only a young girl. Sandy listened with half an ear as he mulled over their situation. It was getting better, but the deck was still stacked against them.

15

THE Goddess watched the battle in her pool of seeing, from first clash to the bloody mopping up, and was satisfied. First at the Well of Shimeeros and now at the Standing Stones, Aku had proved his generalship. The tribesman were flocking to his banners, both from Rithian speaking tribes of the southeast and even from some of the smaller Lugdanian tribes. By these two victories Aku had secured the southern and southeastern borders, confining the revolt to the southwest. He was building a reputation along the frontier and in other places that would stand him in good stead in the future.

The Goddess picked up some pebbles and threw one into her pool of seeing. When it hit the water a scene from the past appeared: the Well of Shimeeros, as it had been two weeks ago. Krizzan Tham-Shanek was sitting by the well drinking bitter-brewed tea with his Chanzi wizards. On a pole nearby was the head of Kas Feldzak, headman of the Shimeeri clan of the Kri Omphor. Tattoo-faced Yartazi warriors were gathering together and standing guard over various groups of the Shimeeri clan: women, children, young men, mature men, and the elders.

The prophet took a sip of his tea and fumed to the Chanzi wizard sitting next to him, "We are fighting a holy war and that misbegotten dog, Kas Feldzak, dared to say no. What are three maids? Nothing! Well, now his head sits on a pole." He added grimly, "The next time I ask for a minor sacrifice from a headman, he won't think twice before he obeys."

The Chanzi nodded and sneered. "These Kri Omphor dirt diggers are hardly worth the killing. Look twice at them and they lose control of their bowels. Show them some blood and they beg for mercy. A pile of dung has more guts than they have.''

"Even dung has its uses," the prophet said, finishing his cup of tea. "When men remember the Kri Omphor, they'll remember my wrath and shudder." He raised a hand and signaled to one of the Yartazi.

The Yartazi, a grizzled warrior with a yellow snake tattooed above his right eyebrow, nodded and stalked over to where the elders of the Shimeeri clan were being held. He barked an order and unsheathed a long kukri knife. Two of his tribesmen grabbed an elder by his arms and marched him forward. The yellow-snake warrior yanked the elder's head back by the hair and with the kukri knife ripped open his throat. Blood gushed from the elder's throat and down the front of his robes. The two Yartazi holding the body contemptuously tossed it to the ground and went back for another victim.

Four times the performance was repeated, while the other prisoners watched in horror. Then there was only one elder left, Yuthman the Smith. He was a short and broad-beamed man as ugly as mortal sin. The many dents and scars on his bald skull and on his face warned that here was no man of peace. The two Yartazi grabbed his arms and marched him forward.

The yellow-snake warrior, now spattered with the blood of his previous victims, gave a savage smile and raised his kukri to slaughter another innocent. But Yuthman was no lamb. His right leg lashed out, catching his would-be executioner in the groin. The yellow-snake warrior screamed and dropped to his knees. Yuthman flexed his massive arms and sent the two Yartazi holding them crashing together. There was a *crack* as their heads hit and they dropped to the ground unconscious.

Yuthman stepped forward and punched the yellow-snake warrior in the throat as he knelt, writhing in agony. The Yartazi dropped dead to the ground and lay there with blood seeping from his mouth. Yuthman laid hold of the yellow-snake's kukri, whirled, and threw it at Krizzan Tham-Shanek. It caught the Chanzi who had been talking with the prophet in the gut as he lunged forward to get at Yuthman.

The smith reached down and grabbed a saber from one of the unconscious Yartazi at his feet. He charged the prophet and his Chanzi cronies, determined to sell his life dear. His chosen foes, wizards and not warriors, scattered. Yuthman's saber lashed out at a fleeing Chanzi; the razor-sharp blade sliced into his neckbone. The body flopped down into the dust. A tall Yartazi, with the sign of the Black Vulture society tattooed above his right eyebrow, came up behind Yuthman and raised his sword; but before he could slay the smith, an arrow pierced his lung. He screamed hoarsely and fell to his knees, grabbing at the arrowhead sticking from his chest. Another arrow caught him in the heart and he pitched over dead.

There was the blare of war trumpets and the roar of battle cries, as Aku and his troops came charging over a rise on their rudhars. They caught the prophet's Yartazi warriors flat-footed, only one or two was still mounted. It was a slaughter as his troops rode down their disorganized foes.

A Yartazi guarding the women forgot his prisoners and hastily raised his bow and let loose an arrow. Before he could shoot again, an old woman came up behind him and hit him with an iron cooking pot. He fell to his knees, stunned. She ripped his knife from his belt and stabbed him in the eye.

Now the rest of the prisoners—even the children—joined in. They grabbed what weapons they could find or used their bare hands if they had to. The Yartazi, beset on all sides by the maddened Shimeeri, were easy prey for the swords and lances of Aku's mounted troops.

The Chanzi shapechangers had no time to work their magic and most were cut down in human form. One was able to start changing, but a Kri Rithi spitted him on his lance, pinning him to the ground. Half man and half beast, he screamed and howled and tried vainly to crawl up the lance. Again and again Kri Rithi warriors lanced him until he was a bloody pincushion. His inhuman vitality kept him alive long after any other creature would have been dead, but finally he died.

Only Krizzan the Prophet fought effectively. With his dragon-bone staff, given him by the renegade god Hothum of the Dark Places, he laid waste to the area around him. His back to the wall of the headman's stone house, he shot ball lightning at his enemies, slaying some and injuring many more.

The prophet took Yuthman out of the fight early, exploding a ball of lightning at his feet. He was flung high, bounced against a stone wall, and came down unconscious. When the smith came to, he found Krizzan fighting nearby—and more than holding his own. Dead and unconscious foes littered the ground around him. Yuthman staggered to his feet and charged at the prophet. There was the sound of breaking bone as Krizzan was caught between this human sledgehammer and the wall.

By a desperate effort of will the prophet held on to his staff. He knocked Yuthman on the head and the smith dropped as though poleaxed. Holding his broken ribs with one hand, the prophet raised his staff with the other. Wheezing and gasping, he tried to say a word of power. A Shimeeri youth grabbed the pot of bitter brewed tea boiling on the nearby fire, ran forward, and tossed it in Krizzan's face.

The prophet screamed and dropped his staff as the scalding liquid scorched his face and went into his open mouth. A Yitheni swordsman tried to cut him down. Krizzan threw out a hand to save himself. The blade sliced through his wrist and then into his throat. The prophet fell to the ground, blood spurting from his wounds, and looked up at his slayer. He tried to scream a curse from his ruined throat, but with a convulsive shudder he died.

Instantly his dragon-bone staff began to glow. In moments it was white-hot, and waves of its furnacelike heat forced back the crowd surrounding the dead prophet. They retreated, dragging Yuthman and their other wounded with them. The staff began making popping sounds; then smoke poured from it, filling the air with the stench of burning flesh. The heat suddenly grew greater and the staff turned black and began to expand.

"Run, you fools!" someone roared.

With a boom and an intense flare of light the staff exploded. Many of those fleeing were picked up or knocked over by the shock wave. Bodies flew through the air and bounced along the ground.

When the survivors picked themselves up and looked where the dead prophet had lain, they saw a scene of devastation. A crater lined with glowing slag now occupied the place where he had made his stand. The stone building behind him had been leveled and now was only a mass of broken rock. Overhead a huge cloud of black smoke was slowly dispersing.

The scene faded from the pool. An unsmiling Goddess tossed another pebble in and a new image quickly formed.

Six clans of Red Branch Zenori were in battle formation on the ridge which bordered the Well of Shimeeros on the north side. Facing them were Aku and his troops—mostly of the Kri Rithi and Kri Yitheni tribes, and well seasoned by war. Behind them the troops who had attacked the prophet and his Yartazi warriors were reforming.

The commander of the Zenori troops looked at Aku's army and apparently didn't like the odds: He was outnumbered by about three to two. He looked toward the Well of Shimeeros, considering. The prophet's murder of their previous commander, several days earlier, had not sat well with the Red Branch clans; he was not going to ask them to avenge his slayer—especially one who had proved so incompetent. This Aku, now, seemed like a man destiny had touched. The commander signaled to one of his kinsman to ride forward with him and parley.

The image faded. The Goddess tossed another pebble into her pool of seeing. The waters rippled and a new vision swiftly formed: Zadar Kray in his tent holding council with his captains.

"The streets of Kimbo-Dashla will become rivers of blood," Zadar Kray was screaming. "Its children will burn on my brother Zuthra's pyre." He turned to one of his captains. "Send a messenger to Kas Makulla. Tell him to send the Black Branch clans to Kimbo-Dashla. Also, tell him to hold the Pass of the Three Winds against the outlander Aku."

"You'll cut our throats if you do that," protested one of his captains, a battle-scarred Kilbri named Raz Hakeem. "We can destroy Aku if we attack him with our full forces. Forget Kimbo-Dashla for now. Destroy this outlander and we can take the city at our leisure. With war in the north and the emperor dying, the Rithians will leave the southern border to fend for itself."

"My brother must be avenged!" roared Zadar Kray. There was fire and brimstone in the glare he threw Raz Hakeem.

The Kilbri, a tall lean veteran with one eye, was not intimidated. "I say avenge him—but destroy our greatest danger first."

"Greatest danger." Zadar Kray sneered. "That incompetent outlander would be dead now if the Red Branch clans hadn't deserted to him."

"Only six had gone over to him until you massacred the Beni Kam and Beni Hojana clans."

"Those traitors," Zadar Kray stormed, "were just waiting for a chance to join their kindred. The Zenori aren't worth spit anyway, and their Red Branch clans are not even worth that. We are well rid of them."

Raz Hakeem retorted, "A sword is a sword. I'd rather our enemies have as few as possible." He paused and gathered his temper. "What's done is done. But we should battle Aku while we outnumber him. As long as he is undefeated, his army will continue to grow. What good will it do to take Kimbo-Dashla and have doom catch us in the rear?"

"We will destroy Kimbo-Dashla," Zadar Kray thundered. "Then we will destroy what rats are left."

Raz Hakeem went white with fury. "You're a fool and you'll take us all with you." He turned on his heel and stalked out.

Zadar Kray glowered after him. He motioned toward the door with an almost imperceptible movement of his head. One of his guards, a Yartazi of the yellow-snake brotherhood, slid out the door after the one-eyed captain. Zadar Kray turned a questioning eye to his other captains, but none dared dispute him.

The scene shifted: It was night and a man lay dead in a gully. A beam of moonlight caught his face, illuminating the yellow snake tattooed above his right eyebrow.

Another pebble hit the water. From the ripples emerged the Pass of the Three Winds. It was mid morning and Kas Makulla waited at the head of the pass for Aku to attack. He sat proud and arrogant in his saddle as though victory already was his. Plainly he expected Aku and his army would have to come up the throat of the pass and through the Standing Stones before they could come to grips with his army of White Mountain Kilbri. History was on his side; more than once armies had become disorganized as they came through the Standing Stones—huge roughhewn basalt monoliths erected by some forgotten people—and were slaughtered on the other side before they could regroup. Behind him massed his White Mountain Kilbri poised to strike the main blow. On the hillsides to left and right were Jadghuli and Yartazi light cavalry ready to strike at the enemy's flanks.

Aku's army drew up in battle array at the foot of the pass and slowly advanced. From his high post Kas Makulla looked at their banners and frowned. He saw the banners of the Kri Omphor, the Kri Yitheni, the Red Branch Zenori, and those of several lesser peoples. Hurriedly he called over one of his runners, a young kinsman, and barked out, "Get my bone-headed spymaster here on the double. Tell him there are no banners for the Kri Rithi."

Aku's troops started moving through the Standing Stones, the huge monoliths now seeming to wait like giant vultures for the feast to follow. As they approached the other side of the Standing Stones, Kas Makulla raised his arm. His Kilbri readied their weapons, waiting to charge when it dropped.

Aku and his warriors began to emerge from the Standing Stones, their line ragged and seemingly disorganized. Kas Makulla dropped his arm. Screaming their war cries, their rudhars' hooves sounding like rolling thunder, the White Mountain Kilbri rode forward like a human avalanche to bury their foes. It was an awesome sight that few in Aku's army would ever forget.

Aku motioned to the rider at his side, a barrel-chested warrior carrying a four-foot-long war trumpet. The warrior lifted the trumpet to his lips and blew a thunderous challenge. Aku's troops fell back to the Standing Stones, leaving the wide avenues between the stones empty.

Kas Makulla cursed when he saw his Kilbri charge down these avenues and then go crashing to the ground by the hundreds as their mounts tripped over the ropes that suddenly stretched from stone to stone. The trumpet sounded again and Aku's tribesmen attacked. Then it sounded once more.

This time it was answered: From Kas Makulla's rear came the piercing blare of a hundred war trumpets. The Kri Rithi had come.

The image faded, another pebble hit the water, and one final scene appeared in the Goddess's pool of seeing:

Aku and Yuthman the Smith were riding through the field of battle. Everywhere were the dead and dying; the scarred ground was black with their blood and the air foul with the stench of their excrement. Vultures waddled along the ground, stuffed with the flesh of the vanquished and the victors. Here and there women and children moved across the battlefield, giving aid to their wounded and collecting their dead—and cutting the throats of any foemen still alive.

"Here's another battle won," Aku said wearily. "Fighting them is no problem; it's the aftermath I can't take. Each one sickens me, and then I go on to the next one." He looked about and gave a tired sigh. "It's what I do best—that's my damnation."

The smith mulled over Aku's words. "The empire needs a few bastards like us. Someone to do the dirty work, someone to be sneered at, someone to give the empire's citizens the peace they crave."

"I wish I had some of that peace," Aku said bitterly. "Some day we'll be angels and love one another." He scowled. "By then I'll be dust, long forgotten."

"It's those idiots in Dar-Esh-Rith who got us into this mess," Yuthman said angrily. "If they'd attended to business instead of stabbing each other in the back the fire would have been put out while it was only sparks. The way to use an army is to have it around to rattle sabres. Makes the vermin think twice, keeps the bloodletting to a minimum, and saves money."

His words cheered Aku, who shook his head and laughed. "You're something, smith. I don't know what, but you're as crazy as the rest of us. It would be nice if things worked the way you say. They don't, though. If there is a way for mortals to screw things up, they will, no matter how good their intentions. If we all worked together we'd have the peace and love we want. But we don't, and I doubt we ever will. There's just too many ornery cusses in this world." He paused, thought a moment, and added, "Maybe we all are ornery cusses."

Yuthman gave a snort. "I don't want that junk. I want a few brawls, more than my share of worldly goods, and something to hate. Don't get me wrong, I want peace and love when I have the time. You study philosophy, like I did, and you find that's what life is all about anyway."

Aku nodded. "I want that, but I want more. Something that satisfies." An image struck his fancy. "You must have been one hell of a philosophy student. These old white-bearded geezers who teach that stuff aren't much for bare knuckles and beer.''

Yuthman laughed. ''You'd be surprised.'' He sighed and said ruefully, ''Those were the days—not that I lasted long. I don't know whether it was my commonsense ideas or the naked whore in my room that got me booted out. Probably the ideas.''

He uncorked his canteen and took a swig of water. Almost immediately he shuddered and spit it out. ''This slop will kill me if I drink much more of it. Let's head for Tam Yarber. Barebottom Babya has the best wine this side of Kimbo-Dashla, not to mention some hussies who can really take you for a ride.''

''What will your wife say?'' Aku shouted as they started off at a gallop: The smith and his wife had a storied marriage.

''What she always says: good riddance,'' Yuthman shouted back.

''You'll lose her if you don't watch it.''

''I'd never be that lucky.''

Aku stopped briefly at his headquarters to give orders. ''Have the troops assemble at Tam Yarber. Get the supply train and the wounded moving toward there as soon as possible.'' Then he, Yuthman, and his personal troops rode swiftly toward the hills to Barebottom Babya's. The stench of death, the moans of the wounded, and the heartfelt curses of overworked surgeons were left behind, forgotten until the next time.

The Goddess stared quietly at her pool, fingering the few pebbles still left in her hand. She blew softly on these remaining pebbles and dropped them to the ground as she murmured, ''Death be kind, for we are not.''

16

SANDY and the Craxidour walked up a broad curved marble stair, chatting amiably. Anala tagged along at their heels, trying to make sense of their conversation and getting more irritated all the time.

"What's he saying?" she finally demanded.

Sandy looked back over his shoulder and said something.

"Idiots!" Anala muttered. She sped up and stepped on Sandy's heels.

He stopped and turned to face her. "Now what do you want?"

"I want to hear what you say—I want to understand it. Not be fobbed off with some mumbled mush you say to the walls."

"I said that the Craxidour is taking us to see his old granny. He's supposedly head of this clan of ningerlings, but I think she has the last word around here. He says she is a sort of seer and wants to take a reading of our future."

He started up the stair again. The Craxidour fell in beside him, an amused smile on his face.

Anala trotted after them, muttering under her breath. "Now we have to see some batty old crone. The world might be coming to an end and he has time for tea, cookies, and petty foretellings."

When they reached the head of the stairs, the Craxidour turned left and led them to a door of honey-colored wood. Every inch of the door was covered with carvings, filling all available space and yet looking uncluttered. This was elf work, not ningerling work; the work of a master craftsman.

Sandy looked at the carvings, enjoying the artistry which had gone into them. Gradually he realized they told the legend of Ithandar and Anishayanda. There was the silver harp, the Fields of Dream, the tears of the Goddess, and the fatal cup of wine.

The Craxidour knocked. There was a whisper which spoke to the mind and not the ear saying *enter* in a high elvish tongue and not the ningerling dialect.

The door swung open on silent hinges and they went in.

Sitting at a round table of blue spicewood, its top inlaid with silver and mother-of-pearl, was the Craxidour's grandmother. Here was no ningerling, but one of pure elfish blood. Where the Craxidour and his kin were knob-kneed and wiry, she was slender and graceful like a well-made dueling sword. Only her eyes were old—sad eyes which had seen the light of a thousand centuries. Otherwise she seemed an elfish maiden in the bloom of her youth, golden haired and with a beauty both otherworldly and yet warm and earthy.

Almost automatically Anala stepped forward and curtsied, then stepped back, not knowing quite what to say. Out of the corner of her eye she saw Sandy just standing there. Unobtrusively she kicked him in the ankle and in a barely audible whisper hissed, "Mind your manners."

The elf woman laughed softly. "He has no manners to mind. He is as he is and you must take him that way." Her voice was warm, sultry, and mysterious, like the air at midnight on midsummer's eve.

Anala blushed, glared at Sandy for getting her into this, and fumblingly tried to make amends. "I meant no disrespect, my lady, I just wanted him to be more—more—"

The elf woman smiled and said, "Sit down, child. I am Ishandis. Just take me as I am and you will find me no ogre." She motioned for Anala and Sandy to sit at the table with her.

Self-consciously, Anala slid into a chair to the left of Ishandis. Sandy stifled a smile and took a seat beside her, amused to see the lulzi speechless.

Ishandis nodded to the Craxidour. The old ningerling bowed and left the room. The elf woman placed her hands on the table, palms downward, and closed her eyes for a moment. When she opened them they had a freshness and excitement that hadn't been there before.

"For a year and more I could feel the whirlwind coming. Now it is almost upon us. You have come, and our life here will never be the same again. But that is always so. The world changes and not even the gods can put it back together as it was."

"We are just passing through," Anala protested. "Our quarrel is with Jara Greenteeth, not you."

Ishandis smiled sadly. "A frog croaks and a fish jumps; because the fish jumped a stone rolls; and because the stone rolls a mountain falls. Now the frog was not trying to make the mountain fall, but it fell nevertheless. So it is with life."

"In other words," Sandy said, "just our passing through is going to make the pot boil."

The elf woman gave a little laugh. "You have a way with words, man. You should be a lover instead of a warrior."

Sandy reddened at her jibe.

"Don't mind me," she said, touching his arm. "I like your words. Yes, the pot will boil. But it has been on the fire a long time. My ningerlings have an old feud with the shee; it is time accounts were settled. Your coming has only decided *when*. You will have our aid and more."

"More!" Sandy said.

Just then Anala jumped into the conversation, seeming more than a little miffed. A lulzi was the proper person to deal with a grand lady, not some lowly soldier. Besides, they were getting along too well. "We will take what help you will give, my lady." Anala's words were gracious, though she had to strain to make them so.

"It is not my help, though I will do what I can, but that of the ningerlings. They have suffered enough from the shee's enmity. Your coming has roused them. Messages have been sent not only to the other Yemsi clans, but to several other ningerling tribes as well."

"We haven't done anything yet," Sandy said.

The elf woman gave Sandy a strange look, an odd mixture of laughter and respect. She motioned toward Anala. "She is a lulzi and she slew the urgach—that is enough to make anyone notice. And my ningerlings see both what is there and what is beneath. Like their kinsmen the elves, they are hard to fool. And each of her companions is more than he seems. Even certain hard-bitten warriors might have done more than they speak about."

Before more could be said, they were interrupted by a nin-gerling maid carrying a silver tray. Sandy ran a appreciative eye over the way her figure was more undressed than covered by her clothes. She put the tray laden with a teapot and cook-ies on the table, curtsied, gave Sandy a sly wink, and hurried from the room.

Ishandis poured tea for them. "You should watch out for Yilla," she said. "She is looking for a good match and you seem a likely prospect."

"He's a good prospect for anyone who asks him," Anala said tartly. "Or anyone who doesn't ask him, for that mat-ter."

"Is that so?" Ishandis asked in a gentle and amused voice.

Sandy was perplexed. How had the conversation gone off on this tangent? True, he had a roving eye, but it was a pretty vice and they had more important things to talk about.

"Why have you invited us here?" he asked, trying to steer the conversation back to more pressing matters.

"To hear about your reputation," Ishandis said, thoroughly enjoying herself.

"What there is of it," Sandy grumbled.

The elf woman turned to Anala. "We will gossip later about our warrior. But, unfortunately, he is right. We have more important matters to see to first."

"If I have a reputation she shouldn't know it," Sandy said.

Anala gave a ladylike snort and turned up her nose.

"Sometimes I can catch glimpses of the future or what might be," Ishandis explained. "Already I sense that your future is fraught with peril, both for you and Zarathandra. If you would place your hands on the table, I will try to see more."

Anala nodded and placed her hands on the table, palms downward. Sandy hesitated and then reluctantly placed his on the table also. The elf woman placed her left hand atop An-ala's nearest hand and her right on Sandy's. Then she closed her eyes and concentrated.

Sandy felt a faint prickle traveling up his left arm. He looked at Anala and saw by her expression she was having the same experience. The prickle reached as far as his shoul-der and went no further, though he could feel feeble surges of power as it tried to push on.

Ishandis nodded to herself and opened her eyes. "Place

your other hand on hers," she instructed Sandy, "and complete the circle."

Sandy, his attention focused on the elf woman, casually placed his right hand on Anala's left hand. There was the faint crackle of static and he jerked away, uttering a mild curse.

Anala muttered, "Men," and grabbed his hand. Again there was a faint crackle. This time the circle stayed complete, both because her grip was like iron and Sandy knew what to expect.

"Close your eyes, blank your minds, and let your thoughts float." Ishandis's voice was soft and throaty, like the caress of a summer night's breeze. "Breathe calmly, breathe slowly." For a brief moment there was only the sound of their breathing. "Breathe slower—and slower," she said, her voice sinking from a whisper down to near silence.

An eerie hush settled over the room as they sat with closed eyes around the table, almost sleeping. Slowly a shimmer of water-blue light surrounded them. Barely a fraction of an inch high, it flowed over their skin, going from one to the other in a continuous and slow-moving circle. A faint but pungent aroma, like cinnamon spiced with ozone, filled the air.

Suddenly Ishandis gave a sigh, breaking the spell. As they opened their eyes, the bluish glimmer faded into nothingness and only a hint of an aroma lingered in the air.

She turned first to Anala and said bemusedly, "Lulzi you are and a lulzi you will be—great lulzi or lesser lulzi, the choice is yours. Perhaps you will be the first since the beginning to know who and what a lulzi is." For a moment she was quiet. "You shall find true love and remember it always. Happiness and sadness, you shall have both, though never as much of one as you would like and no more of the other than your share."

Anala looked bewildered and slightly vexed. "What of our quest? Is there nothing about that? I'm not looking for true love. That's for others. Lulzis have more important things to do than moon over some man."

Ishandis looked at Anala, and her eyes were sad with the hint of some ancient hurt in them. "Love comes; those who have it are blessed. Doubly blessed are those who keep it. You can be a lulzi and not love, but the lulzi who has love is greater. Much greater." Her tone changed, becoming sharper and less reflective. "As for your quest, I can only speak of what comes."

"What of me?" Sandy asked.

There was a mischievous tone in her words as she turned to him. "You shall have many blessings, some of which will arrive much sooner than you expect. You will love and be loved, lose and know sorrow, regret and yet never repent."

Sandy looked at her perplexed. This was like no fortune-telling he'd ever run across.

Ishandis spoke again, but now her tone was darkly brooding. "Death will come for you again and again, but never shall you be friends. Be true and you will be betrayed. Be false and you will have your heart's desire. Be yourself and you will have both."

She sighed and looked up at him, beautiful still, but in some indefinable way older. "You are like one I knew. Fey, with doom ever at your heels."

Sandy took a sip of his tea, savoring its delicate bitterness. "I already knew that," he joked grimly. "But we are all doomed. It's just that some of us die innocent, while the rest of us cheat the hangman for somewhat longer." He held his cup to the heavens and said, "Here's to a life worth the damning and a death worth the price."

Anala looked shocked. "No doubt you will sit on your coffin, getting drunk and making lewd jests at the redeemed, when doomsday comes."

"It's an idea."

Anala sniffed and turned to Ishandis. "Can you provide us with guides? We need someone to lead us to the door of the shee's dungeon."

"Zemmi has already chosen who will go with you. Now he has only the Sandcreeper sept to choose from, but in a few days he will have all of the Yimsi and probably two or three more ningerling tribes to aid you."

Anala looked puzzled. She hesitated for a moment and then asked. "Who is Zemmi?"

The elf woman gave a soft laugh. "That is my grandson. When he was young he was Zemmi. Now that he is the oldest tak among the Yimsi he is too important to have that name. He is the Tak Tak ab Craxidour." She smiled and added, "Though to some he will always be Zemmi."

"He doesn't seem part elvish," Anala said.

"He is where it counts," replied Ishandis, tapping her head and her heart. She went on casually, "Don't be too hard on your companions. They too have been touched by the Goddess, even the worst of them. Each in their own way was worthy to be chosen."

Anala flushed guiltily.

The elf woman rose from the table. When they started to rise, she held out her hand and said, "No. Keep your seats and enjoy the refreshments. I must go now, but I will see you tonight at the feast." Gracefully she turned and walked toward a silken tapestry covering the back wall of the room.

Sandy watched her go with an appreciative eye, drinking in her beauty with its mixture of unearthly elegance and earthy warmth. When she pulled aside the tapestry and disappeared through the door behind it, he gave a small sigh.

"She is not for the likes of you," Anala snapped. "Any man she took as a lover would have to be special, not some down-at-the-heels warrior looking for a rich wife."

Sandy grinned impishly. "It's nice to be wanted, even by a sprig who can't support me in the style I want."

Anala choked. "I didn't say that."

"You meant it."

"I didn't either."

Sandy poured himself more tea. "You should drink what you have in your cup before it gets too cold," he said conversationally.

"Don't change the subject. She is not one to give her love lightly. When she loves it will be with a passion you could not begin to understand."

"You know a lot about her for just having met her."

"I know of the great elves and of the way they think. I am not some untutored skirt-lifter; I am a lulzi, one who knows many things, seen and unseen."

Sandy sipped his tea and thought for a moment. "I don't want love; it hurts too much. She doesn't either. She's had her great love, lost it, and suffered. Now to dally . . . that is a different matter."

"For a simple soldier you know a lot."

"Even us common riffraff have our bits of hard-won knowledge."

Anala snorted. "You're an uncommon pain in the behind."

Sandy scratched his chin and said, "You know, I've always thought the same of you."

The lulzi threw up her hands in disgust. "I am not going to listen to any more of this rubbish. You can keep your mind in the gutter for all I care." Savagely she grabbed her cup of tea and took a swallow, then made a face as she tasted the lukewarm stuff. But doggedly she finished it; she would be damned if she would give him a chance to make some snide comment.

Sandy refilled her teacup. With a straight face he said, "It has a nice flavor, doesn't it?"

"I haven't decided." She changed the subject. "What are our chances of defeating the shee's minions and taking the dungeon door?"

"Better."

She listened, waiting to hear more. He just sipped his tea.

"Is that all you have to say? I could get more advice from a stone."

"There's not much to say." He finished his tea and then relented a little. "With the ningerlings' aid, I think we stand a good chance of taking the dungeon door. But it will be a small victory and we will have to get out of there fast, before the shee has a chance to strike back. We have to keep fighting our battles when and where we want, and never give her time to get organized. Still, getting to her will be hard, and that is the only way we can win."

"What are our chances of that?"

"Not so good." He paused as if he had said all he was going to. When he saw Anala was about to erupt, he went on, "She's been entrenched in this citadel for a long time. Who knows what nasty surprises she had dreamed up to take care of any foes that manage to slip in. If we can get a lot of help from the ningerlings, if we can sucker her out into the open, and if we are lucky, we just might have a chance."

"You'd make taking sweets from a toddler sound like a next to impossible task."

Sandy shrugged amiably. "If you are going to risk your neck, you have to be realistic about your chances and then go and do it anyway."

Anala gave him a puzzled look. He had a certain reputation along the border of being a bad man to tangle with. Very few of the renegades and reavers who had skirmished with him and his troops lived to fight another day. Yet he didn't look, talk, or act like a hero. Or, for that matter, the troublemaker some of the arm brass considered him. Also, rumor and gossip talked of him as a ladies' man, but he was only passably attractive and about as charming as an old shoe. Still, she had to admit, he was interesting.

Sandy tried to pour some more tea for himself, but only a few drops came out. "I'm going to talk to Hojeen. That old scoundrel has skulked about this citadel in the past. I'll see what he remembers about the guardroom and anything else that might help." He yawned. "Maybe I'll get some sleep first. It's hours until the feast tonight."

He got up and started to leave.

"How can you think of sleeping with so much going on?"

"Because I'm an old man who needs his sleep. Maybe you can march all day, party all night, and fight the next day without dozing off, but I can't. Besides, tomorrow comes at the same time whether you run toward it or sit and wait."

Anala realized she was as tired as he was, not that she would admit it. "No wonder the empire is going to pot, if its warriors like to bunk down as much as you do."

He yawned and smiled lazily. "If you ever join the army, you'll learn to appreciate hitting the sack." He started walking toward the door.

She called after him. "You won't get much sleep between the legs of that ningerling hussy."

Sandy stopped and stifled a yawn. "I hadn't thought of her," he mused. "Maybe after I have some sleep." He gave her wicked grin and went out the door.

Anala muttered something about a cantankerous old goat and went after him.

On the table, a bundle of white fur watched them go. Then it started nibbling on the cookies they had left behind, springles made from fine-sifted breadroot and frosted with sparkling sugar.

Sandy found his assigned quarters without any trouble: a long-neglected set of rooms which the ningerlings had refurbished for his use. A bit of dust and a cobweb here and there could still be found, but that was a great improvement over the state of his rooms in Kimbo-Dashla.

He headed immediately for the gigantic fourposter which dominated the bedroom. It was stacked chest-high with feather beds and at the head was a mountain of pillows. He yanked off his boots and jumped up onto it, meaning only to rest for a short time, but in less than a minute he was snoring away.

Bemusedly, Sandy walked and walked and walked some more. Seeing nothing, hearing nothing, feeling nothing; just knowing he must go on. Gradually his senses awakened and he began to be aware of his surroundings. It was a world without boundaries, stretching to the end of eternity and beyond; a place of mists, shadows, and shifting light.

Suddenly he stopped and glowered, fully awake and furious. "Now, where am I?" It looked like a dream world or some type of hell—a miserable place.

He looked around, trying to figure out where to go next. Now that he was aware what he was doing, he was lost. He sensed a cold and snaky something to his left. Sandy hesitated for a moment and then caught a whiff of butterscotch and spice coming from down below.

He looked down at his feet, staggered drunkenly, and quickly looked away. As far as he could tell, he was standing on a misty nothingness—a nothingness even less substantial than air. He sneaked a peek with his left eye and the bottom dropped out from under his feet. Frantically he looked for something to grab on to. The moment he wasn't watching where he was standing, he was no longer falling. Screwing up his courage, he carefully looked downward. He sank to his knees in whatever he wasn't standing on.

After a little experimentation he got the hang of staying or moving where he wanted. All you needed to do was believe there was something under your feet and not pay close attention to what you walked on. Even so, he still had a distressing tendency to sink if his mind wandered.

He felt a cold chill and shivered. The unending nothingness surrounding him tasted blacker, like that eerie green-black before a storm.

Once again he caught a whiff of that sweet and spicy odor he had noticed before. He headed toward it. Moments later he realized he hd passed it, and turned back. He stopped where the aroma was strongest and looked around. He could see nothing. Then he looked down. Far, far beneath his feet he could almost see something, though whether a difference in the light of a difference in the shape of the space, he wasn't quite sure.

Sandy tried to walk down toward what was below, but now the emptiness was as solid as rock under his feet. He muttered a few choice remarks and tried again, this time by relaxing, composing his mind, and thinking of the void under his feet as not existing. The right frame of mind should have let him drop through.

No such luck. The stubborn nothingness under him would not yield an inch.

"Damned ass-backward world." He glowered at emptiness and thought for a while. "If you can't fry fish in water, you try boiling them," he said to himself as he closed his eyes.

He let his mind float and then slowly sniffed the air. Immediately he caught the spicy aroma he sought. Slowly Sandy walked forward, letting his nose guide him. The awareness of up, down, forward, backward, and all other directions were booted out of his mind, letting only smell steer his course.

Gradually the aroma grew stronger. Soon the air had a pleasant warmth as it brushed his skin, and on its soft shoulders carried the perfume of flowers and the sun-cured odor of summer grass. Gravel crunched under his feet, grass swished against his boots, and the songs of a dozen different birds filled the air.

Sandy opened his eyes and immediately liked what he saw. This was the way a world should be, as common as clay and as real as the next minute.

"You took your time."

"You're damned lucky I came at all," growled Sandy. He turned to his left, toward the voice.

Beside a shallow pool, the Veiled Goddess lounged in the corner of a pew-shaped bench. As usual she wore a hooded robe, this one of pale blue silk sprinkled with tiny diamonds, and her face was hidden by the deep shadows of the hood.

The air surrounding her was redolent with the spicy butterscotch odor which had drawn him here. It came from a massive tree which grew beside the pool. The tree was in full bloom, bending under the weight of millions of trumpet-shaped flowers, each blossom three or more inches long. The blossoms varied from a pure virgin white to a pale ivory in hue, but the inner surface of each flower was tinted a rosy pink.

"I knew it had to be you," Sandy told her. "Anyone else would have done it the easy way and asked me."

"Would you have come?"

Sandy scowled. If she was going to be huffy, he could be too. "No."

"Who do you think you are, mortal?"

"I don't know and I don't care," he snapped. "All I know is that I was dead on my feet and you drag me here. Of all the goddesses in all the worlds, I had to get you. The desert folk treat their dogs better than you treat me. At least they throw them a bone once in a while and let them to their snoozing!"

The Goddess bounded to her feet and strode toward him like a mad elephant. "Snoozes!" she said bitingly. "If you serve me, you don't have time for snoozes." She raked him with scornful eyes.

Sandy didn't back down an inch. "I didn't volunteer for the job," he replied. "I'm stuck with it since you won't take *no* for an answer, but that doesn't mean I have to like the bloodletting or give up common comforts to please you."

"But at least you could be good at it," she raged. "What kind of quest is this where you dawdle along the way? By the time you get to the shee, your companions will be dead of old age."

"We'll get the damned thing done," Sandy muttered. "We don't have much choice. Not the way you have been finagling around." As if an afterthought had struck him, he added, "And she *is* an ancient evil that should be removed from Zarathandra."

The Goddess stared at him. "You have the morals of a Shardakkan lawyer. No, less. At least they shed a tear when they send an innocent man to the headsman."

"I do things my way," he said stubbornly. "If you don't like it, get some other poor sucker to do your dirty work." He waited for an answer. When it didn't come, he went on, "Who knows what right and wrong are or if they are unchanging? I don't. I serve you in my way because you are more right than any other I could serve. Maybe you are always on the side of the angels, but you haven't proved it to me."

"You question me!" she screamed.

There was a thunderous silence and then he nodded almost imperceptibly.

"I will remember this," she said in an unnaturally quiet voice. "There will be a day when you will pay for your lack of faith."

Sandy gave a tired shrug. "You're not my god."

"You're a heathen who believes in nothing."

A stormy and uncomfortable silence settled over the world around them. Destiny and magic had brought them together and forged a whole that was greater than either one. Both had profited from this trick of fate; the Goddess by regaining a human part of herself her great enemy Kels Zalkri had destroyed, and Sandy by becoming something more than human. Yet it was an uncomfortable union.

The Goddess looked him over and gave a dissatisfied sniff. "At least you could look like something." She made an offhand motion with her hand. "That's better."

Sandy looked puzzled at her and shifted uneasily on his feet. He frowned and looked down. He was wearing narrow-toed boots, the mahogany leather finely tooled with intricate designs.

"Where did I get these damned things?" he asked, surprised. He distinctly remembered taking his boots off before he flopped on the bed.

"They look good on you."

"Maybe they do, but they feel terrible. My toes feel like they've been crammed into a sardine can."

"Then you don't need them," the Goddess said, miffed. She made a motion with her hand. Instantly the boots were gone, along with the rest of his clothes.

Sandy looked down at himself and then opened his mouth to give her the back side of his tongue.

The Goddess beat him to the punch. "Your dawdling must stop. When you return, rouse your companions and get on with the quest." She didn't wait for an answer, but turned around and was gone.

Sandy stewed silently for a moment and then gave vent to his ire. "That dirty-minded harridan! She'd do anything to get the last word."

He turned around to go back the way he had came. He saw a path of crushed stone, but nothing that looked like the never-never land he'd come from. He looked about and saw a couple more paths and noticed how well kept the parklike landscape was, but got no hint which way to go.

With a disgusted shrug he started heading back along the path of crushed rock—but not for long. He gave a curse and hopped over to the grass alongside the path. Cursing under his breath, he picked pieces of stone from the bottoms of his feet. Still cursing, he started walking on the grass bordering the path. After hobbling a few steps, he stopped, looked at his sore feet, and headed for the pool.

Sandy sat down on the tiled edge of the pool next to the tree and eased his sore feet into the water. He sighed with pleasure; the cool water felt good on his bruised feet. Soon the pain was replaced by a pleasant tingling. He leaned back against the tree and started drifting off to sleep, while a small fish nibbled at his toes.

Suddenly the image of the Goddess appeared, floating in the air over the middle of the pool. "How dare you defile my pool of seeing? I commanded you to return to your companions."

Sandy reluctantly pulled his feet from the water and got to his feet. "It's just a pool. You don't drink from it. Besides, how about the fish swimming in it—don't they defile it?" In a sharper voice he added, "You didn't say which way to go."

"You're no child who has to be led by the hand. You found your way here, you can find your way back." Her image broke into millions of shining motes that disappeared to the four winds as a gust of air smote them.

As the image blew away, he heard one last comment from her. "Death is the price of such sacrilege—and you shall pay it."

"Here we go again," Sandy said, disgruntled. "Hasn't she killed me off enough as it is?" He started walking in what he hoped was the right direction. "Her priestesses babble about her justice and her love for mankind," he said, giving a snort. "They should see her when she's in a bitchy mood."

After a while Sandy saw that he wasn't getting anywhere except to another part of this park or garden. It had a wild and eerie beauty that soothed the soul and made the heart glad, but he had no time for it now. Still, he would have to return sometime to soak his feet in her pool again. He smiled at the thought: She would start spitting tacks when he did it. Then he closed his eyes, turned his mind to the nowhere place he had been before, and started walking again, trusting his feet to lead him the right way.

He shivered and opened his eyes. Mist and shadows surrounded him, so he was back where he wanted to be. Shivering again, he threw his arms about himself. He didn't remember it being this cold before. Damn her and her petty spite, he thought. How would she like to be freezing her tush off?

"If I'm dreaming, I should be able to dream up some clothes," he said, thinking out loud. He concentrated hard, trying to clothe himself with imagination. However, his mind refused to be fooled by him.

He closed his eyes and tried again. In moments he felt warmer, felt garments covering his body. He opened his eyes to see how successful his conscious dreaming had been—and made a sound of disgust. His body was wrapped in fog, which now started to disappear.

A drop of sweat ran down his face and he realized that what passed for a climate in this strange land had taken a tropical turn. He looked about and wasn't sure he liked the change. The shadows were deeper and what light there was had a greenish tinge.

Ahead of him, where the shadows and mists were blackest, he caught a hint of movement. As he watched, he saw a figure walking toward him. It seemed to be coming from the far ends of eternity, yet he could see a distinct outline. The sight of it chilled his heart and made the hair at the back of his neck prickle. Instinctively he knew that the fearsome figure was Jara Greenteeth.

He stood his ground and waited. There was nowhere to run to, nowhere to hide. He grinned blackly to himself. However this came out, it would not be an encounter well met.

The mist thinned and she came through it to face him. She stopped about ten feet away and looked him over. The shee didn't seem to be much impressed.

Sandy was very much impressed, and scared down to his toes. The shee was an imposing figure. She was tall, slim, and regal, looking every inch a goddess. Her smiling teeth were ivory with the slightest hint of emerald, her hair greenish black and trailing like sea foam down to her heels, her skin a creamy green satin beaded with tiny scales, her eyes midnight black and strangely sorrowful, and her lithe body full and yet graceful. She wore a long dress of buttermilk-white silk, the filmy material clinging and emphasizing every curve.

She was breathtakingly beautiful, the kind of beauty that sends shivers down the spine and makes poets weep. It was like cold marble, yet Sandy could feel hot passion smoldering beneath the surface. Her beauty reminded him of the Goddess's, and he would have been hard put to say who was the more comely. She didn't have the earthy bawdiness of the Goddess, but radiated a carnal heat that set his loins on fire despite the fear nibbling at his gut.

"So you are one of the heroes the old bitch has set on my tail," she sneered. Her voice was soft and sang like silver bells, despite the harsh words. "She must be getting desperate."

"A sow's ear can be as deadly as a dragon's claw at times."

An involuntary smile flashed across her face. "You're not quite that bad." A note of reluctant approval was in her voice. She raked him with her eyes, lingering over his naked charms.

Sandy flushed. He didn't mind the lustful glances of some wench he had been dallying with, but this was different, because he hadn't shucked his clothes willingly. Silently he damned the Goddess again: It's hard to stand up to someone when everything is hanging out. Defiantly, he stuck out his chest and faced her with his legs spread. If she was going to look, let her get a good look.

"I like you, man. Must we be foes?"

Sandy thought for a moment. "It's the way it is. You are on one side and I am on the other. I won't change and I don't think you will." The words came hard, as he couldn't take his eyes off her, fascinated by the ruddy nipples showing through the gauzy material of her dress and the dark triangle peeking at him from down below.

"Am I that fearsome?" she asked cajolingly. "Am I that terrible? Have my deeds been any worse than hers? Who has slaughtered more people?"

Sandy did not know what to say in reply. Right and wrong was a shifting ground; they were mixed together in such complicated ways that not even Amaz-Migon the All-Knowing could sort them out completely. All anyone could do was make choices and act according to his heart. If that damned him, it was worth the price. Of course, some people would let others make their choices—but they weren't worth the damning.

Sandy voiced what he felt the best he could. "With her, you can be a little man and be valued. With you, a man has to be a mover and shaker or he's part of the great mass who just follow and aren't worth a tinker's damn."

Her face clouded over with fury. "What do you know of right and the wrongs I have suffered? You have never been denied your rightful place. You have never had immortality stolen from you, forcing you to scavenge life from others just to enjoy your birthright. When I gain the godhead which is mine I too can create peace and reward the righteous; there will be no more of the bloodshed, lies, and double-dealing that's forever been my bane. Give me power and I can be loving, kind, and benevolent. All a mortal could wish for in a goddess."

"And forgiving," Sandy added.

At his words, the shee became abruptly calm. She paused to turn the idea over in her mind. "No, not that," she said in a cold, thoughtful voice. "There should only be right."

Sandy shrugged. "Then we will always be on opposite sides. There has to be some place in life for wrongheadedness and foolishness. And a chance to do it right the next time."

The shee laughed derisively. "You're a dreamer, and dreamers always lose. Dreams rub against reality and are shredded. Maybe it will happen today or maybe in a year or ten years, but it will always happen."

Sandy felt himself getting cold again, either from the climate or the company. Whichever, it was time to go. He decided to back out of the situation gracefully. "I am no dreamer, but that is neither here nor there," he said. "My body wakens and I must go. I've enjoyed our talk and maybe we can chat again sometime." He thought of his bed and started to fade away.

"Hold!" commanded the shee.

Sandy's body obeyed and he solidified again on the plane of reality he'd tried to escape, much to his annoyance. A weird commanding look came into her eyes and against his will he felt an intense lust for her.

"I did not bid you go," Jara Greenteeth said, stepping closer. Her teeth gleamed greenly white between her parted lips. "If I will it you are dead, mortal. You have few choices. Bend your knee or bend your neck to me."

The ultimatum just made Sandy stubborn. This, combined with the fear freezing his blood and the passion she had unleashed in his loins, made him bold.

"So I'm dead. But I will be damned if I will bow my knee to you. You can flaunt your pretty piece at me, you can show those long teeth, you can threaten to suck me dry, but I'll stay what I am." He exposed his neck and loins to her. "Here, wet your whistle."

The shee hesitated, put off guard by his stubborn defiance. She was used to mazing the minds of even the strongest men and bending them to her will. She took what she wanted from her lovers and went on to others when she had had her fill. Sandy frustrated her like a wayward wind she could get to blow any way she wanted for a moment, but could never capture. The more she enthralled him, the less he was hers.

"You are a brave man," she said as she slowly unfastened a gold pin holding her dress together at the left shoulder. "Most would only stare in horror if I came their way." The pin came loose and the dress fell away from her shoulder, exposing the upper part of her breast.

Her unearthly allure and his fascination for naked women kept his eyes on her. "I've had a vampire come on to me before," he said as he watched her graceful fingers play with the gold pin on her right shoulder.

"There are vampires and there is Mem-Jara-Shil, just as there are dragonflies and there are dragons." Her voice was soft and throaty with a faint echo of silver bells. It soothed his fears and sent small fiery thrills dancing along his spine.

Sandy watched the top of her dress slowly shimmy down her body, enjoying himself even though he was being set up for the kill. She had good reason to be proud of what she exposed, and her broad red-brown nipples sat perkily atop breasts even Venus would have envied.

"The vampire died."

"You threaten me, mortal?" the shee said, sidling closer.

"I only slew her mate. She just died." He would have said more, but became fascinated by the way she fumbled at the gold belt around her waist.

"I am deathless." Her belt came loose and she dangled it provocatively in front of him while her other hand lightly held her dress at the waist. As the belt slipped from her fingers, her silken dress slowly slithered over her hips, down her thighs, past her knees, finally settling around her ankles. She stepped out of her dress and into his arms. Gently she rubbed her nipples across his chest and brushed his loins with her bush.

A tiny corner of Sandy's mind told him, *Now you've had it.* He ignored it. The lust she had so skillfully aroused was running rampant.

The shee lightly bumped her belly against him, teasingly pulled it away, and then rubbed it gently across his stand. Sandy responded in kind, too far gone to mind the consequences. He pulled her to him, pressing his chest against hers. The shee held him tenderly in her arms, her skin soft and slippery, but her muscles locked in an unbreakable grip. With lips welded together and tongues darting in and out, he delved and she spanned as they fought the old battle. . . .

As she brought him to a point of unbearable ecstasy, her lips slid down to his neck. Panting with passion, she sank her teeth into his neck. Sandy never noticed. Then they were beyond the point of no return and great shudders shook them.

The shee screamed with pleasure as the fires of Sandy's life gushed into her from both above and below. Then she screamed again: a scream of horror.

Sandy sat bolt upright, scared out of his wits by his nightmare, especially the last and most horrible part. Rivers of sweat rolled down his body, drenching the bed. A shudder shook his body as he remembered the dream. Only the last terrible instant remained hidden, and he knew he never wanted to find it, ever.

Sandy wiped his brow. When he looked down and realized he was naked, he began shaking again. The nightmare had been too real; he remembered falling asleep and that he had only shucked his boots. He looked upward and said vengefully, "I hope it was worth it, because, by damn, I'm going to get it out of your hide someday."

He stood up and went over to the table which stood by the bed. On top were a pitcher and basin, both made from a creamy bluish-white stoneware. Sandy lifted the pitcher and drank great gulps from it, easing a throat that seemed parched into leather. He stood holding the pitcher for a moment and then lifted it over his head and upended it. The feel of the water was bliss, as it not only washed away the sweat, but also the grime he felt coating his body and soul.

He found a towel and began wiping himself dry. Behind him the door of the bedroom opened slowly. A head peeked through, the eyes becoming big and shining as they took in his well-muscled body. The door opened a crack wider and the ningerling maid, Yilla, slide into the room. Softly she closed the door behind her.

She watched him for an instant longer, then with a quick motion she flipped off her light cotton smock, kicked off her slippers, and tiptoed up behind him. She ran a caressing hand down his arm.

Sandy let out a yell and jumped a foot, whirling in the air to land facing her. "What are you doing here?" he shouted, quickly wrapping the towel around his waist.

Yilla stood facing him, completely unabashed. "I thought you might have need of me," she said provocatively. She smiled and cupped her small breasts in her hands for him to see.

"Lord!" he groaned. "When did I say anything about that?"

"Didn't, but Yilla knows. The Goddess has touched you. Throwing a leg over you is a way of worshipping her."

Sandy stared open-mouthed for an instant. "Bullshit! If you want to come on to me, why don't you just say so."

Yilla grinned. "I like big men. Now will you lay me down?"

"No!" Sandy said emphatically. Her wise innocence was a refreshing change from the shee, but he was in no shape or mood for it—at least he thought he wasn't.

"Oooh," she said as his towel slipped for a moment.

"Stop this," Sandy said. "I'm worn down to nothing and I don't go robbing cradles."

"No worry," Yilla said. "I've had three babies." She looked impishly at him. "Looks like you need to be worn down again."

Sandy looked around for his clothes and a way to back out gracefully—or just to back out. He edged around to the far side of the bed to see if he had any clothes there. Yilla closed in, and too late he realized he was boxed in between the bed and the wall.

"You big strong man," she said, running her fingers over his chest.

Sandy grabbed her upper arms and started pushing her toward the door. She gave a joyous squeal and bounced her hips at him. Sandy muttered a curse, realizing he no longer had the towel to protect him. Gritting his teeth, he marched her backward. He ran out of steam as they neared the door and stopped to regain his resolve; she did feel awfully good. Yilla jumped into the breach, sliding out of his grip and the next moment leaping up and wrapping her legs around his waist. Sandy started peeling her away from him, hoping his moral strength would hold out.

Sandy sat in a corner chair watching the ningerlings and his companions having a good time. He was so tired he could hardly move and hoped the festivities would soon be over. His companions had other ideas and seemed ready to dance, sing, drink, and eat all night.

Anala especially was filled with vigor. At the feast she had put away enough food for two grown men. She had joined in immediately when the dancing started and had danced every dance so far and was still going strong. He shook his head. Even as a teenager, he hadn't had that kind of energy. Someday she was going to run some unlucky buck right into the ground.

The feast itself had gone well. The butter popovers and the plum-roasted duck had been especially delicious, not that he'd had much of an appetite after his adventures that afternoon. At least they had got their plans set for the next day. The Craxidour had said they would be leaving at the crack of dawn, though Sandy wondered how you could tell dawn from dusk around here. He hadn't seen daylight since dropping into the dungeon.

"Hey, sleepyhead," a voice yelled at his ear. Sandy jerked awake and saw Anala standing front of him.

"I don't know what has come over you," she said. "You sleep all afternoon and can hardly keep your eyes open."

"I had some hard dreams."

Anala's eyes widened and she whispered, "You saw her too. Hojeen and Shamdad said they dreamed of her. I was scared stiff and hating her, yet her offer seemed so fair and reasonable. It came hard, but I was glad I turned her down." She made a face and added, "You should have seen the fit she threw when I told her so." She fell silent for a moment. "She is so evil, so evil. Yet there *is* something about her." Anala paused, trying to find the right word.

"Sad," Sandy prompted.

The lulzi nodded. "So sad and lost."

Sandy gave a derisive snort. "Whatever she is, she is not lost."

"We will talk of our dreams later." Anala looked impatiently over her shoulder. "They are ready to start the yallodand. I need you to dance with me."

"What is the yallodand?" Sandy asked.

"You don't know *anything*, do you? It's the big dance of the evening. Everybody gets into a big circle, the men in the center and the girls on the outside. The lead couple starts weaving a serpentine pattern across the dance floor and we all follow them. It's fun, especially when the pattern gets so complex it breaks down and you have dozens of different lines constantly joining and breaking apart. You're always losing your partner and picking up new ones."

Sandy remarked dryly, "It sounds like a great mess to me. I have enough trouble sorting out my left foot from my right. I'll sit this one out."

"You've sat out every dance tonight."

"I can't dance and I don't like making a fool of myself. Besides, I'm too tired to lift a foot."

Anala gave him a determined look. "No more of the fool than you have ever been." Without warning she stomped on his toe.

Sandy yelled, hopped to his feet, and grabbed at her. Anala evaded his groping arms, stepped inside his reach, put her one arm around his waist and the other in his hand, and danced out toward the middle of the floor with him.

There were whistles and cheers from the ningerlings. Hojeen let loose a great hootenanny holler and the dance started.

"Just watch my feet," Anala said. "Like this. Three steps, hop, and slide. And once in a while you whirl around."

Sandy followed her lead and shortly was doing as well as his partner. He was even enjoying himself.

"I thought you couldn't dance."

Sandy grinned. "It's a secret. You never get to sit if the ladies know you can put your right foot forward at the right time."

Somewhere along the line—Sandy wasn't quite sure when—he lost Anala in the swirl of dancers going every which way. He paired with an older ningerling lady for a while, though you'd never have guessed her age from her winking eye and saucy tongue. For a while he danced with a shy lass who must have been all of eight. She had all the steps right, but hadn't learned all the clinching and casual body bumping her older sisters had down to a science. It was fun letting her act the grand lady.

There was a confusing moment when several groups of dancers all converged at one spot. When they split apart, Sandy found himself with a new partner: the elf woman, Ishandis.

She was an elegant dancer and though he knew he was good, Sandy felt like a bull stumbling through a china shop. There wasn't the rowdy good time as with some of his other partners, yet he rather enjoyed the cool and distant way she partnered him. In some manner it was more titillating than the open bawdiness the ningerling wenches favored.

As they danced they came near an arched doorway. Gracefully and without missing a step, Ishandis maneuvered him through it.

"Come," she said, taking his hand. "I must talk to you."

She led him up a broad marble stair, each tread inlaid with warriors of green jade fighting innumerable ruby stone beasts. As was everything in this ningerling hold, it was grand and slightly decrepit with age. Many warriors and beasts were missing heads, limbs, or entire bodies. Here and there pieces of the missing stone lay in the cracks and crannies of the staircase.

Ishandis saw him looking at the worn and ancient figures. "The Shooni built this part of the citadel. They were a fierce folk who loved fighting and lived life to the full." She sighed sadly. "They are long gone, destroyed during the War of the Three Twins. I can remember when this stair was new. I was a child then. But the raiders came, and Ush-Mharra, the twelfth and last king of the Shooni, died on these stairs. He took a dozen of his foes with him, but the kingdom died that night.''

She sped up the stairs, as though trying to escape memory, and Sandy followed. A violent shiver shook him as he passed through a cold spot. Sandy turned around to look back and his heart jumped into his throat. A giant of a man stood there, half dressed, covered with bushy red hair, a notched sword in one hand, and dozens of bleeding wounds covering his body. An instant later he realized he could see through this ghastly figure. He shivered again and hurried after the elf woman.

Ishandis led him down a short corridor and then up a long winding stair. They emerged atop a stone platform, open on three sides. The fourth side contained the stairwell and a massive wooden door bound with strips of steel. The elf woman walked over to the stone rail bordering the platform and looked out. Sandy followed and stood beside her.

The air was slightly chill with the smell of coming rain in it. Sandy took deep breaths and watched the ragged clouds scudding across the sky. They were a black roiling mass of beasts fleeing the blind hunter and his wolves. For brief moments a star or bit of moonshine would peep through, to be quickly trampled under their charging feet.

Below a black velvet night enveloped the countryside. Ghostly fires flickered through this dark world, now flaring to dimly illuminate tangled forests, now fading to leave the thickets in profound blackness. To the left, ice-crowned mountains towered into the night, their white tops constantly strobe-lit by dancing bolts of blue lightning.

''I come up here often,'' Ishandis said, ''to watch and remember. It was a stormy night much like this when the shadow owls brought word of Ithandar's death and Anishay-anda was no more.''

Sandy nodded in understanding. ''You live long and you lose friends and those you love.''

''And enemies. You could almost wish they were alive again and your hate fresh.''

Sandy shrugged. ''I wouldn't know.''

Ishandis gave him a strange faraway look. ''You will. I

have seen glimpses of your future. You are blessed and damned as no other mortal man has been or will be. Eternity will be yours unless you are willingly betrayed by one who loves you."

Sandy gave a wry smile. "I would expect no less. The world is cruel and unforgiving. You see friends suffer and die and you wonder at the right of it. You tell yourself there must be some great rightness to this existence of ours and you never see it. Maybe you're blind or maybe there is nothing to see."

Ishandis shook her head and laughed softly. "What is Zarathandra coming to, with warriors who think about the meaning of life?"

Sandy gave a snort. "I'm only a warrior by misadventure. I had plans to be many things, but war and battle never entered my head." He stopped and thought. "And all of us ordinary knuckleheads sometimes wonder what it is all about."

Ishandis gave him a gentle smile. "There is a *geas* on you, a spell partly new and partly what was before."

Sandy started to question her, but a large drop of rain hit him in the mouth. Intermittent drops began hitting around them; soon more and more came.

"Come to my room and we will talk more," Ishandis said.

She turned and hurried to the steel-bound door.

Sandy ran after her. The last few steps were the worst, as torrents of rain mixed with hailstones tried to batter him into the floor. He felt like a drowned duck as he slammed the door behind him. The old-fashioned linen shirt and moleskin trousers Yilla had found for him dripped great puddles on the marble-tiled floor. He wrung out his hair with his hands and looked around for something to use as a towel.

Ishandis stood by a large walk-in fireplace of gray stone. She pointed to a door on the left side of the fireplace. "Strip off your wet clothes and go in there." She turned and went through a matching door on the other side of the hearth.

Sandy went through the door, undressed, and the next moment someone came up behind him and started rubbing him down. He turned and saw it was Ishandis. She was naked just like he was, but on her it looked a lot better.

Sandy looked around and saw he was in a bedroom, the bed large enough to hold a dozen couples. He looked at it again and then at Ishandis and silently cursed the Goddess. Ever since he had hooked up with her he'd had more than his share of bouts and bits, but his streak of luck in the last day couldn't be natural. She'd done something. Whatever devious scheme she had up her sleeve might be all for the good, but he was damned tired of her meddling in his life.

"I suppose we go to your bed and you jump my bones," he said to Ishandis.

The elf woman gave a soft laugh, unfazed by his irritation. "No, we come to know each other and find our way there." She stood before him, enjoying her nakedness and quietly flaunting it at him.

Sandy tried to gently push her away, but quickly yanked his hands away—her flesh was too warm and pleasantly yielding. "Let's not," he said. "Wait for another time, a time when the Goddess is not toying with us," arguing as much with himself as with her.

Ishandis shook her head in a gentle no. "It is our time, our fate. I waited once, but I will not wait again. Long ago I cast the runes and foresaw your coming. This is the Veiled One's will, but it is also my will."

"Everyone's except mine," Sandy fumed. "I don't mind going down and dirty, but I like to do my own choosing. Besides, I am no one to lose your heart to."

"Once I loved, and him I will never forget; but you are here and that counts the most. Memories and ghosts are poor company when you need a man between your legs." She ran a finger along his arm, just barely touching him, and he could feel goose bumps rearing up all over his body.

"No," he said.

"Yes—because you want me. Your mind says no, but your heart and soul say different." She reached out and took hold of his hand, bringing it back to rest on her bare flank.

Sandy started to pull his hand back and then said what the hell. He was enjoying her despite himself, so he might as well do some of the seducing and enjoy himself all the more.

He fondled her flank and quoted some words from "Of

Hymelli and the Rain,'' one of Junnanan's more printable and beautiful poems. She laughed, jiggled her breasts almost imperceptibly, and tweaked his chest hair. One thing led to another and a long night became too short to suit either of them.

17

THE Goddess sat on her ivory throne and smiled up at the night sky as she studied the configurations. The moon was waxing, the Warrior Star was in the thirteenth house, following on the heels of the Seven Sisters were a cluster of new-born stars, and the Lost Star lay within the mouth of the Serpent. The stars boded well for her plans.

Finally there seemed a way to break the bond that tied her to Sandy. He was very useful and sometimes more than merely bearable. But he shared the power that was rightfully hers. That must not be. The bond would be severed and him sent on his way. Still, it would be years before her plans could come to fruition. Until then she had need of him and the rights given her by destiny.

Her thoughts turned to the shee, and the Goddess smiled grimly. Jara had bitten at the bait and had tasted doom. This time the shee had drunk too deeply of life. She had sustained a wound which would eat at her, which would weaken her at the critical moment. She who despised lust and love would find there was a deadly magic in them.

The Goddess thought of the snares she had set and felt a troubling in her soul. She had become that self which was Omyssa, who was both mother and bawd, and had touched Sandy with the magic natural to that incarnation. Once Sandy met those she had set the snares for, nature only had to take its course. She had done what had needed doing; now she wondered if she had done what was right.

Her attention drifted to less bothersome matters. Along the

southern borders of the Rithian Empire events were shaping up well, going the way she wanted them to.

The Black Branch Zenori had turned on Zadar Kray at Kimbo-Dashla. The siege had been broken and the tribesmen still loyal to him had fled westward. Meanwhile, Aku of the Isles had won several small skirmishes. More importantly he had won the hearts of the desert men. From now on he would be a force to be reckoned with in the empire.

As for Zadar Kray, his future was bleak. He still had a formidable force under his command at the Dry Bone Hills, but nowhere near the strength of the forces available to Aku. He must win at the Dry Bone Hills or he would have no tomorrow. Many of the Kilbri now grumbled about his leadership and the way his uncle and cousins had been slaughtered. And the Jadghuli and the Yartazi were like beasts of prey, always ready to turn on a fellow wolf who had proved weak.

Zadar Kray was desperate, ready to call in anyone who would aid him. He had sought help from the Kri Shandri clans. But it was a long way from the central desert and their leaders were too canny to join a losing cause. As for Jara Greenteeth, he no longer had her ring, and the shee was in deeper trouble than he was. Only from Hothum of the Dark Places, the god he had bartered his soul to, could he be sure of help. And that the Goddess had planned for: It had been a long, long wait, but that evil being had finally stuck his neck out too far.

The Goddess picked up her dice, rolled them, and smiled when she saw the result. Destiny was going her way. Let her enemies beware.

18

SANDY, Hojeen, Shamdad, and Anala crouched on a dusty balcony overlooking a broad corridor. About two hundred paces to the right the corridor ended in a broad stair leading upward. To their left the corridor terminated in the steel door which sealed off the dungeons. In front of the door stood two of the undead. Their skins were pie-dough white and waxy looking, but their red-burning eyes were ever watchful.

Across the way were deserted balconies, twins to the one they were on. Below them, at corridor level, was the guard-room. It was a large stone-pillared room, open to the corridor and with several individual holding cells along its wall. At the back were two small staircases, leading upward. Between them was a massive wooden door. Scattered around the room were several tables. At one of them the guard commander and a companion sat swilling ale, refilling their tankards from the large keg sitting in the middle of the table.

The guard commander's companion was a huge man clad in leathers and a steel shirt. He was close to seven feet tall, with muscles that bulged and rippled under his clothes. He looked a fell opponent, but was dwarfed when compared to his drinking partner.

The guard commander was at least nine feet tall, but looked short because of his enormously broad body. He was as wide as three men and had a barrel chest the size of a hogshead. His troll blood was evident in the faint scaling of his skin and the arms that hung almost to his knees.

Sandy whispered instructions to his companions: "Use your fire arrows to take care of those two undead guarding the door first, then any other undead that show up. If you're any good as bowmen, the rest of us won't have to risk our necks fighting them.''

Anala whispered back, "Between us and the ningerling bowmen you won't have to do anything.''

"I hope so," Sandy muttered. "Remember—as soon as you take care of the undead, put a few arrows into that half troll and his companion. I don't want to fight either one of them.'' He paused before adding, "Remember to watch that door. The undead are quartered behind it.''

"You worry too much," Anala said. "This battle is going to be a slaughter.''

"It should be, but I've seen too many walkovers go sour. I'll call it easy when it is over.''

Sandy caught a hint of motion out of the corner of his eye and looked up. Two ningerlings were slipping across balconies on the other side. He nodded in satisfaction. The Craxidour had infiltrated the other side of the corridor and the area over the guardroom.

In fact, everything was going *too* well. Sandy had never had an operation go this well at the start. It helped that the defenses were laughable. The guards were there to keep prisoners in, not to fight off an attack from within the citadel. Well, they were due for a surprise.

Sandy slipped down a rickety stair to join Talim and Jatro. The room below was filled with dust, trash, and empty shelves; and a waist-high counter separated the room from the corridor. Jatro and Talim crouched behind it, waiting to make their move. Sandy crawled to them and cautiously looked over the counter.

He ducked down and turned to his companions. "In a couple minutes Hojeen will let fly the first arrow. After we vault over the counter, I want you two to head for that door. If you can block it and keep the undead bottled up, the battle will be more than half won. I'll watch your backs and be the cleanup man. If our friends put a few arrows in that half troll and his friend we shouldn't have any problem.''

"You get the easy jobs," Talim grumbled.

"That's because I'm boss: there to look important if everything goes right and there to save your bacon if it doesn't.''

For a moment Sandy worried about Zhadnoboth. He'd put the sorcerer back down the corridor, out of harm's way, with instructions not to use his magic unless the situation got desperate. The first hint of magic in this strategic area and the shee might become aware of what was happening. If they could win this battle without it, they just might have some more time. Besides, he had no desire to dive for cover when all hell broke loose, as was apt to happen when the sorcerer invoked a spell. He wished he knew if Zhadnoboth was a great incompetent sorcerer or an incompetent great sorcerer. Maybe it didn't matter.

Suddenly there was the sound of loud voices and a chair went crashing to the floor. Sandy peeked over the counter and saw the half troll and his companion were standing up and yelling at each other.

"Damned if I will," the big man roared, slamming his fist on the table.

"By damn you will!" his companion thundered.

They glowered drunkenly at each other and then started yelling insults. The big man half drew his sword, but stumbled as he came forward. The half troll caught him with a roundhouse swing. The power of the blow lifted him off his feet and sent him sliding across the floor. He hit a table and a couple of chairs and then the whole mess hit the wall with a great crash. Pieces of wood flew in all directions and the man slumped to the floor, unconscious or dead.

"By damn I said I would," roared the half troll. He picked up his tankard, drained it with one swallow, and collapsed back into his chair.

The door at the back of the guardroom flew open and a dozen or more of the undead came boiling out, roused by the racket. A fire arrow hit one of the zombies and he burst into flames. In seconds his whole body was burning like a torch.

Sandy cursed out an obscenity, yanked out his sword, and vaulted over the counter. The fat was in the fire now, and him with it. A dead man charged at him, moving ungodly fast for someone with two feet in the grave. Sandy dodged him and hacked downward, severing the corpse's Achilles tendon. His undead foe crashed to the ground, no more able than a mortal to walk on a hamstrung leg. The sword gave an angry hum, not much liking the taste of flesh that was already dead.

Another foe approached him, trying to run him through with a spear. Sandy twisted and the spearhead scraped along the links of his armor. The sword wailed an eerie song as Sandy slashed at his foe's neck. The magic edge sliced like a hot knife through the undead flesh and the dead man's head went flying. The body staggered away blindly until it stumbled into a wall and fell to the floor.

Sandy whirled just in time to beat off an attack by two more zombies. He was hard-pressed fending them both off and retreated backward. A fire arrow hit one of them in the eye and he went up with a whoosh, burning with a bright blue flame. The stench of charred flesh filled the air.

Sandy was no mean swordsman, but his remaining undead foe tested his skill to the limit. Every attack was frustrated, and twice his foe wounded Sandy slightly. Sandy wounded it several times and lopped off its left hand, but it kept coming. The magic sword buzzed angrily, craving more satisfying prey.

Sandy changed tactics and caught the other's blade edge-on with his sword. The undead's sword was sheared off near the hilt, its ordinary steel no match for the magically honed edge of Sandy's blade. The sword moaned happily. Without pausing, Sandy quickly lashed out with his sword, first to the left and then to the right. The dead warrior's arms dropped to the floor, lopped off at the shoulder.

The red fire in the undead warrior's eyes burned brighter. His lips opened and he croaked out, "Death." There was a barely perceptible pause and the creature spoke again, each word tumbling from his lips after great effort. "Death—for—me." Another pause and then, "Want—death—good." He said no more and the fire in his eyes guttered down to glowing coals.

Sandy lifted his sword to put the thing out of its misery. At that moment a fire arrow struck it in the throat and it went up in a sheet of flame. The creature let loose an earsplitting shriek and then collapsed into a silent burning lump. Sandy would remember that shriek for a long time, for mixed with the agony and despair was joy.

Sandy looked around and saw that his companions had held their own. Nine or ten smoldering piles marked those of the undead hit by fire arrows. Jatro, bleeding like a stuck pig from a wound at the base of his neck, was backed into a corner fighting an undead. At his feet were two more, each with its head missing. At that moment Talim came up behind the creature and severed its neck bone with one stroke. Elsewhere two of the undead, their hamstrings severed, crawled toward Sandy and his companions.

"Watch the door," Sandy yelled to Talim. "We don't want any more of these bastards erupting out of there." Before he could do anything about the two remaining undead, both were hit by fire arrows.

The half troll was slumped back in a chair as though drunk. Six or seven arrows stuck out of his carcass. The two in his chest still smoldered and wisps of smoke rose from his leather jerkin. Talim stepped around him to get to the door leading to the area where the undead were quartered.

Suddenly the half troll's eyes popped open. He stared uncomprehendingly for a moment, then let out a thunderous roar and staggered drunkenly to his feet. Talim whirled to face him. The trollman picked up a massively built table as though it was made of feathers and threw it. There was a thud as it hit Talim, then he and the table went half rolling and half flying down the corridor.

Jatro charged up behind the trollman, his sword held in both hands, and tried to split his skull with a savage chopping stroke. His sword rebounded as though it had hit stone and flew out of Jatro's numbed hands.

The half troll let out a ferocious roar and spun around, catching Jatro with a roundhouse punch. There was the crunch of breaking bone and Jatro went flying, landing in an unconscious heap on the floor.

Sandy entered the fray, swinging his sword up in a disemboweling stroke. By a combination of drunken luck and surprising agility the trollman escaped serious injury, staggering just far enough backward so all he got was a deep cut from right hip to left breast.

The half troll howled and swung clumsily at Sandy, who caught a glancing blow on the side of his head that sent him reeling down the corridor. The trollman roared in triumph, looked around through bloodshot eyes, and then stumbled drunkenly to the nearest wall. He yanked a giant battle-axe from its rack, swung it around his head, and roared a battle cry which shook the foundations of the building. Trickles of mortar sifted down from between the joints of the ceiling. He was answered by a volley of arrows, most of which bounced off his tough hide.

"Come, squishbugs. Come to Chormdag."

Another volley of arrows hit him. Only one stuck, going into his mouth and through his left cheek. He bit the shaft in half and yanked what was left from his cheek, then laughed thunderously, spewing out a mist of blood with each guffaw.

"Come to Chormdag and he will smash you."

For a moment no one answered his challenge. Then Sandy came shuffling forward cautiously, his head still wuzzy from the buffet he had received.

Chormdag laughed in contempt. Sandy kept edging forward, sidling to the trollman's unprotected left. Chormdag laughed again and sprang toward Sandy. The battle-ax came down with a tremendous crash as it smashed into the floor, where Sandy had been an instant before, and split a granite block in half. Sandy made a thrust in return, laying open the ribs on his foe's left side, but missing a killing stroke as the trollman twisted away. His sword yowled in glee.

Chormdag yanked his battle-ax free and charged at Sandy, who danced away. The trollman doggedly kept coming, seemingly unfazed by his wounds. For the next several minutes, Chormdag attacked again and again; only Sandy's nimbleness kept him from being brained or chopped in half. He wounded Chormdag several times with his counterattacks, but the wounds only seemed to make the half troll more angry.

Finally, both of them huffing and puffing, they stopped about ten feet apart and watched each other as they got their wind back. The trollman was still dripping blood, but his wounds were closing quickly.

"You die, man," Chormdag growled. "Your head will hang in the place of honor by the door of my home." He took several deep breaths and added, "For a squishbug you're almost a fighter."

"You're almost one too."

Chormdag's face split in a sudden grin. "Chormdag like you. Will hang your head higher." He sprang forward, swinging his battle-ax at head level.

Sandy ducked down and swung his sword to meet the axe. The sword howled a song of glee and sheared through the haft of the battle ax. The head went flying and buried itself in a wall.

While Sandy was still off balance, the half troll reversed

direction and caught Sandy on the side of his head with the axe handle. He stumbled backward, stunned, only the steel cap on his head saving him from a broken skull. Chormdag dropped the axe handle and stepped forward to wrap his enormous arms around Sandy and lift him up to his chest.

Though still dazed, Sandy instinctively arched his back and braced himself against the half troll's body with his left hand and both knees. Momentarily, he saved himself from being crushed, but he could feel Chormdag's enormous strength beginning to bend him backward.

His sword sang angrily and the hilt bit at the palm of his hand. Suddenly realizing he still held the sword, Sandy yanked it backward and then up into the gut of his enemy.

Chormdag screamed and his grip grew tighter. Sandy ripped out the sword and then rammed it back, this time going upward inside the ribs. The trollman clenched his arms convulsively as the sword pierced his heart and then dropped dead, falling forward on top of Sandy.

Anala and Hojeen came running up, followed by several ningerlings.

"Is he dead?" Anala asked anxiously.

"No," Sandy replied in a muffled voice. "But if you don't get this elephant off me, I might be."

"Oh, you're all right." Anala almost sounded disappointed. "I must see to Jatro," she said over her shoulder as she hurried off.

Hojeen and Shamdad, with some ningerling help, got the trollman off Sandy. He started to stand up, groaned, and clutched at the small of his back. Cautiously he straightened, muttering an obscenity. He hobbled a few steps and then had to stop, his face white with pain. "That bastard troll damn near broke my back."

"Looks like you took a roll on the floor of a butcher shop," Hojeen said deadpan.

Sandy looked down and saw he was covered with blood, mostly troll blood, but also some of his own. "Some piece of cake," he grumbled.

He looked down at the trollman's body. "Rest in peace, you bastard," he said somberly. "You died well. I'd do it again, but I'd still damn the blood on my hands."

Talim stalked over, bleeding from a split lip and holding a broken left wrist.

Sandy could see the crazed look in his eye and jumped into the breach, barking orders before Talim could open his mouth. "Talim, get the dungeon door open. Hojeen, you check to see if there are any more of those undead lurking about. Shamdad, take a couple ningerlings and keep watch on those stairs at the end of the corridor."

Hojeen and Shamdad nodded and hurried off. Talim hesitated, started to open his mouth, then turned and stomped off toward the dungeon. His high dudgeon was quite impressive, even if he did limp slightly.

Jatro was sitting against a pillar with Anala kneeling beside him, checking out his injuries. Sandy walked gingerly over to them. "How is he?"

"Worse than you." She stopped and looked Sandy over. "But more presentable."

"Hell, I'll be all right pretty soon." Jatro started to get up.

Anala pushed him back down. "No, you won't. That left shoulder is broken." She felt his ribs on that side and added, "And you have at least three broken ribs."

"Fix him up as best you can," Sandy said and started to walk away.

"He could die if we move him," Anala yelled. "Those broken ribs could shred his lungs. If you had his injuries you'd be crying," she added unfairly.

"I don't. And we have to move him. Jara Greenteeth is not going to let us lollygag around here long. She'll come loaded for bear and we had better be gone."

He saw Talim heading their way, looking mad enough to chew nails in half. "Take a look at Talim when you have a chance. I think his left wrist is broken."

Sandy moved to intercept his henchman. Behind him Anala muttered, "Bastard," and then started to croon a healing spell over Jatro.

"That damned door won't budge," Talim raged. "There is some sort of spell on it. This raid of yours has gained nothing."

"Go back to the door," Sandy ordered, "and keep an eye on it. I'll bring Zhadnoboth over. If there's magic closing it, he'll get a chance to earn his keep."

Talim saluted stiffly and went.

Sandy found the sorcerer sitting by the ale keg, drinking a tankard down slowly and enjoying every drop.

As Sandy walked over, he started refilling his tankard. "To think those pieces of slop got to drink this black ale. Did you see them swill it down as though it was little better than water? This is genuine dwarf brew with some real kick and flavor."

"If so, it's too good for sorcerers."

"There you go again," Zhadnoboth howled, "making light of your betters."

Sandy jerked his thumb toward the dungeon door. "Get over there and see what's keeping it shut." Sandy started to leave, but turned back to admonish the sorcerer. "And don't do anything until I get there. Just find the problem and figure what to do about it."

Zhadnoboth gave a disgusted snort that said much more than words ever could, and went to join Talim.

Hojeen came up to report. He pointed to the doorway from which the undead had swarmed. "Twenty, thirty dead there— enspelled, but not moving. Shee's not using death-rising spell now."

Sandy saw the Craxidour standing by the dead trollman as a couple of his ningerlings tried to cut Chormdag's head off. He strode over and said, "Leave the bastard's head on. Let him go whole to hell." He motioned to the door gaping open between the two small stairways. "Hojeen says there are un-dead in there. Get some of your ningerlings to burn them up before the shee decides to wake them. I want you and the rest of your ningerlings to guard the stair at the end of the corri-dor. Tell Shamdad to join me at the dungeon door."

The Craxidour nodded and then pointed down at the troll-man's body. "Troll was a great fighter."

"Yeah," Sandy said and left it at that.

The Craxidour started barking orders at his ningerlings. One group headed for the stairway at the end of the corridor while the other group started scampering around looking for combustibles.

As the Craxidour headed off to join the first group, Sandy called after him, "If anyone or anything comes, hold them off as long as you can and then run for it."

When Sandy got to the dungeon door, he saw that Zhad-noboth had been busy. The door was covered with a helter-skelter network of runes, drawn in yellow and blue chalk and in no discernible order. Around the ponderous lock and bolt holding the door shut, the sorcerer had molded a semicircle of what looked like red wax and stuck it to the metal. Zhadnoboth started to lift his staff, saw Sandy, and backed off with a guilty expression on his face.

"I have it all figured out," he babbled nervously as he saw the steely look in Sandy's eyes. "It is an old-fashioned spell, but effective. If I burn the lock out, the bond holding the spell together will be gone and the spell will vanish."

"Getting ready to do it, weren't you?"

"It's a very simple spell; any apprentice sorcerer could do it blindfolded. For something so trivial, I knew you wouldn't want me to ask you." Zhadnoboth continued before Sandy could get a word in edgewise, "And make sure you mark this sorcery down. I expect to be paid my just due for what I have done for you and your empire." He added emphatically, "And for the suffering I've had to undergo."

"You sure you don't want to charge for your time also?"

"And that too."

Sandy didn't bother replying to this latest bit of hot air. He scowled and stared at the massive dungeon door, not liking his options. "The shee and everything she can throw at us will be on their way the moment she feels your spell."

"Pah," Zhadnoboth said. "She won't notice anything this minor, but I'll buffer the spell with a time delay just to please you." He saw the angry question in Sandy's eyes and hurried to explain. "In simple soldier language, any magical vibrations will take much longer to echo through the magical dimensions."

"In other words," Sandy said in a disgusted voice, "it will take her longer to know something happened."

The sorcerer nodded and opened his mouth to say a little more.

Sandy wanted no more of his vague explanations. "However things go we'll have to hightail it out of here. If you give us a few more minutes, that will be all to the good."

He turned to Talim. "Once the door is down I want you and Shamdad to hurry into the dungeon. Find what able bodies there are, especially those who served with you. You can have ten minutes at the most. Then I want you back here.

Anybody left behind will have to pull their own fat out of the fire.''

Sandy motioned Talim and Shamdad to fall back, before turning to the sorcerer. "Get on with your spell. And try not to blow us to kingdom come." He retreated swiftly to the guardroom and stood behind an overturned table.

Zhadnoboth mumbled some comments under his breath and turned to the dungeon door. He checked the runes he had chalked on the door and the waxen semicircle he had placed around the lock, grunted in satisfaction, and pulled a tattered red book from his robes. Wetting his finger, he swiftly paged through it until he found what he wanted.

For the next minute he silently read through whatever magical recipe he'd found. Mumbling instructions to himself, he pulled a brass pot the size of a teacup from inside his robe. Into this he put a pinch of dust, some ashes from what was left of a zombie, and some light yellow salad oil. He swirled this mixture around, spit into it, and whispered a word into the pot. A small plume of vapor curled up lazily from the pot.

Zhadnoboth took a swig of ale from the tankard he was still carrying and reluctantly poured the rest into the pot. Softly, so no one could hear the words, he said a cantrip over it, then placed it on the palm of his left hand and stared at it. In a minute or less sounds of bubbling came from the pot. Then a thick orangish steam billowed up, to form a turbulent oily cloud which swirled in the air over Zhadnoboth's head. He glanced up at it, and though his spell seemed be sailing along in fine fashion, glowered peevishly.

The pot burped up a last gobbet of orange steam and then crumbled into a glittering powder. The sorcerer lifted his hand to his face, moved closer to the dungeon door, and gently blew on the powder. The fine particles spread out into a thin and sparkling mist that coated the door from top to bottom. For a second this mist hovered an infinitesimal fraction of an inch over the metal. Then it gradually seeped into the door and disappeared.

The cloud over the sorcerer's head suddenly started splitting out tiny bolts of black lightning; then it silently exploded. Small cloudlets, ranging in size from hazelnuts to coconuts, shot off in all directions. A rancid stink, reminiscent of burned popcorn and wet feathers, filled the air.

Zhadnoboth wrinkled his nose at the smell, then remembered his audience and hurriedly put on a pleasant and pleased face. He raised his staff and touched its end to the semicircle of wax and spoke a word of power. A tiny green flame flickered at the end of his staff. Where the staff touched it, the wax caught fire, quickly spreading all the way around the semicircle.

The sorcerer spoke a word of ceasing and the flame at the end of his staff winked out, while the semicircle of greenish red flame ate into the metal.

"You will notice how fast and efficiently the metal is being etched away," he announced in a self-congratulatory tone.

At that moment the flame erupted from the groove it had eaten in the metal and spread instantly over the whole door. Zhadnoboth blanched and swiftly backed away, taking refuge behind Sandy's table. The greenish red flame burned on the door for a minute or more, then the metal turned an odd shade of plum gray and the flame disappeared.

For an instant nothing more happened, then the door began slumping. It flowed downward and across the floor in a thick gooey mess. Sandy and the sorcerer started to back off when the metal mud crept to within a couple feet of where they stood. Then the metal suddenly went rigid and a white coating covered the surface. *Ping ping ping ping* filled the air as the metal cracked into small jagged fragments.

"Well, that's one way to do it," Sandy said. He stepped forward and knelt to pick up one of the fragments. He scraped some of the white coating off with his fingernail and tasted it with the tip of his tongue. "Frost," he announced.

"Did you notice how no heat was produced?" Zhadnoboth was obviously trying to make hay from his mistake. "A very efficient spell—removed the whole door with minimum effort."

Sandy nodded cynically and barked his orders to Talim and Shamdad. "Get your butts down there and get who you can. I want you back here in ten minutes or less. And be ready to move out when you do."

He watched them plunge through the dungeon doorway and then turned to Zhadnoboth. "You get over to those stairs at the end of the corridor and watch them with the ningerlings. If the shee comes—or anything else we need magic to stop—be ready with some sorcery."

"I am not one of your flunkies," Zhadnoboth retorted.

Sandy looked at him in exasperation. "No, but you could be one of my victims."

The sorcerer hesitated a moment for pride's sake and then trotted off to the stairs. As always, he knew when discretion might be the better part of valor.

Sandy joined Anala and Jatro. The big man was standing up and moving easily. He was pale and his left arm was bound to his body, but otherwise he seemed in fine fettle.

"The lady," he said respectfully, "has fixed me up fine. If there is fighting, you won't have to worry about me." He looked at a pile of ashes on the floor and shivered. "The shee told me in my dream that the dead would slay me. Well, I proved her wrong. It was her dead who bit the dust."

Sandy nodded uneasily, wondering if Jara Greenteeth had poisoned all their dreams. He sniffed and looked up just in time to see several ningerlings scamper out of the doorway at the back of the guardroom. Faint whiffs of smoke were drifting out of it; the waiting dead had been taken care of.

"Close that door," he told Jatro, "and make sure nothing comes through."

Jatro started to protest. Sandy silenced him. "Somebody has to do it and you're available. We would be up the creek if they burst through and surprised us."

After watching Jatro bar the door and stack broken furniture in front of it, Anala went over to where Sandy was sipping on a tankard of ale. "You got him out of the way."

"I put him where he would be some use," Sandy said as he savored his ale.

Anala gave a disbelieving shrug. "He and Talim were magnificent during the fight. It takes real heroes to face such odds. I am proud to be with them."

Sandy slowly swigged more of his ale. "Sometimes the only way to save your life is to be a hero."

"And sometimes people fight when they could have run," Anala said heatedly. "If you appreciated their courage, maybe you would think better of yourself."

"I did my share. I didn't back down."

"But that's what is expected of you."

"That's good to know," Sandy replied wryly. "And Talim and Jatro did a damned good job. So did the three of you up in the balcony. That won this skirmish for us. Because of your marksmanship the three of us down here only had to fight some of the undead.''

There was a crash and clatter from the direction of the stairs. Sandy dropped his tankard and ran to the end of the corridor. A ningerling lay dead at the foot of the stairs, his throat torn out. Near him, its body skewered by numerous arrows, lay an enormous yellow wolf. On the stairs lay the bodies of three elves, wearing mail shirts and black and green livery.

Sandy stared for an instant, then made a dash for a doorway. An arrow bounced off the stone behind him. A moment later, the Craxidour jumped past him, let fly an arrow, and backed back into the doorway.

''Who are the elves?'' Sandy asked.

''Not elves. Sanhar folk.''

Sandy looked again at the bodies and noticed that although the Sanhar folk looked much like elves, they were thickset instead of slender like the elves he had seen.

''The Sanhar folk joined Mem-Jara-Shil when she revolted against the Goddess. Not many are left—most were slain in her wars.''

''What about the wolf?''

''The Goddess once punished the leaders of the Sanhar for betraying her. Eighty and seven wolves she made. It was thought that all were dead.''

Sandy peeked out the doorway and ducked back in as an arrow came flying his way. He turned to the Craxidour. ''Hold them for a while. I'll go and light a fire under Talim. When you hear my signal, come running, and we'll get out of here through the same hidden doorway we entered by.''

''It will be easy. There are not many Sanhar folk.''

''You better hope it stays that way.''

Instead of going back down the corridor, Sandy went through the interconnecting rooms, until he was back in the room where such a short time ago he had waited to spring his ambush.

Stepping out into the corridor, Sandy saw Anala trying to talk to one of the ningerlings. He ran over to her. ''Hold that room,'' he said, motioning back over his shoulder, ''until we can run for it.''

''By myself!''

"You and the ningerlings at this end of the corridor." He spoke a few words to the ningerling Anala had been palavering with, and turned back to the lulzi. "He and his group of ningerlings will be there with you."

"Good, I can learn some more of their tongue."

Sandy stopped by Jatro. "Keep an eye on things here. If I'm not back in five minutes, blow that conch horn the Craxidour gave you and head for the hidden door."

Not waiting for an answer, Sandy headed for the dungeon door. Suddenly, he stopped dead in his tracks and swore. "Damn that sorcerer, I forgot him." He hesitated a moment longer and then hurried on to the dungeon, muttering, "Why am I worried about him? He could walk over a cesspool and not fall in."

He stopped on the stone landing and looked down into the dungeon. Shamdad was leading a group of prisoners up the stairs toward the door, but there was no sign of Talim.

When Shamdad reached the landing, Sandy barked out, "Where's Talim?"

"He's still searching the dungeon for stragglers."

"Idiot!" Sandy growled. He looked over the prisoners and found them a scruffy bunch, though one or two might be worth their salt. "Take them to the guardroom and arm them with what you can find, then run like hell. We'll meet in that hall of dragons we passed through."

Sandy stepped to the edge of the landing and roared out, "Talim, where the hell are you?"

"The fool is down at the far end," said a voice behind him.

Sandy spun around and saw an old man with a game leg climbing the stairs. By the scars on his face and arms, he had seen more than his share of fighting.

"He had to get something. Doesn't have the sense to know life is worth more than a few baubles."

The walls shook and a grinding screech echoed through the dungeon. It stopped, started again, stopped, and started once more.

"She's trying to open the death gate," the old man yelled, turning and hobbling at full speed out the door.

Sandy cursed and ran down the stone stairs into the dungeon, almost knocking down a couple of stragglers. He dashed

toward the far end of the dungeon's great hall. The few prisoners who were left in the dungeon were running in panic the
other way.

At the far end of the dungeon was a rough stone wall that
looked as though it had been hastily thrown up to close off
what lay behind it. In the middle was a door standing wide
open. Talim burst out of the doorway, a bundle under his arm,
and came running toward Sandy. There was another horrendous screech followed by the steady grating sound of rusty
metal rubbing against stone.

Talim rushed by, shouting, "The shee's got the gate
open."

Sandy turned and followed him, wondering why he had
gone after a fool who hadn't needed his help. Behind them
there was a thunderous rumble and the stone under their feet
shook. Sandy looked back and saw an avalanche of rough
stone blocks tumbling down and bouncing across the dungeon
floor toward them.

For a moment, Sandy did a desperate dance to avoid the
stone blocks which rolled and tumbled by. The sudden onslaught over, he turned and saw Talim lying on the floor.
There was a dent in his helmet and blood oozed down the
side of his face. He cursed his luck and hurriedly slung the
unconscious man over his shoulder.

He looked back and saw the whole wall closing off that end
of the dungeon had collapsed. There was a shrill chittering
sound like the clicking of innumerable tiny teeth and a low
blackness began shambling over the remains of the wall.
Sandy stared at it and could not quite get it into focus, as
though whatever the thing was, was only partly in this world.
Mixed in with the blackness were millions of red coals the
size of pinpricks. Sandy shivered and then hobbled off as fast
as he could go.

As he got to the bottom of the stairs he heard a scream
from the back of the dungeon. One of the prisoners hadn't
had the sense to flee. The agonized shrieks continued as he
climbed, becoming in the end almost a sob. As he reached
the landing, there was a bloodcurdling scream which swiftly
dwindled to a gurgle and was gone.

Sandy hurried through the doorway, dumped Talim on the
floor, and raced back to the landing. He looked back down
into the dungeon. The black tide was lapping at the foot of

the stairs and starting to climb them. Racing back to the corridor, he found Talim sitting up and looking dazedly about. Sandy yanked him to his feet.

"What happened to him?" Anala asked, suddenly showing up at his elbow.

"What are you doing here?" Sandy yelled. "I told you to watch our bolthole."

"I—I—I," Anala stuttered, caught between crying and yelling back.

"Never mind," Sandy said. "Grab Talim and take him to the hall of dragons."

Sheepishly Anala obeyed orders. Sandy never noticed, already on the run again. He hurried over to where Jatro still guarded the blockaded door.

"I don't like it," he told Sandy. "There's been some strange noises on the other side of the door."

Sandy nodded absentmindedly; he had too many other troubles to worry about already. He took the conch horn from Jatro and raised it to his lips. Before he could blow it there was a flash of flame and then a boom from the other end of the corridor. They could hear stone crashing and a cloud of dust and smoke rolled down the corridor.

A dark figure came through the dusty cloud. Sandy started to pull out his sword until he saw it was Zhadnoboth. The sorcerer's beard was singed and several holes had been burned in his robe, one of which was still smoking.

"I just don't understand it," he said. "I used only three drops of oil of amber and it was the right word of power. Must have been using ashes from the undead instead of mummy dust."

Sandy grabbed him. "Quick—block the dungeon door. If you don't we're going to be up to our rears in some hungry black glop."

Zhadnoboth shook Sandy's hand off and drew himself up with as much dignity as his scrawny build permitted. "I never asked to join this expedition, I never asked to be constantly thrown to the wolves, and I am certainly not going to continue."

Sandy didn't answer. He picked the sorcerer up by the scruff of the neck and carried him to the dungeon door, tossed him on the landing, and then stood blocking the doorway.

The sorcerer angrily scrambled to him feet. He opened his mouth, but what was intended to come out, didn't. Instead he saw the evil black tide inching up the stairs and let out a yowl. He ran for the door and bounced off Sandy.

"Do something."

"What?" the sorcerer babbled.

"How do I know?"

Zhadnoboth tottered gingerly over to the top of the stairs and stared downward. Gulping, he raised his staff. Five times he said a word a power and five times a thunderous blast of white lightning shot out from the end of his staff, though the last blast was a bit weak.

Heavy clouds of greasy black hung in the air and a choking sulphurous stench made breathing difficult. The crawling black mass below just kept coming. The thing's tiny eyes burned red with insane rage and ravenous hunger, but mostly hunger.

"It's no use," Zhadnoboth panted weakly. "I could blast to the end of eternity and this stuff would still be coming."

"Then do something different."

"Easy enough for you to say," Zhadnoboth howled. "You don't have to pay the price. Much more of this and I'll be a cripple for life."

"If you have a life."

The sorcerer looked around and thought furiously. "Stand back," he yelled. When Sandy was out of the way, he turned back to the doorway. He murmured a spell and struck the landing hard with his staff. There was an explosion and the sorcerer was blown back into Sandy's arms.

On wobbly legs he staggered back to the doorway. The landing and stair were gone. Below the black thing hissed angrily and slowly inched up the wall.

"That won't hold it for long," Sandy said.

"It wasn't meant to," The sorcerer snapped. He dug a leather bag out of his robe, loosed the drawstring, and threw a dark blue powder on the doorway and the thick walls surrounding it. "Grab that keg of ale," he ordered. "We haven't much time."

Sandy ran over, threw the keg on his shoulder, and staggered back to the doorway.

"Pour it on the floor."

"The hell with that." Sandy lifted the keg over his head

and dashed against the floor. It split and ale flowed in all directions. He turned around and sounded a blast on the conch shell. In moments, ningerlings came fleeing down the corridor.

Zhadnoboth quickly drew some runes on the doorway. Then he lifted his staff and tapped the floor and the wall on each side of the doorway, all the while softly chanting. He said a final word and there was a grinding crash and a swirl of dust.

When the dust cleared there was no doorway, only a solid stone wall. Zhadnoboth stood with his nose nearly touching it and looking stunned. He started to back away and then stopped. He tugged angrily at his robe, swore, and then gave it a hard yank. There was a ripping sound and he tumbled over backward. Protruding from the solid stone of the wall was a piece of his robe.

Sandy helped him to his feet. "Get going. Remember the hall of dragons."

Suddenly the door Jatro was guarding caved in and two Sanhar warriors burst through. Jatro ran one through the throat, but caught a blow from a battle-ax on his bad arm. He screamed and dropped to his knees. The Sanhar lifted his axe to give a killing blow and Jatro rammed a dagger between the plates of his cuirass.

One of the undead came through the door, tossed the dying Sanhar aside, and struck at Jatro with his spear. The spearhead caught the injured man in the chest and he collapsed.

The next instant the undead was headless as Sandy's sword sliced through its neck. As the thing staggered around, Sandy grabbed a torch from the wall and set fire to the undead's waxy flesh. It fell to the floor in flames, setting fire to the broken furniture Jatro had piled there.

A Sanhar tried to jump through the flames and Sandy sliced him open, his magic sword singing in fierce joy. Sandy grabbed a table and threw it into the doorway. There was a crunch and howl as it hit someone before dropping to add more fuel to the fire.

Sandy lopped off the spear shaft protruding from Jatro's chest, grabbed him by the shoulders, and began dragging him across the corridor toward the hidden door they had entered by. An arrow came down the corridor and bounced off his helm; another plucked at his sleeve. He got into the storeroom and the Craxidour and another ningerling each took one of Jatro's legs and helped carry him into a back room.

Sandy slammed the door and jammed a wooden bench against it. Then he and the ningerlings carried Jatro through the back of a huge walk-in fireplace. Sandy yanked down an iron lever protruding from the wall and with a grating sound the back of the fireplace dropped into place.

He knelt beside Jatro. The big man smiled, blood dripping from the corners of his mouth. "Damned if that green-skinned bitch wasn't right," he said with black humor. "One of the undead got me." He coughed and blood gushed from his mouth. "Cold," he whispered, gave a shudder, and died.

There were crashing sounds from the other side of the fireplace. Sandy quickly pried the bloody dagger out of Jatro's hand and jammed it into the slot holding the iron lever. "That should stop them for a while."

In one corner of the room was a round stone trapdoor. Sandy and the Craxidour grabbed hold of the heavy steel staples sticking up from its surface and heaved it up. The hole beneath was dark and dank. From far below came the sound of rushing water.

They dragged Jatro's body over to the hole and laid it out on its back. Gently Sandy closed the eyelids, weighting each down with a silver coin. "This is the best we can do," he said to the corpse. "I didn't know you long, but you were a good man: Scared like the rest of us, but when the pinch came you did what you had to." He knelt silently for a moment, saying a prayer for the soul of his departed companion.

Then he and the ningerlings lifted the body and dropped it into the hole. For a moment there was no sound, then they heard a loud splash. Grunting with effort they dragged the stone trapdoor back onto the hole. "The shee's going to have to do a lot of searching to find that body."

There was the sound of pounding on the other side of the fireplace. The stone rattled and groaned, but the fireplace was made from solid granite. It was going to be a while before anyone broke through.

"Let's go." Sandy headed for the back of the room.

Here a ladder led up to a hole in the ceiling. Sandy motioned the ningerlings to climb first, then he slowly made his way up. After dragging the ladder up after them, they headed down a dark passage toward the hall of dragons and their companions.

19

THE Goddess stared gloomily into her pool. Both in Cimber-Tal-Gogna and along the southern border of the Rithian Empire everything was going her way. Yet a deep sadness ached inside her. With every win there were losses. Most were, in the scheme of things, tiny—but to a child left crying for its father or a mother mourning for her daughter these losses were irreplaceable.

The universe was a bitch and a bastard. There were prices for everything. For a bag of rock candy you paid a copper piece, for a skirmish you paid in lives and maimings, and for a war you paid in shattered hopes and dreams. You won and sometimes what you gained seemed small reward for the agony in your heart. What was a warehouse of great wines if you couldn't drink cold spring water again?

Sandy and his companions had struck a dire blow at the shee. Their attack had shaken her confidence. While she had ruthlessly dabbled in the affairs of the Rithian Empire, both along the border and in the intrigues at court, the tables had been turned on her. Now she had a killer snake crawling within her bosom. Her allies would have to fend for themselves. The shee would lay her life on the line for no one.

Meanwhile, in a series of running battles, Aku and his army had shattered the Kilbri in the Dry Bone Hills. Most were either dead or suing for peace. Only Zadar Kray, two clans of the Kilbri, and some of his Jadghuli and Yartazi allies were still holding out at Fortress Matandi at the foot of the mountain called Tham Og Hothum, the house of Hothum.

The end was drawing near, both along the border of the

empire and along the borderlands of Zarathandra. Both the shee and her sometime ally, Hothum of the Dark Places, had plagued her world too long. It was time to settle with them for eternity.

There was a howl from above her pool of seeing. A raging indeterminate darkness hovered there, striving to break through to her. The Goddess sighed and then, as she had done in times past, let the shee into her presence.

"You did this. Must you always smash me down? Can you never be satisfied with my abasement?" The shee raged, tears streaming from her eyes.

"If a child sticks her fingers in the fire, she can expect to get burned."

"Who are you to tell me what to do? Who are you to be the mother, keeping those who should be your equals as children? You are only an old, old woman tilling one small patch of garden and keeping all its fruits to yourself. You are not forever. Better ones have gone before you and there will be better when you are long dust."

"But I am now."

The shee gave a wild laugh. "You think you will win. But even now those you have sent against me are going to their doom. They have taken deadly hurts you know naught of and I have gained that which will destroy them."

Sneering in contempt she faded from view. The Goddess brooded for many minutes, going over and over her schemes and plans and coming always to the same conclusion. She had no choice; she must do what was necessary or bring damnation to Zarathandra.

The shee had once been a small child, both bad and good. As a child she had received a child's punishment. She had grown and made her choices. Now she must pay the price those choices demanded. Let her die, and let her mother weep for the adult who might have been.

20

SANDY buried his face in the washbasin and quickly jerked it out. "Damn, that water is cold," he complained to himself. Quickly he washed his naked body off until he had removed the blood and grime. He looked bleakly at the three pitchers of clear water standing on the marble-topped washstand. Gritting his teeth, he lifted one of the pitchers over his head, and then slowly poured water over his body. Shivering and shaking he picked up the second pitcher. He glared at it and said, "To hell with this slow torture," and dumped it all at once over his head.

As he began toweling himself down, a voice spoke up from behind him.

"I don't see what they see in you. You're getting a pot, you're only passably handsome, and you haven't much to offer otherwise."

Sandy whipped the towel around himself and turned to face Anala. "What are you doing here?"

"I was curious."

"Be curious about someone else."

"I've seen men before."

"That should have satisfied you."

Anala thought a moment. "No, you always hope for something different."

Sandy scowled at her, realizing he was never going to win this argument, and he didn't want be arguing in the first place. "Just run and stare at someone else. Let me finish my bath."

"But I'll miss most of the fun."

"Get out."

As she left, she said over her shoulder. "And you're a terrible conversationalist."

Furiously rubbing himself dry, Sandy grumbled, "Why can't I be home? I want hot showers and girls too bashful to be dirty-minded. I want to wake up in the morning and know nothing exciting is going to happen."

He quickly donned his clothes, still damp from the brief scrubbing he had given them, and then his armor. He walked quickly down a hall lined with storerooms and hurried up a narrow spiral stair. As he came out into the hall of dragons, the first person he saw was Zhadnoboth. "It's your fault," he growled as he walked by.

The sorcerer stared after him, baffled. "What's my fault?"

"This whole damned world and me being stuck in it."

Sandy quickly conferred with the Craxidour and a couple of ningerling chiefs from other clans. When the plans had been made, the ningerlings hurried off, except the Craxidour.

"The Yellowbird Singer and six of my Yimsi will stay with you. The Goddess go with you, Peaceman." He made a sign of blessing and added, "Until we meet at the Emerald Throne." Then turned and was gone.

"Peaceman?"

Sandy turned and saw Anala. "It's a nickname they stuck on me. Doesn't make sense, but then nicknames hardly ever do." He paused and looked quizzically at her. "I thought you didn't understand ningerling lingo."

"I'm a fast learner." Seeing his disbelieving look, she embroidered the rose somewhat. "The Yellowbird Singer is teaching me. It's not so different from common elvish once you get the hang of it." She gave him the once-over and added, "And you are a peaceman. You bring the long peace to your enemies."

"Yeah, and none to myself," he said blackly. Abruptly he changed his tone. "Let's see how our small army is doing."

As they walked toward the far end of the hall, where Talim and Hojeen were whipping their recruits into shape, Anala rubbernecked.

The hall was an enormous place, with four decks of balconies on each wall and a sort of covered porch on the main floor. Dragons were all over the place, from tiny bird dragons to giant colddrakes and firedrakes. They were carved in high relief on the jade and alabaster of the balconies. The enormous mosaic which was the floor showed them in all their glory: black as night velvet, orange like topaz in the morning sun, scarlet like rubies dipped in blood, the angry blue of the sky before a storm, the dark green of sea agates.

Across the faraway ceiling had been painted a series of murals, depicting the history of dragons from the beginning of time and on into the ages of man. There was Omdad the Creator mixing three drops of his blood with wind, fire, and iron to create the first of their kind. Great Acraginzar again destroyed the Ten Cities of the Far Shore. There was Hobbin One-Eye carving the heart from Ustimag the Destroyer and bathing in his blood. The weeping dragon, Embisharra, stalked through the halls of the mountain kings as she avenged her dead children.

At each end of the hall was a stained glass window, four stories tall and almost as wide. One showed a skyful of dragons as they flew to the dread Battle of the Midnight Fields, where only twelve survived out of the ten thousand who fought. The other window showed a gigantic Acraginzar in all his midnight blue splendor, his belly a fire-orange and stained crimson where the diamond lance had pierced his heart. He was flying up and up, his fading eyes seeking the sun, seeking a fiery burial, seeking a final purification. The light gently filtered through these windows, giving life to the dragons who slumbered there.

"They loved dragons," Anala said in a hushed voice. "Who were they?"

"I don't know. Maybe no one now living knows," Sandy said in a musing voice. "They are dead and nameless, yet their love lives on."

Anala gave him an odd look. "Sometimes you seem to care for nothing; you seem a small man with small worries and small peeves. Other times you surprise me."

Sandy gave a wry grin. "That's what I like about people. You can never be sure you've seen all there is to them."

Talim was giving his men a pep talk. "You're free, you've got weapons, and you've got a chance to send some of the heathen to hell. If you go with us, that's most likely where you'll end up. But that's a damned sight better than yesterday. If no one's got the sand to go with us, I want to know now."

They were a raunchy bunch, unshaven, hollow eyed, and haphazardly armored and armed; yet not one of them moved.

Talim scowled at them. "Fall out and get some food in your bellies. It might be the last you get."

As a man they headed for Hojeen, who had set up a sort of kitchen at one end of the portico. Hojeen was a great field cook, but hog swill would have been fine with them, after the watery porridge the shee had served them every day.

"A bunch of scum," Talim told Sandy, "but they will fight. The shee's fed on their blood and souls; they won't forget or forgive." He pointed at the grizzled hard case limping to a bench with a plate of stew. "That's Hobhardigan the reaver. He and Shamdad are my sergeants. You can trust him with your life, if there is no coin in your pocket."

Sandy nodded. "I've met him."

"We picked up him and ten others. Six soldiered with me, but the others know which end of a sword to hold on to."

Sandy nodded again. "Let's eat. Then I'll tell them what's what and we can move out."

Talim maneuvered Anala into eating with him. Watching her chatting a mile a minute, Sandy was just as glad to be aced out. He wandered over and sat by Hobhardigan. Neither spoke for a while, busy eating and measuring each other up.

"Call me Hob," he said finally.

"I will."

"Heard about you. You had a reputation among the desert folk. Said you were a bad man to cross."

Sandy broke off a piece of bread and chewed on it before answering. "When I ran into trouble, I did what I had to."

"The way I hear, after you did what you had to, there wasn't anyone alive to complain."

Sandy grinned. "I wouldn't go that far, but I was damned hard on anyone who tried to cut me down." He looked his companion over. "You were the one with a reputation. Every caravan master from Kimbo-Dashla to Tamrook shivered when they heard your name."

Hob smiled as he thought back. "It was a good life. Money, women, and the best wine." His face darkened. "The Rithians caught us at Yarmida Springs. Only me and three of my scoundrels escaped. If I ever get back, there is a certain headman who is dead meat."

"We have to get by Jara Greenteeth first."

"I owe her, too. Once I ram a sword up her affair, I'll be ready to leave." He finished his stew. "That scrawny bastard,

Hojeen, can cook. I'll see you around.'' Giving a sort of half salute, Hob went for a second helping.

As Sandy started chewing on his bread, there was a hungry squeak at his feet. He looked down and saw his white furred piglet had returned. He scowled and the piglet sat up on its hind legs and held out its front paws. Suppressing a smile, he said gruffly, ''All right, here's a chunk of bread.''

The little beast grabbed this offering and scuttled away, disappearing with a faint pop just before it rounded a corner. Sandy raised his eyebrows and took a long swig of ningerling beer.

Zhadnoboth wandered over, stopped, and wrinkled his nose as if trying to catch an elusive smell. He shrugged uneasily and said, ''I found some interesting fragments of parchment. I think they contain parts of Kommerdan's lost spell.''

Sandy refrained from asking where he got the fragments. Knowing the sorcerer, there was bound to be something shady about their acquisition. ''What has this lost spell got to do with us?''

Zhadnoboth bent over and whispered slyly, ''It's a spell to transport its user wherever he wants—and from wherever he is.'' His voice sank lower. ''I think I have the lost parts figured out. It needs three people. You, I, and whoever else you want.'' He looked in Anala's direction.

''She won't go,'' Sandy said. ''She's got her principles, unlike certain people I could name.''

''Now look who's being high and mighty,'' the sorcerer said in a huff. ''A cheapjack warrior who has never been better than he has to be.''

Sandy shook his head. ''You just don't understand. She won't go. That's the way it is. As for me''—he gave a shrug— ''I'll stay.''

The sorcerer threw his hands in the air. ''You're either an idiot or she's got you believing in this hogwash.'' He walked off grumbling about crack-brained fools trying to do the impossible.

Sandy wasn't sure that he didn't agree with him. He got up and walked over to the almost empty stewpot, then banged on it with the large iron spoon Hojeen had used to dish out the stew. When he had everybody's attention, he called out, ''Gather 'round.''

After they had made a circle, he went into his spiel. ''We're only a few and the shee is now searching high and low for us. We could run and she might never find us—the ningerlings say this place has beyonds even the gods don't know about—but we will not. We're going to attack her where she is weakest, her center of power. Her throne room.''

''What about her dead men and her other minions?'' Hob asked.

''They'll be searching for us, wandering through the nooks and crannies of this place, where the ningerlings can pick them off.''

Talim asked, ''How come the ningerlings haven't done this before?''

''Because their various tribes and clans have never been of one mind before. Nor has the shee ever before stuck out the necks of her henchmen where they can be so easily chopped off. She's afraid, and she's making mistakes.''

Anala jumped forward to add, ''We're history, we're myth, we're destiny, we're the stories our grandchildren will tell: the brave few who did mighty deeds even when our hearts were sinking into our boots.''

''And we will be the ones to leave our bones in the halls of Cimber-Tal-Gogna,'' Sandy murmured to himself.

None of the others heard him. The magic and enthusiasm in her voice had set fire to their blood and they were ready to go out and slay dragons—even Zhadnoboth.

They headed for the doorway under Acraginzar's window, Hojeen and the ningerlings ranging ahead and Sandy and Anala at the rear. They had nearly reached the doorway when there was a blood-chilling hiss from the other end of the hall. It started below the threshold of hearing, slowly rose to a piercing crescendo, then faded into silence.

They looked back and saw a gigantic snake sliding into the hall. Its head and body were as thick and round as a house, and its tail seemed to go on forever. Its scales were an iridescent armor of gold, crimson, and green stripes which spiraled around its body. Swiftly it slithered toward them.

Sandy drew out his sword and faced it, wondering if his magic toothpick could do more than scratch this monster. Behind him he heard his companions scrambling for cover. ''Zhadnoboth,'' he yelled out of the side of his mouth, not daring to look away. ''Do something.'' No sorcerer showed up and he cursed him roundly, making some choice comments about his ancestry.

Then Anala was standing beside him, trembling, but resolutely facing the serpent. "It's one of the Brood of Omdigad, the legendary enemies of the dragon folk," she whispered.

She began to sing, starting with a soft chant which gradually became stronger and more sure, until it was like a great war anthem. Into this she wove a weird and subtle magic, each word and note becoming soldiers in an army of shadow and sound. As the song wove its spell, the serpent slowed its advance and then stopped, confused.

It was a strange song she sang, a song of dragons and their deeds. She sang of when Zarathandra was young, when the dragons first flew its skies. She sang of battles won and battles lost, of dragons slaying and being slain, of dragons in the egg and dragons toothless and their fires cold, and of a world lost and gone. She sang of their enemies, fierce trolls, wily elves, treacherous men, but mostly of the Brood of Omdigad and their insatiable lust for dragon eggs.

As she sang the dragons in the hall seemed more and more alive; their images seemed to subtly move and breathe. The light shining through the stained glass windows reddened and warmed, becoming like wisps of dragon fire.

The serpent gave an angry hiss, shaking off the spell she wove and slithering forward. Then it hissed again, this time in pain and surprise. Blood leaked down its sides, and desperately it tried to move forward but couldn't, held fast by the talons of the mosaic dragons beneath it. Faint and insubstantial fires streamed from the thousand or more tiny dragons in the far window. The serpent writhed, small spirals of smoke rising from its scales.

Slowly the green-flecked topaz eyes of Acraginzar opened. They looked at the serpent and there was a deep anger in them. Two beams of orange-gold filtered through these eyes, quickly becoming powerful streams of burning light. Where they touched the serpent, it charred and burst into flame. There was a constant agonized hiss as the monster's body became a raging inferno. Then the hiss was gone and soon after the blaze, leaving behind only burned bone and gray ash.

There was a profound silence and then the dragons noticed

Sandy and his companions. The beams from Acraginzar's eyes began drifting their way, the mosaics under their feet started a slow writhing, and wispy strings of fire floated toward them from the window dragons at the far end of the hall. Zhadnoboth let out a yelp as an alabaster dragonet that was crawling up a column opened its mouth and bit his robe.

Anala quickly changed her song, the words and cadences becoming soft and slow. She sang of long nights, of dragons snuggled in their caves, and of dragons leaving the living realms to find the undying land of their destiny. Gradually the fire and life faded from the dragons of the hall and they became no more real than pictures on pavement. Anala's song trailed off into a whisper and there was a profound silence.

"Quit your gawking and get me free," Zhadnoboth crabbed, breaking the uncomfortable quiet. He tugged angrily at his robe, held firmly in the cold stone jaws of the alabaster dragonet.

Sandy strode over to the sorcerer and chopped down with his sword, the blade singing a chuckling song as it sheared through the enchanted cloth of Zhadnoboth's robe. Gold coins streamed to the floor from the hole in the fabric; along with a copper teapot, three pairs of loaded dice, a smoked ham, a candle stub, a small suede bag, and a rather flustered hummingbird. As always, the sorcerer's robe held much, much more than just Zhadnoboth.

The sorcerer yowled angrily and slapped a hand to the hole, temporarily stopping the flow. He quickly touched his staff to the rent fabric and spoke a word. There was the crackling of static, and tiny needles of electricity began reweaving the cloth. In less than twenty seconds the fabric was whole.

Zhadnoboth fell to his knees and began to frantically gather up his treasures. As he crawled along the floor and stuffed them away, he came to a pair of boots. He scrambled to his feet and flowered at their owner, Hobhardigan.

Hob had the suede bag in his hands. He opened the drawstring, emptied some of the contents onto his left palm—and stared at some ten or fifteen cat's-eye marbles, ranging in color from mystery blue to tawny orange. Scowling unhappily, he shoved them in the bag and gave it to the sorcerer.

Zhadnoboth ungraciously accepted the bag and stared around to see if any more of his treasure wasn't where it was supposed to be. Satisfied he had rescued it all, he stalked off.

Hobhardigan watched him go and then moved his left foot. Two gold pieces lay on the floor. The bandit smiled and picked them up.

"I wouldn't tell Zhadnoboth about that if I were you," Sandy said.

Hobhardigan started guiltily. When he saw the smile on Sandy's face and the eye that almost winked, he smiled in return and stuffed the two pieces in his pocket.

Sandy raised his voice and shouted at his troops. "You've had your fun. Now fall in and get moving."

In moments they were moving out of the hall. Sandy, Anala, and Hobhardigan lagged behind as a rear guard. Anala looked weary, but an inner glow filled her. Hobhardigan watched her in worshipful silence, his habitual cynicism washed away by what he had seen in the hall of dragons. Sandy paid small heed to his companions. He was too busy checking their surroundings and keeping his eyes open for trouble.

"If I ever get old, I'll tell my children and their children about the hall of dragons," Hobhardigan said in a hushed voice. "They'll hear of the great lady Anala and the miracle she worked there." He paused, trying to think of the right words. "Before, I only sort of believed in good and the Goddess. Now I know they are true."

Anala smiled wearily. "They are always true, though sometimes we lose our faith."

Hobhardigan nodded solemnly, as though she had pointed out a profound truth.

A wry smile crossed Sandy's face, followed fleetingly by a look of grudging respect. Anala had grown a long way, but he missed the wrongheaded romp he had gotten used to.

After they had been moving for a while, a thought that had been nibbling at Sandy's mind surfaced. "Hob," he said, "go relieve Hojeen at the point and send him back to me."

"You don't seem much impressed with me," Anala said.

"But I am. As Hob said, you did something extraordinary back there."

"But you are not awed like the rest."

Sandy shrugged and said musingly, "I think I am, but I remember the brat I first met." He laughed. "Don't know how I stood you. Now I wonder how I will be able to stand a most reverend lulzi."

Anala gave a snort. "You will have it easy. I have to put up with a rogue who would make a devil pay his due."

"I'm not that bad."

"It must have been someone else who kept me in my place."

"Ah, for the good old days. Now I'll have to kneel and say, my lady."

She put her hand in his and looked him in the eye. "Don't. I'll need someone who knows Anala, not someone who bends his knee to a lulzi."

Sandy's face grew serious and he nodded.

"Thank you."

Hojeen dropped back and fell in at Sandy's side. "You want me?"

"How well guarded is the shee's throne room?"

Hojeen scratched his chin. "Maybe a few guards. If they search for us, maybe less."

"I hope you're right." Sandy did some fast figuring. The odds against them were long, but just might be shorter if they struck directly at the shee. "Is there a way to get to her quarters without running head-on into her henchmen?"

Hojeen thought for a while. "Ningerlings will help. They know the ways of other whens. If they can get to us to the round pool, I know a way from there."

Sandy started to nod, then suddenly stopped and listened. He looked around the pillared hall they were in, then listened again. Silently he motioned Anala to catch up with the rest of the company. For a moment a contrary look flashed in her eyes, then she picked up her skirt and ran ahead.

Without speaking, Sandy and Hojeen concealed themselves behind the pillars on each side of the hall. For long moments it lay open and soundless. There was a slight scuffing sound and a figure, hardly more than a shadow, came stealing down the hall. Soon there were five or six shadows flitting from pillar to pillar.

Sandy strung his bow and lay it on the floor beside him, along with six arrows. A thin gangling man dressed in black velvet and leather slipped out of the shadows toward him. There was a scuffling sound from across the hall and the skulker ducked behind the pillar concealing Sandy. A moment later there was an almost inaudible snapping sound. Sandy eased his foe's body to the floor and waited.

Another black-clad figure came running on silent feet toward him and died with an arrow in his heart. On the other side of the hall two figures rushed toward where Hojeen was concealed. One tumbled to the marble floor, Sandy's arrow buried in his spine. The other disappeared into the shadows, where moments later there was a muffled scream.

Sandy dropped his bow and rolled as another foeman rushed him from behind. A wavy-bladed dagger just missed his throat. Then Sandy was wrestling for his life, both hands holding the wrists of his opponent, while the daggers in each of his foe's hands slashed at his body. A knee almost caught Sandy in the groin. Instead he did a last-second twist and the knee rammed into his thigh. Sandy catapulted himself forward, catching his foe in the face with his steel cap. There was the crunch of breaking bone, a strangled scream, and the assassin collapsed.

There was a shadow behind Sandy and he whirled to face it, only to see Hojeen.

He held up three fingers and then reached down and picked up one of the wavy-bladed daggers dropped by the assassin Sandy had disabled. He looked at the black stain on the blade and then at the foeman who lay nearly unconscious on the floor, his face a smashed and bloody mess. Hojeen ran the dagger lightly over the assassin's arm, just barely scratching him. For a moment there was no sound except the foe's labored breathing, then there was an agonized scream and he went into convulsions. In less than a second he was dead. Hojeen held up four fingers.

"That's cheating," Sandy whispered.

Hojeen just smiled and tucked the wavy-bladed dagger away in his belt.

They caught up with the rest of the company in a broad indoor courtyard. In its center was a large fountain with a headless bronze statue of a woman kneeling in its middle, a trickle of rusty water dripping from her neck. Above, the sun shone through skylights, illuminating the courtyard with gentle light. Here and there a few hardy weeds pushed their way up between the cobbles. Six tiers of apartments surrounded the courtyard, many of their windows broken and the doors sagging on their hinges.

Talim had given the men a break and they were sitting around one end of the fountain, resting and doing some gabbing. Talim sat alone at the other end. Sandy joined him, sitting down at his side.

"We had some trouble back there," he said. "Some Chen men. The last of them are supposed to have died over thirty years ago. The shee must have dug them up from someplace, though I thought they only served Glag Glorgan."

"Shamdad says this citadel is a strange place that goes on forever, that it exists in many times and places at once. According to him, the shee only controls a small part of it, the part that borders on Zarathandra." Talim added bleakly, "I think some part of this citadel belongs to Glag Glorgan and he has struck a bargain with the shee."

The Yellowbird Singer, the ningerling who had been teaching Anala his tongue, came hurrying up. "Many strange folk are wandering the deserted parts of Ab Cimber—folk from the *far* places of the citadel."

"What did he say," Talim said darkly.

"Trouble," Sandy replied. He turned back to the ningerling and asked, "Have you seen any of these strange folk?"

The Yellowbird Singer pointed back toward the way he had come. "We slew some slingers from the Place of Falling Water. They were attacking ningerlings from the Red Wall clan when we came upon them. The Red Wall clan, and other ningerlings we have met, spoke of slingers and others wandering the forgotten parts of Ab Cimber."

Sandy muttered an oath and got to his feet. "Somehow that green piece has got the pot boiling—if we don't move we'll get burned. Well, we're going to tip the pot."

He asked the Yellowbird Singer, "Can you get us to the round pool?"

"Great round pool or dry round pool?"

"Whichever is closest to the shee."

"The way is long and twisting, but there is a way."

"Good." Sandy turned to Talim. "Get the men off their butts and ready to move."

Talim nodded glumly and then began barking orders at the troops, who scrambled to put on their gear. There was a thud and a trooper fell down, a large dent in his skull. A sling stone smashed against the edge of the fountain, sending marble chips flying.

"Get your helmets on," Talim roared. "The stones can't hurt you if you're in armor." A stone caught him on the shoulder and he staggered backward. A moment later he was back bellowing orders, living proof of his words.

Shamdad let fly an arrow and there was a scream. While Hobhardigan led half the troops into the abandoned apartments, the rest formed a bastion at the fountain. Sandy, Shamdad, and the ningerlings provided covering fire and waited for any slingers Hobhardigan flushed out.

They heard screams and the clash of weapons inside the abandoned buildings. Suddenly a slinger came flying out a third-story window, taking a fatal nosedive to the cobblestones. A second later another slinger ran out an adjoining door, pursued by Hobhardigan. He raced across a balcony and desperately tried to jump to the next one—but never made it. Three arrows sent him plunging downward. Hobhardigan threw a curse at his friends and plunged into the building after more prey.

The fight didn't last much longer. In less than half an hour, Hobhardigan and his crew had cleaned out the building. "They weren't worth crap as hand-to-hand fighters," he complained to Sandy as he led his troops out into the square.

Sandy, Hojeen, and the ningerlings did a quick scout of the adjoining rooms and corridors. They found no sign of trouble, which just made Sandy more uneasy. He hurried back to the fountain and asked, "What's the count?"

"Blind Darl and one of the ningerlings are dead," Talim replied. "Aside from that not much. Marvkaye has a cracked left arm, but he can still fight." He paused and added almost accusingly, "Anala got whacked on the head. We're lucky she was only dazed."

Sandy grunted. "We found a crypt beneath the building. Dump the bodies there and move out as soon as you are done; the Yellowbird Singer and his ningerlings will be waiting to lead you. Hojeen and I will cover the rear."

While Talim got things moving, Sandy checked on Anala. She was sitting on the rim of the fountain and seemed to be in fine fettle except for a bandage around her head.

"Next time," he said, "you duck. We can't afford to lose you."

"Or you," she replied.

"Don't give me any of that bull," he retorted. "There aren't many lulzis. You can find a good thug at any street corner. Now watch yourself."

He went off to join Hojeen, not giving her a chance to argue—not that that shut her up. "You're impossible," echoed after him.

As Sandy fell in beside Hojeen, the old scout said, "Don't worry. The lulzi is tough. She has the luck of the Goddess."

"Yeah, but we're up a creek if she dies. She is what holds us together."

"Bad to lose the lulzi," Hojeen agreed. "Worse to lose friends." There was an old grief in his eyes. "Flowers die. Yet spring comes and there are more flowers." He was silent for a moment. "But never the same as the old flowers."

This wisdom didn't sit well with Sandy. "So flowers die— I don't care if they do. What I want is to be old and gray. To sit in the sun with my cronies and tell lies about our big adventure. I want them all to be there, not moldering bones in some forgotten corner of this place. Even that bastard Talim."

Hojeen shook his head sadly. "All want everything. All want to pay nothing. It's not like that—always pay and sometimes you get nothing."

"I know," Sandy agreed. "But you can always hope."

At a sudden shuffle, Sandy and Hojeen both whirled to the left. A strange ningerling came limping from a side corridor, blood flowing from a wound in his left thigh.

He panted out a message. "Jarjanni hounds—back there. Slew most of the pack, but I could hear other packs." He gave Sandy a shrewd look and added, "They are hunting for special meat—not ningerlings this time." He paused for breath. "The Craxidour and Yimsi clans ambushed dead men in the halls of Mammarkadas. Greenteeth has many fewer servants now." Then he limped off the way he had come.

"What are Jarjanni hounds?"

"Bad. Very bad," Hojeen replied.

"I could figure that out by myself."

Hojeen gave a crooked smile. "If you see, you will know."

Sandy cursed him out, ending up with, "If I see them, I know who I'll throw to them."

"They're big lizards with long legs and sharp teeth. Savage and fierce, but not smart. Gol the Huntsman is their master."

"Gol the Huntsman is no friend to the shee."

"Not her enemy . . . not mostly."

Sandy swore. "I wonder what kind of markers she has

pulled in. Next thing you know the kitchen sink will be after us.''

Hojeen raised his eyebrows and looked at him questioningly, but Sandy didn't explain.

For the next hour they had no trouble. The Yellowbird Singer led them through a series of deserted halls and up long flights of stairs, and they saw no one. Sandy didn't like this part of the citadel. There was a prevailing gloominess and despair here that seemed to seep from the walls. Whoever had built this part couldn't have been very happy folk; what few murals remained on the gray stone walls were scenes of death and defeat in battle. There was a sense of relief when they walked around a corner and were in another time and place.

They came through a doorway carved in the shape of a giant snake's mouth and found themselves in the Grand Canyon of halls. They were on a wide walkway along one of its walls. To the left, without any bannister or railing, was the edge of the walkway. A thousand feet below was the floor of the hall. Another thousand feet or more up was the vaulted ceiling, and a gentle light filtered through the translucent blue and amber stone it was made of. Five hundred feet across the hall was the other wall, lined with a hundred or more walkways from floor to ceiling.

Whoever the builders of this place had been, they apparently couldn't abide unused space. Every inch of stone was covered with carvings. Demigods and men romped, feasted, fought battles, tilled fields, built cities, did great deeds, betrayed each other, raised children, grew old, and died. Everywhere, filling otherwise empty space were vines, leaves, and the beasts of field and home. There was so much detail that Sandy could have spent a year just getting to know one small section of wall.

The builders couldn't abide naked stone, either. Every piece of carving was painted, glazed, gilded, or somehow colored. The unending profusion of figures and rainbow hues was overwhelming.

The walkway beneath their feet was covered with tiles depicting an intertwining mess of cats and serpents. The cats chewed on the tails of the serpents, while the serpents in turn were swallowing the cats from behind.

The walkway worried Sandy. It was too open and exposed,

with nowhere to go except straight ahead, straight back, or straight down. Occasionally doorways pierced the right-hand wall, but the rooms beyond were filled with inky blackness.

As they passed one, Hojeen said, "Bad place to go into—the lair of night beasts and night people. They hate light and like nobody. We're safe in the hall as long as the sun is up."

"How can you tell when the sun is up?"

Hojeen pointed toward the ceiling. "When the stones go dark, it's night outside."

After they had been traveling along the walkway for an hour, they stopped for a rest by a spiral stair leading up to the next level. Sandy talked to the Yellowbird Singer and then to his companions. "We've about another two hours before we reach the end of this walkway," Sandy told Talim. "The Singer says we have enough time and a little more to make it before nightfall. From there it is only a short way to the round pool."

"Why before nightfall?"

"That's when the beasties come out." Sandy pointed to a dark doorway a short way down the walkway. "They are no friends to the shee, but they are no friends to anyone. Tell everyone they have fifteen minutes and we are on our way again."

Sandy and Hojeen broke out their canteens, sat down close to the doorway, and shared a loaf of ningerling bread. As they munched they heard a soft noise from the doorway. Startled, they turned and saw a pair of beady red eyes watching them. Hojeen started to draw his dagger, but Sandy put a hand on his arm.

"Put it back. I know this moocher."

Sandy's piglet hesitated a moment and then scurried out of the doorway and sat up on its back legs, keeping a wary eye on Hojeen while looking expectantly at Sandy. He gave a half grumble and threw it some bread. It grabbed the bread out of midair and then sat back to chomp it down, watching Sandy to make sure he didn't go anywhere else while he still had food he could be chivvied out of.

Hojeen laughed. "That's a chubba. If chubba likes you, that is good luck. He's a magic beast who long ago the Goddess blessed. Chubba has no master; he goes where he wants to."

"Bottomless belly too," commented Sandy as he threw the last of his loaf to the chubba.

There was a long bellowing howl, back toward where they had come from. Moments later it was followed by a whole series of harsh yaps, then another long bellowing howl, sounding much like an out-of-tune bell.

"Jarjanni hounds," Hojeen said, unslinging his bow.

Far away toward the other end of the walkway was an answering howl, so faint it was nearly inaudible, but still there.

"Damn, they have us boxed in." Sandy caught the Yellowbird Singer's eye and pointed up the stairs. The ningerling nodded. Talim came hurrying up and Sandy swiftly gave him his orders. "Leave Hobhardigan and a couple of soldiers here and get Anala and the rest to the upper walkway. We'll hold them until you get a good lead. If we don't catch up with you, look for us at the round pool."

The ningerlings were up the stairs in a flash, followed by Talim hurrying along a protesting Anala. Shamdad and the rest of the troops brought up the rear. Scurrying down the walkway toward the stairs was Zhadnoboth, who had wandered off to study some hieroglyphs. He saw Sandy's eye on him and hurried faster.

"Not so fast," Sandy yelled. "We need you here."

"Here?" protested the sorcerer. "I'm no fighter."

"No, but you have your uses. Have a spell ready to destroy the stairs."

"That will take time. It's not like drawing a sword from its scabbard, something that can be done instantly. Let me go; I'm no use here."

"We'll buy you the time."

Sandy turned to Hobhardigan. "Get to the top of the stairs with your two men and hold them. Hojeen and I will spit as many as we can and then join you." He motioned toward Zhadnoboth. "Take him with you and make sure he gets busy on that spell."

He nodded to Hojeen, strung his bow, and turned to face the fast-approaching pack. They were a fearsome sight, looking like long-legged crocodiles. Their noses were shorter, their hides scarlet, their bellies yellow-orange, but their teeth were just as long and sharp as any water-loving crocodile's.

They let out a raucous roar as they saw Sandy and Hojeen. Their bellowing howl sent shivers up Sandy's spine.

"Get as many as you can, then run for the stairs when they get too close," he told Hojeen.

He drew his bow and let fly an arrow that caught the pack leader in the chest and sent him tumbling to the floor. Between the two of them they killed or wounded seven of the hounds in the next few seconds.

Sandy yelled, "Run," to Hojeen, dropped his bow, and yanked out his sword. A hound charged him, jumping for his throat. Sandy ducked and the beast went over him. An instant later there was a terrified howl which quickly faded away as the hound plunged toward the faraway floor of the hall.

Two beasts came at Sandy from each side. He lashed out with his sword to the left, and it howled gleefully as it sliced off the head of one beast. With a backhand blow he severed the throat of the other. A third came flying toward him and caught his armored forearm in its teeth. The impact sent Sandy and the hound reeling over the edge of the walkway.

Desperately Sandy grabbed at a carving with his free hand as he went over the edge. His hand found purchase and he came to a halt with a jerk that nearly tore his arm from its socket. Momentum tore the hound loose from his other arm and it went howling to its death. Sandy wrapped his legs around a pillar and he was safe for the moment. Hastily ramming his sword through his belt, he began crawling upwards, using the carvings as a ladder.

He lifted his head over the edge and saw the hounds surrounding the spiral stair. As he watched one came tumbling down to land with a smash on the floor. The others ignored its bleeding body and struggled up the stairs, hindered more by the pressing mass of fellow pack members than by the defenders above. More than one was shoved off the unrailed stair to hit the tiles below. They kept coming, though, too dumb or too vicious to give up.

Sandy looked upward and saw that his pillar continued up to the next level. He looked toward the hounds and decided to climb; he'd had his fill of fighting for the moment. Grabbing the stone breast of a dancer in his hand, Sandy began pulling himself up. When he was about four feet above the walkway, a hound tumbled off the stair, saw him as it picked itself up, and charged.

Sandy tried to shin up the pillar out of harm's way, but the hound recklessly jumped and sank its teeth into his left boot.

Clinging to the pillar with a slipping grip, Sandy reached down and stabbed the thing in both eyes with his dagger. It still held on. He stabbed again, this time ramming the dagger to its hilt into the beast's left eye. The blade penetrated the brain and the beast gave a convulsive shudder and died, but the teeth kept holding on.

Sandy gave a curse and tried to climb, but the dead hound's weight almost pulled him off the pillar. He yanked at his sword hilt, but the position was awkward and the blade snagged against something. He pulled his upper body away from the pillar, almost falling when he inadvertently caught sight of the floor of the hall so far below. He quickly jerked his eyes away and this time managed to get his sword out. Left-handedly, he struck down at the hound. The blow was weak, but the magic blade easily sheared through the beast's flesh and cut a deep gash in the stone beneath.

The thing's body dropped away, though the stubborn head still was clamped onto his leg. Sandy placed his sword blade in his mouth and resumed climbing, the sword humming happily. Every half second he would remember the gulf yawning below him and he'd get the shakes. He forced his mind to concentrate on one handhold after another, and then he was at the top. A hand suddenly appeared to give him a boost over the edge. He looked up and saw Hojeen's grinning face.

Sandy crawled away from the edge of the walkway. Then he spit out his sword and put his hand to his mouth. When he took it away there was blood on it. The sword crooned a soft and happy tune; blood was blood.

Sandy muttered, "Goddamn vampire," and bent down to pry the hound's head off his boot. It was clamped on like a steel vise. Hojeen bent down and jabbed twice at the back of the beast's head with his dagger. With the second jab, the jaws suddenly relaxed. Sandy yanked the head off his boot and tossed it over the edge of the walkway.

"Never, ever let me do that again," he told Hojeen. "I'll see that damned drop forever in my nightmares."

He heard a snarling at the stairs and looked up in time to see Hobhardigan split a hound's skull. The stairwell beneath him was stuffed with dead and dying hounds, but those below kept forcing their way up. One of the troopers lay dead at Hobhardigan's feet, his throat torn out. The other was on the other side of the stairwell jabbing down with his spear. There was an increased howling from below and an increased frenzy on the stairs.

"New pack," Hojeen said laconically.

Sandy looked for Zhadnoboth and saw him leaning against the wall reading a dog-eared spellbook and mumbling under his breath.

"Hurry up," Sandy yelled. "We haven't all day."

"All right, all right," the sorcerer complained. "I'm coming." A brass censer, puffing out light purple fumes, hung down on its chains from his right hand. He started to swing it over the stairwell and chanted the words of a spell over it, reading from the spellbook in his other hand.

A whiff of purple smoke drifted up into Hobhardigan's face. He sneezed and backed away, coughing. Sandy took a sniff and moved off; the heavy, cloying incense was powerful enough to wake the dead.

The fumes engulfed the head of one of the lifeless hounds crammed into the stairwell and suddenly it roused and snapped at Zhadnoboth's ankles. He hollered, dropped the censer, and jumped back.

A swirling cloud of purple smoke mixed with orange flames rose from the stairwell in great puffs.

The sorcerer's face turned white. He yelled something incomprehensible and ran for his life. Sandy was right at his heels.

There was a dull thud behind them and then a shaking. Sandy was lifted off his feet and sent sprawling. He rolled over on his knees and looked back. Except for a few wisps of purple smoke the area around the stairs appeared the same. But when a hound erupted from the stairwell and charged, a tiny piece of stone fell off the walkway, followed quickly by two more, and then a dozen. With a roar, the whole walkway shattered into pieces and slid downward.

When the dust cleared there was a huge gap in the walkway and a smaller one in the one below. Part of the wall had come away, exposing the empty rooms. Below, the few remaining hounds huddled against the wall and whined.

Sandy looked at the gap, then at the trooper on the other side, and cursed. Only the trooper had run the right way; the rest of them were on the wrong side of the gap. He motioned to the far end of the hall and yelled, "Find Talim." The trooper waved and trotted off.

He turned to Zhadnoboth and said, "You did it again."

"Me!" retorted the sorcerer, his face purpling. "It was the perfect spell for the occasion. Except for an accident it would have stayed perfect. No other sorcerer could have whipped up any kind of spell in the time you gave me." He ran out of steam for a second then added as a capper, "And you didn't have to run the wrong way."

"Neither did you."

The sorcerer didn't know how to answer that so he glowered peevishly.

"We'll have to go back until we can find a stairway to a higher level," Sandy said. He tossed his quiver away and gave his spare dagger to Hobhardigan, who had lost his sword.

With Hojeen leading the way, they set off. Ten minutes later they still hadn't found an upward leading stair. Suddenly, the old scout stopped and pointed off into the distance. Sandy moved up beside him and shaded his eyes. A vague moving mass covered the walkway in that direction.

"Now what do we do?" Sandy asked.

A squeak answered him: His chubba was sitting in a dark doorway.

"We follow the guide the Goddess sent us," Hojeen said, heading toward the chubba.

"You're not going in there," the sorcerer howled. "It's dangerous. You don't know what is in there."

"It's better than climbing one of these pillars to the next level." Sandy set off with Hobhardigan after Hojeen.

Zhadnoboth looked at the black doorway, looked at a pillar, looked down, gulped, and ran to catch up.

Sandy pulled out his sword, which began to glow with a bright ruby light. He grunted in surprise, smiled, and walked on. The sorcerer muttered something behind him and there was a flare of light. Zhadnoboth yowled as if he had been bitten, angrily spat out some more words, and the brilliant glow behind Sandy dimmed to a mellow brightness.

The chubba waddled through the dark rooms, followed by Sandy and his shining sword, Hojeen and Hobhardigan, and Zhadnoboth bringing up the rear with his glowing staff. Out of the corner of their eyes they could catch glimpses of things hiding in shadows or sliding around unseen corners. But nothing attacked them, whether from fear for Sandy's sword, the sorcerer's staff, or some inexplicable other reason.

The chubba led them down a stairway into a wide room. By the echoes they could tell the room had to be gigantic, but all they could see was the floor under their feet. The rest was a vast darkness that seemed to go on forever. The floor was inches deep in dust and Sandy noticed they were following a faint trail. Somebody had walked this way a very long time ago.

Several minutes later, the chubba suddenly swerved off the trail to go to one side of it. A black something lay on the floor in front of them. Sandy brushed off the age-old dust. It was a skeleton in black armor, laying face-down, the black steel axe in its right hand was buried a couple inches into the floor.

Hobhardigan knelt beside the skeleton. "Forgive me for disturbing your rest, warrior," he said in a surprisingly reverent voice. "I would ask the use of your axe. Our need is great and you can no longer swing it."

A soft sigh echoed through the room. Hobhardigan bowed his head and said, "I thank you." He reached down and yanked the axe free from the floor. The finger bones of the previous owner made a clicking noise as they fell to the floor.

As the warrior strode along with the axe in his hand, Zhadnoboth asked, "Why did you do that?"

Hobhardigan shrugged. "It felt right."

"It *was* right," Sandy said. "I could feel anger back there, but it turned to approval, almost joy when you asked."

"Piffle," said the sorcerer, though not too loudly.

At the far side of the room they came to a wide and curving ramp leading downward. A dank wind redolent of the smells of decay and age blew up the ramp. Unhesitatingly the chubba waddled down it. They went down for a long time and then came out into narrow corridor.

Many narrow doorways opened into the corridor from each side. As they passed they could see that these doors opened into side corridors which twisted back to unguessable distances. Shelves had been cut into the stone walls of these corridors. On all of them rested the bones of the dead, sometimes the bones of a dozen or more people.

Just beyond the range of their light, white figures sidled through the shadows and looked at them with hungry red eyes. Behind them they heard a faint shuffle. Zhadnoboth looked about nervously and then moved his mouth close to his staff and murmured a short cantrip. The light brightened slightly and moved to form a shield behind his back.

As Sandy approached a side corridor a woman stepped out. She was wrapped in white silk and slender gold chains encircled her arms and neck. A starvation thinness, skin the pale yellow of old linen, tangled black hair which trailed to the floor, and fine chiseled features all were hers. Yet what he most noticed were her wide black eyes with pinpoint red pupils and her small sharp teeth.

"Join me," she said in a soft and sultry voice. "Come see the wonders that were and shall be again. Come." Her voice wove a powerful spell and their misgivings were wiped from their minds. They saw only an alluring and fascinating woman they ached to know more, not her faded finery or her chill flesh.

In the shadows other figures edged closer, eager to join in the feast. She touched Sandy on the hand, coaxing him to go with her. There was a brilliant flash of blue light as their flesh met. She screamed and staggered back, her arm a blazing torch. In moments her whole body was afire and in less than sixty seconds only ashes and an intense heat remained.

Sandy and the others stared in horror and then turned and fled after the chubba.

For hours the chubba led them deeper into the maze of rooms—out of the catacombs, through feast halls, down twisting corridors, up stairs, down stairs; but always unhesitatingly.

They only caught glimpses of the world that surrounded them—a corner of a giant web; creatures slinking out of sight as their light came close; some gnawed bones; and over everything an unending layer of dust. The chubba moved through this completely unconcerned, and no creature tried to gobble up this fat little morsel or even come close to crossing its path. Several times the piglet munched on something that it found along the way. Sandy never quite saw what it ate, though once it could have been a snake's tail sliding down its throat.

Finally they came to a place where walls of black cut basalt towered high above them and approached to within ten feet of each other. The floor under their feet started sloping downward until it was a steep ramp. They went down for half an hour until suddenly the walls ceased. The ramp continued, but now on each side was a deep abyss. Gradually they became aware of a vertical line of light far in the distance. Almost running, they hurried toward it.

Then they were on the floor of a great hall which stretched unimaginable distances to each side. Across the hall was a great vertical crack through which the light seeped. As they came closer they saw a pair of gigantic bronze doors, several stories high and each about a hundred feet wide, standing just slightly ajar.

The chubba waddled quickly through the open crack. Sandy was right on its heels, followed by Hojeen and the sorcerer. Hobhardigan got stuck for a second, but Sandy grabbed his arm and gave a yank. He popped through, leaving behind a couple of buttons and some cloth.

The light was a gentle glow, but they stood around blinking for several minutes before they could see. To their dark-adapted eyes it was almost a glare.

The chubba squeaked petulantly. Sandy turned and saw it bouncing up and down impatiently on its hindquarters. He searched through his pockets and found a piece of cheese wrapped in waxed linen. He threw it toward the chubba, who gave an it's-about-time squeak and disappeared: one moment there, the next moment only thin air where it had been.

"What was that?" Hobhardigan asked.

"Magical beast," Hojeen replied matter-of-factly.

The round pool was over a hundred feet in diameter, but only about three feet deep. The bottom was covered by mosaics of fish, mermaids, and other sea life. The rim was made from alternating tiles of lapis lazuli, jade, and carnelian. Thirteen bronze fountains in the shapes of various kinds of fish formed a circle in the center of the pool. Only two still dribbled some water and the pool, except for some minor puddles, was dry.

The circular room which lay about the pool had walls made up mostly of marble pillars, stairways, small balconies, and narrow walkways. Everywhere and at all levels small rooms opened off the pool room. Into the marble were embedded panels of alabaster, turquoise, jasper, agate, aquamarine, and other semiprecious stones. Some of the panels were carved, but more were plain, relying only on the natural beauty of the stone.

Suddenly a faint "Damn!" echoed through the room. They

whirled to face the sound, just in time to see Anala hobble in through a door at the opposite end of the pool. Talim, Shamdad, and three troopers came in after her, looking battered and tired. Sandy waited for more warm bodies, but none came.

"It's about time," Sandy yelled.

Anala and her companions looked up and then came running, howling joyously.

21

THE last stroke of midnight came. Old Zorgul, Zorgul of the Twelve Coins, stepped forward and faced Fortress Matandi. He pointed his staff at Hothum's Door, the great gate leading into the fortress. A pale thread of lavender fire arched from the end of his staff and touched the gate. Once, twice, three times it got no purchase on the god-forged metal. The fourth time it caught and held. Zorgul spoke a name of power and then a word of unbinding. A ball of lightning, the color of royal purple, slid from his staff and along the thin lavender line, touched the metal of the gate, and quietly vanished.

For twenty-three seconds an unearthly silence gripped the fortress and the surrounding countryside; then a bestial roar, powerful as an earthquake, erupted. The steel-bound gate exploded outward, sending a deadly shower of metal shards flying into the warriors manning the outworks.

From their prison beneath the foundations of the gate, the Akitazzi—the six demons who are one—burst forth. Six gigantic black shapes quickly shambled across the stone bridge over the dry moat and tore into the outcastle guarding the far end of the bridge. In short moments men, metal, and stone were ripped apart in a fiery storm.

The moon came from behind a cloud to illuminate the top of the mountain. At the sight the Akitazzi howled fire and slobbered brimstone, forgetting the hatred fortress and charging up the mountain toward the being who dwelt there: Kels Hothum, Hothum of the Dark Places. The time for vengeance had come.

The Goddess smiled wolfishly. Hothum wouldn't sleep this

night. The Akitazzi did not forget and did not forgive. The god of the dark places must now face their demonic wrath and pay for enslaving them to the gate so long ago. He might win this battle, but he would be a wounded god if he did, easy prey for his many enemies—and she would be the first of them and the last. The dark places would have to look for another lord.

The Goddess looked again to the fortress. Aku's desert troops, led by Yuthman the Smith, charged over the bridge and through the ruined gate. Zadar Kray's warriors fought desperately, but the heart had been taken out of them.

Zadar Kray fought his way to the old tower, the inner citadel of the fortress, and its black gates slammed shut. For those left outside, it was the bloody peace of the sword, the eternal peace, and only three survived.

The Goddess looked toward Cimber-Tal-Gogna, and it was much the same. What happened in that great citadel, what happened in Zarathandra—each was affected and reflected by what happened in the other, but in odd and unexpected ways. A sneeze in Ab Cimber could be a storm in Zarathandra or a sniffle or a chill morning. Both her foes' defenses had been breached and they had suffered grievous losses, yet in both the outcome still hung on a thread. Defeat in either would change the destiny of the borderlands, Zarathandra, and the other worlds whose boundaries faded into those of the borderlands.

The Goddess looked again at the bloodletting in Ab Cimber and Zarathandra, then looked away. Quietly she walked to a far corner of her garden, a corner filled with the sharp aroma of mint and the gentle sweetness of blooming bragberry. She knelt and prayed for the dead, the living, her children, and herself. . . . Yet the pain remained.

22

"I'M starved," Anala said, as she sat on the edge of the pool and munched on some bread and cheese. "Bat riders ambushed us the second day and we lost most of our food. Yesterday we found a pond stocked with mudfish, but I like my fish cooked, not wiggling as it goes down."

"How many days has it been since we got separated?" Sandy asked in a too-quiet voice, sure he was not going to like the answer.

Anala did a quick count on her fingers "It's almost four days."

"That's not right," Hobhardigan said. "We wandered in the dark a long time, but at most that was only a half day."

"Dark houses are a different when," Hojeen commented. "Here, we are in shee part of Ab Cimber. Time in two whens moves at different speeds—sometimes."

"We're together again," Anala said. "That is what is important, not that I am an older woman."

Talim came hurrying up, his usual sullenness replaced by excitement. "I just talked to the Yellowbird Singer. A great coalition of the ningerling clans and tribes is attacking the shee's bastions. Now's the time to strike, while she is too busy to watch her rear."

Sandy nodded, and then yelled to his remaining troops, "You got five minutes. Finish stuffing yourselves and then gather at the broad stair."

"Stuffing ourselves," complained one of Talim's troopers, an old campaigner by the look of him. "On bread, cheese, and water?"

"It's better fare than we'll get in hell," Hobhardigan said with dark humor.

The broad stair was at the opposite end of the pool from the great doors Sandy and his companions had squeezed through. The broad flat steps were about sixty feet wide and went up four stories before they ended at a line of bronze doors.

"Hojeen knows the secret ways, so he'll lead," Sandy said. "Talim, I want you and your troopers in front. Hobhardigan and Shamdad will guard the rear. Anala and the sorcerer will be with me in the middle. Now, move out."

Halfway up the stairs, a puffing Zhadnoboth complained to Sandy, "This is ridiculous. There's no reason to kill ourselves before we get into battle."

"If there is a battle, I'm sure you'll find enough wind to take to your heels," Sandy commented dryly.

The sorcerer puffed angrily.

"They're called the wizard's stairs," Shamdad said, utterly deadpan. "By the time any fat wizard gets up them, he is too out of breath to say a spell."

The sorcerer's face went red. "I am not a wizard," he puffed. "Nor am I fat."

Shamdad winked at Sandy.

Zhadnoboth caught the wink and spent the rest of the climb grumbling about people who didn't respect their betters.

The landing at the top continued as a broad corridor to both the right and the left. And they were going to have to choose a corridor, because the bronze doors had been melted shut. The reliefs which had been sculpted into the doors had flowed and twisted so much that it was hard to tell what had been pictured: There a man with a drooping sword confronted a blob of something, and here a woman combed her hair while her dress and feet flowed into puddles.

" 'Abrabbas made me,' " Sandy read as he traced some runes in the metal with his finger.

"He'll have to make them again," Hobhardigan joked.

"They were beautiful," Anala said sadly. "Why did the shee do it?"

"Shee didn't," Hojeen said. Abruptly he went down the left-hand corridor.

On the right side of the corridor there were doors or stair-wells leading down to the pool every fifteen or twenty feet.

On the left side, the wall was smooth and unbroken. Hojeen followed it for about fifty feet, then stopped and looked up, moved forward a few feet, and leaped. The old man must have had some kangaroo in him, since he was able to grab hold of a narrow slot in the ceiling. He hung there for a moment. Then there was a grinding creak and a long narrow segment of the ceiling, with Hojeen hanging onto the end, dropped to reveal a stairway.

Hurriedly they climbed the narrow stairs and found themselves in another corridor, this one dusty and unfinished. Hobhardigan was the last one up, as he stepped off the stairway, it quickly rose and snapped into place. He stepped back onto the uneven surface and it didn't budge.

"Don't worry," Sandy told him. "If we leave, it will be feet first or through the front door."

Hojeen led them to a crude wooden door. They went up a short flight of stairs, ankle-deep in dead leaves, and came out into an arbor. Around about them lay a rooftop garden. Once a formal affair with neatly trimmed trees and precisely laid out walks, it had long since gone to seed. Now it sprawled all over the place, the trees ragged and the weeds growing in the walks.

The garden was huge. Behind them lay a corroded copper dome which covered the pool room. Half a mile or more ahead was a square tower, several blocks wide and with an odd dark green color. To their left the garden seemed to go on forever, but only a hundred feet or less to the right they could see a parapet, its crenelated top looking like broken teeth.

Hojeen headed for the parapet and they quietly followed. About fifteen feet from the parapet the garden abruptly stopped, replaced by a pavement of granite blocks. The roadway was still usable, but showed signs of long neglect. In the cracks between the blocks isolated tufts of grass and an occasional flower had begun to grow. Hojeen stopped at the edge of the pavement, pursed his lips, and blew a long trilling whistle.

In the distance they heard a low purring rumble which stopped, started, stopped, and started again—each time stronger and closer. Suddenly, a hundred feet or more ahead, a beast burst out of the garden. It looked like a long and slinky cat, though it was as tall as a man at the shoulder. Its color was a gray and green mottle with an orange-brown crest running from the top of its forehead, along the backbone, and ending at the base of its bobtail.

It stopped when it saw them, then slowly began to stalk. Hojeen stepped forward and whistled softly. With a joyous howl the beast came bounding toward them; coming to a quick and graceful stop inches from Hojeen. A great purr thundered in its chest and it rubbed its head against him, as he reached up and scratched it behind the ears.

Hojeen and the big cat continued their reunion for several moments. Then Hojeen stepped back and spoke to them. "This is Lord Ondaz. He rules the garden. He says who may pass."

He introduced them to the big cat by name. Ondaz looked over each one of them carefully and nodded, his glance cool and intelligent. When Hojeen introduced him to Anala, Ondaz gave a quiet purr and gently insinuated himself into her arms. The lulzi laughed and rubbed his head, and the big cat lapped it up as though it were cream.

Last of all, Hojeen introduced the cat to Sandy. They measured each other warily. Ondaz yawned, showing his needle-sharp teeth, and flexed out his long talons. Sandy stared straight into his lambent green eyes, slowly drew his sword, and then placed it atop his arm. The cat cautiously sniffed at it, smiled amusedly, and rubbed his head against Sandy.

"All right, you big bozo," Sandy said. "We've got us an agreement." There was a wild twinkle in the cat's eyes and Sandy knew the beast understood him. He scratched the cat over the eyes and a purr rumbled through its body.

"Ondaz will guard us. The lesser beasts, who roam through his domain, will show their respect and keep their distance," Hojeen said. Then, followed by Lord Ondaz at his shoulder, he set off toward the green tower, keeping the parapet close on the right.

Several times they saw hints of motion in the tangled brush which bordered the pathway to the left, but no beast came close enough to identify. Once a deep angry growl sounded in the middle of a grove. Ondaz stopped and let loose a soft rumbling roar. Then he stalked forward in all his majesty. The threatening growl abruptly trailed off into a frightened squeal, and an instant later they heard a loud crashing as something huge ran away. Ondaz bared his fangs in a brief smile.

Shortly afterward they rounded a corner and the big cat came to an abrupt stop. Sitting by a bush loaded with strings of red berries was Sandy's chubba. With one paw he held down a branch and with the other he stripped off the berries, shoveling them into his mouth as fast as he could. The fur around his mouth was stained scarlet and strewn with stray bits of his lunch.

Lord Ondaz growled angrily. The chubba looked up, burped contentedly, and went back to eating. With an explosive spurt, the big cat charged forward and tried to bolt down the white-furred glutton in one gulp. Just as his teeth touched the chubba's fur, there was a faint *pop* and the pest disappeared.

A moment later there was an angry chittering off to one side. The chubba was sitting on his haunches, under another berry bush, telling Lord Ondaz what he thought of him.

The big cat gave a lordly sniff and stalked off down the path. The chubba sent a sassy chirp after him, waddled closer to the bush, and began cramming berries in his mouth again.

Sandy smiled. He had the impression that this was an old game to the two of them, a game they would rather play than win.

As they got closer, they could see that the green color of the tower was caused by enormous masses of ivy-like holly growing on it, an ivy with shiny dark green leaves and deep crimson berries. Suddenly, Ondaz gave an outraged roar and bounded toward the tower.

Sandy looked and couldn't see anything. Then he caught a flicker of motion and looked again. This time he saw a clan of ningerlings climbing the holly toward the tower top.

Hojeen said soothingly to the big cat. "They're gone. Don't worry over ningerlings. Hojeen will tell them you're angry, tell them to ask, tell them they must bring gifts for forgiveness."

Ondaz let loose one last angry growl at the interlopers, then he stalked over and lay down at Hojeen's feet.

"Ningerlings will keep the shee busy from above," he said. "We will go another way, a much better way." He pulled a stone out from the bottom of the parapet, reached into the hole, and pulled out a long knotted rope. This he attached to the parapet where it met the tower and threw the free end over the edge. He smiled at his companions, jumped atop the battlements, and then over the edge and down. Ondaz yowled miserably behind him, then suddenly turned and vanished into the garden, as though heading for some definite goal.

Sandy hurried over to the parapet, looked down—and swore. Hojeen was swiftly bounding down along the joint between the tower wall and the wall of the garden, his feet finding footholds sunk into the stone and his hands moving along the rope with lightning speed. A thousand feet or more beneath him was the craggy outcrop upon which Cimber-Tal-Gogna was built; beneath that, the great borderland forest. Sandy looked again at the sheer drop and backed away, white-faced.

He turned to Hobhardigan. "You go next. The lulzi will be coming right after you."

The big man smiled and went over the edge without a qualm. Anala was almost eager when she went over, blowing Sandy a mischievous kiss. He cursed her out and sent the next man over. Eventually, he was the only one left atop.

He looked at the sky and told her what he thought: "This is the last time I go on one of these harebrained adventures for you. From now on I am going to stay where I belong; on good flat ground." Then a big flat . . . something . . . with a mouth a yard wide waddled out of the garden, brave now that Ondaz was gone. Sandy took one look at it, jumped to the top of the battlement, grabbed the rope, gulped, and began to gingerly climb down.

The going wasn't bad. The footholds carved into the walls were deep and the angle between the two walls gave him a lot of purchase. He made a point of not looking down or behind him, keeping his mind on the next foothold and then the next after that. He got to a small ledge and Hobhardigan grabbed him and helped him onto it. Sandy started to say thanks, looked down, and swore once more. The ledge was solid, but hardly two feet wide, with a wall behind and open air in front—and that same damned thousand-foot drop underneath.

Some fifteen feet away the ledge disappeared into the holly which covered most of the tower. Sandy said his prayers and edged along the ledge toward it, keeping his back to the wall and his eyes looking up. After what seemed an eternity he made it to this shelter. It was a tight squeeze between the holly and the wall, a narrow tunnel hardly head high, and Sandy was thankful for every branch which rubbed him the wrong way.

He eased along the ledge until he came to a doorway recessed into the stone. The heavy, inward-opening door had been unlocked. Beyond was a small chamber with stone benches along the walls. At one inside corner was a stairway leading down, at the other was a stairway leading up. Hojeen stood at the foot of the up stairway with the rest of the company. When he saw Hobhardigan come in the door, he started to climb the stair.

They went up the narrow stairway—hardly wider than the span of one's arms—for what seemed hours.

"Some adventure," Zhadnoboth groused between puffs. "All we do is climb stairs."

Finally, they halted while Hojeen fumbled at a door. A moment later he, Talim, and the three troopers eased through. There followed the clash of blades, a choked scream, and then silence.

Sandy pushed Zhadnoboth aside and hurried up the stairs. When he burst into the room at the head of the staircase, he saw the bodies of three Sanhar folk lying on the floor. Hojeen was over by a barely open wooden door peeking out. He nodded in satisfaction and eased the door shut.

Looking around, Sandy saw he was in a sort of mess hall. A heavy wooden table surrounded by twenty-odd wooden chairs dominated the room. Three plates of warm, half-eaten food were on the table. A tankard had tipped over, spilling wine which slowly dripped to the floor. At one end of the mess five huge wooden barrels lay on trestles; at the other were two doorways—one to the kitchen and one to a bunk room. A Sanhar lay half in and half out of one bunk, a large pool of blood on the floor beneath his slit throat.

Sandy went over to the door Hojeen had been looking through and eased it open. Outside was a great hall lined with two rows of old banners near the roof, the walls thick with trophies: axes, swords, halberds, pieces of armor, and innumerable other types of war gear. At the far end, two Sanhar guarded a pair of iron doors; at the near end was a pair of golden doors, two stories high and twenty feet wide. Four

Sanhar, just being relieved by an officer and four fresh soldiers, guarded it.

Sandy muttered a curse as he saw the relieved troopers and the officer heading for his door. Quickly he explained the situation. "Hide those bodies. We'll ambush them once they're through the door."

As soon as the officer entered the mess, he yelled for the missing soldiers. As the last guard came into the room, Hobhardigan, who was hiding behind the door, slammed it shut and attacked with his axe. He got two, while Sandy sprang up from behind the table and gutted the officer. The other two were quickly dispatched by Shamdad and Talim. It had been a fast and brutal fight.

"I wish they were all this easy," Sandy said, cleaning his dagger on the officer's cloak.

"The next story up," Anala said, "there are some loopholes overlooking the hall. Shamdad and I can go up there and pick off those guards by the gold doors."

"I'll take Talim," Hojeen croaked. "I know a hidden way to iron doors. We will slay the guards there."

Sandy motioned for them to go, then turned to Anala and Shamdad. "You two go upstairs. When the two guards at the other end are taken out, let fly with your arrows. The rest of us will come charging out. It should be sweet and bloody." To the sorcerer he said, "It's about time you earned your keep again. Watch for any magic. If it's there, you'll have to save our bacon."

"I've got just the spell," Zhadnoboth said eagerly. "You won't have to lift a finger."

"No! Use sorcery *only* if we have no choice. We want to give the shee as little warning as possible."

Exploring the barracks, Sandy found officers' quarters at the far end. From them a door opened only a few feet from the gold doors, and he stationed Hobhardigan and the three troopers there.

"Get the bastards fast," he ordered. Hobhardigan nodded and shook his axe.

Sandy wandered back to the mess hall and found Zhadnoboth sitting at the table and swilling ale from a tankard. He belched and drank some more. "That middle barrel has some passable light ale. The shee does right by her servants."

Sandy suddenly realized he was dry as old bones. He yanked a tankard off the wall and turned the spigot on the left-hand barrel. A dark beer gushed out. He sipped it, found the smoky bitter flavor to his liking, and drained his tankard in four swallows. "That's the real spoils of war," he said, wiping his mouth.

He motioned the sorcerer to follow, unsheathed his sword, and eased open the door into the hall, just far enough to see out. Suddenly two of the guards were dying with arrows in their throats, and Hobhardigan came charging out to split one guard to the gizzard. The remaining guard was quickly spitted by one of Sandy's troopers.

Sandy entered the hall, caught some motion from his right, and turned to face six undead spearmen who had been standing unnoticed along one wall. Enspelled until now, the blood just shed had roused them. They charged, and Sandy had to roll under their spears, somehow managing to swing his sword in a long sweeping motion at ankle level. With a soft song, his sword sheared off the feet of two of them, sending them tumbling to the floor. He slammed into a third and they rolled along the floor in a tangle of limbs and weapons.

The thing wrapped its dry hands around Sandy's throat, throttling him. He punched it in the gut with his free hand, but that did little good. He tried to get at it with his sword, but the zombie was too close. Desperately he rammed his sword up between them, almost cutting off the tip of his nose. He cut to the left and to the right and magical blade easily cut off the dead man's hands—so it went for Sandy with its teeth. He rolled onto his back, drew his legs to his chest, and let fly with a two-footed kick, catapulting it away.

The undead bounced off the floor, got to its feet, and came right back at Sandy. Then Hobhardigan was there, slashing away with his axe. In moments the zombie was only a grisly pile of twitching body fragments.

But the undead soldiers had exacted a price for their destruction. One of the troopers was down, a spear through his gut. He sat against the wall, moaning and clutching the haft. Zhadnoboth was kneeling by him and examining the wound.

"I don't want to die." The soldier gave a weeping howl. "It hurts, it hurts. Oh Goddess, I don't want to die."

"You're going to," the sorcerer said brutally.

In some strange way his words calmed the soldier. "So

much yet to do. So much more life to live," he said, biting back the pain.

"More wenches to put it to, more wine to souse away, more brawls to fight," Zhadnoboth said cynically—though there was an odd tremble in his voice.

The soldier laughed, his face grimacing with pain. "You got it right, father. You got it right."

The sorcerer placed his hands on the soldier's forehead and gave the blessing for the dead, ending with, "Peace, my brother, peace."

"Thank you, father," the soldier whispered painfully.

Zhadnoboth brought his canteen to the soldier's lips. The soldier drank from it, and suddenly slumped unconscious to the floor, his face no longer full of pain.

Zhadnoboth stood up and saw the others staring at him. "Someone had to do the proper thing," he blustered. "I couldn't let him die unshriven."

Sandy gave a brusque nod of agreement as he watched the sorcerer sneak a small vial from his hand and into his robe. In a black mood he turned to face the gold doors, weary of death and knowing more was to come.

There was a small cry behind him: Anala stood weeping over the dead soldier. "He pulled a sliver from my finger yesterday. The quest was so grand, so right." She wept some more. "Is it always like this?"

"No," Sandy said. "Sometimes it's worse."

"Damn you!" she shouted. "Do you have to be so hard?"

Sandy ignored her and went to look at the gold doors.

"It's like this, miss," Hobhardigan said, coming to stand beside her. "If you are a soldier you either accept death or ignore it, but you go on. Those who can't, die or get the hell out."

She nodded and dried her tears, then knelt and began saying a silent prayer to the Goddess for this dead soldier who had touched her life so briefly.

After fumbling around and trying to open the gold doors, Sandy called Zhadnoboth over. "Take a look at these—see if you can get them open."

The sorcerer shuffled over and began poking, sniffing, and scowling at the door. Soon he was eagerly investigating its lock and the runes cast into it, muttering comments like "interesting" and "my oh my oh my."

Hojeen came to watch. Catching Sandy's eye, he motioned almost imperceptibly with his head toward Anala. "She's less a child." He sighed. "Had to be—but it's sad. Knowing hurt, she's more human, but older."

There was a crack of electricity and Zhadnoboth jumped back from the door, swearing and shaking his hand.

"How soon can you get it open?" Sandy asked.

The sorcerer sucked on his fingertips before replying. "When hell freezes over—twice." He sucked on his burned fingers again. "There is a spell on that door the like I have never seen."

"You need a key," Hojeen said.

His words triggered a memory in Sandy's mind and he reached into his pocket, pulling out the iron key he had found in the armory such a short—and long—time ago. He unwrapped the linen rag he had put around it, held the key in the palm of his hand as though weighing choices, and inserted it into the keyhole. It slipped in easily. He waited an instant and then turned it. There was a sharp click and the doors silently swung open.

With Hobhardigan and Talim leading, they made their way into the throne room. At the far end, on a raised dais, was the massive throne. Unadorned and yet subtly beautiful, it had been carved from the grandfather of all emeralds. Only a great artist could have created such a seemingly artless masterpiece.

Except for the throne, the room was empty. Yet the granites and marbles contained a stunning natural beauty.

The floor was of polished green marble, the walls of a green-gray granite, and the vaulted cathedral ceiling of a green-tinged white marble, as was the stone framing the windows. Its long and narrow proportions reminded Sandy of a church—an impression reinforced by the seven stained glass windows piercing each of its side walls. The large central window on the left wall pictured the shee, her arms raised in blessing, and a multitude of tiny figures tagging along at her skirts. The large window opposite it was much the same, except that the figure was a male whose features had been blotted out by whitewash.

"Where the hell is she?" Sandy asked.

Hojeen pointed toward the far end of the room, behind the throne, where several ironbound doors pierced the wall.

They advanced cautiously, ready to fight for lives and souls. There was no sound but the quiet echo of their own footsteps, yet the further they went the more ominous was the silence and the greater the trembling in their hearts.

At the foot of the throne they stopped, not quite daring to go further, regretting they'd gone so far.

Suddenly one of the doors opened and a small, elderly Sanhar came scuttling out, carrying an armful of scrolls. He hurried along for several paces before he saw them. Then his eyes grew wide, a terrified squawk burst from his lips, and he ran for his life. The scrolls went flying, bouncing and rolling across the floor in every direction. Shamdad's arrow caught the small man in the back and he went tumbling.

"He wasn't worth the spit," Hobhardigan bitched at Shamdad. "Hell, he didn't even have a paperknife."

"He could have been the death of us all," Talim callously.

A large set of doors crashed open and the shee came marching out, followed by several of her minions who were half running to keep up with her angry stride. Sandy was never sure who was more surprised, the shee or those who had come seeking her.

The shee raised an arm and Zhadnoboth panicked. He said a hasty word and pointed his staff at her. There was a roar and the staff began spewing forth an unending stream of fireballs in a scattershot pattern. Red, blue, yellow, orange, green, striped, polka-dotted, and an occasional run-of-the-mill white fireball were flying every which way. They bounded, rebounded, reversed direction, went in circles, exploded, winked out, shattered, burnt holes, split, went mushy, and in general did everything except hit the shee.

—Because Jara was moving her arms in complex patterns, weaving and constantly renewing an impenetrable defensive shield around herself. Any fireball that came close was turned away.

As for the rest of them, both friend and foe, it was everyone for himself and the devil take the hindmost. Hobhardigan yowled and went flying into a wall as a pink fireball caught him a sideways blow. A troll from the low tribes was hit by a silver-stained fireball and shattered into tiny chips. An orange one burst apart over a Sanhar and he sank struggling to the floor, covered by a thick goo.

A turquoise fireball hit the wall behind the throne and exploded, sending deadly pieces of stone shrapnel flying. One of the troopers was virtually cut in half, while a half dozen of the shee's henchmen were cut to ribbons.

A Sanhar officer fled the carnage, racing for the gold doors and blowing piercingly on a brass whistle. But Talim caught up to him and rammed his sword through the officer's back.

A smoky black fireball hit the stained glass window containing the shee's image and it imploded inward, showering them all with needlelike shards. For a few moments the air was a multicolored holocaust like a giant deadly kaleidoscope.

Then the color, the crash and clatter, and the wild fury was over. Only five of them remained standing; Sandy, Anala, Shamdad, Hojeen, and Jara Greenteeth. Talim lay unmoving by the officer he had slain; Hobhardigan was semiconscious by a wall. The remaining trooper was kneeling, holding together his bleeding face, split from top to bottom by a shard of flying glass. And Zhadnoboth lay flat on his back, his face peaceful and his outstretched hand still holding onto his staff. Only one of the shee's henchmen still lived—a blond youth who was blindly feeling his way along a wall.

Jara Greenteeth glared disdainfully at them. "Are *you* the ones I must fear? The old bitch must be getting desperate."

"Where are your soldiers, shee?" Anala piped up, her voice shrill, but getting stronger. "It is you and us. Any you would command are destroyed or fighting the ningerlings. How grand are you without anyone to do your bidding?"

"Quiet!" Jara's face was twisted with hate. "I am enough." She went on sneeringly, "You lulzis think you are so special, so good. You're not. I've always known you for what you are. Who do you think was the first lulzi? What I was, you are, and that makes you nothing."

Anala's face went white with shock.

Hojeen stepped forward, fire in his eyes. "Let her be, Mem. She is not rotten like the first of her kind."

The shee recoiled from his voice, an odd expression of horror on her face. She looked at him closer, and turned livid with anger. "You! I thought you dead. How dare you show your face to me? We could have had Zarathandra—and you betrayed me." Scornfully she said, "And what was the price? *I'm* still young, and you are an old man who smells of death. Which of us chose rightly?"

Sandy watched in awe, silently cursing the old scoundrel. The scout who spoke bastard Rithian had disappeared. Now he was a somebody, and a well-spoken one at that. Sandy shifted position, bringing his sword to bear.

The shee swung toward him and hissed angrily. "And who are you? You swagger and carry a big sword, but you're a small man. And what is your sword? A dangerous toy—no threat to such as I." Her words were contemptuous, but Sandy heard the slightest echo of fear in her voice.

She turned to Shamdad. "I know you, little man. We've had dealings, you and I. You served my purpose and I threw you away when I had wrung you dry."

She laughed wildly. "Not one of you could worry even a minor god. Put together you are even less of a threat."

"You are nothing," Anala's voice rang out, her tones true, strong, and magical.

The shee winced as if the words lashed at her.

"You wanted everything and gave your soul to get it—and lost. You're long dead and don't know it." Her voice wove a powerful spell and the shee shrank away.

Then Jara Greenteeth struck back, sending hazy green bolts of energy at the lulzi. Anala retaliated with her voice, using it to form a shield and simultaneously attack. Stray bits of energy and slivers of magic sound ricocheted throughout the room.

The shee was older, more confident, and stronger; but she was only one. Sandy attacked her with his magic sword, the blade singing joyously. Though his mighty strokes couldn't penetrate the enspelled space around the shee, he kept at it, forcing Jara to divide her attention. Hojeen and Shamdad also joined in, sending an incessant rain of arrows and other missiles which burnt to ashes before they touched her.

The battle seemed to continue an eternity, the four of them holding the shee to a draw. The room was a shambles, the floor scorched, walls broken, and shattered stone kept falling from the ceiling.

Gradually Anala's vocal magic began to gain the upper hand. The sphere of energy about the shee grew smaller, and grudgingly she gave ground. Anala's voice rose to a crescendo and the shee was hammered to her knees. Then there was a strangled gasp and an unearthly stillness filled the room.

Sandy sprang back from the battle and looked for the lulzi.

He saw her and his face went white. The blinded youth had crept up behind her and was choking her. Already her face had turned red and her eyes were bulging.

The shee screamed in triumph and hurled a great bolt of energy at the lulzi. Hojeen reacted instantly, flinging himself in front of Anala. There was an earsplitting explosion—then the shee screamed out her agony, horror, and despair.

Sandy rushed in to attack, putting every ounce of energy and muscle into the blow, catching the shee across the back of her neck.

A flash of energy—and the sword went flying across the room, landing on the emerald throne where it smoked and hissed. Sandy fell to his knees, paralyzed by the shock that had gone through his system.

Shamdad tried to flee and the shee offhandedly speared him with a bolt of energy. She went to Sandy and touched him on the neck. He fell paralyzed to the floor, yet fully conscious and aware of what was going on.

The shee moved slowly over to where Anala lay. Her skin and clothes were scorched, but she still breathed. The blind youth who had been choking her was now a cinder. Hojeen's body was burned and mangled, yet the face was untouched, a face now strangely young and peaceful. Mem-Jara-Shil looked at him silently for a long time, then fell to her knees by the body and sobbed.

After long moments she rose to her feet, tears streaking her face and vengeance in her eyes.

"Halt!" she hissed—for Zhadnoboth had been scuttling away along a wall. Now he turned to face her, looking old and drawn. Holding his staff in front of him he came toward her.

"You are going to die, sorcerer," Jara said savagely. "You'll die a death such as no one has ever imagined. And you will be only the first."

Zhadnoboth frenziedly fumbled in his robe, pulling out the silver ring Sandy had pawned for the sword. Whether through fear or the working of fate, the ring slipped from his fingers and rolled across the floor to the shee.

She picked it up, a gloating look of recognition on her face. "Where did you get this?"

Zhadnoboth lost his nerve and pointed toward Sandy. "It's his; I was just holding it for him. He also has the key."

"What key?" she demanded, a terrible eagerness in her voice.

"The master key to Cimber-Tal-Gogna. The key that gives you full access to everywhere and everywhen it is."

"He stole it long ago." Jara's voice trembled as she glanced toward Hojeen's body. "The one key of the seven I most needed. Get it for me, sorcerer." Her tone was like the lash of a whip.

Zhadnoboth started to protest, but she turned the full force of her gaze on him. He got a glazed look in his eyes, dropped his staff, and began walking haltingly toward Sandy. As he knelt, he whispered, "*Now* see where you've got us."

"Have you got it yet?"

"Only a moment more." The sorcerer fumbled at Sandy's belt and palmed the shee's ring he found there—the ruby-headed ring that had so fortuitously fallen into their hands. "It's poor old Zhadnoboth who has to save the day," he muttered under his breath. Fumbling some more, he found the key, deftly slipped it into Sandy's hand, and said a certain word of power.

A warm glow quickly spread from Sandy's hand, up his arm, and then into the rest of his body—and with it the paralysis disappeared. Grasping the key tighter, he lay there and played possum.

The shee tapped her foot threateningly. Zhadnoboth grasped the leather thong around Sandy's neck, pulled out the pouch containing the other key, and held it up for Jara to see. "Here it is."

"Bring it to me."

The sorcerer rose and reluctantly shuffled toward her. He stopped a few feet away, opened the pouch, and showed it to her.

A cruel smile played upon the shee's face. "Stay," she commanded; and he stood as though rooted to the spot.

She walked over to the throne, stopping at the foot of the dais, and pointed. A thin beam of light flowed lazily from her forefinger and touched the great seat. She raised her arm and the throne rose several feet, stopping when her arm stopped. Her arm moved sideways and the throne did likewise. She lowered her arm and the throne floated down to settle on the scorched pavement.

Grandly Mem-Jara-Shil mounted the dais, moving with all

the grace and power of the heavenly queen she knew she was. She curled her finger and beckoned to the sorcerer. "Come."

"Don't trust the she-bitch," someone croaked.

Sandy looked toward the weak voice from where he lay on the floor and saw that a blood-spattered Talim had staggered to his feet. Sandy cursed inwardly, hoping the damned idiot wouldn't queer whatever plot the sorcerer had cooked up. He readied himself to move and move fast when things heated up—and they were bound to, with Zhadnoboth involved.

The shee looked contemptuously at him, raised an arm, and made a throwing motion. Talim was picked up and flung across the room, smashing backward into the throne. He slid downwards to sit, unconscious, with his hand resting limply on the hilt of the magic sword.

The shee said a word and the top surface of the dais crumbled into dust. From the ruined stone a block of rock crystal slowly rose, locking into place with a click when it was waist-high. The clear crystal was inset with hundreds of silver keyholes, and atop it lay a pair of long supple gloves fashioned from green leather.

Jara reached down and picked up the gloves and slowly donned them, flexing her hands in triumph after she had them on. Then the shee motioned for the sorcerer.

Zhadnoboth reluctantly mounted the broad stair leading to the top of the dais. His right hand held the pouch and its key, his left hung by his side, the fingers loosely clenched. She held out her hand and he emptied the key into it.

She looked at the key, which was now glowing with a faint blue light, and quietly gloated. Then she murmured, "So long . . . so long . . . now you are finally mine." Turning her back on the others, utterly confident of their powerlessness, she randomly picked a keyhole and inserted the key.

Behind her, Zhadnoboth backed down off the dais, moving quietly but quickly. Sandy also made his move, rolling to his feet. Hobhardigan, from where he lay slumped against the wall, did the same. Even Talim stirred slightly as he lay dying on the throne.

There was a sudden flare of blue light as Jara turned the key and staggered back, screaming. Where her left hand had been, there was only a smoking stump.

Then the floor bucked and heaved—a small earthquake followed by a much greater shock wave. A wall collapsed, and the ceiling at the far end of the throne room fell with an avalanche roar.

"The wrong key," Jara screamed in fury. She raised her right hand and flung a bolt of energy at the sorcerer, putting all her hate, all her being into it.

Sandy saw Zhadnoboth fling up his left hand—saw the ruby ring on it—saw the look of horror on the shee's face. The energy bolt engulfed the sorcerer, forming a maelstrom of swirling light which rose to the heavens, then rebounded toward the shee.

There was a brilliant, soundless explosion. Intermingled gobs of ruby and emerald light shot off seven ways to sunset; then Cimber-Tal-Gogna ceased to exist for them. There was only an all-encompassing blackness, violent and turbulent. Like the birds of ill omen they were, they were flung back to their roost: to Zarathandra.

23

THE massive battering ram smashed against the gate of the inner keep again and again. As the great tower rocked and shuddered, stray bits of stone fell from the battlements.

"It won't be long now," Yuthman the Smith remarked to Aku. "In a couple hours we can nail Zadar Kray's hide to the door. I'll do the skinning myself—I owe him that favor."

There was a sudden yell from the battlements and then the clash of weapons. A defender came tumbling down to smash against the edge of the great shield protecting the battering ram.

Yuthman grinned wolfishly. "Kas Ozaxas and his Black Branch Zenori must have made it up the back wall. Now if the gate goes, their nuts are in the grinder."

The ram hit again, and with a thunderous roar the gate tore loose from its mooring, taking part of the wall with it. The next moment the left-hand gate tower collapsed, half burying the ram. Cries and screams rose from the ruins.

Aku raised his arm high and brought it down. Thousands of desert warriors rose from their places of concealment and charged toward the keep like an irresistible wave. They asked no quarter and they gave none. Their trapped foes fought desperately but, outnumbered by more than ten to one, they were quickly cut down.

Aku and Yuthman the Smith, with a group of picked warriors, led the charge into the central chamber of the keep. There Zadar Kray with his remaining Yartazi raiders and Jadghuli hirelings met them in a fast and furious battle.

Just when it looked hopeless for him, with nearly half his

remaining troops cut down, Zadar Kray sprang a surprise. Sidestepping a thrust by a Kri Rithi tribesman, he ran him through; then, abandoning his sword, he raced to a corner and turned to face his foes. He drew a gray glass vial from his waistband and smashed it to the floor. A cloud of gray smoke spread through the chamber.

There was a savage chorus of bestial roars, and out of the smoke twenty odd Chanzi shapechangers came charging. Most were sand leopards, but one came as a wingless cave dragon and another as a bear-wolf. Aku and his men fought bravely, but they were in desperate straits.

Not content with the destruction he had unleashed, Zadar Kray ran to the black basalt altar dominating one end of the room. Drawing two more vials from his waistband, he held them high. "Come, o great ones," he yelled. "Come to the aid of thy servant. Destroy my enemies, wipe their seed from the face of Zarathandra, bring victory for thy faithful." He smashed the vials against the stone floor, and great billows of green and black smoke rose in huge spirals up the tower.

Then all hell broke loose.

From on high Kels Hothum was called, but so were the Akitazzi—and they had been set free of the enchantment that had bound them to the dark god's will.

Kels Hothum was in his guise as the great seven-headed black hound of hell. He let loose a roar that stopped mens' hearts, and charged into the fray. The next instant the vengeful Akitazzi arrived and fell upon him. The Six Who Are One surrounded him in a cyclone of teeth and talons.

The monsters ripped and tore savagely at each other, and whoever else got in their way. Gouts of fiery green demon blood and great splatters of Hothum's burning golden blood flew in all directions, slaying and maiming friend and foe alike, burning great scars into the stubborn stone of the fortress.

The shee came too, along with Sandy and his companions and an avalanche of debris torn from the wreck of Cimber-Tal-Gogna. The emerald throne smashed against the floor, crushing a Chanzi, and split into millions of fragments. The dying Talim staggered from the wreckage holding the ruby sword. A Yartazi backed into him and Talim instinctively swung, cleaving his foe in two. The sword sang a wild and drunken song, a doom song full of mindless rejoicing.

Sandy came down among a group of Chanzi. A leopard grabbed his hand in his mouth. Ignoring the pain, he wrapped that hand around its lower jaw and grabbed the upper jaw with the other, ripping the werebeast's jaws apart. It screamed horribly and fell, convulsing. Another Chanzi sprang at Sandy and they went rolling to the floor. Sandy's legs were wrapped around its middle; one hand held its slavering jaws, while with the other hand he thrust his dagger again and again into the beast which raked at his mailed back with its claws.

Hobhardigan landed on the back of the cave dragon just after it had incinerated a couple of Aku's men along with an unlucky Jadghuli. Briefly they looked at each other in mutual surprise. As the dragon tried frantically to stoke up its inner fires again, Hobhardigan brained it with his axe. The were-dragon let out an agonized roar and charged brainlessly through the room, squashing the hindquarters of a wereleo-pard on its way. Hobhardigan held on for dear life until he saw the dragon heading at full speed for a stone pillar. He flung himself off just before the beast plowed into it. The impact cracked the pillar in half and ser⁺ several tons of stone roof falling to bury the weredragon.

Lord Ondaz appeared, looked about puzzledly, and then charged into battle. One swipe of his paw disemboweled a wereleopard and another sent a Chanzi crashing into a wall. He fell on a third, severing its spine with one snap of his jaws.

The trooper with the ripped-open face came down behind Yuthman the Smith. He cut down two foes coming at Yuth-man from the rear, while the smith spitted a wereleopard on his spear. Yuthman turned around, saw the two dead foes, and nodded a brief thanks. The trooper nodded in return and then fell unconscious as shock and blood loss got to him.

Zhadnoboth, singed but otherwise uninjured, landed on Zadar Kray and knocked him over. He shook his head daz-edly, and then simultaneously saw his staff and the utter may-hem around him. He picked himself up, grabbed his staff, and scuttled for cover behind the altar. Behind him a crazed and bewildered Zadar Kray stared uncomprehendingly at the carnage.

The shee joined the party late, crash-landing onto the altar a moment after Zhadnoboth had hidden behind it. She lay there a charred and smoking heap, hardly recognizable; then stirred, sat up, and fell forward off the altar. Screaming in mindless agony, she fired off bolts of energy with machine gun rapidity, riddling the tower around her so that it looked like Swiss cheese. One blast caught Zadar Kray, burning his legs off at the knees.

Talim staggered toward her, his breath coming in great ragged gasps and bubbles of blood oozing through his clenched teeth. Blasts of energy tore through the air all around him, but none hit him and the shee seemed unaware he was even there. He drew up before her, raised the magic sword above his head in a two-handed grasp, and drove it through her.

A great scream echoed through the keep . . . and sudden silence followed as every being looked her way. She tottered forward on unsteady legs, the sword buried in her breast, and blindly knocked Talim down. She stood silent a moment and then moaned, "Mother." The sword turned blue hot and disappeared in a cloud of fiery plasma, a last clear note of victory ringing in the air. The next instant, what had been the shee drifted to the floor as tiny particles of ash. A fine green haze floated on high and then swiftly disappeared.

Something dropped from above, hit the floor with a ringing sound, and rolled across it to come to rest near Sandy's hand: the silver ring of Uncertainty seeking its master. He slipped it on and pushed the dead Chanzi off himself.

The battle was almost over. In one corner several warriors were finishing off a trapped wereleopard. Near a stair leading to the upper reaches of the keep Aku was chopping off the head of a gravely wounded, but still snarling bear-wolf. In a far corner a seven-headed beast, its body torn by great gashes, lay twitching.

Sandy heard a moan and turned to see Anala—burnt, battered, but still alive. He limped over and picked her up, holding her to his breast. She moaned again.

Behind him he heard awed gasps. He turned, holding the injured lulzi, and saw the Veiled Goddess advancing on him. She wore a hooded robe the color of death. Then she was before him; he looked and beneath the shadows saw her face— he stepped back involuntarily. She held out a hand and slipped a key into Sandy's palm. "Hold this until it is time."

"What time?"

The Goddess spoke a few last words, but did not answer

his question. Then she reached out, touched the lulzi, and vanished.

For a thousand years and more, folk would speak of the miracle at Fortress Matandi: how the Goddess came and healed her lulzi, and how Aku the Great carried her from that place of death as it collapsed behind him. They would sing of Talim the Good and how he slew the great shee; and of Hobhardigan the reaver who redeemed himself and became the Dragon Slayer.

And they would tell darker tales of how sometimes travelers could hear a great hound howling in agony from the ruins; or how if you come there at midnight, you can hear the shee weeping . . . and if you do, you can never rest easy again.

24

THE Goddess sat on the edge of her pool, running her fingers through the cool water and mourning for her children. The ache in her heart was a void that could never be filled. Long ago she had lost them both, and the agony of that time was still with her. Hojeen had found himself, but her daughter had stayed lost. They were beyond her ken now, and only her prayers were with them. But they were her children and she still loved them, no matter how cruelly life and destiny had misshapen them.

A fierce surge of emotions flowed through her. "I forgive not, forget not. A price will be paid," she whispered to the silent pool.

Then she wept.

25

SANDY rode down the streets of Kimbo-Dashla toward his quarters, thinking about the Goddess's last words. They still rankled—though damned if he knew why. He was free of her at last, if he had understood her. Now he could have the life that best suited him: calm, unexciting, and with a certain amount of good food and good women. Yet hearing her words again in his memory, he felt the odd pain.

"You have done what was needful," she had said. "From this moment be gone from my life and its pain. Live with mortals, know their joys and sorrows. I have blessed you, I have given you what you most need. I bid you go." After a poignant silence she had added, "You have done what had to be done, but I will not forget."

He remembered the tears that slowly trickled from her eyes. Her last words had seemed a pronouncement of doom, and he felt an ache which would not go away.

"It's all your fault," Zhadnoboth crabbed. "If you had talked to your Rithian masters the way you should have, I would have been a rich man, instead of a poor sorcerer wandering through the streets of a backwater city wondering where my next meal will come from."

Sandy looked at the sorcerer riding beside him and raised his eyebrows. "You do have that small villa on the outskirts of the city and if I remember right a bit of gold."

"Humph," the sorcerer snorted. "A yearly stipend of two hundred gold pieces and a piddling reward for my services of one chest of gold isn't even worth speaking about. I could

273

do better traveling around with some flea-bitten circus and dumbfounding dim-witted peasants with small magics.''

Sandy smiled. When the sorcerer *didn't* complain, then something was wrong.

They drew up in front of his quarters, a pleasant town house with a walled garden, and dismounted. His landlady, a plump busybody who had buried two husbands and was looking for another, came bustling out.

''The Goddess bless me,'' she said, ''if it isn't Master Sandro. A bit of a hero aren't you?'' She gave him a wink. ''What was it like, fighting with a great hero like Talim? You must be proud to have known him.''

''Yes, I am,'' Sandy said after a moment, managing to lie with a straight face.

The door of his town house opened and a young man came out with a woman on his arm. He saw Sandy staring at them and patted his wife's washtub-sized belly. ''Twins.'' They both beamed at him happily and toddled down the street together, obviously very much in love.

Sandy stared after them open-mouthed.

''I rented to them after your wives came and moved your stuff out,'' his landlady said. She got misty-eyed and added, ''And your babies were so cute. I just wanted to hug and cuddle them.''

Sandy stared at her. Slowly he asked, ''Wives? Babies?''

Five minutes later he was riding his rudhar hell-for-leather towards Ree-Mahim's villa—his villa—and muttering furiously under his breath. Zhadnoboth followed half a block behind, fruitlessly trying to catch up.

''I went to the best witch woman in the city. I *can't* have children!'' He scowled as he remembered his landlady's words about the Goddess especially blessing his wives with children. She would, that bitch. ''Ree-Mahim I can understand,'' he muttered. ''And even Belissa and Sheelimar. But the greatest madam in Kimbo-Dashla—that's too much. Not to say anything about this child bride from Ekbadikar. I haven't been within a hundred miles of that damned place, let alone her.''

He stewed some more. He was stuck but good. Shoe marriage, with children and the blessing of the Goddess thrown in, was nearly impossible to get out of. Now, maybe he needed a wife, but he certainly did not need a whole gaggle.

One wife and a mistress or doxy now and then—that was fine. He'd settle for that. He'd get this situation straightened out and settle down with whichever of them seemed the most comfortable. The rest would have to hook some other poor sucker.

He lifted his head to the sky and yelled, "You palmed me off! I am not going to forget this!"

DONALD AAMODT works for the Social Security Administration, and lives in the far northern outliers of Minneapolis with his wife, two daughters, a cat, and a dog. He began writing the adventures of Sandy MacGregor in his first published novel, *A NAME TO CONJURE WITH,* also available from Avon Books.

Mr. Aamodt writes, "I was born in Minnesota on May 17, Norway's equivalent of the Fourth of July, so every year Norwegians around the world make me feel good as they celebrate my birthday. By hook and by crook I graduated from the University of Minnesota in only seven years—taking a forced vacation in the army between entering and graduating. (My military time was very uninteresting except for the plane crash I survived.) I majored in anthropology and history while in college, especially enjoying the hard-digging archaeological summer projects (with especial fond memories of a site located between two breweries)."

The Epic Adventure

THE OMARAN SAGA
by
ADRIAN COLE

"A remarkably fine fantasy...
Adrian Cole has a magic touch."
Roger Zelazny

BOOK ONE:
A PLACE AMONG THE FALLEN
70556-7/$3.95 US/$4.95 Can

BOOK TWO: THRONE OF FOOLS
75840-7/$3.95 US/$4.95 Can

BOOK THREE:
THE KING OF LIGHT AND SHADOWS
75841-5/$4.50 US/$5.50 Can

BOOK FOUR: THE GODS IN ANGER
75842-3/$4.50 US/$5.50 Can

Buy these books at your local bookstore or use this coupon for ordering:

Mail to: Avon Books, Dept BP, Box 767, Rte 2, Dresden, TN 38225
Please send me the book(s) I have checked above.
☐ My check or money order—no cash or CODs please—for $_____ is enclosed
(please add $1.00 to cover postage and handling for each book ordered to a maximum of
three dollars—Canadian residents add 7% GST).
☐ Charge my VISA/MC Acct#_____ Exp Date _____
Phone No _____ I am ordering a minimum of two books (please add
postage and handling charge of $2.00 plus 50 cents per title after the first two books to a
maximum of six dollars—Canadian residents add 7% GST). For faster service, call 1-800-
762-0779. Residents of Tennessee, please call 1-800-633-1607. Prices and numbers are
subject to change without notice. Please allow six to eight weeks for delivery.

Name_____

Address_____

City_____ State/Zip_____

OMR 0391

RETURN TO AMBER...
THE ONE *REAL* WORLD, OF WHICH ALL OTHERS, INCLUDING EARTH, ARE BUT SHADOWS

ROGER ZELAZNY

The New Amber Novel

KNIGHT OF SHADOWS   75501-7/$3.95 US/$4.95 Can
Merlin is forced to choose to ally himself with the Pattern of Amber or of Chaos. A child of both worlds, this crucial decision will decide his fate and the fate of the true world.

SIGN OF CHAOS   89637-0/$3.95 US/$4.95 Can
Merlin embarks on another marathon adventure, leading him back to the court of Amber and a final confrontation at the Keep of the Four Worlds.

The Classic Amber Series

NINE PRINCES IN AMBER	01430-0/$3.50 US/$4.50 Can
THE GUNS OF AVALON	00083-0/$3.95 US/$4.95 Can
SIGN OF THE UNICORN	00031-9/$3.95 US/$4.95 Can
THE HAND OF OBERON	01664-8/$3.95 US/$4.95 Can
THE COURTS OF CHAOS	47175-2/$3.50 US/$4.25 Can
BLOOD OF AMBER	89636-2/$3.95 US/$4.95 Can
TRUMPS OF DOOM	89635-4/$3.95 US/$4.95 Can

Buy these books at your local bookstore or use this coupon for ordering:

Mail to: Avon Books, Dept BP, Box 767, Rte 2, Dresden, TN 38225
Please send me the book(s) I have checked above.
☐ My check or money order—no cash or CODs please—for $_____ is enclosed
(please add $1.00 to cover postage and handling for each book ordered to a maximum of three dollars—Canadian residents add 7% GST).
☐ Charge my VISA/MC Acct#_____ Exp Date_____
Phone No _____ I am ordering a minimum of two books (please add postage and handling charge of $2.00 plus 50 cents per title after the first two books to a maximum of six dollars—Canadian residents add 7% GST). For faster service, call 1-800-762-0779. Residents of Tennessee, please call 1-800-633-1607. Prices and numbers are subject to change without notice. Please allow six to eight weeks for delivery.

Name_____

Address_____

City_____ State/Zip_____

AMB   0391

Magic...Mystery...Revelations
Welcome to
**THE FANTASTICAL
WORLD OF AMBER!**

ROGER ZELAZNY'S
VISUAL GUIDE to
CASTLE
AMBER

by Roger Zelazny and Neil Randall
75566-1/$8.95 US/$10.95 Can
AN AVON TRADE PAPERBACK

Tour Castle Amber—
through vivid illustrations, detailed floor plans,
cutaway drawings, and page after page
of never-before-revealed information!

Buy these books at your local bookstore or use this coupon for ordering:

Mail to: Avon Books, Dept BP, Box 767, Rte 2, Dresden, TN 38225
Please send me the book(s) I have checked above.
☐ My check or money order—no cash or CODs please—for $_____ is enclosed
(please add $1.00 to cover postage and handling for each book ordered to a maximum of
three dollars—Canadian residents add 7% GST).
☐ Charge my VISA/MC Acct#_____Exp Date_____
Phone No _____ I am ordering a minimum of two books (please add
postage and handling charge of $2.00 plus 50 cents per title after the first two books to a
maximum of six dollars—Canadian residents add 7% GST). For faster service, call 1-800-
762-0779. Residents of Tennessee, please call 1-800-633-1607. Prices and numbers are
subject to change without notice. Please allow six to eight weeks for delivery.

Name_____

Address_____

City _____ State/Zip _____

GAM   0391

Avon Books Presents

THE PENDRAGON CYCLE

by Award-Winning Author

Stephen R. Lawhead

TALIESIN

70613-X/$4.95 US/$5.95 Can

A remarkable epic tale of the twilight of Atlantis—and of the brilliant dawning of the Arthurian Era!

MERLIN

70889-2/$4.95 US/$5.95 Can

Seer, Bard, Sage, Warrior... His wisdom was legend, his courage spawned greatness!

ARTHUR

70890-6/$4.95 US/$5.95 Can

He was the glorious King of Summer—His legend—the stuff of dreams.

Buy these books at your local bookstore or use this coupon for ordering:

Mail to: Avon Books, Dept BP, Box 767, Rte 2, Dresden, TN 38225
Please send me the book(s) I have checked above.
☐ My check or money order—no cash or CODs please—for $_____ is enclosed
(please add $1.00 to cover postage and handling for each book ordered to a maximum of
three dollars—Canadian residents add 7% GST).
☐ Charge my VISA/MC Acct#_____ Exp Date_____
Phone No_____ I am ordering a minimum of two books (please add
postage and handling charge of $2.00 plus 50 cents per title after the first two books to a
maximum of six dollars—Canadian residents add 7% GST). For faster service, call 1-800-
762-0779. Residents of Tennessee, please call 1-800-633-1607. Prices and numbers are
subject to change without notice. Please allow six to eight weeks for delivery.

Name_____

Address_____

City_____ State/Zip_____

PEN 0391